FALSELY ACCUSED

ALSO BY THE AUTHOR

#8

ROBERT K. TANENBAUM

FALSELY ACCUSED

A SIGNET BOOK

SIGNET
Published by the Penguin Group
Penguin Putnam Inc., 375 Hudson Street,
New York, New York 10014, U.S.A.
Penguin Books Ltd, 27 Wrights Lane,
London W8 5TZ, England
Penguin Books Australia Ltd, Ringwood,
Victoria, Australia
Penguin Books Canada Ltd, 10 Alcorn Avenue,
Toronto, Ontario, Canada M4V 3B2
Penguin Books (N.Z.) Ltd, 182–190 Wairau Road,
Auckland 10, New Zealand

Penguin Books Ltd, Registered Offices:
Harmondsworth, Middlesex, England

Published by Signet,
a member of Penguin Putnam Inc.

First Signet Printing, October, 1997
10 9 8 7 6 5 4 3 2

For those most special:
Patti, Rachael, Roger, and Billy

With affection to my partner and collaborator, Michael Gruber, whose genius flows throughout this book, and who is primarily responsible for this manuscript.

Special heartfelt appreciation must be extended to the best Penguins you'll ever meet: Laurie Parkin and Mayann Palumbo, both of whom would be my first picks for a schoolyard game of three-on-three basketball at the Avenue P park in Brooklyn; Eddie Stackler, like Henry Robbins, one terrific editor; all of the Penguin reps stationed around the country—you guys are special; and especially Ellen Silberman, whose guts and courage make us all proud— you're a sweetheart.

ONE

With a wet and embarrassing sound, a sound like no other, a human brain came loose from its skull and, dripping thick, clotted blood and fluid, hung suspended in the hands of the chief medical examiner of the City of New York. The brain's former owner (or rather, the being that once sprang from it) was named Jeffrey Zimmerman, late a stockbroker and arbitrageur, and a famous near-billionaire of the day, which was one reason why his autopsy was being performed by the chief medical examiner himself, Dr. Murray Selig, instead of by one of Selig's many subordinates.

Another reason was that Selig loved doing autopsies. He especially loved probing the *kishkas* of the rich and famous, or of those meeting their ends in some spectacular or bizarre manner, but he would also drop into the morgue of an afternoon and whip through a couple of overdosed whores with as much elan. He was good at it too. Dr. Selig was generally considered by his profession to be one of the half-dozen best forensic pathologists in the United States, an opinion that Selig himself rarely lost a chance to share with others. As a result of this skill and fame, Selig often had an audience of med students, trainee pathologists, or visiting coroners to watch him work. He didn't mind that either; a bit of a showman, Selig, another reason why he had chosen this particular branch of medicine. He liked appearing before press conferences and giving the straight poop on how some particular leading light had been switched off.

The audience today, three first-year Downstate students, one now looking quite green, and the medical examiner of a county in Texas, saw a shortish, perky-looking man in his late forties, with an aureole of frizzy hair over a balding forehead, big black horn-rims, and a neat brush of a mustache. Dressed in a slick rubber apron and green scrub clothes, he moved with a springy step across the damp floor of the autopsy room. They watched him weigh Zimmerman's brain.

Selig read the weight into a microphone suspended over his head: 1,352 grams, about average for a man. He then placed the organ on a steel tray and began to investigate what had until the night before last been quite the most valuable three pounds of meat in Manhattan. Now he became totally absorbed. The morgue staff, the deiners and the other medical examiners, knew that Dr. Selig was in no circumstances to be interrupted during an autopsy, which was why when the call came through from the Mayor's office that afternoon, nobody roused the pathologist from his close examination of the stockbroker's brain.

Selig continued to probe and snip at the thing, assessing the extent of the damage to it and telling the tape what he was finding. The audience watched, breathless. The Cause of Death, the apotheosis of any autopsy, was about to emerge. Zimmerman had received a heavy blow to the base of the skull. Selig had already recorded the depressed fracture of the right posterior fossa and the attendant tearing of the membranes surrounding the brain. Now he peeled away those membranes, the dura, the arachnoid, the pia, to expose the cheesy substance of the crown of creation itself. He noted the swelling, the extensive hematomas of the occipital lobes. He chased a ruptured artery and the purplish damage it did deep into the midbrain. He announced: death from massive cerebral hemorrhage. The only problem remaining was to determine . . . ah, here it was: bruising and smaller hematomas at the point of the frontal lobes, the part of the brain just behind the forehead. There had been no injury to the forehead itself, which meant that these particular bruises were contra-coup injuries. Zimmerman's brain had been violently thrust against the inside front of his skull, evidence that this injury had been caused by a fall. Nobody, it seemed, had bashed Zimmerman's head in, although there were plenty in town who wouldn't have minded the chore. Mr. Z. had fallen, like a great tree, and cracked the back of his head against the porcelain rim of one of the six toilets in his Sutton Place duplex. How he had come to fall like that still remained a puzzle, the solution to which Selig believed waited on the completion of the various drug tests he had already ordered. That the late Zimmerman enjoyed a creative use of the pharmacopeia, both legal and illegal, was a fact well known in Manhattan's tonier haunts.

A half hour later, Selig was back in his office, having put away his apron and green scrubs, but still exuding a faint redolence of the morgue.

"The press is out in force," said his secretary.

"What, on the Zimmerman?"

"Uh-huh. Crews from the three networks and a local, plus the print people. They're in the big conference room. And the Mayor wants to see you. It's urgent."

Selig laughed. "I bet. Zimmerman was a big contributor. Well, he can catch it on TV like everyone else."

"What was it?" asked the secretary. A neat part of her job was being the second person in the City to know how famous people died. She had worked for Selig for the whole year he had been C.M.E. and had developed a mild crush on the man, not least because of his free and breezy manner and his willingness to share tidbits of information with the peasants.

"Fall," said Selig. "Probably doped to the gills, but we won't know that for sure until tomorrow. Get the car around, would you? I'll leave for the Mayor's right after I get rid of these guys."

Later, relaxing in the back of the official car as it sped downtown, Selig thought that it had gone reasonably well, and that, had the Mayor actually caught the press conference live, he would have had nothing to complain about. Selig rather enjoyed the repartee with reporters and flattered himself that he was good at it. He had restricted himself to what he actually knew about Zimmerman's death, and declined to speculate about the rumors of wild drug orgies in the broker's home. For the hundredth time he had lectured the press that the M.E.'s job was solely that of determining cause and circumstances of death; whether that death included foul play or not ("Could he have been pushed, Dr. Selig?") was a job for the police.

So if the Mayor wanted to talk to him about Zimmerman, he was clean, except for the drug business, in which case he could truthfully say that he didn't know—yet. When the results came in, the Mayor might want him to cover them up, which, of course, he would refuse to do. Although on paper the medical examiner reported through the health commissioner to the Mayor of New York, Selig held to the older and unwritten tradition that the coroner was, as that older title implied, the agent of the crown, of the sovereign alone—in England, the King, in America the People. If the Mayor did not understand this yet, too bad for him.

As the car swung into the South Street Viaduct for the run up to City Hall, it occurred to Selig that tomorrow, July 21, would mark exactly a year since he had taken over as chief medical examiner. Maybe the Mayor was planning a ceremony. A little chat about the deceased contributor, followed by a little wine and cheese? The Mayor had a fondness for ceremony, or rather, for having his face exhibited on television during ceremonies. Selig caught his reflection in the glass of the window; he adjusted his tie and brushed off his lapels. He was somewhat miffed at not having been told about it in advance, although that too was typical of this Mayor. Selig sniffed at his hands, which he had remembered to scrub thoroughly before leaving Bellevue. No remnant of the morgue remained, just a faint scent of green soap.

They arrived. Selig got out and was shown directly to the Mayor's great office, where there occurred a ceremony of a sort after all. In the presence of Angelo Fuerza, the commissioner of Health, and on the basis of letters of complaint from that official and from the district attorney of New York, Sanford Bloom, the Mayor told Selig that he was fired.

And that was not the worst. The same evening, Murray Selig sat with his wife, Naomi, in front of their television and watched a press conference in which first the Mayor and then the district attorney denounced him as an incompetent, and as someone with whom, in the Mayor's words, "the most important district attorney in the city" could not work. Selig was therefore to be demoted to the rank of ordinary medical examiner. Selig sat quietly while this went on, as if in a trance, a stiff scotch in one hand and his wife's hand in the other, until it was announced that he was to be replaced by one Harvey Kloss.

"Kloss!" screamed Selig. "That *patzer*! I wouldn't hire him as a deiner on the graveyard shift!"

"Who is he?" asked Naomi Selig.

"Oh, he's some putz from upstate, a pal of Bloom's. Bloom was pushing him like crazy last year for my job—my ex-job, sorry. Not only does the guy not know what the hell he's doing, but when Sandy Bloom says, 'Shit,' he says, 'What color?' " He punched the power switch and flung the remote at the darkened screen.

"Breaking the TV is not going to help," observed Mrs. Selig, and after a moment asked, "So what *are* you going to do about it?"

"What *can* I do? I got canned. At the end of the day it comes down to the Mayor signs the check."

"And all the garbage they were saying just now about you? You're going to let that just go by?"

Selig considered this, his face flushing. "No. I was defamed. That wasn't true, what they said, but . . . God! I can't figure it out." He jumped to his feet and began pacing. "It's like something went insane. I work for a year, I think I'm doing okay—I mean, there are the usual little squabbles, with the D.A.'s, with Health, but nothing serious, nobody says a word to me that anything's seriously wrong, not the Mayor, not Bloom, not Fuerza, and now, boom! I'm out on my ass and they're on television saying I'm some kind of bum."

"It's Bloom," said Naomi definitively.

Selig stopped pacing. "Why do you say that? I never did anything to him."

"It doesn't matter. Look, Fuerza's a nonentity who doesn't roll over in his sleep without checking it out

15

with His Honor. And, no offense, but the Mayor could care less about the M.E. You barely appear on his radar screen. If he moved on you, it was because Bloom made a stink and said you had to go."

"But why?"

"Because Sandy Bloom's a dickhead. He was a dickhead at Dalton forty years ago, and age hasn't improved him."

Selig stared at his wife. She rarely used salty language, and when she did, it meant that she was very angry indeed.

"You knew Bloom in high school?"

"Prep school we called it, little *yiddisheh* aristocrats that we were. Yes, I knew him. I even dated him once, my freshman year. No, don't ask! The point is, he developed a problem with you for some reason, and in typical Sandy fashion, instead of coming to you like a mensch and talking it out, he engineered this ream job. Well, we're not going to let him get away with it."

Naomi Selig had enormous black eyes, and as she said this they flashed sparks, and her bony jaw became set in a grim line. She was a small, tightly knit woman with a perpetual tan and a thick cap of dense black hair that flipped as she nodded her head twice, with vigor. Half the charity committees in New York, not to mention the staff of the P.R. agency she operated, knew that look and those nods. It meant that an object stood between Naomi Selig and something she wanted, which object could expect shortly to be reduced to glowing radioactive ash.

Selig had not missed the significant "we" in his wife's last statement. He didn't mind in the least; in fact, he was relieved. His marriage was based on a reasonable division of labor: he cut up dead bodies, and Naomi took care of nearly everything else, especially politics, at which Selig had to admit he was less than talented.

"So what do we do?" he asked, and then, in the pregnant silence, uttered the distasteful monosyllable: "Sue?"

"Goddamn right we sue. Not only are we going to get your job back, but we're going to make those slime-meisters stand up in public and admit they lied about your performance."

Selig sat heavily on the couch and finished off his drink in a gulp. His stomach was feeling hollow, and there was a vile taste in his throat. "God, lawsuits! One of the things I thought I wouldn't have to screw with when I became a pathologist. I guess this means your cousin Sidney?"

"Oh, Sidney!" said Naomi contemptuously. "It's Sidney if you break your leg in the hospital driveway. No, we need a much heavier hitter for this one. I want Bloom to writhe."

She sat for a while thinking, and Selig watched her think, very happy that he was not on the business end of those thoughts, if the frighteningly stony, calculating expression on her face was any indication of their content.

"Karp. We'll get Karp to do it," she said at last.

Selig's head snapped back in surprise. "Butch

Karp? God, that's a shot from out of left field. Isn't he still in D.C.?"

"No, he's been back for ages. He works for Bohm Landsdorff Weller. Steve Orenstein got him the job when he came back to town."

Selig looked at his wife in amazement. "My God, Naomi! How do you know this stuff?"

"Because I'm on Cerebral Palsy with Jack Weller, and once in a while I let him pat my fanny accidentally-on-purpose and he tells me stuff. Karp's been there since, oh, around March of last year. Apparently he's a hell of a tort lawyer, although Jack says he'll never be a truly great one."

"Why not?"

"Because he doesn't lust after money enough. He has a killer instinct, though, especially when he thinks some little schmuck is getting a royal screwing."

"That's why we want him, because I'm a little schmuck getting screwed over?" Selig snapped, coloring brightly.

His wife's jaw dropped briefly, and then she laughed and kissed him on the cheek. "Of course not, you kugelhead! No, we want Karp because he's got a reason to get Sandy Bloom. It'll be a blood match."

Selig knotted his brow; this was getting hard to follow, and it seemed to him that his wife had entirely too much information at hand, as if she had been preparing dossiers to be consulted in the event of a whole range of potential catastrophes. "Karp has a thing against Bloom?"

"Of course he does! The whole town knows it. It's a famous feud. There was an article in the *Times* magazine a couple of years ago. It was supposed to feature Sandy, but she wrote almost entirely about Karp. Sandy went ballistic. That reporter did it—big gal with a funny name . . ."

"What's it about? The feud, I mean."

"Who knows?" she replied with a shrug. "With Sandy, you hardly need a reason. In any case, you'll call Karp."

It was not a question. Selig nodded. She really was better at this stuff than he was. He rose and picked up the remote control from where it had landed and examined it closely. Besides cutting up bodies, he was in charge of fixing things around the house; this seemed to him a sufficient load. The gizmo appeared undamaged. He pressed the power button and the television flashed on. For some unexplainable reason, this tiny success made him feel better than he had all day. Still, something nagged him.

"Okay, say Karp'll do it—he's a homicide prosecutor. What if he doesn't know anything about defamation or employment law? That stuff."

"So he'll learn," said Naomi Selig blithely. "How hard could it be? He's a sharp cookie, according to that article. God, what was that woman's name? Maybe we should contact her. As I recall it, she didn't like Bloom much either."

"Contact her?"

"Dirt, darling, dirt. On Sandy. They flung enough at you, we'll fling some back. Oriana? Ariel? Something like that. I'll get the girl to look it up tomorrow."

The offices of Bohm Landsdorff Weller were located in a red-brown sixty-year-old building at 113 William Street. The firm occupied two floors, eighteen and nineteen. The building was undistinguished, as was the firm itself. A very small nuclear blast set off at the junction of Wall and William would destroy several thousand such firms, each with their one or two floors of offices, their ten or so partners, their tax or merger or tort departments, their fake English paneling, their Aubusson or oriental carpets, their well-framed *Spy* caricatures or Daumier prints or sporting paintings, their starched secretaries and exhausted paralegals, their remarkable annual incomes. Such firms almost never have their names displayed in the pages of the *Times* or the *Wall Street Journal*; nor do they appear as the main contestants in the famous cases of the day, where giant corporations meet in titanic battle. Yet so incalculably immense is the river of money that flows through lower Manhattan that even the most delicate, pigeon-like sips from it, of the sort taken by such modest enterprises as Bohm Landsdorff Weller, were sufficient to keep the twelve partners thereof in stupefying wealth.

These firms are like wildebeestes or buffalo in a herd, all the same yet all slightly different to the naturalist's trained eye. Some are preeminent in taxes, others in trusts or torts or contracts; some will destroy a union for you, others will be happy to create a corporation. (But if you're thinking of getting rid of your spouse, by murder or divorce, or selling the story of how you did it to the movies, you want a different kind of law firm. If you are a good client, firms such as Bohm Landsdorff will supply you with a reference to lawyers of that sort from the fat Rolodexes they all maintain.)

In this office, in a cherrywood-furnished room on the nineteenth floor, Karp worked, not happily, but well and lucratively. He was making more money than he ever had in his life, except during the six weeks he had spent as the twelfth man on an NBA basketball team, investigating a murder and getting paid to play the game.

Karp was unhappy because he had in his life found only two things that he could do a lot better than most people and that he genuinely enjoyed doing: playing basketball and prosecuting criminals, and fate had dealt him a hand that prevented him from doing either. It was basketball, however, that had, in an indirect way, landed him his present job. He had been shooting baskets one Saturday at the Fourth Street courts in the Village, and a slight man with a friz of ginger hair around his bald pate had approached him on the asphalt with a "you won't remember me" and a look of something close to worship on his thin face. It was certainly true that Karp didn't remember him, but Steve Orenstein remembered Karp. Orenstein had spent one season warming the bench on the suburban high school team of which the young Karp had been the chief ornament. That morning they played an easy game of horse while chatting and discovered that Orenstein was working at Bohm Landsdorff Weller, or B.L., as he called it, and that Karp was at liberty. Orenstein asked whether Karp had ever thought of going into civil litigation, to which Karp had frankly replied that it had never once crossed his mind, and Orenstein had mentioned that if it ever did happen to cross, his firm was badly in need of someone who knew what to do in a courtroom. Two weeks after that, Karp, bored with unemployment and stony broke, had come by for an interview and been snapped up.

At B.L., Karp found that he was as much a specialist as the little men that NFL teams hire to kick field goals. Most lawyers of the type that populate downtown law firms never come anywhere near a trial. There are quite distinguished and successful lawyers in that milieu who have never once argued a case before a jury during a long career. Among such lawyers, therefore, trials signify a breakdown of the gentlemanly process of negotiation whose aim is settlement out of court, during which agreeably long process both sets of clients can be gently fleeced and neither law firm embarrassed by the possibility of a public defeat. But this glowing surface of collegiality is, of course, underpinned by the grim cast-iron structure of the trial system, and so it is necessary for the firm to have at its disposal at least one litigator who is not strictly speaking a gentleperson at all, and who, it may be given out along Wall and William and Pine streets, is kept chained in a tower room and fed raw meat against the day on which he will be unleashed against the firm's rivals in an actual courtroom, to raven and destroy. At B.L., this was Karp.

Karp had tried but one case in the sixteen months he had been at B.L. This was an affair in which an investment house had run an initial public offering of stock in a technology firm known to have a set of potentially lucrative patents. It turned out that the firm did not quite have all the said patents and that the ones they did have were not quite as succulent as advertised. The investors cried foul when later the stock prices went into the toilet; the investment house claimed breaks of the market. B.L.'s negotiators offered an out-of-court settlement—restitution plus interest. When the investment house declined this civilized deal, B.L.'s people sighed and rolled out Karp. Six months later, he had won not only restitution plus interest but a punitive award, of 4.3 million dollars. It turned out that the investment house had known all about the defective patents before offering the stock. A criminal fraud case was pending, and the head of the investment house, whom Karp had treated, during a hideous day and a half on the witness stand, to the sort of cross-examination usually reserved for members of the unmanicured classes, was resting in a convalescent home.

Since then it had not been necessary to use Karp again. He kept busy, however, keeping track of a variety of cases where the threat to go to trial was a useful ploy, much as the men who, in those waning days of the 1970s, sat in North Dakota missile silos and practiced the annihilation of Kiev.

The major on-deck case at the moment was *Lindsay et al.* v. *Goldsboro Pharmaceutical Supply Company*, a cat's cradle involving tainted insulin, three multinational drug companies, the largest insurer in the nation, eight thousand or so aggrieved diabetics, their families, heirs, and assigns, and approximately 1.6 billion dollars in claims and counterclaims. Karp had mastered the case with a speed that amazed his colleagues and had expressed confidence that, should the elaborate negotiations then ongoing break down, he was prepared to try the case and win. Nobody at B.L. wanted that to happen, least of all Karp. Such a trial could take three to five years, and he preferred the challenge of the new. When he had been in charge of the Homicide Bureau, he might, during an average killing year, have been involved in several hundred trials and might have actually prosecuted as many as twenty.

Being a sort of utility for B.L., Karp was considered part of the overhead and was not expected to drum up business. Nor did he. Thus he was startled when Murray Selig called him on the phone to say he needed a lawyer. After recovering from his amazement, Karp was actually pleased, and told Selig to come by and chat.

Selig came in the next morning. Karp rose from behind his desk and greeted him warmly and invited him to sit. Selig was glad to do so. Like many men of less than moderate size, he was made uneasy on a visceral level by males the size of Karp. Karp was a little taller than six foot five, with big shoulders and long arms and legs and first baseman's mitt-sized hands. The two men made small talk for a few minutes—sports, their families, mutual friends. They had any number of these, since Selig had worked closely with Karp on dozens of cases when Karp had been with the D.A. and Selig was an assistant C.M.E. During this time Selig took the opportunity to focus his keen observer's skills on the figure of his interlocutor.

Karp had cut his crisp brown hair shorter since D.C., and Selig noted with rue that it did not seem to be climbing back along his forehead with the velocity to be expected in a man past thirty-five. Underneath the forehead was a nose that had started out as something of a beak, but Selig's practiced eye estimated that it had been broken at least twice. It now resembled several small potatoes in a sock. The face had in general an odd, nearly oriental cast—high cheekbones and eyes set aslant in their deep sockets. The skin was rough and yellowish. If Karp had been dead on a slab, Selig might almost have called him a central Asian.

Selig began now to recite the reason for his visit. Karp's eyes fixed on him as he spoke, which the doctor found unsettling. Officially hazel, Karp's eyes had yellow flecks in them that seemed to glitter, like those of a feral animal. Selig thought that it would not be much fun trying to slip a lie past those eyes.

Selig came to the crux of his story, the two letters of complaint on which his dismissal had been based, and Karp stopped him.

"You have copies of those letters, Murray?" Selig did and handed them across the desk. Karp read through them quickly. "Any of this crap true?" he asked. "For example, did you actually say that this purported rape victim might have inserted snails in her vagina?"

"Oh, for Pete's sake, of course I didn't say that," Selig cried. "The thing happened in *People* v. *Lotz*. That was when you were in D.C. Lotz was a junkie burglar who broke into an apartment in Peter Cooper. He thought it was empty, but the tenant was at home. A woman named May Ettering. Lotz panicked and strangled her. They caught him about ten hours later buying stuff on her credit cards. Not exactly a rocket scientist, Lotz. So they had a good circumstantial case, but this kid D.A., Warneke, wanted to make it even better by making it out that Lotz was a rapist besides being a strangler and a burglar."

"Was he?"

"I didn't think so. The serology from the vaginal sample of the victim contained acid phosphatase, and since semen contains acid phosphatase, Warneke wanted me to say that evidence of sexual intercourse was present. But I pointed out to him that there are any number of food substances that contain it. Broccoli and cabbage, for example."

"And snails."

"And snails. I also pointed out to Warneke that Ettering had an intact hymen. She was a virgin. That usually rules out rape. Bloom claims in his letter that Warneke told him I had flippantly remarked in a conference about the case that the victim might have put snails up her vagina and that this could account for the phosphatase. Which is complete horse manure."

Karp made a note. "There were other people at this meeting?"

"At least half a dozen."

"Good. What about this one on our late vice-president? Did you really stand up in front of grand rounds at Metropolitan Hospital and tell the folks that the great man had expired porking someone?"

"Oh, God, no! I just did my usual dog and pony about the evolution of the M.E.'s office, and at the part where I say that one of the problems of the job is doing autopsies of notable people, I may have mentioned him. He'd died a couple of days before the presentation."

"But no death in the saddle?"

"Of course not!"

"Wise. I expect we can corral enough distinguished physicians who were at the meeting to confirm it. In fact, when shown false, the charge is so infamous that it'll help with damages."

Selig suddenly realized the import of this remark. "You're taking the case?"

"Oh, yeah," said Karp. "You'll make an appointment, and we'll go over this stuff line by line."

Karp shifted his swivel chair so that it faced the window and fell silent. He seemed deep in thought. After a minute or so, Selig cleared his throat and asked, "So—you think we have a good case?"

"Oh, no question. I'm a little rusty on employment law, but I'm certain that a public official can't be fired for cause without some sort of hearing."

"The Mayor claims I'm—I *was*—a political appointee serving at his pleasure."

Karp shook his head dismissively. "That's something we'll duke out. Even if they *could* fire you, I'm almost sure they *can't* fire you for cause without giving you a hearing. It's not a *Roth* case. God, I can't believe I remembered that!"

"Who's Roth?"

"Teacher at Wisconsin, early seventies. Untenured. The school didn't renew his contract, and he sued. He claimed that they didn't renew because he'd pissed off the university authorities by criticizing the administration. Defendants came back with the argument that they didn't have to give any reason at all for not renewing, and the Supreme Court agreed."

"This is *good* for us?"

"Yeah. The Supremes decided he didn't have what they call a property interest in his job, because they didn't fire him, they just declined to rehire him. You did have such an interest. Also, and probably more significantly for our purposes, when they declined to rehire Roth, they made no statement that would impugn his good name and prevent him from getting a job elsewhere. And from what you tell me, the press conference and all, that's very far from your case. They canned you for cause, and went public that they thought you were a bum. They can't do that, not without giving you the right of rebuttal. We can work a little deprivation of liberty action in here too."

To Selig's questioning look Karp added, "Liberty. Under Fourteenth Amendment case law, liberty includes the right to seek your customary employment. By maligning you without due process, they've limited your liberty in that way." Karp stared out the window again.

"What are you thinking?" asked Selig when the waiting became too much for him.

Karp spun his chair slowly around until he faced Selig. "What I'm thinking is, why? Bloom doesn't like to make waves. He made plenty over you. And he must have used some pretty big chips with the Mayor to get you out of the C.M.E.'s slot."

"Naomi said it's because he's a controlling asshole."

"That's true enough, but . . ."—Karp flipped the copies of the complaint letters on his desk—"this crap, this snails nonsense, isn't enough to warrant the hatchet job Bloom did on you."

"The reason's important?"

"Oh, yeah. I think in a way it's the key to the case. Not the case we'll argue in court, necessarily."

Karp fell again into a silent study, and Selig, starting to become irritated with what seemed to him vagueness, changed the subject.

"So. What do you think this is going to cost me?"

Karp regarded him blankly. "Hmm? I don't know, Murray. Don't worry about it. We'll win, you'll *make* money."

"But if we don't win," Selig persisted.

Something hard congealed in Karp's yellowish gaze. "Murray, I said, don't worry about it. I'm taking the case."

"But . . ."

"Murray," said Karp with finality. "I'll pay *you.*"

TWO

Two women, one very tall, one of ordinary size, both dressed in silk kimonos, sat talking and drinking champagne on a bed in a loft on Crosby Street in lower Manhattan. They were wearing the gowns because they had been caught unprepared in a summer downpour and were being languorous before getting dressed again in dry clothes. The tall one was the freelance journalist whose peculiar name Naomi Selig had tried vainly to recall the previous evening, Ariadne Stupenagel. She was, to look at, quite as odd as her name. Over six feet tall and leggy, with broad mannish shoulders and wide womanly hips, Stupenagel had facial features in proportion. Her mouth was wide and lippy, her jaw strong, her nose generous. Her eyes, dark, knowing, heavily mascaraed and shadowed green-blue, looked as large as a pony's. She wore her dust blond hair piled up on top of her head in the manner of Toulouse-Lautrec's barmaids, which added another several inches to her height. If not beautiful in the conventional sense, she was hard to miss and memorable.

Marlene Ciampi, her hostess, was, in contrast, beautiful in the conventional sense, looking, as an artist friend of hers had once noted, exactly like Bernini's statue of St. Teresa in Ecstasy. St. Teresa was not, however, a smart kid from Queens with adorable black ringlets and a glass eye.

The meeting was in the nature of a reunion. Stupenagel had just returned to New York from a year covering the guerilla war in Guatemala. The two women were at the point of drunkenness in which confidences may begin to flow, and everything seems vastly funny.

"I can't get over what you've done with the loft," said Stupenagel, refilling her glass. "It must have cost a fortune."

"Yes, it did," agreed Marlene, gazing contentedly out the open door of the bedroom at her remarkable dwelling. She had lived in this place since the days in which it was illegal to do so. She had with her own hands ripped out the ruins of an old electroplating factory and installed simple plumbing, electricity, heating, and cabinetwork. Necessarily, this had been crude work; as a junior assistant D.A., she'd had little cash to spare on comforts, although the mere size of the space—a hundred feet by thirty-three—made up for a lot. Nevertheless, she had lived ten years in what was little more than a shabbily furnished nineteenth-century factory: rusty tin ceiling, the floor of splintery planks where it was not concrete slab, tepid radiators, a tiny, fetid toilet, raw drywall partitions instead of proper rooms.

Now, however, she looked out on an expanse of satiny Swedish-finished oak flooring, glowing under the track lighting that hung from the smooth dropped ceiling. She had real rooms with doors and brass hardware. The creaky inconvenient sleeping loft was now a handsome bedroom, w/bath. The kitchen was right out of *Architectural Digest*, oak cabinets, a double stainless reefer, a Vulcan stove. Lucy, the Karps' seven-year-old daughter, had a cozy, carpeted bedroom and a well-stocked playroom. The stingy gas radiators were gone, and the whole vast space was heated and cooled in season by a climate control center that had its own little lair in a corner of the loft.

"Luckily," continued Marlene, "we *had* a fortune. Last year Butch made about twice the *combined* total of what our two salaries were when we both worked for the D.A. It was like Monopoly money; we couldn't believe the numbers. Especially coming from D.C., where we were practically sharecroppers. So we figured while we were flush, and who knew how long it'd last, we'd better fix up the place. And there it is."

Sounds of giggling floated through the open door. Lucy was entertaining a friend.

"Why wouldn't it last?" asked Stupenagel.

"Oh, I don't know," replied Marlene. "It doesn't seem right, somehow. All that dough. And Butch is not a happy camper, not really. He was born to put asses in jail. One day he's going to come home and tell me he's quit Bohm Lansdorff What's-his-face and gone for a job with the Brooklyn D.A. or the Feds, and it'll be back to genteel poverty and the joys of public service. Meanwhile, hi-ho!" She poured herself another glass of Moët.

"Why doesn't he just get his old job back?" asked Stupenagel. "Assuming he wants to be a D.A."

"Long story," said Marlene dismissively.

"Mmm," said Stupenagel, for whom no story was too long, and shot Marlene an interested look. When this prompted no revelation, she changed tack. "Well, you certainly seem to have taken to the life of a bourgeois matron," she observed in a needling tone. "I never would have thought it, the way you used to carry on at Smith. Little Ms. Feminist—"

"Fuck you, Stupe," replied Marlene amiably.

"Supported by a man. Dependent. Want to go shopping? We could buy slipcovers. We could play mah-jongg—"

"We could strike one another over the head with empty champagne bottles, me first."

"Oh, is it all gone? That's almost as bad as your pathetic domestic slavery," said Stupenagel, and then she called out, *"Marcel! Encore de champagne!"*

"I notice you don't mind sharing in the tainted largesse," Marlene observed.

"Leeching off friends is completely different. There are numerous other people I could leech off of; I choose to leech off you from a position of absolute freedom. You expect nothing from me in return."

"I'll say!" said Marlene dryly.

"That did not come out precisely as I intended. As you know, I would give you the shirt off my back, speaking of which . . ."

"I'll check the dryer. You can get your own wine. There's another bottle in the fridge, but you'll have to drink it yourself. I have to make dinner." She got up and walked out of the bedroom.

"Oh, yes, God forbid hubby won't have his meat and two veg on the table," Stupenagel called after her. Then Marlene heard the sound of a bottle being taken out of the refrigerator and the pop of the cork. She sighed as she removed her friend's dry clothes from the dryer. Ariadne was going to get pissed, and she could be a mean drunk. The last thing she wanted right now was to have to handle a gigantic drunken woman, two seven-year-olds, and a hungry and unhappy husband. Maybe Ariadne would just pass out. From habit, Marlene sniffed the warm clothes and wrinkled her nose. Personal hygiene was clearly not one of the journalist's strong points and hadn't been at college either, Marlene recalled.

"I could have washed these," Marlene said as she tossed the clothes (black jeans, red Solidarity T-shirt, underpants, and socks) on the bed where Stupenagel was reclining, now swigging champagne directly from the bottle.

"Oh, God, never! Not a jot will I add to your domestic slavery," exclaimed Stupenagel in ringing tones, and then, dramatically, "I'd rather wallow in filth."

"You are," said Marlene. "Get dressed. You can help me cut stuff up."

Stupenagel groaned and put her bottle on a nightstand, then stood shakily and dropped her robe. She staggered nude to a full-length mirror, struck a pose with her chest thrown out, and groaned again. "Good Christ! What a great foundation for such tiny edifices!" She turned to stare appraisingly at Marlene, who was trying to slip into her own clothes as quickly and privately as possible. "Jesus, is there no justice? You haven't sagged an inch, and you're a mom! Marlene, if you die, can I have your tits?"

"Oh, grow up, Stupe!" snapped Marlene, tucking her blouse into a long denim skirt. "What would Gloria Steinem say if she knew you were still lusting after big knockers?"

"Easy for her to talk! She's got nice ones." Stupenagel collapsed on the bed again and reached for the bottle. After a lengthy swallow she said, "So. This is it for you? Cook, clean, read bedtime stories?"

"Are you going to get dressed?"

"I will, I will. Don't nag me. No, really, tell me."

Marlene recalled that this was one of her friend's little oddities. In college she would stride through the dorm hallways stark naked, frightening the freshmen and, on Sundays, annoying those who were entertaining men in their rooms with the door opened the prescribed eighteen inches. Another was also observable now: her ability to carry on a normal conversation while drunk, a quality she considered essential to success as a journalist.

Marlene sat on the bed and turned her real eye on her friend, being careful to keep in view the bedside clock-radio. "Okay, Stupe—here's the story. The loft in which we now sit is a condo. It's worth approximately three hundred and fifty thousand dollars and was purchased and sold to me for one dollar by an old Armenian gentleman, in return for services rendered."

"Jesus! What the hell did you do for him?"

"I stole something back from someone who had stolen it from him. And yes, it's a great story, and no, I'm not going to tell it to you. The point is that my financial contributions to this family have been very substantial, when you add it all up, probably more than Butch's. So the fact that I'm not bringing in cash right at this minute has no significance. I bought this time and I'm enjoying it, without guilt, thank you. I like cooking. I like hanging out with Lucy. I like not having to deal with scumbags and assholes all day. It's improved my disposition considerably. So you can cut out all the 'dependent' horseshit."

"Oooh, she's wailing now!" hooted Stupenagel. "But admit it! Aren't you just the teeniest bit bored? Wouldn't you like to be back at the D.A.?"

Marlene considered this seriously, although she understood that Ariadne was merely baiting her. Did she feel bored?

"Frankly? Yeah, sometimes. I have a brain, it wants to be used the way it was trained. But a couple of things: one, it turns out I'm not that great a D.A. I don't mean in terms of skill or knowledge or success. All that's fine. I mean in terms of temperament. I'm too impatient to be really happy in the legal system." And too vindictive, thought Marlene, without saying it. "And two . . ." Marlene stumbled on what *two* was. She really shouldn't have drunk so much wine. "Oh, right . . . two, if I went back to the D.A., I'd have to commute, because I can't work for the New York D.A. anymore."

"Like Butch," said Stupenagel, driving to the point of the elaborate manipulation she had been carrying on for the past half hour, the goal of which was to find out why two of the most prominent prosecuting attorneys in the recent history of New York were no longer prosecuting. "And why would that be, Marlene? Why the big career change?"

Marlene laughed in spite of herself, understanding very well what was going on and, in an odd way, admiring it, and Stupenagel's brazen awfulness. Karp already knew the story, but no one else did, and Marlene in an instant decided to tell it to Ariadne, who, although certainly the world's least reliable confidante, was at least a woman.

"This happened," Marlene began, "when Butch was in D.C. I was running the rape bureau. To make a long story short, Bloom essentially asked me for a proposal that would have tripled my staff and made sex crimes a really big deal. He invited me to dinner at his place to discuss the project, filled me with booze, and, I think but can't prove, slipped a little something extra into the brandy. In any event, I passed out, and when I came to, he had my blouse unbuttoned, my tits out, my panty hose down around my kneecaps and his hand on my pussy."

"So you fucked him," said Stupenagel. "Then what?"

"Oh, for crying out loud, Stupe! I certainly did *not* fuck him."

"You didn't?"

"No! He tried to rape me. I mean, I assume you're familiar with the concept?"

"Don't be vile, Ciampi. Okay, so what did you do then?"

"I shoved him off me and gave him a couple of good shots to the nose. He ended up in a cheesecake. I pulled myself together, got out, and puked my guts on the sidewalk."

"I assume this was not a career-enhancing move."

"No. In the clear light of hindsight, I should have at least tried to nail the bastard for it. But . . . oh, shit, the embarrassment! The head of the rape bureau charging the D.A. with attempted rape? Attempted, mind you. No pubic hair, no sperm, no proof. He would have smiled and said something like, this bitch came on to me with a ridiculous plan for her own self-aggrandizement and I turned her down and she got drunk and made this absurd accusation. Or he would have said that Butch put me up to it. But it was mostly the shame—I wasn't thinking legal strategy at the time. I just wanted *away*. So, a couple of weeks after that I quit and moved down to be with Butch in Washington. Are you going to get dressed?"

Stupenagel ignored this and sucked again on the Moët, a little too vigorously, because the wine foamed and ran up her nose and down her chin. She sputtered and coughed. When she recovered, she said, "So *that's* the story. God, Marlene, what a mess! Why the hell didn't you let him pork you?"

"What!" cried Marlene. Long association with Ariadne had diminished her friend's ability to shock her, but this last question, delivered in a matter-of-fact tone, made Marlene's stomach churn. "I told you, the slimeball tried to rape me. *Please* tell me you're not giving me that relax and enjoy it horseshit . . ."

"Oh, hell, Ciampi, we're not talking about some pervert sweathog climbing through your window with a knife. This was a guy who could do you some good. What the hell does a fuck mean anyway? Lie back and think of England."

"*You* would have let him?"

"Of course!"

"I can't fucking believe this! This is the woman who's telling me *I'm* not living up to feminist ideals?"

Stupenagel uttered a dramatic sigh. "Oh, don't be such a baby, Marlene! What's feminism? Feminism is about getting ahead. Achieving power. And *using* sex, using our luscious young bodies for the pathetically few years they remain luscious to climb a little higher up the pole. Like men. You do what you have to. What, you think *men* don't? Men suck ass instead of cocks, except for the ones who suck cocks too. They let their egos be ground into powder by their bosses. For years. You think that's preferable to eight minutes of wiggling your butt and groaning?"

"You've done this? This is not just theoretical?"

"Marlene, darling, how do you think we went from a city reporter on an Ohio daily to the Moscow bureau of the Associated Press in four years? Journalistic brilliance? Yeah, that too . . ." She laughed. "But even journalistic brilliance sometimes requires that we drop our panties. Guys will tell you stuff across a pillow they'd never let go of across a desk. Besides, I *like* to fuck. And it clears the air. What you don't want is some guy with a hard-on following you around, mooning. *That's* annoying. It's a pity so many of the ones who can help you happen to be little short persons."

"Butch doesn't," Marlene blurted out.

"He doesn't what? Have hard-ons?"

"No, suck ass."

"No, I'm sure he doesn't, which is why he doesn't get to do the one thing he likes doing, and is better than practically anyone else in the city at, and why he's chasing ambulances for a second-rate tort factory. Whereas I, slut that I am . . ." She paused, as if performing an instant analysis of her current status. Her nose wrinkled involuntarily. She took a swallow of wine and giggled. "Whereas I . . . have to take a whiz. Excuse me."

Stupenagel rose with the stately, over-controlled movements of the experienced lush, threw her kimono around her shoulders, and swayed into the bedroom's toilet, still holding the champagne.

Marlene bustled into action, irritated at Ariadne and angry at herself for letting the woman get under her skin. Again. Why do I put up with the bitch?

she wondered for the ten thousandth time since her freshman year. To which she knew the answer very well, but was not disposed to think about it just then.

She went to the kitchen and began to rattle pots. "Little girls! Little girls! Come and help!" she shouted. Giggles and pounding of feet on the hardwood: Lucy Karp with Janice Chen trailing behind. Marlene took a lump of pasta dough out of the refrigerator and set up the machine. Lucy officiously supervised the process, allowing Janice to crank while she herself arranged the long, pale strands of linguine on the wooden rack. Marlene busied herself with clam sauce, keeping an eye on the children from time to time. Lucy was becoming a little Marlene: bright, pugnacious, with a tendency to boss. She had her mother's pure bisque skin and curly dark hair; her eyes, yellowy gray and slightly tilted, were out of Odessa and points east by way of Dad.

You wind them up, Marlene thought, and they go off by themselves, and then they start to wind themselves up, which was the stage Lucy was moving into now. She had friends; sleep-overs were starting to become more important than having Oz books read at bedtime and being tucked in. As much as she hated to admit it, with Lucy away in first grade for the full school day, the hours were starting to hang. This thought reminded her of Ariadne, and she called out, but got no answer. She continued her chopping and stirring.

The girls helped her set the table, and then Janice Chen's mother arrived to take her home. Mrs. Chen smiled a good deal and looked wide-eyed around the loft. People lived in factories in Guandong, where she came from, but not factories like this one. Some remarks were exchanged in primitive English about noodles—a point of cultural intersection—and then the Chens left.

Marlene went to check on her friend, and found her, as she had feared, curled around the toilet, snoring gently, tenderly cradling the empty bottle in her arms. Marlene removed the bottle and shook Stupenagel. No reaction. She cursed, and was considering stronger measures when the sound of the door opening and Lucy's "Daddy's home" announced the arrival of Karp.

She left the bathroom and went to greet her husband. The greeting was an unusually warm one, and Karp looked at her closely. "That was a hot kiss," he said huskily. "Did I do something right for a change?"

"The other possibility is that I want something expensive from you," said Marlene in the same tone. "Did you make lots of money today, Daddy? Millions?"

"Only thousands." He sniffed the air. "Not Italian food *again*!" The family joke. They sat, Karp admired the linguine and heaped praises upon its little manufacturer. Then he glanced around.

"She left?" he asked, his voice hopeful. The visit from Stupenagel, which was supposed to have included dinner, had been announced well in advance. Karp was not one of the journalist's numerous fans.

"She's blotto on our bathroom floor," said Marlene.

"What's blotto, Mommy?"

"Very sleepy from drinking too much wine, dear," Marlene answered her daughter, and then to Karp, who had assumed a sour and unpleasant expression, said, "She's had a rough time, Butch. She can get her load on in my house if she wants."

"I don't see why you put up with her, Marlene," said Karp defensively. "She's always dumping on you and then passing out."

"Well, since I see her about once every couple of years, 'always' is not the best word. And as far as dumping goes, maybe I occasionally need dumping on."

"From your friends?"

"Who else? I seem to recall someone else in this family who has friends who are not models of supportive behavior."

"Who in this family, Mommy? Me?"

"No, not you, sweety. Your father."

At the word "sweety" a Neapolitan mastiff the size and blackness of a classic R69 BMW twin-cylinder motorcycle padded into the dining room from its rug in the kitchen and stood panting redly at Marlene's elbow. Lucy laughed.

"Sweety thought you meant him, Mommy."

"Oh, Sweety, go back to bed. I'll take you out later," said Marlene. The dog gave her a heartrending look of disappointment, deposited a dollop of drool on the carpet, and departed.

Karp was glad of the interruption. Marlene's dart had struck home; he did indeed have several close friends from his days at the D.A., men whose little ways re:support made Ariadne Stupenagel look in comparison like a golden retriever. For this reason he was content to drop the subject entirely, but Marlene seemed determined to press on in the woman's defense.

"I realize," she said, "that she's a pain in the behind on occasion. She's tricky and unreliable. On the other hand, I'm probably the only old friend she has left—yes, don't say it, there's a reason. But she makes me laugh; and if she pees me off . . . I don't know, maybe it's a message. Maybe I'm getting too self-satisfied. She described me as a bourgeois matron—"

"What bullshit! Why do you listen to that crap?"

Marlene raised an eyebrow. They had agreed to lower the level of foul language at the dinner table.

"May I be excused?" asked Lucy wisely.

"Sure, baby. Get ready for bed and you can watch some TV."

The child took her dish to the kitchen to be pre-cleaned by the mastiff, and trotted off to her room.

"As I was saying," continued Marlene, "there's something in what she said."

"Can I say 'bullshit' now?"

"If you choose."

"Okay, bullshit! You know damn well she only says stuff like that because she's jealous of you and wants to make you feel bad."

"Her intentions are not germane, counselor," replied Marlene coolly. "We're talking about veracity here. In fact, it's time for me to make some changes. Lucy's in first grade and I'm getting antsy."

Karp thought carefully before replying. The last eighteen months had been very nice for him indeed, and, he supposed, for Marlene and Lucy as well. A nice meal on the table every night; no hassles about leaving work and picking the kid up from school; an unexhausted and unharried mate. And while he knew that this would not be a permanent state, that Marlene was a bright and talented person and would not wish to live the sort of life her mother (or, more to the point, *his* mother) had lived, the inevitable change had, in his secret heart, been pushed into the indefinite future, almost like death itself. Justice and selfishness therefore waged brief war within him, justice winning but taking heavy casualties.

"What," he ventured, "do you think you'd like to do?"

"I'm not sure. D.A.-ing is out for now. I don't want to be tied down to regular hours and court dates. Aside from that . . ."

"I could talk to Orenstein. They're always hiring associates."

Marlene's wide brow darkened. "No, you will not talk to Orenstein or anyone else. I am never again going to work in the same place you work."

"Sorry. Another firm, maybe."

Marlene shrugged. "I don't know. It doesn't exactly make my heart leap. I think what'll happen is, now that I'm ready for it, something will turn up. Uh-oh, I think our guest is conscious again."

They could hear the sound of water running, and groaning, and cursing, quite imaginative obscenity in three languages. Five minutes later, Stupenagel appeared in the dining room, dressed, made up and coiffed, only a slight dampness on her neck and hair indicating the velocity with which she had brought herself up from nude stupor.

"Jesus, Marlene, why the hell did you let me drink so much? I got an appointment uptown in an hour. Hi, Butch. Yeah, I could eat something. In fact, I'm starving to death. What is this, linguine and clam sauce? Marlene, you're such a little guinea! Nobody eats this stuff anymore . . ." With which, and similar, Stupenagel sat down at the table and ate a mound of cooling pasta approximately half the size of her own head, with the remains of the salad, three chunks of bread, and a pint of medium-good Soave.

In between bites she talked. ". . . Christ, you see I'm itching? Some kind of parasite I picked up, it's probably turning my liver into sludge. I wanted to visit this massacre site, the Red Cross guy in Guat City told me about it, also the nuns. There was a teaching order near San Francisco Nenton, where the massacre happened, the Sisters of Perpetual Dysentery, no kidding, that's what they called themselves. Great bunch—anyway, they took me under their wing, a nice Catholic girl like me, and they introduced me to—"

Marlene interrupted, "Stupe, you're not Catholic."

"Sure, Marlene, by the *pope* I'm not Catholic, but, believe me, in Guatemala they only have the two flavors, communist and Catholic, and they shoot the communists. They shoot the Catholics too, as it turns out, but I didn't know that until later. Anyway, of course the army wouldn't let us get anywhere near the place, but the nuns had a school near there, and they let me and the Red Cross guy go up on a supply run, in this jeep that they had converted into like a two-ton truck, and of course it was raining, so we had to practically build the roads as we went along, and by the time we got to where we were going we found the army had closed the convent school down so they could kill more Maya without anybody finding out, so we were stuck there, in this place San Luis some-fucking-thing, for six weeks until the rain stopped, living in the truck, during which time I picked up this damn parasite. Burrowing worms will probably pop out of my eyes on *Meet the Press*. Meanwhile, I managed to piece together the story from survivors drifting by, or relatives, not that anybody cares, it's like the classic Earthquake in China eighty thousand Die story, an inch and a half on page seventeen, although, of course, there's the angle that we put these bastards in there, in sixty-four, and we keep giving them guns and stuff, so maybe I'll write a book or a searing essay for *Harper's*, although between us girls, I'm not much of a book or searing-essay type, more of the you supply the war and I'll supply the story sort of thing, hard news and all.

Meanwhile, do you guys know a cop named Joseph L. Clancy? Sergeant at the Twenty-fifth Precinct?"

"Wow, *that* was a change of pace," exclaimed Marlene. "Swung on and missed. Why do you want to know this for?"

"Um," said Stupenagel, swallowing a lump of bread, "okay, I get here and I look up some people I ran into in Guatemala City—Guats, a lot of them illegals, and gringos helping them. I'm still interested in Nenton. These people are not easy to find or talk to, for obvious reasons. So one day, I'm down in a garage in Queens talking to this bunch of gypsy cabbies, mix and match Latinos, Salvadorans, Dominicans, Panamanians, and this Guat all of a sudden says something like, hey, what you bothering about Guatemala, lady, the same thing's going on here. All the other guys looked at him like, oh, shit! Now he's done it! So, of course, I asked him what he meant, but he wouldn't give anything else, just threw it off, like, oh, well, the cops hassle the gypsy drivers, what else is new? So, one thing I know is what really scared people look like. There's a smile they get, like, please please please don't push on this phony mask or it'll break into pieces. Is there any more wine?" Marlene found an opened bottle and passed it over. "Thanks. Anyway, a little later I'm in this grease pit, eating rice and goat, and the little brown guy comes up to me, looks like Cochise, but with the clean white shirt buttoned up to the collar. Asks if I'm the *journalista* asking questions about the *pendejos* in the *calabesas Nuevayorquenos*. So of course I am. And the story is, after he checks I'm not a cop or *la migra*, the story is his brother and a bunch of other gypsies working up in Spanish Harlem are getting shaken down by the local police, and what happens, they don't pay up, they get arrested. Only, it's not just getting arrested: it seems these guys end up dead. He gives me the names of three guys, and the name of this cop, Clancy, who's supposed to be investigating or involved or something. The kid won't give his own name. I tell him I need his name, but I won't use it if he doesn't want me to, but no, no. I pressed him a little too hard and—wham!—he's smoke. So all I have is this Clancy. I call him up at the precinct. He says he doesn't talk to the press, it's policy, I should go see Public Affairs at Police Plaza, which I go do, and I get a smoothie who tells me that of the three Latin gentlemen in question, two hanged themselves in the precinct tank and one died of natural causes. He says the M.E.'s reported on the three of them, two as consistent with hanging and the third as heart failure, and the cops closed the cases without action. And that was that, except I'd still like to get with Joe Clancy, about the shakedown side of it at least.''

"Don't know him," said Marlene.

"The name rings some kind of bell," said Karp, "but there's a lot of cops. Lots of Clancys, if it comes to that. One thing, though: I'd believe a shakedown racket; I'm not sure I'd buy that cops were knocking off people in the cells."

"Yeah, I'd tend to go along with that," said Stupenagel, surprising Karp, who had expected a bleeding-heart attack on the police from the journalist, and was, truth be told, rather looking forward to a row with her. Stupenagel continued, "It's tragic. The rich world is full of young guys from poor countries doing the shit work that the rich poor people won't do. They come from villages where they knew everyone and everyone knew them, for generations back. Suddenly, they find themselves in a place like New York, six to a room, surrounded by strangers, no hope of any emotional relationship, working at exhausting jobs for twenty hours a day, or else not finding work at all and slowly starving to death, scared of any authority, exploited by everyone. One day they get arrested. They're locked up. They have no goddamn idea in the world of what's going to happen to them, but they know it's the end of everything. Of course they hang themselves. Christ, in Bangkok and Hong Kong they don't even have to hang themselves. They just go to sleep and don't wake up. Nobody knows the cause. It doesn't even make the local papers anymore it's so common. Maybe it happened to the third guy up there."

"You could ask Roland Hrcany," suggested Karp. "If something's going down with cops, he'd probably know about it. Or someone he knew would."

"Who he?" asked Stupenagel.

"A guy we used to work with at the D.A.," said Marlene.

"Yeah? Cute?"

"Some might say so. On second thought, it might

not be such a good idea. Roland has unreconstructed ideas about women."

"You mean he'll want to screw?"

"He may insist on it," answered Marlene, with a side glance at her husband. *His* rat friends.

"Is he tall?"

"Actually, wide," said Marlene.

"Oh, God, not a porky!"

"The furthest thing. Roland's a weightlifter. Washboard stomach, pecs of iron, buns of steel. Brain of toad . . ."

"I'll look him up," said Stupenagel, polishing the last of the clam sauce from her plate with the last scrap of bread. She had eaten and drunk literally everything remaining on the table except the salt, pepper, and Parmesan cheese. "Mmm, the little woman sure can cook!" she said, with a broad wink at Karp.

"Knock it off, Stupe," said Marlene.

"I bet you get your underwear ironed and folded too," said Stupenagel, ignoring her.

"I *said*, knock it off!" They both stared at Marlene in the ensuing silence. Her jaw was clenched and she was white around the nostrils. After a brief staring contest, Stupenagel turned her eyes away and said lightly, "Oh, my, I think I hit a nerve there. My big mouth . . . sorreee!"

"Didn't you say you had an appointment uptown, Stupe?" Marlene inquired.

Stupenagel laughed and pushed her chair back. "Oh, and now I'm getting the bum's rush, and don't

I deserve it! Thanks for the delish dinn, and the tip about the cop." She pouted. "You're not *really* mad at me, are you, Champ?"

Marlene sighed, and smiled and shook her head.

"Oh, good!" cried the journalist and rushed around the table to give Marlene a hug and a kiss. She gave Karp a hug and a kiss too, and Marlene saw from the way her husband's body went stiff that Stupenagel was putting a lick more into the transaction than was required by convention.

"Well, that was fun," said Karp after Stupenagel had trotted down the stairs.

"Yes, delightful. You never have to worry about whether Stupe will wear out her welcome because she always does. Yes, I know, she's *my* friend. As so she is, for my sins. Let's clean up—no, *you* clean up. I'm going to walk the dog, lounge in the bath, and then lose myself in a trashy romantic novel."

Later, the two of them lying in bed, Karp was aware of a dense psychic cloud, oily smoke and troubled lightning, emanating from Marlene's side of the bed. Her jaw grinding, her brow furrowed, she was rapidly snapping the pages of her paperback at a pace too quick for reading. At last she tossed the book aside and drew a deep sighing breath.

"What?" he ventured.

"Oh, nothing, just the usual pathetic dissatisfactions of the bourgeois matron."

"She really got to you this time, didn't she?"

"Yeah, but I was ready to be got to." She shifted in bed and gazed into his eyes. Out of long habit, and love, he no longer registered that one of her eyes was not real, but imagined expression in both of them. "Look," she said, "I'm not saying this hasn't been sweet, this last year and a half. I *like* cooking. I even like ironing. It's sort of calm and dreamy and sensuous, when you have plenty of time, and I like having kids in the house and being the place where the kids come, and Lucy loves it too. And I think I needed it, after what went down in D.C. I deserved it. But now . . . I don't know. Something's stirring. Dragons." She paused, then laughed briefly. "My vocation."

Hesitantly Karp asked, "You're saying you want to get back on some kind of career track, right?"

"Yeah, 'career track.' That's just what I *don't* want. I want my blood stirred. I want to feel the way I felt when I was with the rape bureau and I had some scumbag in my sights and I was going to send him away for eight to fifteen, and he knew it and I could see it in his eyes. Or even chasing down that stuff in D.C."

"You could land a D.A. job in a second. As you never fail to remind me, there are four other boroughs."

"Yes, but I already explained why that won't work," replied Marlene impatiently. She flung herself back on the pillows and let out a puff of air. Suddenly she rolled closer to him, flicked her fingers over his lower belly, and nuzzled into his chest. "Ah, shit, we might as well start another baby. Close your mouth, Butch; flies will fly in."

THREE

Marlene shook her daughter into grumpy wakefulness, and then tripped lightly to the toilet and puked again. It was a glorious Monday, the fourth week of first grade and Marlene was pregnant.

"How are you feeling?" asked Karp solicitously across the *Times* and was rewarded with a wordless snarl and a poisonous look. He shut up and raised the wide sheet of newsprint like a drawbridge. Marlene dragged on an ensemble made up of scruffy, striped OshKosh B'Gosh overalls, a T-shirt, and basketball shoes and had her usual fight with Lucy about appropriate school clothes. Lucy refused to wear skirts, and Marlene would not let her wear jeans to school. After a brief contest of wills, they compromised on corduroy slacks and a heavy red turtleneck with embroidered birdies, too hot for the season, but let the little rat sweat her butt off. Lucy brushed her own hair and shrieked when Marlene attempted to correct the snarls. By this time Karp had wisely departed the loft. Breakfast, a war between Froot Loops and a proper breakfast, with the basic food groups, was unpleasant, as was the argument about what would go into the purple Barbie lunch box.

Marlene took a deep breath, fought to control her liquefying gut, and held her hands up in a referee's T. "Okay, time-out. I don't want to fight with you anymore. I'm feeling sick and short-tempered and you're probably picking it up, and it's making you all crazy. I tell you what: Mommy's going to wash her face and brush her hair, and while she's doing that, you can pack your own lunch box with anything in the house."

"Anything?"

"Hey, go for it! As long as it fits."

After that, it went more smoothly. Marlene finished her toilette, including another little spew, and fed the mastiff a quart of kibble. Lucy, for a wonder, remembered her homework, still something of a prized novelty in first grade. It was a large collage of pictures clipped from magazines and pasted on red construction paper, which bore the legend MY NEIGHBORHOOD in careful block letters. Lucy's neighborhood comprised a large midtown bank building, a car, a pizza, a sliver of Chinese writing, a fire engine, and a cat, all of which, except the bank, were undeniably to be found in the environs of Crosby Street. She had done it entirely by herself, including the doily-work border, making very little mess with the rubber cement, and so was inordinately proud of the thing.

The door was thrown open, and the huge dog leaped out and clattered down the stairs, followed

by Lucy at a trot and Marlene at a more dignified
pace. Lucy went to P.S. 1, the City's oldest school
and one of its best, rather than a somewhat closer,
but undistinguished, institution. Marlene had con-
trived this irregular arrangement not only to provide
her darling a better start up life's slippery slope but
also to partially block the outrage of the child's maternal grandmother, to whom all schools not conducted under the auspices of the Church were nests
of vice and crime. (Ma, it's a great school; all the
Chinese kids go there.) As a result, Marlene had
taken upon herself not only the additional burden of
fighting each morning over school clothes (surren-
dering the great and ever underestimated advantage
of school uniforms) but also the responsibility for
transport.

Marlene had a car for this purpose, a beaten-up
VW hatch-back, yellow in color, that she had bought
in D.C. The vehicle was parked illegally in an alley
at the foot of Crosby Street, which Marlene rented at
the cost of about ten traffic tickets per year. Marlene
knew the beat cops, and took care of them, and only
got a ticket when a substitute came on duty, or when
there was a ticketing drive on. There was no paper
under the wiper this morning, which improved her
mood. The dog defecated promptly by the storm
drain, which improved it even more.

Then Marlene, the dog, and the child piled in and
drove off with a rattle, enveloped in blue stink.
Though relatively rich now, she kept the beater, as

she maintained that anyone who ran a decent car in the City was a moron. Which she was not.

Eight minutes—east on Canal and south on the Bowery—brought them to the school, to which, in fact, all the Chinese did send their kids. P.S. 1 was about eighty-five percent Asian, the remainder made up of the children of striving Lower Manhattan moms like Marlene, who had worked a scam to get their kids into this font of Confucian order, discipline, and achievement.

A few of these aliens stood out—blond and auburn accents—among the sable tide of little heads that bobbed above the noisy throng milling along the gate and arched entranceway of the venerable building.

"There's Miranda Lanin!" cried Lucy, pointing at one of these, a blondie. She was out of the car in a flash, clutching her homework project but leaving her lunch box on the seat. Sighing, Marlene switched off the car and trotted after her with lunch.

There were Chinese moms at the entrance too, of course, all of them, Marlene noted with shame, better turned out than she was, although nearly all of them worked a job or two, or three, in addition to running a household. She saw Janice Chen and Mrs. Chen and waved. Janice exchanged a rapid trill of Cantonese with her departing mother and then joined Lucy and Miranda on the steps, switching effortlessly to idiomatic American English, a feat that always knocked Marlene out. As the three girls stood chattering and comparing their neighborhood-view projects, Marlene spotted another familiar face.

"Hey, Carrie," she called.

A pretty blond woman wearing a blue head scarf gave a violent start at hearing her name called, and uttered a sigh of relief, holding her hand dramatically to her breast, when she saw who it was. Marlene had known Carrie Lanin, Miranda's mother, for some years now, in the casual manner of women who live in the same neighborhood and have children of the same sex and age. They had sent their daughters to the same day-care center and play groups and had exchanged pediatrician intelligence. Marlene recalled that she lived in a nice Tribeca loft, without husband, and did something arty with fabrics.

Marlene passed the lunch box to Lucy, who took it without a word, being now immersed in kidworld. A bell rang inside the building, and the children vanished in a murmurous rush.

"Are you okay?" Marlene asked the woman. She was pale and her small features were marked with strain. She seemed to be looking past Marlene down the street, casting anxiously in all directions like an infantry point man seeking snipers.

"Yes," said Lanin, then "No." She stared blankly for a moment before her gaze settled on Marlene's yellow VW.

"Is that your car? Could you, um, give me a lift?" Her blue eyes were red-rimmed and pleading.

"Sure. Get in."

Marlene cranked the engine and moved off down Henry Street, made a four-corner at Catherine, and headed back up Henry for the Bowery. Lanin sat stiffly in her seat, eyes fixed on the passenger-side mirror.

"Where's your car?" asked Marlene conversationally.

"In the shop. We came by cab."

"Uh-huh." They were headed west on Canal. "You're on what? Duane, right?"

"Yeah, 152, off West Broadway."

Marlene hung a left on Greenwich and turned downtown. The closer they got to Duane Street, the more nervous her passenger became. As they passed Jay Street, she was twitching like a trapped rabbit and craning her neck in an attempt to cover all directions at once.

"Who are we avoiding, Carrie?" Marlene asked gently.

"Oh, God, this guy. It's been going on for a month. I'm losing my fucking marbles behind it." She sighed heavily and moisture pearled on her golden eyelashes.

"You called the cops?"

"Oh, right, the cops!" snapped Lanin contemptuously. "The cops do not think this is a high priority. Wait, just pull in front of this red truck." Marlene brought the VW to the curb. Lanin gazed into the car's mirrors and looked out the window, checking the street and the nearby cars.

"Who *is* this guy? Jack the Ripper?" asked Marlene.

"Don't joke! We're talking somebody with a serious screw loose. Look, you're going to think I'm crazy, but could you walk me up to my loft? I have a funny feeling—"

"No problem," said Marlene, and started to get out of the car. Lanin seemed to notice the big dog for the first time. "He'll be okay in the car? I wouldn't want him to get stolen."

"I wouldn't worry about that," said Marlene confidently. She popped the rear hatch and massaged the dog's floppy neck. Sweety sighed and sprayed drool. "Sweety is a doggie-college grad," said Marlene, ruffling the dog's ears. "Aren't you? *Aren't you?* Yeah, I sprang for the whole nine yards: obedience, guard, attack. Now that I have some assets, all I need is for this monster to take a chunk out of a citizen. Without good reason, of course. So, guaranteed, anybody who broke into that car, we'd find a neat pile of cleaned bones."

Carrie Lanin's building was a fine old cast-iron-fronted commercial building that had been bought by a speculator a few years back and turned into floor-through condos. Marlene vaguely recalled that Carrie had married some serious money and had done well in the divorce. There was even an elevator, which Lanin summoned with a special cylinder key.

Lanin uttered a loud wail and then a string of curses when the elevator door slid open at her floor. Marlene pushed forward to see what the problem was. It was apparently the long-stemmed rose wrapped in green cellophane, with an envelope attached, leaning against the metal door to Lanin's loft.

"That's from him, huh?"

"Yeah, God damn him! That means he's figured out how to work the elevator." She snatched up the rose and unlocked her loft door. Marlene put a restraining hand on her shoulder and said quietly, "Why don't you wait here and keep the elevator? If he figured how to work that, he could have figured your door lock too. Let me just check it out."

Lanin's eyes went wide and she froze, holding the rose in front of her like the prom queen in a horror movie. Marlene went into the loft.

She was not frightened at all. Rather, she found herself wondering why she was not, and why she was putting herself into this peculiar situation for a woman she hardly knew. She took a breath, cleared her mind, and went in.

The loft's main room was a lovely space, full of light from the huge semicircular window facing the street. The floors were shiny oak accented by bright Rya rugs; the furniture was fashionable Danish teak and Haitian cotton. It was an easy place to search: the only private rooms were two bedrooms and a small office-studio. Marlene went through these swiftly, peering under beds and into closets. She had no idea what she would have done had she found an obsessive man lurking there, but, as it turned out, the place was empty.

"Marlene?" a quavering call from the doorway.

"It's okay, there's no one here. I'm in the bedroom."

Carrie Lanin came stomping into her loft, cursing

under her breath. Marlene heard the sound of a sink running and the grind of a disposal. She went out to the kitchen, which was a slick number built around a sink-and-cooktop island, and was in time to see the last of the rose disappearing down the sink.

"What did the note say?" asked Marlene.

"Fuck if I know. It's in the trash. Jesus, I need a drink, I don't care how early it is." Lanin reached a half-full bottle of Jack Daniel's down from an upper cabinet and poured herself a large one over ice. "Want something?" she asked after a deep swallow and a mild coughing fit.

"Not for me, thanks," said Marlene. "Where's the trash?"

Lanin gestured at a chrome can; Marlene opened it and lifted out the crumpled envelope. "Ecch! What are you doing?" Lanin exclaimed, wrinkling her nose.

"Just curious. I think, by the way, if you're going to have any chance of stopping this guy, you'll want to keep his little offerings." Marlene smoothed out the envelope and opened it. Inside was a plain card, unsigned and inscribed in black ink, "Love Til the End of time." The writing was rectilinear and excessively neat, like the inscriptions on a blueprint or circuit diagram.

"Stopping him? What do you mean?" Lanin took another sip and, as the light dawned, she suddenly pointed her finger at her guest. "Oh, I remember now, you're some kind of cop . . . no, something to do with raped women—"

"I was an assistant D.A. I used to run the rape bureau."

"But you know people!" said Lanin excitedly. "You can pull some strings . . ."

Marlene shook her head. "No—hold on, Carrie! My string-pulling days are over. In any case, even if I was still with the office, there probably isn't a whole hell of a lot I could do. Being an annoying asshole is not against the law—unfortunately, maybe, but there it is."

"But, Marlene, the guy *won't leave me alone!* He calls me every night, sometimes more than once. He uses up my answering machine tape playing 'Twist and Shout' over and over—"

"Why 'Twist and Shout'?"

"Oh, because it was 'our song.'"

"Was it?"

"*Was it?*" Lanin's voice rose to a screech. "*Was it?* Marlene, I don't even *know* this son of a bitch. It's all *in his head!*"

"Wait a minute—he just, like, *seized* on you on the street?"

Lanin sighed deeply and rolled her eyes. "You want the whole story? You got an hour?"

As it happened, Marlene's calendar was free for at least the next eight months, so Lanin made some coffee and Marlene sat down on the Haitian cotton sofa, and Carrie Lanin settled herself on the bentwood rocker across from her, sipping from a steaming mug enriched with a tot of sour mash bourbon and told her tale.

"I went to high school in Jersey—Englewood Cliffs. I was sort of a player in high school—captain of the cheerleaders, junior prom queen—like that. People knew me. Okay, a couple of months ago, it must have been before we went to the beach, like June, I'm in Gristede's on Sixth, picking up some things, when this guy comes up to me in the dairy department. 'Carrie Tiptree?' he says—my maiden name, right? He holds out his hand and says his name's Rob Pruitt, he went to high school with me. So I sort of smile back at him. Of course, I don't remember him at all. I mean, if I ever actually saw him, he was just a face in the crowd. So we started chatting, he carried my packages for me, and I thought, okay, a pleasant guy, chance meeting, nothing special to look at but neat. I mean, he didn't have red eyes and fangs. After I got home, I was curious, so I dragged out the old yearbook and looked him up."

She paused, and Marlene asked, "He was there? In the yearbook?"

"Oh, yeah. Want to see?" Without waiting for an answer, Lanin went to the bookcase and brought back a volume bound in maroon imitation leather and marked CLIFFHANGER in faded gold. She riffled through it and handed it, opened, to Marlene.

"That's him—Robert T. Pruitt, no nickname, no friendly little tag line, one extracurricular activity," said Lanin.

"The rifle team," read Marlene. She examined the tiny photograph: Pruitt was a close-faced youth who looked more than usually stupid in his academic cap. Dark and unruly hair squirted out from under this headgear, and the retoucher had not been entirely able to disguise a bad case of acne.

"See? A geek," said Lanin.

"Is he still geekish?"

"No, and that's what sort of threw me. He looks regular, normal. I mean, he had a neat haircut, and he was wearing, like, chinos, Nikes, and a white shirt. And it made me feel sort of sad—I mean, high school is such hell. I was in and he was out, and I guess the in-crowd just doesn't think about what it's like for the nothing people, the ones who aren't rich, or bright, or gorgeous, or funny. So, uh, I don't know whether it was guilt or what, but he asked me for my number and I gave it to him."

"And he called, of course."

"The next day. Asked me out for dinner that Friday. In retrospect, needless to say, I should've heard the alarm bells going off. But I figured, what the fuck, right? New York is not exactly full of straight guys dying to buy nice meals for thirty-one-year-old divorced ladies with kids. Plus, he was at least presentable, and there was that expiation thing, being a little princess in high school and ignoring kids like him. And he lost the pizza face—I figured he deserved something for that, too. So, Friday, he arrives at the door, dead on time. He's still got the chinos and the white shirt, but now he's wearing a leather jacket, not the cool kind, but the kind that looks like a sports jacket. It's like brand-new and shiny. And he's got a fucking Whitman's Sampler box of chocolates and a huge purple orchid in a plastic box."

Marlene could not suppress a snort of laughter.

"Yeah, *you're* laughing," said Lanin, whose mood had much improved. "As a matter of fact, I thought it was pretty funny too, at first."

"Sorry," said Marlene. "So then what?"

"So then, after I put the goddamn orchid in the fridge, we went out. He's rented a *limo* for the evening. With a driver. Okay, to be brutally honest, this is not something that happens to me a lot. I'm dying of curiosity. So I try to pump him on the ride up, what does he do, where does he live, what's happened since high school. He's not saying. What does he do? A little of this, a little of that. He lives 'uptown.' Actually, it turns out he only wants to talk about me, and what happened to the people in my crowd back then. So I perform, I bullshit away, but meanwhile, I'm thinking, uh-oh, please let this guy not be in the dope business, because that's all my ex needs to hear, I'm keeping company with Mr. Coke, it's court again and maybe good-bye, Miranda."

"Where did he take you?"

"Elaine's. Where else? Of course, there's a line outside, and when our limo pulls up, they're all gaping. The doorman looks at us funny, but he lets us past—I guess a limo is a limo. Also the geek's got reservations, which means he's not a regular, but we go up to the maître d' and Rob says he wants us to have a banquette table, where all the celebrities sit. The guy smiles and shakes his head, and then Rob pulls out a roll of bills, Marlene, I swear it was the size of a pastrami sandwich and solid twenties, and he starts peeling them off one by one onto the maître d's little lectern. And the guy's embarrassed, you can tell, but all the same, he can't take his eyes off the pile of bills."

"So you got the good seats?"

"Oh, yeah, the best. Burt Reynolds was at the next table. And we saw Bill Murray and a bunch of people from *Saturday Night Live*. I was looking for Woody and Mia, but they didn't show."

"Poor you," said Marlene. "Let me understand this: you are *running away* from this guy? This is your *problem*?"

"Oh, God!" Carrie wailed, "I *knew* you were going to say that. Okay, listen to the rest of it. There we are, and, to be frank, I'm pretty excited. I mean, the Bread Shop on Duane Street is my usual speed since the divorce, and I'm trying to get a conversation going. But there's nothing coming from him. Zip. He's not looking around. He's barely interested in his food. He's just looking at me, as if he's finally achieved this big dream and I'm just some kind of trophy. The geek bagged the prom queen? Right about then the little buzzer started to go off: *wronggg! wronggg!* And after that all I could think about was, this guy must have blown a grand tonight, he's going to expect his money's worth, being, as I now realize, the same old geek but with money, and how the hell am I going to keep him out of my panties?"

"And did you?"

"Oh, yeah. As it turned out, that wasn't a problem. We get back here. I turn to him, grab his hand, give it one shake, say 'thank you very much for dinner, Rob,' and I'm gone. And he took it, didn't say a word. So, I pay the sitter, have a bath, go to bed. Around three a.m. the phone rings. I let the machine take it. In the morning, I see the blinker and I play the tape. It's him, and it's weird. In this voice, 'Hi, it's me.' Like we've been married for six years, and then he starts talking about what a great time we had and how he'll be around to pick me up at eight, and a lot of other crap about how he always knew I liked him in high school but he had to get his shit together before he was worthy of me, and how, way back when, he was in this place, this joint we used to hang out at in high school, Larry's, and somebody played 'Twist and Shout' on the jukebox and I looked at him and he knew that our love was real. It was incredible. It just went on and on like that, and then he played the song."

"What did you do?" asked Marlene.

"I got out of town is what I did. I called up my friend Beth in Southhampton and said it was life or death, and I grabbed the kid and took off. Okay, we get there, we swim, around six we're out on the deck in our bathing suits having a drink, when the doorbell rings and in walks Pruitt, like we planned it all. Beth gives me a look, but what could I say to her? So I take him aside and give him a piece of my mind. It's like talking to a wall. He just smiles. He says he just wants to be with me. So I leave. He follows me, of cours He's been following me ever since. I go out on a date, for dinner, he's sitting at a table in the back, staring. Once I ran up to him on the street and started screaming at him to leave me alone. People were staring at me. He just kept smiling, like it was a lovers' spat, for Christ's sake!"

She finished her drink in a gulp. "I'm going crazy."

Marlene said gently, "Okay, let's look at this realistically. So far, except for this trespass today, which we can't really prove, he hasn't done anything criminal. I say that because you'll have to nail him for an actual crime in order to get him to stop." She halted—something had passed over Carrie's face. "Or am I wrong—has he done something else?"

"I don't know. There's a guy I see, Don Grier, nothing earthshaking, just a nice friendly relationship. Anyway, I saw him last week, Saturday. Sunday somebody blew up his car—sneaked into his garage and stuck a signal flare in the gas tank."

"You think it was Pruitt?"

"Um, yeah, actually I do. I mean, Don's a production manager at *Vogue*. You think somebody at *Mademoiselle* was trying to send him a message?"

"You tell the cops about this?"

"I told Don. God, Marlene, the embarrassment! I think he told the cops. They weren't impressed, apparently. He hasn't called since then, by the way."

"Who, Pruitt?"

"No, Don. Pruitt calls every night. What?"

Marlene had involuntarily creased her face into a

concerned frown. She said, "I think you could have a serious problem here, Carrie. This guy, if he did the car arson, well, we know he's capable of committing a felony. If he did one, he could do another."

"What, you mean I could be in *danger*?"

"It's a possibility. We had cases like this when I was at the D.A. Stalking cases. Sometimes the guy's just a pathetic asshole, and he gives up or gets drunk and forgets it, or drifts away or lands in jail. Or it could happen that the guy decides that if he can't have you, nobody else can."

Lanin had gone deathly pale. "You mean, he could, like *attack* me?"

"Yeah, but let's not get ahead of ourselves, okay? I said I couldn't pull strings, but that's not completely true. I know cops, actually one cop in particular, who'd be willing to help out. Let me take a day or so to look into it, see if this bozo has a sheet on him, find out where he's coming from. He knows a lot about you, and our first step is to find out something about him."

"But what'll I do meanwhile?" Lanin cried.

"Nothing different from what you're doing now. I'd suggest you keep your social contacts limited, especially with guys—not for your sake, for theirs. And let me pick up and drop off Miranda for a while. You should stick close to home and work until we can get this sorted out. You should get your phone number changed too."

"Oh, Jesus, I can't believe this is happening. You're sure you want to get involved. . . ?"

"Oh,   problem," said Marlene lightly. "I was looking   something to pass the time. I'm pregnant.

Lanin' mouth opened, then closed, and then opened again to let out a spluttering laugh, not that far from hysteria. "Congratulations!" she said, and giggled.

"Thə   you," said Marlene, and then, "Could I use yo   bathroom?"

Marlene left Carrie Lanin's shortly after throwing up the remains of her light breakfast, did some quick food shopping, carefully averting her eyes from the display   meat at DiAngelo's, and returned to the loft, where she immediately put in a call to Harry Bello at the D.A.'s office. Bello was a former Brooklyn homicide detective whom Marlene had recruited to work with the Rape Bureau when she had been in charge of it. He was also Lucy Karp's godfather. Bello agreed to check out Robert Pruitt. He didn't ask any questions or require any covering small talk to get him in the mood to help. That was one of the nice things about Bello, who did not have that many other nice things about him.

At two-thirty, she left to pick up the two kids at school. Carrie Lanin had called ahead, and Miranda was waiting with Lucy in the schoolyard. As she put the kids in the car, she noticed a man leaning against an old blue Dodge Fury. He was looking at them, or rather,   as looking at Miranda, because when she ran back   the chain-link gate to pick up a paper she had forgotten, shoved into the links of the fence, the man's eyes followed the child.

Marlene made sure the children were belted in and said, "Girls, just give me a minute, I have to walk Sweety," and then went around and popped open the hatchback. Sweety, who did not need a walk at all but who was not going to turn down a freebie, leaped out. Marlene snapped the short leather lead onto its collar and headed down Henry Street. She went once past the schoolyard and then crossed and came back down the other side. The dog snuffled along the curb, marked a power pole, sniffed the tires of the Fury and the shoes of the man leaning against it. Marlene looked him straight in the face. His hair was shorter and thinner than it had been in high school, and his skin was clear and tanned, but the eyes, pale and a shade too close together under straight, heavy brows, were the same. It was Pruitt. He returned her look with a blank stare for a moment and then opened his car door abruptly, so that she had to pull the dog sharply away from its swing. Then he sat down in the driver's seat and started the engine. As she walked back to her car, she could feel his eyes on her back.

All in all, Marlene considered that the heroism she was displaying in involving herself in the confrontation of a potentially dangerous stalker was as nothing compared to what she went through in preparing a nice dinner for her family that evening. The odor of broiling lamb chops went right to her gut, and it was only with the greatest of self-control that she managed to cook, serve, and sit through the meal. She herself consumed only a few small chunks of Italian bread.

"Not eating?" observed her husband.

"Can't slip anything past you," replied Marlene tightly.

"Are you sick, or. . . ?"

"It's definitely 'or.' I made an appointment with Memelstein to confirm."

Karp beamed and leaned over to kiss her cheek. "That's great, babe."

"What's great?" asked Lucy Karp.

"Mommy's pregnant," said Karp, and, seeing the blank expression on her face, added, "She's going to have another baby. It'll be your brother. Or sister."

"Which one?" asked Lucy suspiciously.

"We don't know yet."

"Could she sleep in my room?"

"We'll see."

"I made my own lunch today," said Lucy after a pause.

"Really? What did you have?"

"Chocolate chip cookies and ice cream. And a celery," Lucy said and added, "For health."

"Didn't the ice cream melt?"

"No," said Lucy straight-faced. "Can I watch TV? I mean, may I be excused?"

After the child had dashed off, Karp said, "That was a competent lie."

"What do you expect from the spawn of two law-yers? And what did *you* do today, dear?"

"Among many other duties, I filed Murray's suit first thing this morning. The Bloom thing."

"Bloom? I thought the Mayor and the health department were the defendants."

"Legally, yes. But Bloom is behind it all. Which I will demonstrate. And find out why. Speaking of which, do you remember Phil DeLino?"

"Vaguely," said Marlene. "He worked for you when you had Criminal Courts. He didn't stay long, did he?"

"No, he was one of those guys who zip through to punch their ticket. But a good guy. A great deal maker. Even if he had a losing hand, he'd tough it out with the defendant. And he'd go to trial too; he had the balls for it. I was sorry to lose him. Anyway, he called me late today. He's a special assistant in the Mayor's office."

"Yeah? What did he want?"

"To talk about the suit. Off the record. The Mayor apparently is not pleased. I'm seeing him tomorrow."

Marlene got up and started clearing dishes. "Speaking of former acquaintances, I spent the morning with Carrie Lanin. Did you ever meet her?"

"She was in that play group, right? Madeleine?"

"Miranda. She was spooked. It seems somebody she went to high school with is stalking her." She filled Karp in on Lanin's story while she washed and he dried.

"You think the guy could be dangerous?" asked

Karp as he tossed chop bones to Sweety, who crunched them up like Fritos.

"That's what I'm going to try and find out. I got Harry in on it."

Karp paused in his wiping as a familiar and unpleasant thought sprang into his consciousness. "Uh, Marlene, this isn't going to, um, get you into *trouble*, is it?"

"It's too early to tell. And what if it is? You know I—" She stopped talking and grimaced as a spasm of nausea passed.

"What's the matter? Still feeling sick?"

Marlene groaned. "Yes. They call it morning sickness for a good reason. It's not supposed to last all fucking day."

"Maybe it's different when you're carrying a first-round NBA draft choice in your womb. Extra male hormones. . . ?"

Marlene giggled in spite of herself. "You're going to be pissed off if it's a short, neurasthenic poet."

"That won't happen if you do your part, Marlene. You have nine months. Think tall, think moves, think hands."

He dropped the dishcloth and moved around behind her, embracing her from in back. She leaned back against him comfortably and said, "Maybe I should consume old sweat socks and jockstraps too, diced."

"If you think it will help," said Karp lovingly into her ear.

FOUR

Phil DeLino was a big, open-faced man with dark, humorous eyes. He wore a nice gray double-breasted three-piece suit that was working hard to cover the weight he had put on since he played tight end for Fordham. His greeting to Karp in his office was warm and seemed sincere.

The small office in City Hall was suitably elegant. It had a window, the appointments were made of wood or leather, and there was a genuine oil painting of a minor nineteenth-century civic luminary on the wall, looking smug and well grafted. Seated, they passed the time in obligatory catching up and discussing the prospects of the various New York teams.

When this pleasant diversion had gone on for ten minutes or so, there was a pause, and DeLino picked up a blue-bound legal notice from his desk and tapped it a few times. "This thing here, Butch. This is a problem."

"Yes. You mentioned that the Mayor was not pleased."

"You could say that. He called Josh Gottkind as

soon as he found out, and I think they had to replace the phone wires; they were fried. Our corporation counsel is not in favor this fine day."

"You mean it took His Honor by surprise? What did he think Selig would do? Say, 'Gee, thanks for the job, sorry it didn't work out'? It's hard to believe Gottkind didn't discuss the issue with him before he decided to go ahead."

DeLino paused judiciously and smiled before saying, "I think 'before' is the operative word. Those of us who serve His Honor rarely get a chance to advise him *before* he makes his mind up. Our job, and he's made the point more than once, is to keep him out of trouble when he does what he's decided to do anyway."

And take the crap he hands out when it goes sour, thought Karp. He said, "So he wishes this had never happened?"

"Profoundly. And he intends to be forthcoming and cooperative in every way, so that as little of the poo that's going to be flying around sticks to him."

"Dr. Fuerza's been nominated to carry the can, in other words," observed Karp. "But there's going to be a lot to carry. The Mayor will not look great under the best of circumstances."

DeLino nodded and considered this for a long moment. Then he asked, "I guess there's no way to solve this little problem in a civilized way?"

"Well, yeah, actually there is. If Dr. Selig could be reinstated, with back pay, and with a public acknowledgment that the accusations about his professional and personal behavior were entirely groundless and the result of misinformation purposely conveyed to the Mayor by the parties that wrote the two memos . . ."

But DeLino was already smiling and shaking his head. "Yeah, right," he said, "Gottkind would really go for that; we fire somebody for cause and as soon as we get threatened by a lawsuit, we announce that the cause was trumped-up? The City would look like an asshole."

"The Mayor would, you mean."

"Is there a difference? Okay, granted, we may have to go to the mat on this one, but"—he glanced again at the legal form on his desk, and at a sheet of paper that seemed to have notes scribbled on it—"do you really think you have a Fourteenth Amendment liberty claim here?"

"Yeah, we do," said Karp.

"Really? What the hell's the theory? It sure as shit isn't a *Bishop* case."

Karp grinned and replied, "You know, I still like the Celtics for the NBA title this year. They picked up Parrish and McHale, and if Bird is hot again . . ."

DeLino chuckled. "Okay, okay, I wasn't trying to pump you. This is off the record anyway, just a couple of old jocks talking about sports and the grandeur of the law."

Karp saw DeLino glance at him expectantly. Karp was familiar with the look of men wanting to pass him information, if he would only ask in the right way. He said, "Off the record, huh? Okay, Phil, off the record, I would like to know why."

"Why what?"

"Why this happened," said Karp. "Why the Mayor bought himself a bunch of problems by firing a man well known as one of the best forensic scientists in the country. It doesn't make sense."

"It does if you think the C.M.E's slot is more than forensics. And the Mayor never impugned his forensic skills. He just said Selig was administratively sloppy and had an attitude problem. He was arrogant and—"

"Oh, horseshit, Phil! Arrogant? Well, compared to most of the people working for the Mayor, including Dr. Fuerza, he at least had something to be arrogant about. And since when is administrative competence a qualification for a job in New York?"

DeLino laughed. Karp continued, "No, really! And don't give me the party line—you know there was political clout behind this, and Fuerza doesn't have much to speak of, which leaves one person."

The other man dropped his eyes and pursed his lips and then looked up again and said, "He's been after the Mayor for months on this. We ran on a strong anti-crime platform, as you know, and this year we're running on it again. We can't have anyone big in criminal justice saying the Mayor is soft on crime or not supporting the work of the district attorney. Bloom claimed Selig was impossible to work with. He was inefficient, he lost evidence, his people were screwing up cases. The argument was made that we might get into a situation where a big, high-profile case went down the tubes because of an M.E. problem and that all of this would come out: the Mayor knew about it and didn't act on time, and now a dread killer is back on the street, and so on, and so on. We were assured that the guy was, I mean—whatever his slice and dice skills in the morgue—he was a bum as a leader, and when the stuff we had on him was presented, he'd just slink away. I mean, it wouldn't be the first time that a technician got promoted over his head and fucked up. So Fuerza got the job of digging up supporting stuff that'd make him look bad, and wrote his memo, and Bloom wrote his memo, and so here we are."

DeLino looked at his visitor, examining his reaction to this information. He saw Karp staring blankly at the window, his cheeks sucked in. It was a characteristic pose that he recalled from his days with the D.A., one that signaled intense thought. It lasted for a long fifteen seconds. Then Karp asked abruptly, "When did it start exactly? How long has Bloom been nudging the Mayor to can Selig?"

"Gosh, I couldn't say," said DeLino, surprised. "Why does it matter?"

"Can you find out?"

The man laughed nervously. "Uh, yeah, I could probably find out, but—"

"But why should you help me?" Karp asked rhetorically. "Well, look at it this way, Phil. I believe my case is good enough to rip the City a new asshole, and you know I'm a pretty good judge of cases. I think you guys screwed up royally, on Mr. Bloom's bad advice. Now, the Mayor doesn't want to carry the can for it, and we agree that poor little Angie Fuerza *can't* carry the *whole* can, so who's left? And I'm sure you'll want the Mayor's experience on the witness stand at the trial—because, believe me, we're going to trial on this one—to be as dignified and unstressful as possible. In fact, I think you'd like to be able to go in there right now and tell His Honor that the deal is done in that department, wouldn't you?"

DeLino smiled the rueful smile of a fixer who has himself been fixed. "I take your point," he said. "Let me get back to you on that."

"Is it Sunday already?" asked Lucy Karp when she awakened to find her mother wearing a dark suit, a blood-colored silk blouse and stockings.

"No, baby," Marlene laughed, "it's a school day. I just have some business downtown. I put your clothes out for you."

Lucy glanced over at the top of her bureau, where a red jumper, white shirt, and yellow- and red-striped tights were neatly arranged. She grimaced but said nothing. Ten minutes later, she appeared in the kitchen and sat down at the table. Marlene noted that instead of the pretty tights Lucy was wearing her worn jeans under the jumper, but decided to say nothing; healthful eggs, toast, and milk were going down without a murmur, and she did not have time for a major battle this morning. With a tiny pang she realized that a certain perfection in child rearing was going to go by the boards as she started working again, and hoped Lucy's psychiatrist would explain this to her twenty years hence.

Keys, raincoat, slicker for Lucy were gathered up and the dog was marshaled, panting and dripping slime at the door. A grocery bag was found for Lucy's project, a shoebox diorama depicting the purchase of Manhattan Island from the Indians by Peter Minuet. She had used one of her prized possessions, a plastic wedding-cake groom, as a stand-in for the canny Dutchman, who stood proudly extending a mass of cut-up Monopoly money to several glum paper Manahattas, while in the background ranged the forest primeval, populated by plastic animals: an armadillo, a polar bear, and a lavender warthog. Marlene was surprised to see that Lucy had done a second shoebox, in which Minuet was a tiny pink baby doll wrapped in cloth and glue, with a beard made of a swatch of Lucy's own black hair, and the Indians were red modeling clay.

"You did two projects?"

"Yes."

"What, for extra credit?"

"No. I made one for Bobby Crandall."

"Why couldn't he make one himself?"

Lucy shrugged. "He said he couldn't. He wanted one like mine."

"Um, darling, I don't think you're supposed to do other people's work for them. I think it's against the rules, you know?"

At which point Lucy shrugged again and uttered a stream of twittering Chinese.

Marlene's mouth opened in stupefaction. "What the f—, I mean, what was *that*, dear? Chinese?"

Lucy looked away, as if bored by her accomplishment. "Janice Chen says it."

"But what does it mean?" asked Marlene.

An impatient grimace. "It doesn't *mean* something, Mommy, it's just a *saying*."

Marlene experienced another of the peculiar feelings she was having about Lucy in recent months, compounded oddly of loss, fear, and pride. Her daughter spoke Chinese! Her daughter had a secret life at seven years! The birth closeness was fading, was almost gone; what would replace it was at the moment still in flux.

They left the house early to pick up Miranda Lanin on Duane Street. Carrie Lanin was waiting by the door with her daughter. "Any contact?" Marlene asked.

"The usual. He called a couple of times last night."

"You have the tapes?" Carrie nodded and handed Marlene a cassette. "And this." She gave Marlene a box containing a cheerleader doll and a note in the same precise writing. It said, "My Love is strong and True. I'd do anything to be with You. Love always."

"Unsigned, as usual. Did you see him?"

"No, this was left on the seat of my car. I almost fainted."

"Was the car locked?"

"Of course!"

"Okay, that's good. A little B and E never fails to impress. You know what to do?"

"Yeah, go to work and come home."

"And stay there. Things may start to heat up."

Marlene gathered the two girls and drove them to P.S. 1. She looked for Pruitt's blue Dodge but didn't see it. Maybe stalkers took a day off; she hoped he hadn't picked this one.

Two hours later, Marlene was waiting impatiently at a scarred metal desk in the nest of cubicles used by the D.A. squad, a group of detectives that did special tasks for the district attorney's office. In the main these involved corruption investigations, but squad members also took on the jobs that in private practice fell to private detectives: finding and bringing in witnesses, looking things up, and other official minutiae. Marlene was waiting for one detective in particular, who was engaged, she hoped, in none of these official duties.

She saw him come in the door, a compact man in a rumpled gray suit and the traditional gum-soled black shoes. Harry Bello was in his early fifties but looked older. He had a face like a fallen leaf in a gutter, brownish gray and drooping and crumpled with lines. If he stood on a corner, or in a doorway, or sat on a park bench, not one in a thousand would see him, or would notice him only as part of the furniture of the street, a trash basket, a standpipe, which was one reason why he was a great detective.

He had been known for it in Brooklyn for twenty years until his wife had gotten sick and Bello started to drink heavily, and then his partner was killed in a shoot-out, while Harry sat hung-over in the car, and then his wife died and he drank more heavily, and during a long bout of this he gunned down a kid who might or might not have been the kid who killed his partner. The cops had covered that up and shifted Bello to a quiet precinct to log hours until retirement.

From this living tomb Marlene had redeemed him, if not to full life, then to a useful sort of walking death. Bello no longer drank, but neither was he working a spiritual program at A.A., unless you figured that his relationship with Marlene and her daughter filled that purpose. His eyes were like cinders, burnt and dangerous.

Bello approached his desk, acknowledged Marlene's presence with a nod, and handed her a slip of paper. She looked at it and, rolling a legal form into the old Royal on the desk, typed for a few minutes.

"You have any trouble?" she asked.

"No. The guy followed her cab until she went into the building. He parked the car and followed her in there too, and a security guard booted him out. He got a ticket."

"Good. Then?"

"He drove around for a while and then went home. I came back here."

Marlene looked at the address on her form, which was an application for a protective order. "Avenue D? I thought the guy had money. It must be a dump, in that neighborhood, right?"

"The pipeline," said Harry.

Marlene stared at him. She was by now used to Bello's habit of announcing a conclusion without any intervening explanation, the result of having worked the street for many years with a partner to whom he was exceptionally well tuned. Although she often found, to her surprise, that she could follow him in these logical leaps, this particular one left her baffled.

"What pipeline, Harry? What are you talking about?"

"Alaska. He worked there a couple, three years. Made about fifty K a year, didn't spend a dime. No sheet. It was in the car."

Marlene rapidly translated this into human speech. Harry had broken into Pruitt's car and found some papers, probably old pay stubs, that had enabled him to make some phone calls. Harry was inarticulate by choice, not through defect; he could charm and bully people as the need arose with the best of them, and he had obviously wormed his information out of some clerk in Prudhoe Bay. And he'd run Pruitt's name through the NIC computer and come up blank. Marlene imagined Pruitt wrestling giant pipes under the midnight sun, lost in a fantasy of reclaimed nonexistent love; she thought such a man unlikely to be seriously dismayed by a protective order. Nevertheless, that was the next step.

She collected her papers and stood up. "Thanks, Harry," she said and kissed him on the cheek. "Let me go and file this, and we'll see what happens."

*   *   *

What happened was that a few days later Marlene received from a bored and harried judge a protection order forbidding Robert Pruitt from approaching or attempting to communicate with Carrie Lanin on pain of contempt of court, which event was duly celebrated by Marlene and her client with a delightful dinner at Rocco's on Thompson Street; after which, Marlene, who had crashed heavily into sodden sleep, was awakened at a quarter to three in the morning by the phone ringing in her ear.

It was Carrie Lanin, crying and screaming by turns.

"Calm down, Carrie, I can't understand what you're saying," Marlene said.

"What is it? Who's that?" asked Karp, startled out of his own deep sleep.

"Carrie Lanin," answered Marlene shortly, and then said into the phone, "Carrie, calm down and tell me what happened."

"Christ, doesn't she own a clock? It's three in the morning," Karp mumbled, and put a pillow over his head.

"He was here!" Lanin sobbed. "You said it would be *over*, but he came *here!* He sat on my *bed* and talked to me and *stroked my fucking hair!"*

Marlene felt her stomach roil, and a sour bubble of used food rose into her throat. She was out of practice, but she remembered how to suppress the empathy and get the facts from the vic. She sharpened her voice to penetrate the blubbering. "Did he assault you? Were you raped?"

"No! No, he just stroked me. He said . . . he said he was saving it for when *we got married*! Oh, God, make this stop! I want my life back!"

More crying. Marlene relaxed slightly. If there wasn't a rape, there was no immediate need to get Carrie Lanin picked up and packed off to a hospital rape center. "Carrie, listen to me. He broke in to your home at night. He touched you. That's burglary and assault right there; plus he violated the protection order. We've got him. He's going to jail."

Lanin didn't seem to hear. "He kept saying you were keeping us apart, like in high school. 'Your snotty friends.' He said, 'You shouldn't have done it, darling. Going to court. We can solve all our problems ourselves. You don't need that bitch lawyer.' I was paralyzed. I didn't want to scream. I didn't want to wake Miranda. God, can you imagine? What she'd think? The effect. . . ? So I just let him talk. I played along with his crazy rap. I thought he might get violent."

"You probably did the right thing," said Marlene. "Look, from one point of view this is the best thing that could've happened—"

"Oh, right! It would even've been better if he'd raped me and carved his initials on my forehead. Then he would've gone away for a long time—maybe. What do really bad rapists get nowadays? Ten years?"

"About that. It depends," Marlene replied, uncomfortable in the knowledge that, to judge from the statutory sentence ranges, the state of New York considered selling marijuana in bulk a lot more serious than first-degree rape. A really horrendous, violent rapist might draw six to eighteen, and be paroled right after the minimum, and people who raped women they knew, especially women of the same age and race and class, usually got a lot less. Or walked. But Marlene kept all that to herself, instead pumping assurances over the wire for all she was worth, ignoring for the moment the possibility that she would not be able to deliver on them. After forty minutes of this, she had calmed Lanin down enough to end the conversation in good conscience, with a promise that she'd see her in the morning.

Which was not that far off. Marlene could not fall back asleep and stared resentfully at Karp, who could and had, pillow still in place over his head. She rose, showered, dressed, made coffee, and drank it in her little office at the far end of the loft, watching dawn come up Crosby Street and listening to the late-night sounds of the City, the sirens, the occasional roar of a car, slowly build to the crescendo of a working day.

She was slow and stupid as she pressed through the morning chores. Karp was up and out early, with only a perfunctory word and a hurried kiss. He obviously had a full plate with the Selig case, and Marlene was reluctant to worry him with Carrie Lanin. And if she allowed herself to think about it, she *was* worried, because if ever she'd seen a ticking human grenade, it was Pruitt, and she'd seen a lot of them in her work, of the DAD KILLS MOM, TOTS, SELF variety, and she *wanted* to share the problem with Karp. That's what marriage was for, in her opinion, or would be, were the marriage not between a basically cryptic and surreptitious woman and a man for whom the expression *straight arrow* might have been especially devised.

As she drove to the Lanin residence, she was therefore running through her head one of those fictitious conversations that are the chief barrier to actual communication between people married to each other. She told Karp what was going on, about her fears for Lanin, about her general frustration with a system that seemed incapable of protecting women from the lethal fantasies of certain men, about her fears of being sucked into a cycle of violence, about her inexplicable fascination with deadly risk. In her head, Karp answered logically, maddeningly obtuse: you know the law; some get away with it, some don't; work inside the system; we've got our own lives to worry about; do what you can, but don't go crazy. But what if doing what you can *made* you crazy? To that the mentalized Karp had no answer. Nor did Marlene.

Carrie Lanin was drunk when Marlene came to her door; it was clear that she hadn't slept either, and she hadn't spent the small hours calmly watching the dawn break. She looked at Marlene with a hard eye, her face saying, you should have saved me from this. And there was nothing Marlene could reply to this, except hollow, comforting banalities, as we do to a friend's news of cancer.

Marlene dropped the kids off and went back to her loft to work the phone. The first person she called was Luisa Beckett, once something of a protégée of Marlene's, and now in charge of sex crimes at the New York D.A.

"What can I do for you, Marlene?" Beckett asked without preamble as soon as Marlene had announced herself. The two women had become estranged after Marlene's sudden unexplained exit from her job, a move that had left Beckett with an impossible burden and a radical, and equally unexplained, dimunition of support from the district attorney. Beckett was a true believer; Marlene, having bugged out to wealth and indolence, was clearly not, and her tone indicated that she had little time for chat with well-off housewives.

"I did some work recently for a friend of mine," began Marlene, and tersely laid out the facts of the case. As she feared, Beckett was not impressed.

"You say she wasn't raped."

"No, but the guy broke into her car and then her loft and assaulted her—"

"Assaulted her by . . . what was it? Stroking her hair?"

"Luisa, I realize it sounds odd, and low-priority, but believe me, I've met this guy, and he's a disaster waiting to happen. Maybe for once we can do something besides shampoo the carpet after the guy's done what these guys always do."

There was a pause on the line, and Marlene imagined what was going through Beckett's head, which was not hard because it was probably what would've gone through Marlene's head a couple of years ago when she had been sitting where Beckett was now and someone had called with a story like this. She knew Beckett's desk was covered with files representing first-degree rape and aggravated-assault cases, hundreds of them, the walking wounded of the sexual wars, and here was this bozo-ette bending her ear about some rich bitch having a little trouble with her boyfriend.

On the other hand, five years ago Marlene had seen the talent in a skinny black kid from a third-rate law school and made Luisa Beckett her assistant chief, so there was a debt and probably always would be. Marlene heard a faint sigh over the wires. "Okay, okay, what do you want me to do?"

"Just make sure the case doesn't drop through the cracks. This is the kind of thing worth fifty seconds in a calendar court. He could just walk."

"You want him to do *time?*" Beckett's tone was incredulous.

"Of course I want him to do time."

Beckett laughed. "Honey, you got me confused with Super Woman. Is there something wrong with your memory? You know what this place is like. What if he pleads not guilty, which you know he will, because these assholes never think they did anything wrong. You think I'm going to get a trial slot for a case of *hair stroking?*"

"Okay, Luisa, I understand all that," said Marlene

resignedly. "Just do your best, all right? I appreciate it."

When she got off the phone with Beckett, Marlene immediately redialed the same number and asked to be connected with Harry Bello. He wasn't in, and she left a message. While she waited, she rushed around the loft, making beds, picking up after Lucy, and running a load of dishes through the washer. She was just taking a container of soup for her lunch out of the refrigerator when Bello called back.

She told him what Pruitt had done. "I talked to Luisa, Harry. You can pick him up."

"Uh-huh." The tone was not enthusiastic.

"Yeah, yeah," said Marlene, "I already got the line about it's a shit charge from Luisa. But maybe the judge who issued the protection will be hard-assed for once. We could get lucky. And Harry? I want him to know he's been arrested. Also, if any illegal items are lying around in plain view—"

"Right," said Bello. "In plain view."

Karp looked at the chart he had constructed and tapped out the rhythm of "The Yellow Rose of Texas" on his bottom teeth with a pencil. It helped him to think. The chart consisted of two sheets of legal paper taped together. On it Karp had written, among other things, the statements contained in the memos and letters to the Mayor from Dr. Fuerza and District Attorney Bloom that comprised the charges against Murray Selig, the "cause" for which he had been fired. Next to each was a list of people he wanted to depose in relation to the veracity thereof, together with notes on relevant case law and statutory references. Karp always made charts like this when he was organizing the presentation of a case. As the thing progressed, the chart would accumulate notes, in increasingly smaller writing, and balloons and red arrows and legal references. It would become furry with constant handling, and Karp would carefully repair the inevitable tears at the edges and folds with cellophane tape until the thing looked like something that ought to be preserved in an argon chamber at the National Archives. What he never did was copy the chart onto new paper. This was only partly a superstitious act. In fact, Karp's memory was eidetic for patterns in space; he could remember the moves of every basketball game he had ever played in, and the layout of every place he had ever lived. Not so his memory for things told to him (like names) or for faces, which was dreadful, and accounted for much of his reputation as a somewhat cold and distant man.

Thus his recall of the facts and personages of every case he tried was keyed to the position it occupied on that double sheet of yellow lined paper. By the time he had to stand up in front of a judge to argue a motion or in front of a jury to plead his cause, the chart, the body of the case, would be set into his mind like a bronze casting, and the chart itself would be folded away in its file, never to be looked at again. But he never threw them away either.

He was shaken out of a state of extreme tooth-tapping concentration by the phone. The receptionist announced that a Mr. Hrcany wished to speak with him.

"You sicced that reporter on me," said Hrcany when he came on the line.

"How are you, Roland?" said Karp. "Long time, no hear."

"Well, you know we public servants get real busy, not like you guys in white-shoe law firms."

"This is a gray-shoe law firm at the most, Roland. White-shoe law firms don't hire Jews."

"And very wise of them too. What's the story on this cunt reporter? *Mzzz* King Kong?"

"It was Marlene, and I wouldn't say 'sic.' Stupenagel asked if Marlene knew anyone knowledgeable about cops and your name came up. Why? Did you talk to her?"

"Did I talk to her! Jeez, it was up to her I wouldn't do anything else. The bitch won't leave me alone."

"You could hit on her. That usually gets rid of them for you pretty good."

Hrcany ignored the last part of this. "Come on, Butch, I have standards. You may not think I do, but there's a limit."

"What's wrong with her?"

"Get out of here! She's closing in on menopause, she's got a big nose and no tits . . . need I go on?"

"Actually, she's around thirty and the real reason is because she's taller than you. A *lot* taller."

There was a pause, during which Hrcany decided not to pursue this line of conversation. Instead he said, "She wanted to know about Joe Clancy. You got any idea why?"

"Didn't she tell you?"

"No, all I got was a load of horseshit about a feature on traffic cops."

"Clancy's a traffic cop?"

"Not really," said Hrcany. "He's a patrol sergeant in the Two-Five, uptown. But he could have something to do with traffic, with parking, with hack violations—"

"It was the latter, I think. Something about shaking down gypsy cabs up by there and some Spanish guys who died in custody. She thought Clancy was in charge of the case."

"Yeah? That's stupid. Clancy wouldn't have been in charge of any investigation. He's *patrol*, for chrissake, not a detective."

"What about the shakedown?"

"The fuck I know. What I told her was as far as I knew, Joe Clancy of the Two-Five was prime. Got the police medal of valor in seventy-one: ran into a burning building and came out with three little kids hanging off him and his hair on fire. Family man, got a bunch of little paddies and so on. A churchgoer."

"So? What's her problem with that?"

"Nothing except she wants to talk to him direct, and Clancy, being a *Patrol Guide* reader, won't talk to the press without authorization. And she keeps bugging me to get her together with him. And . . ." Hrcany paused significantly.

"And now you're bugging me about it. What do you want me to do, Roland?"

"You're a famous big cheese—"

"Medium-size cheese. *Ex*-medium-size cheese."

"Famous ex-medium-size cheese. You know the big shots up on the twelfth floor in the P.D. Make a call. Get Clancy to see her. Get the bitch off my case."

Karp considered this request for a long moment. Ordinarily, he would not have minded doing a favor like this for Roland Hrcany. He liked Roland, especially when Roland was in this kind of faintly embarrassing bind. And he had the contacts. He had been very close for a long time to the chief of detectives, and as head of the Homicide Bureau he had been a major player in Manhattan's criminal justice bureaucracy. He had met most of the current superchiefs and their aides. Even if he was no longer a player, there were people who owed him favors. The only thing that made him hesitate was the suspicion that Ariadne Stupenagel had figured this out too, and was using Roland, all unconscious, as a means of manipulating Karp. On the other hand . . .

"Butch? You still there?"

"Yeah, Roland. Okay, no problem. I'll call Barry McGinnity at Public Affairs. It shouldn't be any big deal."

FIVE

Pruitt looked good in court for his arraignment, so good that Marlene's heart sank when she spotted him moving with his lawyer through the thronged courtroom. He didn't have long, greasy hair, he was not dressed in filthy leather garments, he did not have a teardrop tattooed on his cheek, or LOVE and HATE inscribed on the knuckles of his hands. He was not wearing the oversize sneakers the cops called perp shoes. He lacked, in short, all the obvious stigmata that would tell a casual glance that he was a dangerous man, and in this court a casual glance was all he was going to get. Pruitt was dressed in his honest, somewhat ill-fitting, workingman's best suit, in dark blue, with a white shirt and a red striped tie. He had heavy black lace-ups on his feet. His hair, cut in humble, honest, Italian-barbershop style, was combed flat with water.

A court officer yelled out a docket number and Pruitt's name and the charge. Pruitt and his lawyer stepped in front of the judge's presidium. Marlene's heart sank further when she saw who was representing the People of New York. She didn't know him, of course. The turnover in the lower reaches of the Criminal Courts Bureaus was too great to make this at all likely, but she had hoped at least that Luisa had been able to talk one of the more senior people into taking an interest. She pushed forward and touched the A.D.A.'s arm. He was a weedy kid with a mottled nose, a moderate Jewish afro, and thick glasses marked with fingerprints, who obviously wanted to be a lawyer when he grew up but was still struggling with the basics. "Excuse me? I'm Marlene Ciampi, I used to work here. You're on the Pruitt case? Did Luisa Beckett talk to you about this one?"

"Beckett? Oh, yeah, she called. I haven't been able to get back to her yet. Sorry, I'm real busy now."

He turned to find out what was going on, at the same time wrestling the half dozen case folders he was carrying so as to float the instant case to the surface.

The judge was saying, "You're charged with burglary and assault, and criminal contempt in that you've violated the terms of a protective order. How do you plead?"

"Guilty, Your Honor," said Pruitt, then added, "With an explanation."

The judge shot him a sharp look. "This is not traffic court, sir. You stand accused of serious felonies."

"I love her, Your Honor. I've loved her for years. I know I shouldn't have gone in there. I know it was wrong, but I couldn't help myself. I just wanted to see her.

The judge resumed a stern look. "Well, she didn't

want to see *you*. That's why there's a protective order. You still want to plead guilty? You understand what it means?" He looked at the defense lawyer. "Does he understand what a guilty plea means?"

The lawyer assured that the consequences of such a plea had been explained in detail to Mr. Pruitt.

"Okay, let's dispose of this right here. Do the People intend to prosecute these felonies?"

"Um . . ." said the People, shuffling his notes. The judge refocused his stern look on him. "Was the girl hurt? What was the nature of this assault?"

"I would never hurt Carrie!" cried Pruitt.

"Quiet, you!" said the judge. To the People, "Well?"

"No, Your Honor, the complaint says he stroked her hair. And her arm."

The judge snorted and looked down at Pruitt. "Stroking, huh? Mister, don't you know stroking is bad for your health?"

Polite titters. The judge grinned and addressed the People. "Okay, let's say, criminal trespass, assault in the third degree, and the contempt, I'd say that was good for about a year, wouldn't you?"

"Um, yeah, I mean, yes, sir, Your Honor," said the People. Marlene could only with difficulty stifle her shout of protest. They were dropping all the charges to misdemeanors, a common method of disposing of cases in the Criminal Courts. She knew what was coming next.

"And I'm going to suspend that sentence and give

you three years' probation," the judge continued. "I assume that's agreeable?"

The defense lawyer's head had started nodding as soon as the word "suspend" had first danced upon the air, and it kept on bobbing.

"Okay, Mr. Pruitt," said the judge, "I want you to stay away from this girl. If I see you coming through here again, you're going to be in serious trouble."

Marlene was out of there almost before the sound of the gavel had ceased reverberating. She did not want to see Pruitt, nor, for that matter, to see Carrie Lanin. Who she wanted to see was Harry Bello.

Karp was not surprised when, several days after his meeting with Phil DeLino, he received an urgent summons to the office of his firm's senior partner, Jack Weller. He had been naughty and was about to get his deserts.

Weller was a hefty man in his early seventies, and looked, if you didn't look too closely, ten or twelve years younger. His thick gray hair was expertly stitched to his scalp, and the perpetually tanned skin of his face had the slick surface signifying expensive little surgeries and peels. He had, naturally, the perfect pearly teeth and shiny fingernails of the well-cared-for wealthy. A shiny man, was what Karp always thought when he saw him, and he thought it this morning in Weller's huge corner office. His teeth shone, as did his nails, the surface of his Sheraton desk, the brass fittings on his yellow suspenders, and his diamond and gold cuff links. His face, however, did not shine; it was dark with displeasure.

Karp was motioned with a curt wrist flick to a tan leather side chair. He was made to wait while Weller finished flipping through a document. Karp watched the cuff links twinkle as the pages snapped. He thought he knew what the document was. While he waited, he studied Weller's tan. The man was just back from St. Barts. Weller took a lot of vacations, and the year at B.L. was divided, like the medieval liturgical year, into before-and-after St. Barts, Aspen, East Hampton, and the Foreign Trip, Europe or Asia in turn.

Karp didn't dislike Weller, although he might have if the man had spent more time around the office. They were polar opposites as lawyers, of course, but Karp was by now used to being a quarter-turn different from most of his colleagues, and he was prepared to render Weller the sort of bland deference we reserve for someone who has made it possible for us to earn vast shitloads of money.

Weller finished reading and looked up at Karp. He sighed. "This won't do, Butch."

"I'm sorry? What won't do?" asked Karp.

"Suing the Mayor. Didn't you realize that I was vice-chairman of his re-election committee?"

"No, I didn't realize that. But I don't see what it has to do with Murray Selig getting his day in court."

"You didn't get clearance from the executive committee either."

"No, I didn't realize I had to. I've never brought

in any business before. It never came up." This was
a lie, of course, but a plausible one. It made Karp
look like something of a jerk, but this had never bothered him much, especially when the lookers were
people like Jack Weller.

Weller's face darkened beneath the tan, and he
looked like he was about to say something nasty, but
reconsidered. He had not spent much time with
Karp, but something vestigial in him signaled a
warning that Karp was not somebody who was prepared to take a lot of verbal abuse without returning
it, and possibly some actual physical abuse as well.

"Who's the judge?" Weller asked instead.

"We have selection today," answered Karp.
"Craig, Roseman and Hollander are on the wheel."

"Well, I know Joe Hollander and Larry Roseman
pretty well, and I know people who're close to Craig.
He's brand-new. It shouldn't be hard to get you out
of there without prejudice to us, or causing a problem for the client."

Weller then launched into a long, detailed statement about what he was going to do and what he
wanted Karp and some other people to do in order
to cancel the firm's role in Selig's case. It was an
admirable plan and Karp might even had admired
it, had he been listening at all. But he was not. Instead, as Weller spoke, Karp was adding up columns
of figures in his head. His available cash, plus what
he could raise from a loan on the loft against monthly
living expenses between his last check from B.L. and
the time when he could expect to see some money

from the Selig case. It worked out pretty close, but it was still feasible, always assuming he'd win Selig. Which he did not doubt.

"So, you understand what has to be done, go do it!" Weller said, and added, "And for God's sake, Butch, in future—"

"Actually," said Karp mildly, "I don't intend to drop the case."

Weller gasped. "You don't? *You* don't! Who the fu—sonny, read the goddamn letterhead! Read the goddamn brass fucking sign on the front door! It's my goddamn law firm, and I say who we sue and who we do not sue! Is that clear?"

"Perfectly," said Karp. "I'll resign, effective immediately." He stood up, and Weller had to lean his judge's chair back a little to see Karp's face. "I'll turn all my Goldsboro stuff over to whoever you think will try the case. Because Steve and Toby think it's pretty sure to go to trial early next year." Karp paused significantly. "Who would that be? Trying it, I mean. Yourself?"

Weller ignored the absurd question. He had not been in front of a jury for years and did not intend to derail his extremely pleasant life to start now. Neither was the possibility of losing Karp seriously to be entertained. There were attorneys at B.L. who knew more about Goldsboro than Karp, but the firm did not have anyone who was his equal in the art of standing in the well of a court and convincing twelve ordinary people that although someone had done a bunch of awful things to the plaintiffs, that someone was not the Goldsboro Pharmaceutical Company, their client.

After a brief pause Weller said, "That's absurd. You're the only trial lawyer we have who's prepped on Goldsboro. You can't just drop it." Then he had a happy thought. "And in any case, you couldn't run both Goldsboro and this Selig thing. You'd have to drop him eventually."

"Not necessarily," said Karp. "I expect *Selig* to go quite rapidly. We can fast-track the whole thing. The case is straightforward, and there's little room for maneuver on either side. It's September now. With the holiday slow-down, preliminary motions and discovery should bring us into next February. Federal jury selection is fast, a couple of days, and we should be in trial by early May, maybe earlier if we draw Craig, who's new, as you say, and who'll have a light calendar. Twelve weeks for trial, max. I can't imagine Goldsboro getting started much before late summer."

"I don't like it," said Weller, a trace of helpless petulance creeping into his tone. "Quite aside from the personal embarrassment and lack of consideration involved in pursuing this, by the distraction of your energies you're potentially jeopardizing the firm's most important case. And I don't understand it at all. Haven't we been good to you?"

"Yes, very good," admitted Karp. "This is a nice place to work."

"Then why? Is this Dr. Selig a friend of yours?"

"Not particularly. But something very nasty was

done to him for no reason and I said I would fix it, and I intend to."

"Butch, Butch," said Weller placatingly, "you're not with the D.A. or some congressional committee now. You can't go running around town righting wrongs whenever you feel like it."

"Gee, that's an odd thing to say. I thought that was the damn *point*. Of the law, of judges, courts, juries—"

"Oh, don't pretend to misunderstand me," Weller snarled. "And I don't need any sanctimony from you. You know very well what I mean."

"Yes, I do," said Karp. "And I'm still not dropping Selig. So, was that all?"

It was.

Marlene went directly from court back to the loft and there sat by the answering machine, screening her calls. There was one message already from Carrie Lanin, and while she waited, Marlene's mother, a charity, and the insurance man called and Marlene let them all leave messages. The phone also rang four additional times, but the party calling hung up when the message tape came on. Marlene guessed that it was Lanin, and she was praying that Bello would call back before she had to pick up the kids and see Carrie and tell her that her sweetheart had picked up a walk from the criminal justice system.

Ring, ring, pause, clickety-click, beep. "It's me," said Harry Bello, confident that Marlene would be poised at the phone. She picked it up immediately.

"He walked, Harry."

"I heard. She tried."

Meaning Beckett. "What are we going to do, Harry? What'll I *tell* her?"

"It depends," said Bello.

Yes, it did depend, on what Marlene herself was willing to do, which simultaneously infuriated her and excited her.

"We should talk," said Marlene. "Eight-thirty?"

"Paglia's," said Bello and hung up.

When Marlene picked up the girls at the P.S. 1 schoolyard, the teacher on yard duty called her over and informed her that cap pistols were not approved accessories, and that her daughter should not bring hers to school again. When Lucy was settled in the front seat of the VW, Marlene looked her over and saw a silvery butt protruding from the pocket of her red corduroys.

"Is that a gun in your pocket, dear?" Marlene asked sweetly.

Wordlessly, her daughter yanked it out, showed it briefly, and stuck it back in her pocket. It was a battered metal six-shooter with plastic grips, about two-thirds full size and quite real-looking.

"Where did you get it, Lucy?"

"Bobby Crandall gave it to me."

Light dawned. "The kid you did the project for, huh? This is the payoff?"

Lucy nodded. After a pause she said, "Girls could have guns."

"Yes, they could," said Marlene, disturbed and proud at the same time. "But some girls have daddies that might think that kids shouldn't play with guns at all, boys *or* girls. I wouldn't go waving that around the house, and you can't take it to school again, understand? The teacher will take it away from you. Plus, no more doing school stuff for other kids. It's against the rules too, okay?"

Marlene was hoping for another burst of Chinese, but Lucy just nodded, her hand deep inside her pocket, from which issued little clicking sounds.

"Well?" Carrie Lanin's face was bright with hope as she met Marlene and the children at the door to her loft. Marlene noted that she had installed a heavy new police lock on it.

"I think we did pretty good, considering. He got a year and three years' probation."

"Yippee!" Carrie shouted. "He's really in jail?"

"Well, actually, no, they suspended the sentence," said Marlene too quickly, "but now it's on record and if he ever comes near you again—"

"If he *ever*. . . ! What are you saying, he's *free*? He's *out there*?" Both women's eyes involuntarily flicked to the door and lock for an instant, and when Lanin turned her gaze back onto Marlene it was vibrating with fear and, naturally, anger, not at Pruitt nor at the criminal justice system in general, but at Marlene, as being the only vaguely responsible adult present to take the shit.

Marlene braced herself. She was used to this, bored

with this even, from the old Rape Bureau days. You would expect violated women, women whose essential self-confidence had been stripped away by a practical demonstration of exactly how vulnerable they were to any asshole who cared to make the effort, to appreciate a sympathetic and willing listener. But no; those who weren't nearly catatonic were looking for someone on whom to take out their rage and, absent the perp himself, the lucky winner was more often than not Marlene or one of her people.

Carrie Lanin was not as bad as some. There was a lot of nasty language, a lot of look-what-you-got-me-into, and a glass and a picture frame got broken. The girls came running out of Miranda's room and stood for a moment in shocked silence in the doorway, until Carrie caught sight of her daughter. Then, with a groaning sob, she swept up the frightened child into her arms and collapsed against the wall, weeping.

Marlene took charge. She grabbed a handful of paper towels from the kitchen and handed it as a nose wipe to the afflicted woman. She took Lucy aside and gave her a child-size version of what was going on: a bad man was after Miranda's mommy and Mommy was going to make him stop and Lucy had to take Miranda away and watch TV or play and keep out of the way while Mommy talked with Miranda's mommy.

To Marlene's delight and pride, Lucy took this all in without a murmur and, taking Miranda by the hand, proposed playing Barbies in her bossiest tone. Miranda was quick to acquiesce, and the two of them ran off. Marlene got Carrie settled on the couch and put some water on for tea.

"I'm sorry," said Carrie after a while. "You've really been great. I don't know why I said all that horrible crap to you." She laughed humorlessly. "I must be going crazy."

"No, you're not. It's normal; forget it! Now, are you ready to listen to my plan? Good. Okay, what we need to have happening now in his twisted little mind is that I become the big barrier to happiness with Carrie. It's started already, but we want to push it."

"We do?"

"Yeah, because it takes the pressure off of you. And off the other barrier to happiness."

"What do you mean, other—"

"Miranda. I don't think she fits into the fantasy. He was stalking her too, the other day at the school."

"Oh, Jesus. . . !" Carrie said in a strangled voice and began to cry again. Marlene ignored this and continued, "What I think is, he's going to start stalking me. He's going to try to hurt me in some way, get me to lay off, like he probably did to that boyfriend of yours. But, basically, he won't be able to."

"Why not?" asked Lanin, curiosity penetrating through the misery.

"Because I'll be stalking him," said Marlene, with rather more confidence than she was feeling.

"I have a thing I have to do tonight" was how Marlene broached her plan to Karp that evening as they put away the dinner dishes together.

"Oh?"

"Yeah, I'm meeting Harry down the street. To talk. You know this guy I told you about? He's been harassing Carrie Lanin?"

"Yeah, what about him? I thought you had a protect order on him."

"We did, but he violated it and did a lot of other stuff. He went to arraignment today. Copped to misdemeanors and walked."

Karp shrugged. "What else is new? How did Carrie take it?"

"Not well. That's, um, I mean, Harry decided he wanted to check the guy out some more. That's what we're going to talk about."

Karp carefully put down the dish he was drying and gave Marlene a look.

"What?" she complained to the look. "What? Harry's going to fuck a little with this guy's head. And I'm going along for the ride. Christ, Butch, the way you're looking you'd think I never went riding out with a cop before."

"You were a D.A. It was your job. Now what is it? Your hobby?"

Marlene's eyes narrowed dangerously. "Excuse me, was that a put-down? Was that delivered in a how-silly-you-little-woman-you manner?"

"Oh, come on, Marlene, don't start—" began Karp, regretting the fatal words.

"Because if it was, if that's going to be your attitude, then I will no longer inform you about what I'm doing. Is that what you want?"

"No, of course not," said Karp automatically, "but . . ."

"But what?"

"It's just . . . I'm sorry, I worry about you. It's natural, isn't it? It's in the genes or something. Men worry about their wives when they're pregnant."

"Ah, the Pleistocene argument, very good," snarled Marlene, and then, seeing his expression, she softened and touched his arm. "Okay, you're worried, but I can take care of myself, as you very well know, and I'll be with a heavily armed and extremely competent cop. Jeez, Butch, old ladies from the League of Women Voters get to ride with cops nowadays. It's no big thing."

Karp nodded, resignedly, and forced his face into a stiff mask that might have been taken as agreeable by anyone other than his wife. "Sure," he said, and afterward, not being able to help himself, he asked, "Why is Harry doing this? I thought the case was closed. I mean, there's no investigation . . ."

"That's right," said Marlene cheerfully. "Technically, we're illegally harassing a citizen. You going to turn us in?"

Karp rolled his eyes and put his hands over his ears and walked out of the kitchen.

Marlene went to the bedroom and pulled a seaman's sweater over her T-shirt and tied black hightop Converses on her feet. She caught her hair up in a rubber band and pulled a dark blue wool watch cap over it. A short black leather coat completed the outfit.

She went back to the kitchen, searched briefly, and took a bottle out of the grocery cabinet and stuck it in her coat pocket. She checked on Lucy, who was sleeping heavily in her typical running-at-full-tilt position. Marlene pulled the kicked-off pink quilt over the child, kissed her forehead, and went out.

She stuck her head through the living room door. "See you later, Butch," she said.

Karp looked up from the papers he had spread on his lap and the couch around him, his face lit oddly by the muted television. He took in Marlene's costume and shook his head. "You forgot the cape," he said.

She stuck her tongue out at him and left. As soon as she was on the stairs she felt the familiar sense of release, the tingling in her limbs, the expansion of her lungs, that she had felt when, as a proper Catholic schoolgirl in Queens she had climbed out her bedroom window at night to meet bad boys.

Of course, she was not meeting a boy now, or a lover of any age. It would never have occurred to Marlene to violate her marriage vows—well, *occurred*, yes, but not actually to follow through. And in the old days, what she had been after down the family drainpipe was not precisely sex, although that was fascinating, but risk. And not merely risk, because she had never been one for simple daredevilry. She had no interest in say, skydiving, or motorcycle racing. No, it had to be prohibited risk, risk in the teeth of decent expectations.

It had started, really, at age twelve, she reflected

on the stairway, when an aunt had escorted her and a group of cousins to the famous off-Broadway production of *Threepenny Opera*. By the end of the show, St. Teresa of Avila had been eclipsed by Pirate Jenny as Marlene's ideal of womanhood. She had purchased the cast recording, and then the German version, and for the next few months she made everyone around her sick of Brecht and Weill. She found herself now humming Jenny's song about the pirate ship and then, as she reached the last landing, singing the chorus in a loud voice with a fairly accurate Lotte Lenya accent.

She laughed to herself, thinking that it had worked out more literally than she might have liked. She could wear a pirate's patch for real now, and had the letter bomb that destroyed her eye and maimed her hand been a little more powerful, she might have been sporting an actual hook.

She let the big steel door slam behind her and walked out onto the damp and chilly street. There she paused, sucking in the night through flared nostrils. Marlene had long since given up the hope of leading a life that made conventional sense, settling instead for one with two irreconcilable but complementary modes: the Good Mom Desperado, not, she thought, a character much to be seen in opera. Or life. *A woman must have everything*—that was also a line from a song, she thought, as it flashed through her head. Joni Mitchell. I'm trying to, she thought.

Marlene made her way up Grand to Paglia's restaurant. When she had first moved to this neighborhood, the place had on most nights been full of local Italians and cops from the old police headquarters down the street. Now it had become SoHo-ized, like most of the places in the area. There was a maitre d' and a line of elegant couples waiting for seats. Marlene pushed past these to the bar, where she found Harry Bello waiting, staring blankly at a club soda.

Marlene sat on a stool beside him and ordered the same, wishing, not for the first time, that fetuses enjoyed booze. When it came, she finished it in a few gulps and said, "You up for this?"

Harry ignored the question. "He's out."

"Driving?"

"Eating. A Spanish joint on C."

"You know where his car's at?"

Harry nodded.

They paid and left. On impulse Marlene swiped a big white chrysanthemum from the large vase in the restaurant's entranceway.

They waited in Harry's old Plymouth and watched Rob Pruitt walk down Seventh Street to where he'd parked his blue Dodge. He got in and cranked it up and drove off.

"What do you figure, a quarter mile?" asked Bello.

"Maybe less, but after it happens he'll probably futz around for a while trying to fix it. Let's go."

They left the car and entered a tenement building. Pruitt lived in the front apartment on the third floor.

Harry picked the lock in two minutes, and they went in.

The apartment was simply furnished and remarkably clean and neat. Pruitt had obviously patronized several of the many used- and unpainted-furniture stores in the neighborhood. He owned a gold velvet easy chair and a scarred thirteen-inch TV on a battered tin stand, and a table, chairs, and chest of drawers in unpainted pine. He slept on a box spring and mattress, neatly made up with gray military surplus blankets. The closet and drawers held an odd combination of worn work clothes and brand-new dressy casuals, many with the store labels still attached. Like the furniture, these last were clearly purchased from shops in the immediate area: colored silk shirts, stiff leisure suits, and the tan leather jacket Carrie had described, clothing suitable for a visit to one of the local salsa clubs. Pruitt was good at taking on the local coloration.

In the bedroom also, Marlene's flashlight picked up a corkboard, covering nearly an entire wall, on which was arranged a photographic homage to Carrie Lanin: yellowed and faded clippings from student newspapers, showing her cheerleading and prom queening; some pages neatly cut from the same high school yearbook Marlene had already seen, ditto; a wedding photograph (sans groom); an 8 × 10 glossy high school photo in cap and gown. There were also a dozen or so recent photographs, candids obviously, of Carrie on the street. Pruitt had some skill with a camera.

Harry came up behind her and took in the scene. He shone his light on the top of the chest beneath the corkboard. There were two candles in red glass containers, bought at a local *botanica*, flanking a little museum of Carrieana. Some keys. A pair of blue lace panties. A lipstick. A receipt from Elaine's.

"Her place," said Harry, pointing his penlight at the keys.

"Yeah. He must have taken an impression of her keys during their date. Maybe she went to the ladies' and he waxed them. Once he had a set, he could visit whenever he wanted, and he took souvenirs. Okay, let's make a donation to the shrine."

She removed from her pocket the empty Karo corn syrup bottle whose contents she had poured into Pruitt's gas tank. The syrup was at this moment (she trusted) turning to hard candy in the cylinders of his car. She placed the bottle on the bureau and stuck the mum from Paglia's in it. Then, using the bedroom window as a mirror, she applied the lipstick to her mouth, removed one of the photos from the board and planted a red kiss on the back of it. She took a ballpoint from her pocket, wrote a short message in neat block letters, and propped the photo up against the bottle.

"What did you write?" asked Harry when they were back in the Plymouth.

"Forget her! Come to me, my darling. Only I love you as you deserve."

He gave her a complex look, which from long experience she could read: a blend of doubt and worry.

It also meant that Bello had fathomed what she was up to.

"It'll work, Harry."

He was silent for a moment and then he said, not as a question, "You're going to have to take a shot."

"Yeah, I know," she agreed. "But I can't think of another way."

SIX

Moore's Bar and Grill is on Lexington Avenue between 119th and 120th streets, right around the corner from the Twenty-fifth Precinct, which occupies a four-story building on 119th. Moore's is a cop bar, owned by an ex-cop and patronized almost exclusively by cops. There is at least one like it a short walk from each of the City's station houses. At a quarter of four in the afternoon the place is usually jammed and noisy with the day shift taking off and the swing shift getting up attitude before starting work.

Ariadne Stupenagel chose this time to make her entrance. She was wearing tight red jeans jammed into black and silver cowboy boots with two-inch heels, and a pale gray silk blouse. Over this she wore a Soviet military greatcoat with colonel's pips and blue KGB flashes on the shoulder boards. She carried a stained khaki haversack that had once held a medical kit. The loud male hubbub in Moore's diminished perceptibly as she passed through.

"What the fuck is that?" asked the cop standing at

the bar next to Roland Hrcany. He was not the only one asking the question either. Hrcany looked up from his scotch and looked away. He rolled his huge shoulders as if shrugging off a burden. Although Hrcany was not a cop, he spent a good time of his spare time in cop bars. He liked cops, and cops liked him, not a usual state of affairs between members of the police force and the prosecutorial bar. The cops liked Hrcany because he treated them like the men they were, because he was a real man himself, because he was a rake of legendary reputation, not averse to sharing his collection of willing girls with favored policemen, and because he was more tolerant than most other prosecutors about the universal and necessary perjury of the police. So tolerant was Hrcany that cops would often reveal to him just where they had violated the rules of evidence and arrest, and Hrcany would go so far as to advise them on how to bring off these fairy tales on the stand. On the other hand, he drew the line at actual fabrication, and knew enough about the ways of the police so that no one but a practicing idiot would try to sell him a total load of manure. The cops respected this. He was a very successful homicide prosecutor.

Hrcany replied, "It's a reporter. I said I would introduce her to Joe Clancy."

His companion gave him a cop look. Hrcany caught it and explained, "It's okay. The bosses cleared it. It's just some kind of hero story."

The cop grunted and stared again at the woman, who had by now spotted Hrcany and was approaching. "Christ, you'd need a fucking ladder," the cop muttered.

"Hello, Roland," said Ariadne. "What a charming place!" she added in a tone implying the opposite. Stupenagel had, in her colorful career, met any number of men who hated her, but almost invariably it had been for good cause. She hadn't done anything to Hrcany, however, yet, but he had been rude and uncooperative from the first moment. It surprised her but did not particularly dismay.

"Glad you like it," replied Hrcany in the same tone.

"Buy you a drink?" she asked.

"I'm fine."

"Well, let's get started. Where's Clancy?"

Hrcany got off his bar stool and walked off without a word. Stupenagel followed him across the floor and into a large back room. Like the bar proper, this was full of off-duty cops, but cops much drunker than the ones in the front. They were sitting at a dozen or so round wooden tables or swaying happily among them. Those at the tables were pounding their glasses and bottles to the beat of an amplified Irish band set up on a small stage in the front of the room. It was a retirement party, a racket, as the cops say, for one of the cops in the Two-Five. The air was thick with noise, smoke, and beer fumes. Someone had decorated the walls and ceiling with green and white crepe paper, and shiny paper shamrocks and leprechaun hats.

"He's over there," said Hrcany, indicating a tall

man leaning against the wall, alone, waving a brown bottle of Schlitz in time with the music.

"Introduce me."

"You want me to *introduce* you? Why, you want to date him?"

"That's the point of this, Roland," said Stupenagel patiently. "You're a regular guy—you introduce me to him and then he'll know I'm a regular guy, too. If I wanted to walk in here cold, I wouldn't have been on your ass making myself unpleasant all these weeks. It's nothing personal."

Hrcany opened his mouth, but stifled the remark he had in mind, which was personal in the extreme. Instead he marched up to Clancy and held out his hand.

"Hey, Joe. Nice racket."

"Yeah," said Clancy. "Jerry's a popular guy."

The two men chatted about Jerry, a detective second grade who was retiring after thirty on the job. The reporter hung behind Hrcany and pretended to be fascinated by the anecdotes about old Jerry, and studied her quarry. Clancy was a large man in good shape: his gut did not hang puffily over the belt line she could see under the tan suit jacket. The jacket itself, though plainly off the rack, hung nicely on his square shoulders, and Ariadne concluded that he was one of those fortunate men whose physiques fell precisely into the dimensions of the standard sizes, a 44R in his case, she reckoned. His hands were large and calm and covered with crisp, short red hairs, as was his skull. He wore his hair in a Marine Corps buzz cut, which revealed patches of twisted scar tissue. Not a man to shrink from honorable blemishes, thought Ariadne, an observation that recommended him to her. His face was the traditional map of Ireland edition: square jaw, softening a little underneath, snub nose, lipless, wide mouth.

After a minute or so of chatter, Hrcany became aware that the Aqua Velva-colored eyes that went with this face were resting ever more often on the large woman standing behind him, whose head, he was uncomfortably aware, was hovering an unacceptable distance above his shoulder.

He said, abruptly, "Joe, I'd like you to meet Mzzz Stupenagel. Mzzz Stupenagel, this is Joe Clancy."

The woman extended her hand, said, "I'm glad to meet you. I've heard a lot about you," and received a firm, formal grasp. Clancy was not the sort of man who either gripped too hard or sent a sexual message. Another point scored.

At that moment three men drunk enough to think wearing shiny green paper leprechaun hats amusing rolled up, hailed Roland as a lost brother, and urged him away to the free beer. He left with no discernible reluctance.

"You got to the bosses," he said.

"I did." In the pause that followed Clancy seemed to be concentrating on the music. Stupenagel read it as demonstrating that although he was now cleared to talk to her, he had not been ordered to do so, and was doing it of his free will.

"You're a friend of Roland's?" Clancy asked. His

voice was soft, but it seemed to cut effectively through the clamor. Stupenagel had spent considerable time among men whose work required them to make themselves clearly heard in extremely noisy and violent places, and she recognized the trick. She could do it too.

"Like a brother to me," she lied. "He said he would introduce me to you, so you could tell me all about being a hero cop—"

Clancy uttered a derisive snort. "You believe everything you hear?"

"You ran into a burning building. You rescued those kids from that fire."

Clancy shrugged. "Hey, I was there, I was helping them evacuate the building, I was leading some kids down a hall. The fire was in the building next door. There was an explosion. The next thing I knew I was on fire, so I picked up the kids and ran out. They played it up big, because we were in the middle of the Knapp scandal and they needed a cop who saved a bunch of P.R. kids."

He told the story wearily, as one who wishes it would go away. Stupenagel had seen this before as well. The denigration of heroism by the hero is often a form of boasting, and she wondered whether it was that in Clancy's case. The man was starting to interest her. Time for a pinprick.

"Speaking of Hispanic kids, they seem not to do well in your lockup. Why is that?"

Clancy remained calm. "You read my report?"

"No."

"I'll send you a copy."

"Thank you. What's the short version, for now?"

Clancy looked out again at the revelry. He asked, "Do you want a drink?"

Stupenagel nodded. "Sure. A beer'd be fine."

Clancy walked off through the crowd to a cloth-covered table on which a tin tub full of ice and beer bottles rested. A large, dark-haired man in a blue sports coat hailed him, and they spoke a few words. The dark man looked briefly over at her, but she was too far away and the room far too dim and smoky for her to be able to read any expression on his face. Clancy returned with a cold bottle and a paper cup. Stupenagel remarked the cup. She poured her beer into it and sipped it, like a lady should. Then she took out her notebook.

"It was a real bad thing," said Clancy. "The first one, Ortiz, we thought it was a fluke. Bring a gypsy cabbie in for a hack violation and he kills himself? Unbelievable. What, he had remorse because he picked up a fare on the street? Okay, there's an investigation, like there always is, we lose somebody in custody, and they cleared us. Guy hung himself on his shirt, the M.E. confirms it. Suicide. The next one's a couple of weeks later, same thing. Jorge Valenzuela, his name was. Now we're going crazy. We got bosses up the ying-yang, running around trying to find, did we follow procedure. And we did, to the letter. These guys, they weren't considered suicide risks, like a guy gets drunk and wastes his wife and kids, he sobers up, you figure he might try for a hat trick, do himself too. But these were bullshit charges, maybe a fine at most. So we—I mean, the detectives—investigate. Okay, it turns out these guys are not your regular Hispanics, they're more like Indians, from down in Central America somewhere, Guatemala, I think. Salvador. And they're wetbacks. So they, like, have a psychological problem with jail."

"The detectives told you this?" asked Stupenagel.

"Yeah, they interviewed some professor up at Columbia. They get into a situation they can't handle, they just check out—I mean, more than regular people."

"I've heard the theory. What do *you* think?"

Clancy chewed his lip and then shrugged heavily. "Look, lady, I'm just a cop, right? What do I know?— you get all kinds in the City. The fact is, we can't watch everybody in the cells, every minute. We don't have the troops. And we can't strip the prisoners buck naked, the civil liberties people would go nuts. We frisk them and take belts and laces and move them out to Central Booking as soon as we can. And the third one of these guys, he didn't hang himself at all."

"What happened to him?"

"Roberto Fuentes. He just died. He went in there at eleven-ten at night. At six-thirty in the morning, when they went to wake them up for the trip down to Central, he was cold. Not a mark on him—just curled up and died. Sad. The kid was—what?— twenty-two. But . . ." He shrugged again and sighed.

"That's it. There's some more detail in the report. Meanwhile . . ."

He put his beer down on the table and picked up a raincoat from a chair.

"I got to go," he said and hoisted on the raincoat.

She eyed the beer bottle, which lacked but a few swallows. "Not much of a party animal?"

"Not much."

"My, my, a non-drinking Irishman! This is a better story than I expected. Hold the front page."

He smiled a tight smile. "Nice meeting you. I'll send you that thing if you give me an address."

She fished a card out of her bag and handed it to him. She did not want him to leave, and not because she thought there was specific information she needed from him. There was something wrong about the vibrations she was getting from him, some blankness in the picture. Stupenagel did not expect every man in the world to come on to her. Hrcany, for example, hated her. But she expected there to be something, some response to the electrical probes she was constantly emitting via voice and look and body language. Either Clancy had some dead circuits or she was losing her touch.

"Where are you off to?" she asked casually.

"Work. Around the corner. I usually take the swing shift if I can get it." He started to walk away, and she set off after him.

"Four to twelve? Must be hard on your wife."

He looked at her, into her eyes, and she thought

she saw something unexpected flicker behind the un-revealing blue—duplicity? Or pain.

"As a matter of fact, it works out for us," he said. "With the kids and all."

"Oh? How many do you have?"

"Four. Joe Junior is ten, then there's Bridie, she's eight, Terry is six, and Patrick is two and a half." He paused. "Patrick is a Down's kid."

"Oh," she said, "that must be rough."

He asked, "Want to see a picture?"

She nodded and smiled encouragingly, and he pulled a color snapshot from his wallet. She studied it: three little snub-nosed, grinning extroverts, and a worn-looking but still pretty blond woman smiling uncertainly, holding the dough-faced baby that would never grow up. She handed it back to him, and as she did she caught on his face an odd look, almost an expression of triumph, as if he had played a card that couldn't be trumped.

A well-honed instinct led her to pounce. "Oh, one more thing: the detectives who arrested the boys who died—what were their names?"

He didn't stumble, which almost disappointed her. "Paul Jackson."

She wrote it down. "And . . . ?"

"And his partner, John Seaver." He started to move away again.

"Are they here?"

"No. I mean, I haven't seen them. You could ask around. Look, I got to—"

"Anything to these rumors about your guys shaking down gypsy cabbies?" she asked abruptly, her voice with a bright edge.

Was that a thin smile as he turned away? She couldn't tell. She experienced briefly an urge to run after Clancy, like Lois Lane on TV, grab his arm and become a pest. She quickly suppressed it; that was not her style. On the other hand, her style was not generating the usual results. In Stupenagel's experience, men in the various macho trades were not famous for marital fidelity, and she was surprised that she had not been able to raise even a flirt from the cop. An unusual specimen, she thought, or maybe it was guilt about wifey at home with the bent kid. Or fidelity? Did that still exist? Or maybe she *was* losing her touch. She drained her beer and headed for the bar to eliminate that dread possibility.

Between the two of them, Marlene and Harry Bello kept Rob Pruitt pretty well stalked. Marlene took the shift between suppertime and the small hours of the morning, so that Harry could obtain the unnaturally tiny amount of rest that he needed. Harry objected to this—there was no telling when Pruitt might turn on his tormentor—but relented when Marlene agreed to take her dog along in her car. Karp knew better than to object.

They were not tailing Pruitt, precisely, only making sure that he understood that he was under observation. Carrie Lanin had been supplied with a new, unlisted phone, and she reported happily that she had not been bothered by the man either over its wires or by any additional personal invasions.

Pruitt had a new car, a dingy green Toyota Corolla. When Marlene took up her station outside his building, she could see him watching it from his window or from just inside the street door of the tenement. He was waiting for another sabotage attempt, which Marlene had no intention of providing. On several occasions, she followed him on long, seemingly aimless car rides through lower Manhattan, making only desultory attempts to keep him in sight. She was not interested in where he went. When she lost him, she would just drive to Duane Street and park in front of Carrie Lanin's loft. Often on these occasions Pruitt would come by, and then she would wave gaily, and have the pleasure of seeing him roar off with squealing tires.

This went on for a week. Two weeks. Then Harry Bello called one evening and reported that Pruitt had started to drink heavily in a local saloon.

"You think?" asked Marlene.

"Your call," said Bello.

"Let's do it. Say, ten."

Marlene fed her family and then tried to watch television with Karp, unsuccessfully. Nothing held her interest. She kept getting up and pacing, doing little meaningless errands and chores. Karp finally asked her what was wrong.

"I have to go out," said Marlene.

"All right," said Karp.

"Not now, a little later. I'm meeting Harry."

Karp nodded. No news here.

"I have to get dressed," she said, and hurried away to the bedroom.

No ninja look tonight. A sweet vulnerability, somewhat antique and out of fashion. Marlene had several elderly great aunts who, on each Christmas and birthday, supplied her with the sort of clothes a nice Catholic girl might be expected to wear on Queens Boulevard should 1955 ever make an appearance again. Marlene was thus able to dress herself in a white frilly blouse with a Peter Pan collar, a heavy tan wool skirt designed to conceal the lines of the body, and a white angora sweater that closed with a little gold chain. Her hair, which usually framed her face in a shaggy mane of natural curls, cut to shadow her bad eye, she now pulled back into the old schoolgirl center parting, held in place by industrial-strength plastic barettes on either side. A dab of pale pink lipstick and a pair of round spectacles completed the image. Marlene thought she looked a lot like her cousin Angela, who was a bookkeeper for the archdiocese.

"I'm going now," she said, presenting herself at the door to the living room. Karp looked away from the set and cast an appraising glance at his wife.

"Could you do 'A Bushel and a Peck' before you go?"

"What?"

"What. Okay, let's see," Karp remarked, "nearly every other night this past couple of weeks you slip out of here looking like Richard Widmark going up against the Nazis, and now you look like Rosemary Clooney. Is there something going on I should know about?"

"Not really," she said.

The bar was so small and crummy it hardly had a name, just a dingy white sign supplied by a mixer company and a fizzing neon that said B R. Inside, a bar ran nearly the length of the room, which was about the size and shape of a railway car. Most of the lighting, dim and reddish, came from a collection of beer company signs hung on the wall. Sitting at the bar when Marlene walked in were three Latina whores, a short, dark man in a suit of aqua crushed velvet (their business manager), a pair of deteriorated alcoholics in grimy rags, and, at the extreme end of the bar, almost invisible in the shadows, Harry Bello in his usual gray suit. The barkeep, a chubby Puerto Rican with a shaved head and a wad of hair like a toilet brush under his nose, looked up as she entered. So did the whores and the pimp. The drunks looked at their drinks, as did Bello.

Marlene took off her raincoat, further astonishing her audience. It was not a venue that went in much for frilly blouses and white angora sweaters. She walked to one of the two round plywood tables and took a seat across from Rob Pruitt. He was drinking straight, cheap bourbon behind beer, and he stank of it across the table. He looked up woozily when Marlene sat down, and focused his eyes with some effort. Marlene noted that his clothes were soiled and his eyes were red-rimmed. Nor had he shaved in a couple of days; Marlene wished she had him in court this very minute.

"What the *fuck* do you want?" said Pruitt.

"You don't look so hot, Rob," Marlene replied. "I think you were a lot better off up in Alaska. I think it might be time for you to leave."

"You're following me around," he said. "You're . . . and that cop, following me. I saw you."

"You think I'm following you, Rob? We live in the same neighborhood. We're neighbors. Our paths cross."

He stared at her, his jaw working.

"And why that accusing tone, Rob?" she asked. "Wouldn't you *like* being followed? Didn't you think Carrie liked it?"

"I love her," he said, his voice robotic and dull.

"But she doesn't love you."

"She loves me," in the same tone.

Marlene glanced at one of the beer clocks. "No, she thinks you're a schmuck and a pest. She hates you."

He looked at her, his eyes narrowing. "Why are you doing this? Why are you trying to break us up?"

"I don't know, Robbie," she replied lightly, "maybe because *I'm* obsessed with you. Maybe I want you for my very own." She paused and then said, very carefully, "Forget her! Come to me, my darling! Only I love you as you deserve."

It took several seconds for it to register. Marlene thought he hadn't gotten the point and was about to say something further, as a result of which her guard was down when Pruitt snarled and lunged at her across the table.

He grabbed the front of her sweater with his left hand and swung a roundhouse right that landed on the side of her jaw, not a solid blow because of the clumsy angle, but hard enough to make her see red. The table went over, as did her chair. Pruitt was yelling something. He was on top of her on the beer-stinking floor, his left hand on her throat now, and his right crashing down on her mouth, this time a solid hit. She tasted blood. She tried to claw his eyes, but he knocked her hands away and struck her again as she turned her head, landing a good one on her ear. Sound vanished into ringing. His knee pressed into her chest; her breath failed and she saw his rage-distorted face begin to gray out.

Then she heard, through the ringing, a sharp crack, a sound like a bat hitting a ball or a book falling off a table. Instantly, his weight was gone. She coughed and gasped and rolled onto her side, trying to get the air flowing again and her vision working. Blood was flowing down her chin in a steady stream. She caught a pool of it in her cupped palm and wiped it off on her white sweater, and then she pressed the satin hem of the sweater tightly against her mouth.

As the ringing faded she became aware of a grunting, shuffling noise, punctuated with meaty thuds. She struggled to a sitting position and looked around the barroom. A tableau: the patrons and the bartender frozen in place, their expressions ranging from avid to dull; at stage center Harry Bello calmly breaking Rob Pruitt to pieces with a short length of lead-loaded one-inch pipe wrapped in neoprene. Pruitt was on his knees, held up by Harry's hand on his collar. Marlene saw at once that Pruitt's jaw was out of line and his right wrist hung at a bad angle. As she watched, Harry's pipe swung out in a short, precise arc and cracked his client's collarbone. She watched him for a moment, both horrified and awed. Harry wasn't even breathing hard. He was beating a man to death with the same effortless skill that Fred Astaire used when he began the Beguine.

"Enough, Harry," she croaked. She rose to her feet, trailing drops of blood and put a restraining hand on his arm. "Enough," she said again, louder.

He looked at her and said, "Are you okay?"

She said, "Yeah, it's just a cut lip. It looks worse than it feels. You better make the calls."

Harry nodded and let go of Pruitt's collar. The man collapsed at her feet like a sack of golf balls. Harry cuffed him to the bar rail and went off to phone. Marlene sat down. One of the whores gave her a damp cloth. Marlene smiled thanks at her and dabbed at the dried blood. She checked the beer clock and looked at the door expectantly. Right on schedule, in walked Carrie Lanin.

After the cops and the ambulance and the emergency room and swearing out the multiple complaints against Pruitt, it was two-thirty before Marlene walked into the loft. They'd cleaned up her face and put a few stitches into her mouth, but she was turning interesting colors. Her lip looked like a raw Italian sausage, her outfit like a butcher's apron.

Unfortunately, Karp had dozed off in front of the TV, and was awakened by her return.

"Jesus Christ, Marlene. . . !"

"I don't want to hear about it, not tonight," she said, moving past him toward the bedroom. He followed close behind.

"Wait! What the hell . . . ?"

"I'm okay, I'm not badly hurt, I've been to the emergency room . . ."

"But what *happened*?"

She stripped off the gory angora and blouse and tossed them into a corner. "It was Pruitt. I went to meet Carrie, he followed her, we went into a bar, he followed us in and he jumped me."

Marlene was stripping off her filthy skirt as she uttered this whopper, the official tale she had concocted and sworn to, and had her back to Karp, so she did not observe the expression on his face as he took it in. She would have been dismayed to have seen it.

"And . . . ?" he said.

She slipped into a robe and turned to face him. "And what? Harry was backing me up and he arrested Pruitt. He's in jail now. Look, it hurts when I talk, and I want to take a hot bath—can the interrogation wait?"

"No, it can't," said Karp, blocking the door. "Let me understand this. This guy comes strolling into a bar where you and his girlfriend are sitting and just cracks you in the face? And your tame cop is just standing by waiting to arrest him? Do I have this right? Why did he hit you?"

"Why?" cried Marlene on a rising note. "Because he's a nut, that's why. He thinks I'm standing in the way of true love. We were just talking and—"

"Oh, horseshit, Marlene! You set this up. You concocted a trap for this bozo to generate an assault charge and a probation violation. And you're going to go to court and swear to a pack of lies to put him away, aren't you?"

Karp's voice had risen to a shout, and Marlene unconsciously retreated a step.

"He belongs in a cell," she snarled through clenched teeth. "What do you want? For me to wait until he kidnaps her, or rapes her, or murders her? He's a *stalker*, for Christ's sake!"

"Right, and who're you?" Karp yelled. "God almighty? Deciding who gets put away, who's the unacceptable risk?"

"Oh, you know, I can't stand you when you get this self-righteous attitude. Like you never cut a corner in your life to nail some scumbag."

He stared at her and she at him for a long moment. Then he said, slowly and carefully, "You don't fucking understand, do you? There's a difference, Marlene. I cut corners, you're a *felon*."

The word hung in the air like sewer gas. Karp turned and left the bedroom. She heard his heavy steps and the slam of the little guest room door.

SEVEN

Karp was gone by the time Marlene awakened the next morning, which she did not at all mind. She looked blearily at the clock and uttered a small shriek of alarm. Fifteen minutes to get ready and off to school. She sat up quickly and let out another shriek, of pain this time. It felt as though the flesh were being wrenched from her face with a dull spatula. In the bathroom she took one look at the Technicolor glory of her face and completed the rest of her toilette with her eye averted.

Lucy gave no trouble about being jammed by brute force into her clothes and eating her breakfast (banana and bran muffin to go) as she did not want to rile the angry and hideous stranger who had mysteriously replaced her mom during the night.

"Aren't we picking up Miranda?" the child asked meekly, when it had become clear that they were heading directly for P.S. 1.

"No, we're not. Miranda can get to school by herself."

"What about the bad man?"

"The bad man is in jail," Marlene replied in a tone that did not encourage further questions.

After the drop-off, Marlene shopped briefly on Grand Street and went back home. There she found the message light on her answering machine blinking, which she ignored, and also discovered that she had been traipsing through her neighborhood with her sweatshirt on inside out and the fly of her jeans gaping. She cursed and tore her clothes off and threw on a black sweatsuit, the right way, and then allowed herself a good, heaving, mucousy cry.

In the midst of this the phone rang.

"What?" Marlene shouted into the receiver.

"Uh-oh, she's got the rag on," said Ariadne Stupenagel. "No, it can't be, you're knocked up, aren't you? You're supposed to have a peaceful glow, unless that's a lie too."

"What do you want, Stupe?"

"We need to talk, girl. Can I come over?"

"Not today. I'm not receiving visitors."

"Oh?"

"I'm washing my hair. Those split ends? There's a new conditioner I want to try."

"Mmm, yes," said Stupenagel after the briefest pause, "and I might have believed that, and I might have been hurt, thinking that you thought so little of me as to use such a moronic excuse to shine me on, had I not drifted by the old courthouse this morning and had a chat with Ray Guma . . ."

"Oh, shit!" said Marlene, with feeling.

". . . and Guma filled my ear with a strange tale—

my little housewife friend with her face rearranged coming into the complaint room in the small hours to swear out a complaint against a nutcase who was stalking another woman. Sisterhood is powerful."

"Everybody knows about this now, right?"

"They will after I finish writing the story, which I will after you give me the details, which is why I'm coming over. I'm at Foley Square—I'll be there in ten minutes. Shall I bring you some nice soup?"

"How about a nice quart of bourbon?" said Marlene gloomily, and hung up the phone.

She checked the messages. They were all from metro reporters or TV stations asking for an interview, except for one from Carrie Lanin and one from someone named Suzy Poole, a name that rang a bell but distantly. Marlene could not quite recall where she had heard it. She called Carrie and got *her* machine, and left a message, and called the Poole person, and got an answering service with a crisp British accent, which assured her that her message would be passed on to Miss Poole.

Shortly after she hung up, the front doorbell rang, and there was Stupenagel, grinning and waving a quart of Ancient Age.

"I can't drink any of that," Marlene said. "I'm pregnant."

"Oh, don't be silly, you can have a *little* drink," said Stupenagel, entering the loft and focusing on Marlene. "Oh, God, look at your face! At last I'm more beautiful than you! I ought to send this bum a box of candy."

"Thanks for your support, Ariadne. You always know how to say the right thing."

"Oh, come on, it was just a joke." She waved her bottle again. "Get a couple of mugs and we'll forget our troubles."

"Sorry. I meant it. You go right ahead, though." Marlene turned away and walked toward the living room.

"You know, Marlene," said Stupenagel, following, "I hope you're not turning into one of those health fascists. Good God! My dear mother used to tell me she never passed a sober day during the whole time she was preggers with me."

Marlene gave her a baleful look and said, "No further questions, Your Honor."

Stupenagel snorted a laugh. "I guess I waltzed into that." She strode into the living room, flung her greatcoat onto the couch, sat down, and placed the bottle on the coffee table. "Well, shall we get started, then?"

Marlene fetched a tumbler and sat down in the bentwood rocker. "What are we starting, Stupe?"

"The story I'm going to write about you, of course." She reached into her canvas bag and drew out a steno book and a pencil.

"There's no story, Stupe. I helped out a friend is all," said Marlene wearily, and looked with longing at the bottle.

"Don't tell me my business, girl. You're news. Okay, let's start with when this Lanin character first told you she was being stalked."

Marlene looked at her friend, at the sharpened pencil poised quivering over the pad, at the bright and merciless gleam in her eye. The thought entered Marlene's mind that it was like having a pal who became a gynecologist: whatever the prior relationship, it inevitably became different when you were up on the table with your legs spread, watching her approach with the shiny instruments of the profession.

"What's funny?" Stupenagel asked, seeing the expression that now crossed Marlene's face.

"Oh, nothing," said Marlene, putting her mug into neutral. Then she began the tale of Carrie and Rob, the official version, of course, and hoped that Stupenagel was not as perceptive as Karp.

Someone had once told Karp that clients were to the law what the serpent was to the Garden of Eden. Heretofore the truth of this had not been pressed upon him, as he had spent virtually all of his professional career as a prosecutor, for whom the client is the People, a pleasant abstraction having no propensity to deviousness or complaint. It was different now that he had a real client breathing, complaining, and being devious in his office. He did not much like it.

"Murray," said Karp in a soothing voice, "it won't matter. We'll get by."

"Yeah, you say that," replied Selig. "How're you going to do all the things you need to do for this trial without support from your firm? It'd be like trying to do a solo on a coronary bypass."

"Right, and if I needed a coronary bypass, I'd take your advice. You need this trial, so take mine!"

A moment of glaring, and then Selig shook his chunky frame and grinned sheepishly. "Oh, crap, Butch—look, I didn't mean to give you a hard time. I just hate this."

Karp smiled back. "That's because you're a decent human being involved in a lawsuit. You're *supposed* to hate it. If you liked it, I wouldn't have anything to do with you. Anyway, as I was about to point out, we can hire support on the outside. I have a freelance paralegal lined up, and a steno who's going to come in a little while and take the Mayor's deposition. That's part of what's happening now, at this stage of the proceedings. I'll be deposing the defendants—"

"Just the Mayor?"

"No. Fuerza too. And the D.A."

"What's the point of him? I didn't work for the D.A."

"No," said Karp smoothly, "but his defamation helped form the basis of the firing, and added to the stigma you're suffering now." This partial truth was accepted without demur, and Karp continued. "We'll also depose all the people who supplied information in the two letters that formed the basis of the decision to fire you."

"The lies."

"As we will prove," said Karp. "Also, the defendants will get a crack at you and all of our witnesses, and they're obviously going to concentrate especially on you."

"That's okay," said Selig lightly. "I have nothing to hide."

Karp shot a stern look across his desk. "Wrong thinking, Murray. Everybody has something to hide—Mother Teresa, the Lubavitcher Rebbe, I don't care—*every*-body. The issue here is, you want to win this case, you don't hide it from me."

Selig nodded soberly. "I understand."

"Okay, let me make sure that you do. This case is about reputation. They said you're a sleazeball, you say you're not. It is to their very great advantage to blacken you even more than they have already. Now, they've restricted the calumny to your professional behavior as C.M.E., but at this point any sleaze will do, because they're trying to paint a picture for the jury and they want to make it the portrait of Dorian Gray. Look, let's say for the sake of argument that you enjoy fucking chickadees in the privacy of your own home . . ."

Selig guffawed.

". . . okay, you're a little embarrassed, you don't tell me. So at deposition, they got this, oh, say, some secretary up there on what looks like some minor paper trail matter and they ask her, did you bring those papers to Dr. Selig? Yes. And what was he doing when you got there? Oh, he was fucking this chickadee out by the birdhouse. Now, at that point I object, of course, but it's now part of the public record, and unless I can get it thrown out by the judge via a motion *in limine*, the jury will hear about it, and that's what they're going to see when they look at you, a guy with a vice he's ashamed to admit, and they're going to *inevitably* think, if he's covered this up, what else is there, and even if we destroy all their charges one by one, they're still going to think, hey, where there's smoke . . . You follow the logic?"

"Uh-huh. Okay, but I have this secret, what does it matter if I tell you first? What can you do? It'll still come out."

"Maybe, maybe not," said Karp. "The point is, if I'm not surprised, then *we're* in control, not them. We can do a deal. Let's say we find out the Mayor likes to get sucked off by a python, he keeps it in a bathtub down at City Hall . . ."

"I love your imagination. Snakes can't suck anything, though—they have no lips."

Karp rolled his eyes. "Let me write that down, I never want to forget it. It's just an *example*, Murray, for chrissake. Okay, we tell the D.: forget the chickadees, we won't touch on the snake. Alternatively, we bring up the chickadees ourselves."

"What's the point of that?"

"Anything you bring up voluntarily has less sting than it does if the other side brings it up. In the hypothetical we're discussing, we'd go in with a shrink: Dr. Selig has this chickadee problem, he's fighting it, he's in recovery. In your professional opinion, did it affect his work one iota? No. No further questions. Now the jury sees a courageous guy who's trying to conquer an embarrassing fault, and isn't afraid to admit it. Shit, if he'll come out about the chickadees, he's sure as hell not hiding anything else. Get the point?"

"Point got," said Selig. "But I'm sorry—right now no secret vices spring to mind. I'll talk to Naomi, though. She knows my faults better than I do."

Karp gave his client a hard and unamused stare, but his client's eyes slid away. Karp was about to say something when the buzzer on his desk bleated, and the receptionist announced the arrival of the Mayor of the City of New York.

Stupenagel stuck her pencil behind her ear and flipped through the pages of her steno pad. The story she had just heard was consistent and logical, but still it stirred some reportorial instinct of suspicion. "It was lucky that this cop Bello was there when this guy started to beat on you," she said, trolling.

"There was no luck to it, Stupe. I told you, he was shadowing her. We figured Pruitt would make a move sooner or later."

"Sounds almost like you baited a trap."

"Carrie Lanin is not a criminal," Marlene said with some heat. "She has the right to go anywhere and see anyone anytime. She doesn't have to live like a hermit because some asshole is harassing her. Besides"—here she pointed at the livid bruises that covered most of her face—"do you think I planned for *this* to happen?"

Stupenagel did not. She had a good imagination and considerable experience with violence, but this experience did not support the notion that someone who looked like Marlene Ciampi would risk her face to put some jerk in prison. She nodded slightly and changed her tack.

"How long do you think he'll get?"

"Oh, maybe five years, maybe three."

"Is that worth it?"

Marlene took a deep breath and searched for an answer. "Maybe," she said. "Maybe somebody will shank him in prison. Maybe he'll discover he likes fucking punks up the ass."

"Not very likely, is it? The guy sounds truly obsessed."

"Yeah," Marlene agreed. "Maybe that's why I got involved. Maybe I thought that the only thing that worked against an obsession was a counter-obsession, a stronger one. I just felt . . . *impelled* to stop him, you know? Do you ever get feelings like that? Yeah? Anyway, it felt good."

Stupenagel wrote this down and then put her pad on the coffee table. "Speaking of obsessions, I think I'm getting one over this gypsy cab business. And the jailhouse suicides."

"Why? I thought you said it was likely that they really had killed themselves."

"Yes, yes, I did," said Stupenagel impatiently, "but . . . I have a feeling that not all is as it should be in the old Two-Five. I went to a retirement racket the other night—your good buddy Roland set it up— and after I talked to Clancy, I lounged in the bar, keeping my little ears open and engaging in good-natured sexist banter. There was so much testosterone in the air, I felt myself growing a beard. Anyway . . ."

"What about Clancy?"

"Clancy's just a bureaucrat. Nice guy, knows nothing. This Jackson character, on the other hand—"

The phone rang. "I better get that," said Marlene, and left for her office at the end of the loft. Stupenagel refreshed her drink and began to compose in her mind the story she would hand in later that afternoon. After five minutes, Marlene returned and sat down with a puzzled look on her face.

"Who's Suzy Poole?" she asked. "I know the name."

"Of course you do. She's the super model. Cover of *Vogue* this month? Why do you ask?"

"Oh, that was her."

"Suzy Poole called *you*? What did she want?"

"Oh, you know—fashion tips, my famous makeup secrets—"

"No, *really*!"

"Off the record, Stupe," said Marlene heavily. "I mean it."

"Swear to God."

Marlene gave her a hard look. "If this gets out, it will not be God who will punish you." She leaned back and lit a Marlboro, only her third of the day, she was happy to realize. "Well, she's being stalked. By this guy she had a fling with. And she wants me to help her out. Carrie Lanin knows her—from the rag trade. That's how she got my name. Carrie was talking up my prowess in some ladies' john on Seventh Avenue.''

"Wait a second—models at that level must have security up the ying-yang. Doesn't she have, like, a regular bodyguard?''

"Oh, yeah, that was my thought too. She said she'd tried that. It's like living in jail, she said. The guy is everywhere. He's got some money too. Somehow he always gets her number no matter how many times she changes it. And he's smart too. There's no physical evidence, no threats.''

"What does she expect you to do?''

"Get rid of him, of course.''

"Will you?''

Marlene watched the smoke from her cigarette circulate up to the ceiling and said lazily, "Oh, I might. I just had the thought when I was talking to her that it could be an interesting thing to do. I mean, as a business.'' She turned an interested face to Stupenagel's bemused one. "So, what happened with the gypsies?''

"Oh, yeah. I was telling you about Jackson. Paul. The cops at the Two-Five are not anxious to talk about Detective Jackson, even when a little drunk and getting any number of cheap feels off the kid here. Something's smelly going down up there in Spanish Harlem. This morning I got with a guy I know at Internal Affairs, Tommy Devlin. They have their suspicions, but nothing solid. Jackson lives a little too well, but that could mean he's just lucky at the track. They haven't had any complaints, not that a bunch of illegal Guats are going to make much of a stink if they're getting shook down by a cop. They think that's how the government collects taxes. I asked him about the suicides too. Those he swears're strictly kosher. The M.E. autopsied the first two as genuine hangings. Apparently there's ways to tell hanging from getting strangled. The third kid just stopped breathing like the ones I told you about in Asia. They called it 'panic death.' "

"So where are you going with it?"

"Oh, I think I'll work the gypsies a little more, see if I can find someone who's not too scared to help." She finished her drink, stood up, and shrugged into her coat.

"In fact, I'm off now. I'll let you know when the story comes out." Marlene walked her to the door. "You know, we should really get a picture of you for this piece."

"Never!" said Marlene vehemently.

"Suit yourself." Stupenagel paused by the door. "You know, you may think me a cynical bitch, but my heart really goes out to those poor bastards. They escape from total hell down there, and they come up here and some fucking scumbag cop takes their few pathetic dollars, when a rookie cop's base salary is about eight times the per capita income of Guatemala. If that fucker is running a racket, I'm going to have his ass for it."

"Good luck," said Marlene, pleasantly surprised by the cynical bitch reporter's words. The two women hugged and Stupenagel stepped out of the door. She felt in her bag.

"Oh, crap, I left my pad on your sofa," she said.

"I'll get it," said Marlene.

Stupenagel waited in the shadowed hallway, pulled from her bag a Leica M3 loaded with ASA 400 black-and-white film, and looked through its eyepiece. As Marlene, returning with the pad, stepped into the light from the track unit outside her living room, Stupenagel silently snapped two frames and put the camera back into her bag.

"I thought that went pretty well," said Murray Selig. The Mayor had just been ushered out amid a flurry of false smiles and the usual faux collegial banter between Karp and his opposite number, the corporation counsel, Josh Gottkind.

"You did, huh?" replied Karp sourly. He was thinking that at this moment the Mayor was visiting with Jack Weller, accepting apologies and being assured that the firm was not involved in this sad and *messhugah* affair.

"Yeah, I thought the guy was, you know, more cooperative than I thought he would be," said Selig in an uncertain tone.

"Oh, he was cooperative, all right. On the other hand, he doesn't know much, and I didn't push him very hard for it. Did you notice that he got annoyed every time Gottkind told him not to answer?"

Selig nodded. "But he didn't want to talk about the probation business."

"No, he didn't, because the City changed the probationary period from six months to one year *after* they hired you, and he never officially informed you of that fact. You had a reasonable expectation that your probationary period was over. I needed to pin him down that he never told you."

"And you did."

"That's right. He's in a tough position, which is why, when he refused to answer, I told him I would be in Judge Craig's chambers this afternoon and walk out with an order to compel in my hand, and this evening the news would be 'Mayor Refuses to Answer Questions in M.E. Case.'"

"So we're doing good?"

"Oh, the Mayor's easy. Pinning down the other people will be a lot harder. Speaking of which, the fun's about to begin on your end. Tomorrow Gottkind gets his crack at you."

Selig shrugged. "Let him take his best shot."

"It's not that simple, Murray," said Karp, a hint of irritation in his voice. "You're under oath, and they'll be scrutinizing every word you say for fishhooks to hang favorable precedents on. I know we've been through this a little before, but let me lay out the legal situation as it affects what you're supposed to say."

Selig looked at his watch. "Will this take a long time?" The doctor, having placed his affairs in Karp's hands, had shown little interest in the nuts-and-bolts aspects of the case.

"No, Murray, about as long as an autopsy," said

Karp. "Okay. You know we're suing under the Fourteenth Amendment because we hold that you've been deprived of liberty and property without due process. The property part is your interest in your job; you can't be deprived of it without a formal hearing beforehand, which you did not get. The liberty interest involves the stigma created by the charges made against you, which has deprived you of your ability to pursue your normal occupation. The classic case is *Bishop* v. *Wood*: a cop got fired for insubordination and ruining morale. Plaintiff argued that accusing him of that behavior in public constituted a 'badge of infamy,' such that he could never again pursue his usual occupation as a cop, hence deprivation of liberty without due process. Same with you. Liberty to pursue your normal occupation, a chief medical examiner of a major city, was taken from you without due process of law. What we'll be asking the court for is, on the property side, reinstatement and back pay, and on the liberty side, damages, to recompense you for that damaging loss of reputation. Stigma plus, as we call it."

"That's what pays you, the damages."

"Right, Murray, that's what pays me. Now, the defendants are going to try to demonstrate two things. The first is that you did not have a property interest in your job. The Supreme Court gives a lot of leeway to states for determining if an employee actually has such an interest. They don't want a situation where every town clerk who gets canned thinks he has a federal case. The idea is that coincident with your taking a public job, you admit to understanding that there are legitimate causes for dismissal, as established under statute. It's called the 'bitter with the sweet' doctrine. There are two ways the City can do this. One, they can show that you were still on probation and hadn't yet acquired any job rights. They say it's a year, we say it's six months. I think we can roll them on this. It falls on employer to inform employee of any probationary period, and they told you it was six months when they hired you, and that should be it. The more serious problem is whether you in fact had a rational expectation of a right to a job that couldn't be taken away without a hearing. That is, we have to point to actual rules that say whether the C.M.E. position requires a formal hearing before dismissal."

"Of course it requires one," said Selig vehemently. "It says so in the position description in the City Green Book."

"So it does," Karp agreed, "and we have general support for right to hearing before dismissal in several sections of the state Civil Service Law. But section 557 (a) of the Administrative Code says the Mayor can boot you out just by telling you why. Which, of course, he did."

A puzzled frown appeared on Selig's face. "But that doesn't make any sense. How can the law say two different things?"

Karp laughed briefly. "How indeed? Now you know why lawyers make the big bucks. Look, Murray: doctors wear white coats because they have to make sure there's no dirt on them. Judges wear black robes so the dirt don't show. The job here is to devise some way of saying that although there appears to be conflict, precedent tells the judge to resolve it in our favor." Karp studied his yellow crib sheet and made a note on its margins. Then he handed his client a document of some twenty or so closely typed sheets. "This is how I think the questioning is going to go. What I mean is, those are the questions I'd ask you if I was on the other side. Let's go through them one by one, because I want to hear your answers."

"Don't I swear to tell the whole truth?" asked Selig lightly.

"Only if they ask for it, Murray," said Karp. "And if I let you."

Before her visit to Marlene's loft, Stupenagel had no thought of doing anything dramatic with her evening. She had planned to return to her West End Avenue sublet to work on her story over a bag of take-out Chinese. Marlene's tale, however, and the evidence of her damaged face, had gotten under her skin. Although she was genuinely fond of Marlene, she was most fond of her when Marlene kept to her place, which in Stupenagel's mind was Mom, Wifey, and at the most, Legal Drudge. It was entirely unacceptable for Marlene to have the sort of adventure she had just experienced, except, of course, by accident. That Marlene had *planned* to risk her neck in this way vexed the reporter no end, because if Marlene could have her luxurious and now trendy loft, and a baby, and a husband whom she did not despise, then she simply *couldn't* be allowed to embark on that kind of adventure, the kind that Stupenagel herself routinely arranged to have. That was the deal that Stupenagel had made with life, and it did not bear thinking that it might not be universally valid.

To her credit, she did not have for Marlene any ill will because of this; nor did she plan to discommode her in any way, beyond the sort of nastiness native to the profession of journalism. But she did enjoy twitting Marlene for being a hausfrau, and planned to continue to do so, and this was only feasible if she continued to outclass Marlene in the adventure business.

These thoughts occupied her as she strolled aimlessly up Grand Street and across Mulberry, past the shuttered groceries and import shops, and the storefront social clubs around which clustered groups of flashy young men, leaning on their double-parked cars. *There* was trouble, she thought, but not precisely the right kind. She received a good deal of commentary as she walked past these knots of wise guys. One of the men, short, hairy, and drunk, stood grinning in her path, demanding an obscene favor and handling his genitals, while his pals urged him on. Stupenagel had in her bag, beside camera and notebook, a short, razor-sharp, bone-handled Arab dagger she'd picked up during her first visit to Syria, and she considered briefly gutting this man with it and then escaping from the country with the Mafia on her tail, and whether that would make a good story. That such an action would cross her mind at all showed how irritable she had become out of this silly Marlene thing. She straightened herself, gave the man a withering look, and walked around him as if he had been a load of dog poop on the pavement.

It was at that moment that it popped into her head that she would go undercover as a gypsy cab driver and catch Detective Paul Jackson at whatever it was he was doing.

EIGHT

Marlene waited a couple of days, until Karp was more or less over the snit he had got into over the Lanin affair, and they were comfortably settled in the marriage bed, before she sprang it on him. He laughed and said, "Yeah, right!" before it struck him that she was not laughing along.

"You're not serious?" he asked.

"Yeah, I'm serious. I think it's a good idea."

"It's the worst idea you ever had, Marlene," said Karp, "and that's a tough league."

"Why? Why is it such a bad idea?"

He sighed. "Babe, private investigators are high school graduates. You went to Yale Law. You were on law review. You have a *mind*. I can't believe you're actually thinking of spending your life following sleazes around with a camera."

"You're not listening to me," said Marlene in a controlled voice. "Listen to what I said. I want to start a service that specializes in helping women who are being harassed, and that'd include legal rep as well as straight P.I. I'm not talking about tort or divorce work."

Karp shifted in bed and gave her a searching look. "When you say P.I. work, you mean stuff like what gave you that face?"

"Not necessarily."

"No? Then what? What are you going to do within a legal framework that the cops can't do a whole lot better?"

"The cops do hardly anything, and you know it," she retorted. "Enforcing protective orders is down below littering on their priority list. As for what I'm going to do, I'm going to do whatever it takes."

"You and Harry Bello are going to do this?"

"Yeah. He likes the idea. He's going to hand in his tin this week."

"Oh, terrific! Marlene, he's a psychopath."

"He's *not* a psychopath! How can you *say* that? He's your daughter's godfather."

Karp tried another tack. "And the two of you think you can make a living from this?"

"What living? Harry's got his pension, and as far as I know, *we* certainly don't have any money problems. Why, is Daddy going to cut me off without a penny if I do this?"

"Oh, of course not, Marlene," said Karp, starting to feel trapped. "But . . . God, with just the pair of you . . . I mean, it's going to be an all-hours thing. What about Lucy?"

"What about her? We seemed to do okay when we were both at the D.A. working crazy hours and she was a lot younger and needed more attention."

"And the new baby . . . ?"

"I'll deal with that when it happens," she snapped, and then, in a more even tone, "Look, this isn't about money or domestic arrangements. If I had a job with a firm or a prosecutor's office, you'd be buying champagne. So what is it?"

"Oh, for crying out loud, Marlene, look in the mirror!"

"What, I got hurt? Jeez, Butch, so I got hurt. I've been hurt worse. I thought we had a deal on that."

Karp paused before answering, trying for a locution that wouldn't send this discussion off into a raging fight. Still, he could not keep a trace of bitterness from his voice.

"What deal was that, Marlene? The one where you get to do all the irresponsible stuff and I get to eat my heart out?"

Marlene looked at him soberly and nodded, twice. "Yes, I understand that it's hard for you. But, look, Butch—right after we started going together, I got myself blown up by a bomb. A year later, more or less, I got myself kidnapped and tortured by a gang of satanists. That was *before* we got married. You must have had a hint, at least, that I wasn't going to be like your mom."

Karp did not respond to this verbally. Instead he riffled the pages of the law book he had been reading when this conversation began, and arranged his face in the mulish, tight-jawed expression that he adopted when Marlene was pressing him to come clean with some negative thought.

"Well?" she said, after a minute of strained silence. "Is that what it is? The danger business?"

"No," Karp admitted. "Not that that doesn't suck too, but no."

"What, then? Christ, Butch, come out with it!"

It came, in a rush. "All right. What you're doing, what you're planning, it's not just going to be P.I. work. It's going to be more of the kind of thing you pulled with Pruitt—"

"Not necess—"

"Let me finish! When it comes down to a case of letting the law take its course, or making sure that some woman doesn't get hurt, I know what you're going to do and so do you. It's going to involve taking out the male party, Marlene. And some of these guys are persistent. So maybe in the back of your mind, there's a thought about making it permanent. In some cases. I'd bet my next three paychecks that stuff like that would not faze Harry one little bit. And it's wrong. Don't you think I know the law's fucked up in the domestic area? Jesus, Marlene, I was a homicide prosecutor for twelve years! There are probably five domestic homicides for every crime-connected murder. But if you want to change that, do it right! Run for office, lobby Albany, be a legal counsel at one of those shelters, anything, but don't do this, what you're thinking about. Because as sure as my ass is on this mattress, you're going to get in trouble, not little trouble, but big trouble, disbarment trouble, Class A felony trouble. And the worst thing is, while you're getting in this trouble, you can't talk about it with me. We can't be—I don't know—*together* in the way I want us to be, because I can't know about that kind of shit. You understand what I'm saying? *I can't know about it.*"

"Why? Because you'll turn me in?" She asked this lightly, not at all liking how this conversation was turning out, but Karp answered with grim seriousness.

"Yes," he said, grimly. "In a heartbeat. Christ, Marlene, you know the damn law on conspiracy and accessory to felony. You got away with this goddamn Lanin deal because Harry's a cop and he covered for you, but if he's private, he won't be able to do that."

"Butch, this is a ridiculous conversation. You sound like I'm planning to set up Murder Incorporated. It's a security and investigation service."

"Is it?" he asked coldly. "Fine, then. I beg your pardon. Just so you know that there is no way in hell that our child—excuse me, our *children*—are ever going to end up with *both* their parents in jail." Karp let a long breath out through his nostrils and propped his book up on his chest and started to pretend to read it. Marlene stared at him for a while and then plumped her pillows and got out a magazine. For a long time, until they switched off their lights, the only sound was the turning of pages.

Stupenagel's article about Marlene's work on behalf of Carrie Lanin was published two weeks later in the *Village Voice*. It was a good piece, Marlene thought, almost good enough to make her not hate the reporter for publishing a photograph of what Pruitt had done to her face. Marlene had not been the only interview: Stupe had broadened the article to cover the whole phenomenon of women being stalked in New York, and seemed to have ferreted out anyone in the greater metropolitan area who had ever thought seriously about violence against women resulting from that peculiar obsession.

Marlene read the article twice, underlining here and there and making marginal notes. Then she called Stupenagel.

"You total shit," she said when the reporter picked up the phone.

"Marlene! You saw the article?"

"Of course I saw it, you jerk! How could you do that to me? Oh, crap! Why do I even ask?"

"What's wrong? I thought you came out of it very well," said Stupenagel. "They even put a sidebar in there describing your colorful past."

"What's wrong is that I'm going to have to carry this face to my mom's house on Sunday, and it's improved enough to give me a shot at passing it off with a white lie about a car wreck, which you have rendered impossible by printing that picture and dwelling on how it happened."

"Yeah, but how did you like the piece?" said Ariadne.

Marlene bit back a ferocious response. There was as much point in getting angry with Ariadne for the wreckage she occasionally left in her wake as it would be to get miffed at a typhoon; the woman was as insensitive as a tropical low.

"I loved it," said Marlene. "I'm going to have it bronzed. I was especially fascinated with that NYU woman you dug up—is she legit?"

"Professor Malkin? Oh, yeah, legit up the wazoo. Did you like the typology? Slobs, sadists, and strangers. I love it!"

"Yeah, but what I wanted to know was, did she have some way of telling them apart, I mean at the beginning?"

"Hmmm, interesting question," said the reporter. "To tell the truth, I didn't get into it with her that deeply. I went to her because she had the statistics I needed, and I just threw the three-types thing in because I thought it sounded neat. Why are you asking?"

"Oh, just curiosity," said Marlene disingenuously. "Do you happen to have the good professor's number?"

Clunk of phone and rustle of paper while she fished it out. After Marlene wrote it down she asked, "And what's with you, Stupe? Anything happening in the great world?"

"I cut off all my hair," said Stupenagel, to Marlene's surprise. She was not surprised that she had done it, just that she thought it worthy of mention.

"Did you?"

"Yes. And dyed it black. Very punky."

"Getting interested in fashion, are we, in our old age?"

"One must keep up," said Stupenagel airily. "For some of us, the ability to make tempting popovers does not suffice. Speaking of fashion, though, did you ever get back with Suzy Poole?"

"Uh-huh."

"And?"

"Bye, Stupe."

Marlene pushed the button down in the middle of Stupenagel's outraged squawk, and immediately dialed Professor Malkin's number. She got a secretary and made an appointment for a week hence. Then she dressed carefully, with as much fashion as she could manage, and called a cab.

The model, Suzy Poole, lived in a high-rise apartment building on Fifth Avenue at Seventy-first Street. The security was about what you would expect in a government installation holding mid-level nuclear secrets. Marlene was examined, checked over the intercom, and elevatored to the fifteenth floor by a manned car, whose operator waited to see her admitted to the Poole apartment.

Which was largely white and black, with splashes of meaningless abstract color and neon sculptures on plain stands, an obvious package by a decorator at the forward edge of au courant. Poole herself was garbed in black—tights and a sort of loose Chinese jacket in heavy cotton, an outfit that, in combination with her essential physique, made her look like a recent releasee from a Japanese prison camp. Her face, despite the famous razor cheekbones and a nose that appeared to have more than a normal complement of tiny, angled bones, seemed, without the intervening miracle of photography, curiously malformed, like that of an embryo bird.

Marlene was seated in a complicated chrome and leather sling, offered a drink, stared at with frank horror, and subjected to a long story of persecution. She took notes. The gentleman was named Jonathan Seely. He was an account executive at a big ad agency that had hired Ms. Poole to associate her cheekbones with an upmarket new perfume. A romance had blossomed, then faded, when Ms. Poole had discovered the gentleman was, as she put it, a sadistic son of a bitch. He had hit her. In the *face*. Now he wouldn't stop calling. Somehow he was able to obtain her private, private number, however often she changed it. Every time the phone rang she jumped. It was interfering with her work. She was a prisoner in her own home. And so on.

Marlene closed her notebook. The model stopped talking and looked at her expectantly. Marlene said, "Well, I think I have enough to go on. Let me do some nosing around and get back to you. Tomorrow?"

Suzy Poole let a crease of doubt mar her perfection. "Umm, sure, but what do you think now? Will you be able to help?"

"Oh, yeah, I think so."

"Like what? Not guards."

"Oh, no. You don't need me for guards, and the point is not to make a more secure prison for yourself, but to make him stop bothering you. For example, I noticed you haven't filed for a protective order. That'd be one of our first steps."

Poole made a moue of distaste, charming. "Ooh, do we have to, like, *involve* the courts? I mean, can't we handle it in a more discreet way?"

"You're concerned about this guy messing with your career if you name him publicly in a legal action?"

"I guess."

Marlene fixed the woman's enormous dark blue eyes with her solo jet one, and said, "Let's get one thing straight before we go any further, Ms. Poole. This man has declared war on you. He is torturing you. He is beyond decency. Pleas haven't helped. In order to make him stop, we must therefore make his life as unpleasant—no, *more* unpleasant—than he has made yours. Now, I think I can do that, and going to court is—"

The phone rang. Suzy Poole uttered a little startled noise and touched her hand to her heart.

"I'll get it," said Marlene, and picked up the nearest phone before Poole could say a word.

"Bitch!" said a hissing voice in Marlene's ear.

"Mr. Seely?" said Marlene pleasantly. "This is Ms. Poole's protective service. We ask you please not to call this number again."

Silence, and then the click of a disconnection.

"He'll call again," said Marlene. "If you're going to go ahead with this, I'll have my partner make an appointment to rig up a recording device on your line. It's critical that we get a physical record of him annoying you. So, are we hired?"

Suzy Poole nodded. "Yes. You're hired. Do you, ah, want me to give you a check?"

"Not right now," said Marlene. "I want to get my license first."

When Marlene left Suzy Poole's she cabbed downtown (marking the cab ride as a legitimate expense in a little book she had purchased for this purpose) and filed a P.I. application at the New York State Building on Foley Square. It was a formality. The state of New York does not want lowlife types carrying guns and poking into the private affairs of its citizens, and so keeps its private-investigator licensing laws strict. The stringency is, however, greatly reduced for former members of the NYPD, and a cynic might see a connection between the verve with which the police resist any relaxation of the City's laws against legal gun ownership (in a town where any fifteen-year-old can pick up a piece for pocket change) and the ease with which retired cops float into the armed security business. Harry would have no trouble getting a P.I. license, and, of course, neither would the respectable lawyer and former prosecutor Marlene Ciampi.

After that, she walked a few blocks south and met Harry Bello at a cop bar near One Police Plaza, where he had just finished the act of handing in his gold potsy. There would be no big retirement racket for Harry. He had used up his friends on the Job. Harry had shot a kid, a kid who might or might not have killed his partner, killed him in cold blood and then dropped a cheap pistol on the corpse, and the cops knew it and covered for him, to protect the department, but people didn't want to know him after that.

The place was busy, yet Harry had two empty stools on either side of him at the bar. He was drinking club soda and shuffling through a set of retirement papers.

"How's the pension?" she asked as she sat down.

"I got Lucy as my beneficiary," he said. "Is that okay?"

"It's fine, Harry. I just this minute came from our first customer."

Raised eyebrow.

"I think we can help her. The guy is a taxpayer; he won't stand up to a serious nudge."

Harry said, "No way. Not again."

"I wasn't thinking about anything as elaborate as the Pruitt thing, Harry. This guy is a different type. There's a woman I need to see at NYU; apparently she's got a line on who stalks and why. I think this model's bum is going to be easy money. Oh, by the way, I got these."

Marlene reached into her bag and brought out a small brick-shaped box. She opened it and handed Bello one of the business cards it contained, printed with:

Bello & Ciampi
Investigations • Security

with the Crosby Street address and an unfamiliar phone number.

"The number's an answering service," Marlene explained. "We'll work out of my place until we're rich enough to spring for an office. What do you think? Bello and Ciampi, pretty classy, huh?"

"Fresh fish," said Bello, deadpan.

"Why, Harry," said Marlene in a tone of exaggerated wonder. "I believe that you have just made a light or humorous remark. You know, I think retirement is going to do you some good."

Phil DeLino's call caught Karp just as he was about to leave. He stood in his office holding his coat and took it.

"May twenty-third," said DeLino.

"What's May twenty-third?" asked Karp.

"What you were so hot to find out. I spoke to His Honor and went over his calendars. May twenty-third is the first date that we can remember Bloom bringing up that we ought to fire Murray Selig. After that it was the subject of lots of calls and at least three meetings."

"Why?" Karp asked with growing interest. "What was the reason? And why just then?"

"I drew a blank there, buddy. The Mayor doesn't know either. Guy just got a bug in his bonnet."

"Mmm. Maybe. Look, thanks, Phil, and if you chance across anything else, I'd appreciate knowing about it."

"Will do. By the way, the Mayor enjoyed his session with you. It made him wish he was still practicing law. And he told me to tell you, quote, when Jack Weller fires his sorry Jewish ass, he can come by and work for me, unquote."

Stupenagel drove slowly up Lexington Avenue in East Harlem, trying to steer the ancient black Chevy around the worst potholes. The shocks were nearly gone, and when she went over a bad one the jolt made her teeth clatter. It was her third night on the job, and she had by now acquired the greatest respect for the way in which gypsy cab drivers made their living.

She was wearing a tattered leather jacket and had a greasy Mets cap pulled down over her eyes. It did not do Stupenagel's vanity much good to be able to pass as a man so easily, but it had often been useful to her professionally. She was good at it too. The guy running the garage, a Dominican, had barely looked at her before sending her out in his worst beater.

The garage boss was, in fact, only interested in the phony license she presented, and her demonstrated facility in both Spanish and English. Gypsy hacks didn't last long in New York, and bilingual ones were a prize. She had a crackling dashboard-mounted radio that occasionally squawked her number and told her where to go for a pickup. The gypsies, she was learning, fulfilled an essential social purpose, in that they were the only automobile transportation available to the City's legions of poor. Into her cab whole families had piled, clown-car fashion, to go to a christening or a funeral, and when the poor moved, which was often, they loaded their entire worldly store into the gypsies for shipment from one rotten apartment to another. This much was legal.

The other side of the gypsy business (illegal) arose from the reluctance of the real taxicabs, the yellow ones with the high-priced official medallion from the hack bureau on their hoods, to travel in upper Manhattan, or other rough regions of the City, or to pick up from the street members of the darker-hued minorities.

It was, of course, well known that gypsy cabs picked up people who hailed them on the street. Since their cabs had no meters, each driver would engage in a brief negotiation with the passenger for the fare and then pocket it. The garage that owned the cab only had claim to the radio pickup fares, and it was understood that gypsy cabbies would supplement their fares in this way; indeed, it was virtually a necessity of survival, given the miserable wage paid by the garages.

Stupenagel had done plenty of street pickups, far more than was usual for real gypsies, who had constantly to worry about being pinched by hack bureau inspectors or cops. She, on the other hand, was looking to get caught, and in three days she had taken in over two hundred dollars.

There was a man standing in the avenue at 147th, under a streetlamp, with his hand up. Stupenagel swerved and slowed and looked the man over. A short man, vanilla gringo or P.R., with a mustache, wearing a raincoat and a leather porkpie hat with the brim turned up. She figured him for a musician; uptown musicians made up a considerable proportion of the gypsies' late business. She stopped and the man got in.

"Where to, man?" she asked, pitching her voice low.

He leaned forward and held out a gold shield in a leather holder. "Make this next right and pull over," he said.

"Ah, shit!" she said. "You from the hack bureau?"

"Shut up and move it!" he replied.

She made the turn, and her passenger directed her to park behind a black Plymouth Fury.

A man got out of the Fury. The passenger said, "Get out!" and she did and he did too. The man from the Fury was large and dark and wearing an expensive tan topcoat. He had a broad, heavy-browed face, on which he carried that peculiar expression, both amused and predatory, characteristic of men confident in some arbitrary power, shortly to be used. Stupenagel had seen it dozens of times around the world, on Eastern European apparatchiki and policemen, on guerillas at Central American crossroads, on the officers trying to extirpate those guerillas. She had not encountered it before in her own country, however, and she felt the beginnings of fear.

"You been a naughty boy, Pedro," said the big man, coming closer and looking her up and down.

"You picked up a fare off the street without a license." He held out a meaty hand. "Give it over!"

"What?" asked Stupenagel stupidly.

The hand flew up in a blur and cracked her across the jaw. She sprawled backward against the cab's fender.

"Hey, he ain't a spic, Paulie," remarked the other man.

"No, he sure ain't," agreed the big man. "Hey, shitface, what's a white man doing driving a gypsy up in greaser heaven?"

Stupenagel's head was still ringing from the blow, and she didn't answer. The big man kicked her painfully in the ankle.

"*Pzhalsteh, gospodin, pzhalsteh . . .*" she gasped in the most obsequious voice she could manage.

"What's that, Polack?" asked the other man.

"Or Russian. You a Russky, shitface?"

"Yes . . . Russian," Stupenagel answered.

"Jesus, the fuckin' foreigners are taking over the damn country," said the big man. "You understand money, right? Stand the fuck up when I talk to you! Let's have the money."

Stupenagel stood and dug into the pocket of her leather jacket, coming out with a thick wad of bills, which the big man snatched from her hand.

"Hey, hey, look at this!" the man exclaimed. "You been a hard worker, boy." He separated out most of the bills and let the rest, mostly singles, drop to the pavement. After a second's hesitation she stooped and picked them up.

"That's for your license. You understand license?" the big man said in the unnaturally loud voice used to communicate with idiots and foreigners. "But look, Ivan, you got to renew it every week, understand? Today's Wednesday—you understand?"

"Yes, Vednesday," said Stupenagel.

"You come back here every Wednesday, this time. You have a hundred for me, yes? Understand?"

Stupenagel nodded.

The big man grinned at her. He had white, evenly capped teeth, she noticed, the kind that very few of the people who drove gypsy cabs had in their mouths. "Good," he said. "But if you drive in my neighborhood without a license . . . not good." He popped her on the shoulder a couple of times, playfully but hard. "Boom, boom, go to jail. Understand? Okay, get the fuck out of here! Back to work!"

He turned away, dismissing her. She climbed back into the Chevy, cranked it up, and drove off. She went directly to the garage, which was in Inwood, by the river, parked, and went into the tiny garage office. When she turned her keys, money, and trip sheets in to the night man, he looked meaningfully at the clock.

"Your shift ain't over until four," he said.

"I'm quitting," she said. The man shrugged, counted her cash, peeled off some bills, and shoved them across the grimy desk at her. She pocketed the cash without bothering to count it. The night man whistled, as for a dog.

A small man, with red-brown skin, with high

cheekbones and crow-wing hair stood in the door-way. The night man asked him in Spanish if he wanted a ride. The man said yes. Stupenagel wanted to tell him, to warn him, but couldn't think of what to say, how to explain what was going on up there. And he wouldn't understand. Even ripped off, the man would make in a month what would take him a year to earn in Central America. Instead, what she said, in Spanish, was, "You can drive me home, brother. I can be your first fare."

NINE

Professor Gloria Malkin of the New York University sociology department was twenty-nine years old, not bad at all for an associate with tenure. More remarkably, she looked about twelve. Not more than fourteen, Marlene thought, a little foxy in the face but nice clear brown eyes, the slightest indication of breasts under the prim white Oxford shirt and grass green sweater. She had frizzy pale tan hair yanked back into an old-fashioned ponytail tied with a bead and elastic holder. She was one of those women who fell into their look in sophomore year and found thereafter no reason to change.

Unlike Marlene. She had chosen to appear for the interview in her biker gang momma thug outfit: knee boots, black jeans, a Navy sweater, black leather jacket with the shiny zips. Her hair had grown out into thick, springy sable coils, which bounced around her face, Medusa-like. Also, she was wearing a patch over her eye rather than the glassie, and not a drugstore black paper model either, but a narrow, soft-leather item of the type favored by actors playing

German officers in the last war. She told herself that it was a professional look, considering her new profession.

"My secretary said you were a private detective," said the professor by way of opening. "I don't think I've ever actually met a private detective before. It sounds romantic."

"Yes, that's odd, isn't it?" said Marlene. "The professions that have attracted the interest of romance writers are a funny bunch. Pirate. Cowboy."

"Spy. Artist. Yes, I imagine for the people who actually do them, they must be the same as—I don't know—tax accountancy or installing washing machines."

"Yes, that's what you're supposed to say," said Marlene, "but in fact, it's unutterably romantic. Rushing around in cabs following people. Wearing black clothes and sneaking into places. Violence."

"I'm impressed," said Malkin. "The violence. Is that how you . . ." She gestured at Marlene's face.

"Yes. I got beat up."

"And the eye the same?"

"No, that was a while ago. I was a prosecutor then. Somebody sent a bomb in the mail."

Malkin's eyes widened. "Oh, you're *that* one! In the article in the *Voice*. I should have made the connection."

"Yes. In fact, Ariadne's a friend of mine. How I got your number."

"Speaking of romantic occupations. Well, my gosh, this is just like being in a comic strip. First Brenda

Starr and now a female crime fighter . . . Wonder Woman? No, the Cat Lady!"

They laughed at that together and then talked casually for a while, trading career backgrounds, until Malkin said, "Well, unless you're recruiting for a mousy sidekick, you must have had a reason for coming to see me. I imagine it was that article."

"Yeah, it was," said Marlene. "I'm trying to develop a service that specializes in stalking cases."

"Really? That's fascinating. Do you have some kind of foundation support?"

"No, why?"

"Well, because most women whose lives have deteriorated to the point where they're being stalked or brutalized are usually in no position to lay out any money for protection."

"Good point," said Marlene. "My husband raised it too. I guess it hasn't been a problem yet. As a matter of fact, I just finished a case that was very lucrative. A fashion model."

"You stopped whoever was stalking her?"

"So far. My sense of this guy is that he won't be back. I don't think he was a true obsessive, just a nasty who liked to torture the animals. Which is really why I came to see you."

"Yes, the typology," said Malkin almost dismissively. "But tell me, how did you do it? Make him stop."

"You want to hear this? Yeah, well, briefly, first we got out a protective order. The guy called anyway, and we had him on the recorder. I got the client to egg him on, insult him, and he got really vile—totally lost control. Threats, obscenity—he really started wailing on how he was going to mutilate her sexual organs. Funny, because he was supposedly this classy guy. Drunk probably. In any case, we take the tape to the judge, and he issues a contempt citation, and the cops pick him up at work. Handcuffs, the whole nine yards. Of course, he makes bail and goes back to the office to straighten things out. I guess he figured he could use the hysterical woman mad with jealousy gambit."

"And didn't he?" Malkin asked. Her eyes were sparkling, and she had curled herself up in her chair, like a Girl Scout listening to ghost stories around the fire.

"No. Actually, my partner walked into his office while he was out and put a copy of the tape on the office P.A. system. I don't think it did his career much good. He specialized in fashion advertising, and a lot of the heavy hitters in that business are women. Anyway, when he found this out, he threw caution to the winds and went straight for her. To her building, I mean. And he got in."

"My God! Didn't she have security in the building?"

"Oh, yeah, plenty. But it turned out the doorman was distracted for the moment, and Mr. Nice got up to her apartment by the fire stairs. Fortunately, my partner was there with the client. The guy became violent and had to be subdued."

"Subdued?"

"Yeah. He broke his arm and his jaw in the struggle. Lost a number of teeth too. He's in the prison ward at Riker's, charged with assault, criminal trespass, and contempt. What is that look for?"

"I imagine that you are referring to the look that we sociologists give to our informants when our informants have chosen to leave valuable information unvoiced. For example, to take the present case, we observe a remarkable and unlikely set of circumstances. The culprit is enraged, the doorman is distracted—by what, we may wonder—the former victim is at home. Strangely enough, she lets him into her apartment, and by another great coincidence there is a guardian capable of subduing the culprit and causing him severe injury. The word setup springs to mind."

"The police are satisfied that we acted within the dictates of the law," replied Marlene primly. "Scumbags who get their lumps tend to be even less of a priority than women being stalked, if you can believe that."

"I can, barely," said Malkin. "So, is making sure that scumbags get their lumps going to be your usual service?"

"Not at all, although I should point out that if some unpleasant and reckless person wants to walk into a doorknob, I don't think it's our obligation to yank it away. I'd like to be able to adjust our service to the degree of risk to the client."

"I see. That's where the typology comes in, you think?"

"Yes."

"Okay—briefly, my belief is that there are three separate types of stalkers. What the article called the slobs are blue-collar types with a history of batting the girls around. When the women get tired of it and want to leave, they become insanely jealous. Why would they leave unless they want to screw somebody else? So they stalk, and they sometimes kill, and when they do they often kill themselves too. The sadists are usually white-collar or better, control freaks, who get their kicks out of torturing the ladies, and the stalking is just a refinement of the torture. The strangers are wackos who fix on some woman as part of their twist. Could be a movie actress or a rock star, or somebody they saw on the street that triggers the twitch."

Marlene broke in. "Yeah, okay, three types—and what I'm asking is, is there, do you have some way of, like, taking some data from the guys—appearance, activities, how they do the stalk and so on—that would let you decide which type they are?" She took a notebook and a pencil out of her jacket pocket.

Malkin thought about Marlene's question, staring up at a corner of the ceiling and knotting her brows in an appropriately professorial manner. At length she said, "For what I think are your purposes, the answer is no. That is, the typology isn't firm enough to use as the basis for a predictive model. We're talking about a much broader population than we are for, say, serial killers. We can look at a murder set, for example, and say with a pretty high degree of confidence, a serial killer did these and he's going to kill again. In the same way, serials form such a small, tight group that we can make good generalizations about them: white male, twenty-five to forty, middle-class, menial work, lives alone or with Mom, and the rest of it. Stalkers, we're talking about a much, much more ill-defined bunch of people. First of all, the act itself: what's stalking? Driving by the old girlfriend's house a couple of times? How many unwanted phone calls, how many unwanted bouquets do we have to have before we call it pathological? Okay, to start breaking down the problem, I developed these three groups. I don't know if they're *organic* groups or not, whether they're different because there's something really different going on in their heads, or whether the apparent differences are superficial. That's because I don't know enough about the causes and etiology of obsession. Nobody does. There's no . . . natural history, no close observation over generations, like there were when biology, say, first became a real science. You could say that we're back there where Aristotle was with nature. Some trees are pointed, others are bushy. Some animals have four legs, some two, some none. Okay, given those caveats, let's take the slobs first. Those are *her* names—the reporter's, by the way—not mine. The slob is into romance, big-time. You know what they say, in real love you want what's best for the loved one; in romantic love you just *want* the loved one. The romantic construct is created in the mind, of which the actual woman is the living symbol. The construct offers unconditional, infinite love, transcendent love. It's a substitute for religion, in fact. But the loved one is an actual woman made of meat. She has needs, a personality. Sometimes she has to withdraw from the relationship, from her symbolic role, in service of her own ego. This is a disaster for him. He can't handle the dissonance between his romantic construct and its symbol. Why would she withdraw? he asks, and since he doesn't see her as a real person who might have a perfectly good reason for withdrawing, such as a need to work, or child care, it must be another man who's stealing his possession. So now we're in *Othello*. The escalating violence begins; the escalation is diagnostic, by the way. Shouting, to hitting, to serious injury, maybe. So she leaves, and then the stalking starts. Continued profession of love throughout, another diagnostic. He literally *would* die for her, and he often does, after he's killed her, naturally. In maybe eighty percent of these things we have drugs or alcohol involved. The good news about the slob type is that if you catch it early enough, and you get tough, and you have the right situation, you can penetrate the illusion, establish a considerate, humane relationship. The bad news is that a certain percentage of these guys will never stop until the woman's dead."

"Or *he's* dead," said Marlene.

Malkin seemed startled by this, as if it had not occurred to her. She nodded. "Of course. Or he's dead. Okay, sadists. The sadist is rarer. Here the operator is not romance and jealousy, but domination.

By the way, we're not talking about consensual sexual games, which is an entirely different bunch of people, the S-M crowd. No, here we have a psychopath and his victim. Often we have a respectable citizen, a taxpayer. We have cold, dispassionate punishment, not hot rage and jealousy. You've been a bad girl and Daddy has to punish you. They have actual torture implements sometimes. The woman has to fetch them from the closet and so on. The rule is control, the woman reduced, once again, to an object, and since that's the case, we don't see quite as many homicides here. What we get is suicide; the woman can't take it anymore, he's stripped her so far down that she really *is* a nothing, and she checks out. Then he goes and gets another one, or maybe he doesn't wait, he goes after the daughter, or somebody else. Here's where you get your bigamists, your secret families. This guy is a narcissist too; he'll stalk because he's into torture, but he doesn't want to deal with any punishment, so he can be turned aside from a particular woman, as you may well have done with your Mr. Seely. If you find a nasty kid tearing wings off flies and you take the fly away from him, he's not going to break his neck chasing after that particular fly. He'll get another fly that's just as good."

"You think they're not as dangerous as the slobs?" Marlene asked.

"It depends. On the one hand, if you expose the dirty secret, threaten him, the guy will often back down. On the other hand, I suspect that this type shades into a heavier psychopathology and your true serials. They dispense with even the pretense of an actual relationship and move into a stereotyped pattern of stalk, torture, murder, dispose. Jack the Ripper. Ted Bundy. But that type wouldn't come into your purview, would it?"

"I hope not," said Marlene with deep sincerity. "And what about the strangers?"

Malkin stretched and performed an elaborate shrug. "Who knows? They're even rarer; there's practically no data. I think we're looking at a variant of the slob, except the relationship is *entirely* in his head. Sometimes they'll fixate on a movie star or a singer and follow her around. Or him: John Lennon. These guys are generally disorganized individuals, drifters. But sometimes not. I happen to think that a lot of rape comes out of this kind of psychology."

"Me too," said Marlene. "I think these guys sometimes become what we used to call 'gentleman rapists.' They assault the woman and then they want to make polite conversation, like they were on a nice date. Some of these guys actually have made dates with the women they raped and we grabbed them when they showed up with candy and flowers. Go figure."

"That's what I try to do," said the professor, smiling. "And you've just had the lecture, in short form. I give a course on patterns of sexual pathology at the New School. You saved yourself ninety dollars."

"It would've been worth it," said Marlene. "I appreciate the time." She put away the notebook she'd been using.

"And now you're going back to your crusade?"

"Is it a crusade? Unfortunately, you can't smite everybody who might be wicked. The law frowns on it. And by the time they've shown their worst, the woman's dead. How many is it getting to be now?"

"Nationally? Between thirteen and fifteen hundred, year in and year out. Slain by their loved ones. Do you know who Simon de Montfort was?"

Marlene started. "That was from left field," she said. "Hmm. Crusader type? Not a sweetheart as I recall."

"No. He was in charge of the crusade that suppressed the Cathar heretics in southern France. Thirteenth century. The story is his men asked him how they could separate the heretic captives from the good Catholics, and he said, 'Kill them all. God will know his own.'"

"Sounds like my kind of guy," said Marlene lightly. It was the wrong tone; Professor Malkin was giving her a peculiar look, admiration mixed with a horrified avidity. The humor had drained out of her face. Marlene had to look away. She wants me to kill them, thought Marlene, and imagined what it would be like to spend all one's time as the clerk in the abbatoir, the keeper of the rolls in our mild, domestic Belsen, immersed in case histories, in the horror stories of implacable men, of perverted love, of tortured and slaughtered women. Kill them all. Marlene did not have to plumb too deeply to reach those same feelings; she had to suppress a shudder.

"There's somebody I think you should meet," Malkin was saying as Marlene snapped back to attention. "If you're going to be a crusader, you should meet the others." She riffled through a Rolodex and wrote something on an index card.

"I didn't know there were others," said Marlene, taking the card. "And I'm not sure I'm a crusader." The name on the card was Mattie Duran, and the address was the East Village Women's Shelter, on Avenue B.

"You and Mattie should have a lot to talk about," said Malkin confidently. "She's quite a character. They call her the Durango Kid."

When Marlene left the professor's office and walked out into Washington Square, she was thinking that Professor Malkin probably considered Marlene quite a character too. A wave of regret passed over her, and she suddenly felt ridiculous: her outfit, her recent activities, her plans, all seemed at that moment absurd. She cursed under her breath, put her head down and her hands in her pockets, and strode off down the street, kicking the damp piles of fallen leaves. Respectable people moved out of her way.

Karp said, "Would you please state your name for the record?"

"You know who I am," said the district attorney, Sanford Bloom. He smiled his famous perfect smile at his lawyer. His lawyer smiled too. Bloom's lawyer was named Conrad Wharton, and he smiled with the purse-lipped pucker of an old-fashioned kewpie doll, which, with his puff of colorless hair and round pink

face, he disturbingly resembled. He was not a particularly good lawyer (it was Karp's opinion that the
D.A. would not know a good lawyer if one bit him
on the ass), but Wharton had once been Bloom's administrative chief and hatchet man, and Bloom, for
whatever reason, trusted him. Besides that, Wharton
probably disliked Karp with an intensity greater than
that of any other person in the state of New York,
not excluding the several score people Karp had sent
to Attica for murder. Karp thought that this was a
big part of why Bloom had chosen Wharton. He
wanted to piss Karp off. He wasn't taking this deposition or the case very seriously.

Karp repeated the question calmly and got the
same answer. He said, "Mr. Wharton, tell your client
that if he doesn't give me his name, I will leave these
proceedings right now and go over to Judge Craig
and get an order requiring him to do so, and when
the press asks me what's going on, I'll tell them that
the D.A. required a court order to reveal his name."

Bloom rolled his eyes at Wharton and said, "Sanford L. Bloom."

"Thank you," said Karp, and swore him in. The
stenographer's keys clattered. Karp handed Bloom a
Xerox of the letter Bloom had written to the Mayor.
"I give you a letter dated June twentieth of this year.
It's addressed to the Mayor and signed by you. Did
you write it?"

"Yes, of course I did," said Bloom after glancing
at the document.

Karp consulted his notes and began with the most

inflammatory charge. "In this letter you state that in late May of this year Assistant District Attorney James Warneke apprised you of deficiencies in the performance of the chief medical examiner, the present plaintiff, Dr. Selig, in reference to a homicide case, *People* v. *Lotz*, to wit: that he had failed to properly supervise the person who made the initial examination; that he had lost certain evidence in the case and threw other evidence away; that he altered the logbook at the morgue to conceal this; and finally, that he made remarks of an unprofessional nature, insulting to the dead victim in this case, namely that a positive acid phosphatase test performed on the victim's vaginal secretions might not have been the result of seminal fluid but of snails. Mr. Warneke told you that Dr. Selig had said, quote, maybe she put snails up her vagina, unquote. Is that substantially correct?"

"Yes. That's what's in the letter."

"Good. When Mr. Warneke conveyed all this to you, what action did you take?"

"Action?" asked the D.A.

"Yes. These were serious charges against a prominent official. Did you investigate them to see if they were true?"

Whispered consultation with Wharton. Bloom said, "I had no reason to doubt the report of Mr. Warneke."

"Did you confront Dr. Selig with these charges?"

"No."

"Why not?"

"I was not under any obligation to do so. And besides, Dr. Selig was often arrogant and dismissive when confronted with the failings of his office."

Karp felt a stirring to his right. Murray Selig was getting steamed.

"Was he arrogant and dismissive to you personally, at face-to-face meetings?" Karp asked.

This required a consultation too, after which Bloom said, "Not to me personally, no, but to my people."

"To Warneke?"

"No, Davis."

"Oh, you're referring to Miss Marsha Davis, the A.D.A. in *People* v. *Ralston*?"

"Yes."

"I see. Now, according to Mr. Warneke's deposition, which we have already taken, he brought these charges to your attention on May twenty-eighth of this year. Is that correct?"

"Yes, around about there."

"All right. Referring now to the charges in the letter regarding the *People* v. *Ralston* case, Miss Davis accuses Dr. Selig of not making himself available to her in this case, of being late for a trial, although she gave him—what was it?—four weeks' notice of the trial date, and also that on one occasion when she went to visit him in his office, he humiliated her in front of another gentleman. Is that what you meant by Dr. Selig's arrogant and dismissive attitude?"

"Yes, that's an example."

"I see. But according to Miss Davis's sworn deposition, you were not informed of these problems until mid-June at the earliest. Yet you still declined to investigate Mr. Warneke's serious charges of late May, because Dr. Selig was arrogant and dismissive? Is that correct?"

The district attorney huffed and made an impatient gesture with his hand. "The details of when somebody came to me about this or that problem are not the point. It was well known that there were plenty of problems."

"Was it?" asked Karp, leafing through a folder on the table. "I give you a copy of a letter dated February 11, commending Dr. Selig for the timely and expert assistance of his office in several difficult cases. It's signed by you. Do you recall this letter?"

"I sign a lot of things," said Bloom. He did not look at the letter.

"I'm sure you do. Can you account for the deterioration of Dr. Selig's performance from exemplary in February to incompetent and worthy of dismissal in late May and early June?"

"I have no way of answering that."

"Are you familiar with the letter written to the Mayor by the commissioner of Health, Dr. Angelo Fuerza, dated June fifth, containing a number of complaints about Dr. Selig's performance?"

"I've seen it."

"Did you at any time meet with Dr. Fuerza and the Mayor with the purpose of developing a case against Dr. Selig?"

"No."

"Did you solicit, did you demand from your subordinates in the D.A.'s office, damaging information about Dr. Selig?"

"No, I did not."

That's a lie, thought Karp with satisfaction. Now let's try for a few others. "Did you meet with the Mayor on May twenty-third to discuss your problems with Dr. Selig?"

Consultation with Wharton. "I'd have to consult my calendar."

"No need. I give you a copy of the Mayor's appointment book page for that date. You met with him. And did you discuss Dr. Selig?"

"I may have."

"And isn't it true that for your own reasons you decided that Dr. Selig had to be fired well before you received any complaints about him from your staff . . ."

"Don't answer that!" said Wharton.

". . . and that you are in fact the source of this conspiratorial vendetta against Dr. Selig?"

"This is preposterous!" said the D.A. A flush had spread across his smooth pink cheeks.

"I take it you are answering no to my last question."

"Of course, no!"

"Thank you. Turning now to the charges in your letter related to the case *People* v. *Mann*. When did you first become aware of the charges that Dr. Selig had allegedly lost evidence in that case?"

Bloom seemed to relax as he answered the question, and the next, and the next. Karp took the D.A.

over the four homicide cases mentioned in the letter to the Mayor. The questions were routine; Karp knew all the answers, having already deposed the staff people responsible for supplying the information. The purpose of the questioning was to establish the full involvement of the D.A. himself in the conspiracy to unseat Selig.

The questioning continued for some hours, until late in the afternoon. The windows in Karp's office had already gone dark. A dullness had settled over the group. Karp had made his voice monotone. The questions were repetitive: when did you, what did you, I show you this letter, this memo, have you seen, are you familiar with?

And then, in the midst of this ennui, not changing his tone at all, casually Karp asked, "What occurred during the second or third week in May that convinced you that Dr. Selig had to be fired?"

A frozen moment. The tap of the steno's fingers petered out in a dry rattle. Everyone looked at Bloom. Karp saw what he was looking for, the startled flick of the eyes, the movement at his throat as he swallowed hard. Karp looked at Wharton too, and he saw that Wharton had his little cherub's mouth open, and that he was looking at his patron with confusion on his face.

This took only a second or two. Then Bloom cleared his throat, smiled, and shrugged. "I'm sorry, I don't know what you're talking about."

Karp stared briefly at him and then continued, as if nothing had happened, with a question about some petty point about the chain of custody relative to a bloody shirt in *People* v. *Mann.*

Bloom and Wharton left soon afterward. The steno packed up her machine and left too. When they were alone, Murray Selig said, "I thought that went okay. You shook him up a couple of times."

"It went about like I thought it would," said Karp flatly, not looking at his client, arranging papers into piles.

After a pause, Selig asked, "You're still pissed off at me." It was a statement, not a question.

Karp said, "We're not married, Murray. You're the client. It doesn't matter if I'm pissed off at you. The opposite, *that* would matter."

Selig laughed unconvincingly. "You're a hard guy, you know that, Butch? I told you, I forgot about those jobs."

Karp looked up from his papers. "Murray, look: this is how it is. We prepped like crazy for your deposition by the defendants, and I remember telling you, I believe, numerous times, that a critical part of your case for damages was a showing that you could not be employed as a chief medical examiner, or as a competent authority in the field, because your reputation had been so badly besmirched by these *momsers*, and that therefore, if you had taken employment in your field, I needed to know about it, so I could advise you as to how to answer their questions relating thereto. Imagine how surprised I was, then, when the Mayor's counsel asked you if you were negotiating for the job of chief fucking medical examiner of Suffolk County, and you said yes, you were."

"I explained that, Butch. It was my in-laws doing me a favor. They're big shots out in Suffolk."

"Murray, it's fine, God bless them. I just needed to know that beforehand. That, and the other little zingers that came out in deposition. A book contract you didn't tell me about. That job you did up in Tuxedo—"

"That's chickenfeed!"

"To you it's chickenfeed. To a jury that we're asking to give you a couple of million 'cause you've been hurt so bad, fifteen hundred bucks for a day's work doesn't sound like injury. Most of them, they don't make a yard and a half a day."

"Okay, you made your point. But the rest of it, my deposition, I thought it went okay. Better than Bloom just had, I mean."

"Of course it went better, Murray. You were telling the truth and he was lying. We're the good guys. But I have to know what's going on, or good guys or not, we're going to look like dog shit at trial."

"Okay, guaranteed, cross my heart," said Selig, who had brightened considerably. "By the way, speaking of which, I thought Bloom was trying to slip one past his counsel. When you asked him that one about mid-May and why he wanted me fired. His lawyer looked like he'd been cold-cocked for a second there. What was that about, anyway?"

"See? That's how *I* felt," said Karp.

"Butch, enough already! You want me to squirm?"

"Yes."

"But really, what do you think all that was about?"

Karp shrugged, as if he didn't care, and made some dismissive remark and they passed on to other subjects, but in reality there was nothing he cared about more at that moment than whatever it was about the middle of May that had brought that transient look to Bloom's face, what it was that he had not shared with his closest political and legal adviser, a man with whom the D.A. had conspired, to Karp's personal knowledge, in a half dozen serious malfeasances. But although he didn't yet know what it was, he knew for certain what it meant. It meant that whatever Bloom had done, it was worse than a malfeasance. It had to be bad. Felony bad, going to jail in handcuffs bad. The thought warmed him like a log fire.

TEN

Old St. Patrick's Cathedral, on Mulberry and Prince Street, had been built as the archdiocesan seat in 1815 when the surrounding area had been the heart of the City. The area had gone downhill since then, as the surrounding tenements had first filled with Irish and then Italians. Both tides had rushed in and aged and become rich and ebbed out to the 'burbs. Now Old St. Pat's was just another church, its parishioners now few and largely Latin American. Every Sunday they were joined, at the latest possible Mass, by Marlene Ciampi.

Who maintained, as she had since the age of fourteen, a complicated, variable, and heterodox relationship with the Holy and Apostolic Church. She tended to treat the various contradictions she found in her religion—all that business about women and who was allowed to place what sexual part in what opening and when—as she treated those in her quotidian life: with cavalier disregard. If she could be a good mother and an irresponsible rakehell, she could also be a weekly communicant and a kick-ass feminist. In her secret heart she believed that were she allowed a half hour with the pope, no holds barred, she could straighten him out, but failing that, she refused to either give up the Church or go along with it.

Beyond that, Marlene's natural cast of mind was contrarian, the single aspect of character that she shared with her husband. As a girl at Sacred Heart, she had read proscribed books and carried herself like an infant Voltaire; at liberal Smith, and later at cynical Yale, she had dragged herself up out of Saturday night debauches and, dressed in sober black, sporting a Jackie Kennedy-style lace mantilla, had floated off to early Mass, quite astonishing the circle of godless musicians and artists she frequented. Over the years she had drifted in and out of regular communion, although she acknowledged an increase in constancy since her marriage to Karp. It might have been, at first, merely a resurgence of her contrarian spirit—marry a Jew, become more Catholic—but lately she had felt a vague discomfort of soul, the sort of thing in which the Church was supposed to specialize, although it had been years, decades, since Marlene had actually brought such a problem to a priest. On recent Sundays, looking at the dull, sheep-like face of Father Raymond at Old St. Pat's, Marlene tried to imagine what he would say if she revealed to him her recent quasi-legal doings—and more disturbingly, her bloodthirsty prospects. Although she was barely able to admit it to herself, she had begun to hope for—in some undefined fashion—moral guidance.

And, of course, there was Lucy. Quite apart from her own beliefs, Marlene had made a solemn commitment when her family's parish priest had agreed to marry her to a non-Catholic that she would raise her child in the bosom of Rome, and she intended to do so. Happily, St. Pat's had an excellent Sunday school, where she deposited Lucy while she attended the service. The girl had taken nicely to the Sunday ritual (her only bitch being the necessity for unnatural cleanliness, and the wearing of a succession of darling dresses, lace-collared velvets or elaborately ruffled muslins, lovingly purchased by her mother and a supporting body of female relatives), Lucy having reached the age where theology was of interest.

This morning, entering the car in a glory of dark velvet, camel-hair coat, and wool hat, Lucy asked Marlene, "How come God has three names?"

Marlene shot her daughter an inquiring look. It seemed unlikely that Sister Theresa, who ran the junior Sunday class, had exposed her charges to the mysteries of the Trinity.

"What do you mean, dear?" asked Marlene.

Lucy counted the persons off on her fingers. "One is Jesus Christ, right? Two, is baby Jesus. Three: Harold."

"Harold?"

"Uh-huh. AreFatherwhichArtnHeaven, *Harold* Be thy name."

"Ah, mmm, I think that's 'hallowed,' baby. It means blessed. Also, Jesus Christ and baby Jesus are the same person."

At this Lucy gave Marlene a disbelieving look. She said, "I'll ask Sister Theresa," and withdrew into what seemed like religious contemplation for the remainder of the ride.

Throughout the service, Marlene made a greater than usual effort to open herself to divine guidance. A faint headache was, however, the only result. Afterward, the sermon was on one of Father Raymond's two favorite themes: the need to support the foreign missions as a front line against the spread of godless communism (the other being the Evils of Unsanctified Sex). The featured mission today was the Missionary Sons of the Immaculate Heart of Mary, this particular Sunday being the feast day of St. Antony Claret, its founder.

Marlene let the words wash over her, hardly hearing, as one waits for a TV commercial to end. Fr. Raymond was, on this Sunday as usual, dull but thankfully brief, and Marlene was inclined to reward the brevity at least with the acknowledgment that St. Antony C. was the devil of a lad and his Charetians deserved at least a sawbuck. She reached into her wallet when the collection started, yanked forth a bill, and saw that her fingers had also plucked out the very slip of paper upon which Professor Malkin had written the name and address of Mattie Duran. A sign, was Marlene's first thought, and then she carefully put that thought aside. But she gave twenty dollars to the mission when the plate came around.

After church, Marlene found herself driving east on Houston. Lucy glanced out the window, recognized the route, and asked, "Are we getting knishes?" A swing by Yoneh Schimmel's for a bag of the tasty bricklike pastries was a frequent coda to their Sunday devotions.

"Maybe later. I want to stop off someplace first."

"Where?"

"A place. It's a women's shelter I want to take a look at. It won't be a long visit."

"What's a women's shelter?"

"It's a . . . sometimes there are bad men that like to hurt women and kids, and this is a place they can run to and hide."

"Are we going to hide there?"

Marlene laughed and gave her daughter a squeeze. "No, silly! Daddy wouldn't hurt us."

"If he did, Uncle Harry would shoot him with his gun," said Lucy matter-of-factly. "Then I would take care of him, and you could hide in that place."

This comment produced enough distraction from the task of driving to have caused a serious accident on any day but Sunday. As it was, there was a squealing of brakes and a honking of horns.

"Good plan, Lucy," said Marlene upon recovery, to which her darling returned a glance both blank and sweet.

The East Village Women's Shelter was on Avenue B off Sixth, occupying the whole of a store-fronted six-story tenement. The former shop windows had been covered with steel plating, painted black, upon which the institution's name was neatly lettered in white. There was an *iglesia* on one side of it and a shoe-repair shop with a traditional hanging shoe sign on the other. Most of the businesses on either side of the street—stores selling salsa records, cheap clothing, and furniture on credit—had their corrugated steel shutters down, and these were covered with graffiti, much of it gang spoor. There were graffiti on the *iglesia* too, but none on the women's shelter—not a one, despite the blank, smooth expanse of black steel.

Marlene observed this and thought it significant. She parked and ushered Lucy up to the door, which was solid, also black, and equipped with a peephole. She rang the buzzer. A voice emanating from a little box affixed to the doorframe asked her business. She said she wanted to see Mattie Duran. The voice told her to wait, and she was aware of being observed through the peephole.

Shortly she heard clankings, as of heavy locks being disengaged, and the door opened. In the doorway was a young woman in her late teens, with a long, thick braid in her black hair and a suspicious look on her face; the face, which was thin and biscuit brown, had darkened channels cut under the eyes, as if by corrosive tears. She was dressed in a black sweatshirt and jeans. This person looked Marlene up and down, and was clearly unimpressed, although she smiled and said hi to Lucy. Without another word she barred the door with a dead bolt and a police lock and turned away, allowing Marlene to follow her if she would.

A short corridor made from plywood led to a glass

door. Marlene and Lucy followed the teenager through it and into a room carved out of the center of the former retail store. The room was clearly an office: four unmatched filing cabinets stood along one wall, and another wall held a corkboard covered with messages. Two battered steel desks in the center of the room were occupied by a pair of women, one black, one white, who were talking on telephones. Another phone rang unanswered. There were grubby toys strewn in odd corners. The place smelled of cooking soup.

"She's in there," said their guide, pointing at a door.

Marlene knocked and, in response to a vague noise from within, opened it, revealing a tiny office, no larger than an apartment bathroom. It contained a rack of steel shelving overflowing with stuffed manila files, a scarred wooden desk, one leg of which was missing and replaced with phone books, a miscellany of straight chairs in dubious repair, and, affixed to the walls, an office clock, a calendar, much inscribed, and a color reproduction of one of Frida Kahlo's self-portraits, with mustache. On the desk was a rough-looking, large black Persian tomcat, nesting in a wire basket full of what looked like official manifold forms. Behind the desk was a swarthy woman of about forty.

Or Marlene guessed her age at about that; she could have been any age from a hard thirty to a light fifty. She was a Latina of some variety, but probably not a Puerto Rican. Her skin had a cinnamon sheen to it, her cheekbones were broad and sharp, and her mouth had that lovely, lanceolate sculpting of the lips that said Mexico. Her eyes, oddly, were gray-blue.

The woman was giving Marlene the once-over too, and Marlene could see that she was somewhat put off and confused by the fancy clothes. Her gaze, however, softened when she examined Marlene's face, which still bore the yellowing bruises left by Pruitt's fists.

"Can I pet your cat?" asked Lucy, who had wormed her way past Marlene's hip.

The woman smiled at this, showing powerful teeth and a flash of gold, and beckoned the child forward. Lucy stroked the cat, who spat briefly and then submitted to a stroking. The woman stood and held out her hand to Marlene. "Mattie Duran," she said. Her hand was large and rough, with thick, square-cut nails. She was dressed in a black cotton turtleneck under a cover-all garment of vaguely military cut, with many pockets and zips on it. It was also black, which seemed to be the color of choice at the Women's Shelter.

Marlene said her own name, and Duran gestured her to one of the straight chairs. She sat down again behind her desk and said, "Look, we're a little jammed now, but I'll try to help." She pulled a clipboard from a wall hook and took a pencil from behind her ear. "Where are you living now?"

"In my loft," answered Marlene, puzzled.

"Is he still there?"

"Who?"

"Your husband, your boyfriend—the guy who beat you up," said Duran.

"Umm, I think we're off on the wrong foot. I'm not a client. Professor Malkin suggested I come talk to you, and since I was passing by . . ."

Duran laughed heartily and tossed the clipboard down. "Oh, yeah, the little professor. You're *that* one . . . in the article. That's where you got the face. Well, well! Yeah, we should talk . . . don't do that, honey, he'll scratch the shit out of you."

Lucy had been trying to lift the cat out of his basket, and the animal was making increasingly more aggressive noises.

"He doesn't like to be hauled around," explained Duran.

Lucy asked, "What's his name?"

"Megaton," said Duran, and then, to Marlene, "You know, we have a playroom upstairs; there's kids and a bunch of toys. Maybe Lucy would like to go up and stay there while we talk?"

"How about that, Lucy? Would you like to play with the kids who live here?" asked Marlene.

"The ones who're hiding from the bad men?" asked Lucy.

Duran gave Marlene a quick sidelong glance. "Yeah," she said to Lucy, "those're the ones."

The woman took Lucy by the hand and led her away. She was back in a few minutes. Sitting down again in her chair, she considered Marlene thoughtfully for a moment and then said, "You don't look like what I thought you would."

"Oh?"

"Yeah, all this . . ." She fluttered her fingers up and down her chest to indicate Marlene's careful navy suit and silk blouse.

"I just came from church," said Marlene, feeling defensive, and absurd because of feeling so.

"Church, huh. A good Catholic girl."

"I try to be," snapped Marlene. "You have some kind of problem with that? I have a butch black outfit too, you know; maybe I should've come in the right costume, get a little less heat."

They locked eyes for a few seconds, glaring, and then Duran flashed her golden smile again. "Hey, no offense. I don't get along with the church, it don't mean you can't. Anyway, it was a neat number you did on that piece of shit. In the *Voice* article, I mean. You want to go into that business, I got a list for you about eight feet long."

She said it jocularly, but Marlene answered her in all seriousness. "As a matter of fact, I do."

Duran cocked her head. "Say, what?"

"I want to be, I *am,* in the business. I want to protect women from stalkers."

Duran's eyebrows rose and her mouth twisted quizzically. "You're not kidding, are you?"

"No."

"Honey, most of these ladies don't have a pot to piss in. How're you going to make a living off of protecting them from men?"

"Money's not a problem. Not right now."

"Rich lady, huh? What is this, a hobby?"

Marlene kept her voice even and responded, "Ms. Duran, I'm not an asshole, and I suspect you're not either, so could we cut the horseshit? You want to trade working-class credibility, we could be here all day."

Duran seemed startled for a moment and then grinned and let out her big, hearty guffaw. "All right!" she said. "The girl means business! Okay—what is it—Marlene? Okay, Marlene: what you're telling me is, you want to run, like, an agency that does protection. You don't mean like, guarding the victims, because that's what I do, me and the other shelters, and there's no way you could afford to put a seven 'n' twenty-four guard on more than a couple of women. So what you mean is, you want to take the bastards out."

"If they commit crimes, if they violate protective orders—"

Duran waved her hand dismissively. "Nah, nah—I mean, *take them out.* You know damn well you get one of these bastards for assault, he's away for eighteen months at the most, less for a contempt cite. And when he comes out, what's the first thing he's going to do? He's going to get even with the woman. And he's going to keep it up until she's dead. You know that's the way it is. I can see it in your face."

"Not all of them are like that," said Marlene.

"Hah!"

"Yeah, well, if you start with the premise that the

solution is wholesale slaughter, you're finished before you start. But there must be hundreds of thousands of cases of battering in the country and maybe thousands of stalking incidents. We have only about fifteen hundred, two thousand homicides in that class across the country per year, maybe a couple of hundred in the City."

"That's some 'only.' "

"That's why I went to Malkin," explained Marlene, unable to keep some sharpness out of her tone. "I was looking for some way of predicting real danger in these cases."

"So? Could she?"

Marlene shrugged. "Not really. That's why I came to see you."

"You think I have some kind of . . . system?" Duran said, and then laughed. "Hell, girl, I got all I can do to keep this place from closing down, getting women relocated with new ID, getting them jobs or welfare. Christ on a crutch, I get five minutes to think a week, I'm lucky. You think I can figure out which of these wackos is going to do something bad and which won't?"

"No, not really," said Marlene with a sigh. "Look, it was just a thought—I'm sort of new at this. I'm sorry I wasted your time."

She started to rise, but Duran waved her back and said, "No, sit. This is sort of interesting. Maybe I *should* think about the problem more, I wouldn't be getting my ass in a sling as much as I do." She glanced at the wall clock. "Look, we'll shoot the shit,

I'll take you around and show you the setup, introduce you to some of the women. You like hard-luck stories? I can tell you do, a good Catholic girl like you. We'll have lunch."

So they did. Marlene met most of the thirty or so women in residence, and heard their hard-luck stories and met and admired their children (almost all the women had children) and, where appropriate, examined their wounds: Donna with the wired jaw, Maria with the separated shoulder, Maureen's broken nose, and Vickie, whose husband had set his pit bull on her, mangling her knee. Toward the end of the tour, Marlene was feeling more like St. Catherine of Sienna licking her way through the *lazaretto* than she liked, and had decided that massively viewing misery was not her line of work.

Lunch was served in one of the apartments of the former tenement, which had been fitted out as a common area, the remaining apartments being used as dormitory space. The kitchen had been enlarged and the interior walls knocked down to form a dining room. The rest of the floor was devoted to a playroom for the children. Duran led Marlene there to gather her daughter for the communal meal.

Marlene's heart sank when she entered. It was a tawdry place, and it smelled strongly of the little accidents of childhood and strong disinfectant. The children, who ranged in age from toddler to preteen, fussed with the few, dirty playthings, and quarreled and cried, while the moms on playroom duty struggled to keep some order and prevent injury. In fairness, she thought a moment later, although it was dreadful as a playroom, it was not half bad as a prison, which is what it really was. The thirty-eight children resident in the shelter could not go outside to a playground or to school for fear of their fathers or their mother's boyfriends. The playroom was also a lot better than being dead, or motherless.

Marlene looked around for Lucy and couldn't find her. After the usual stomach-roiling burst of panic, she waited until the place had emptied out for lunch and then crossed to a refrigerator carton that had been laid on its side and converted into a playhouse, with painted walls and flower pots and cut-out windows. She knelt and peeked in one of these.

Her daughter was sitting on a cushion declaiming the story of Cinderella to two older children, a girl of about fourteen and a boy who looked twelve. These two had covered themselves with a ratty pink blanket, and were clearly riveted by the tale. So sweet was the picture that Marlene was reluctant to interrupt, but Lucy noticed her face peering through the window and stopped.

"We're playing house," said Lucy. "I'm being the mommy."

"That's nice, dear," said Marlene, "but we're going to have lunch now."

"Here?"

"Yes, here. In the room next door."

"Can I eat with Isabella and Hector?"

"Of course. Come on along." Marlene smiled at the two children. To her surprise, the girl gave a start and pulled the blanket over her head. Lucy and Hector both began talking to her and gently tugging the blanket. After a few minutes of this, the girl emerged and followed the other two out of the carton.

Later, when the three children were sitting at a card table, eating vegetable soup and bread, Duran leaned over to Marlene and said, "You know, that's amazing. This is the first time Isabella has eaten in the lunchroom. Usually, she grabs food from the kitchen and runs to eat it in that carton."

"Yes, I think Lucy's made a conquest. It's not the first time either. The kid is clearly destined to sell insurance big-time. Is she all right, though? Isabella? I mean, mentally?"

"I have no idea," said Duran. "She's obviously scared shitless of everything and everybody. Except Hector, of course, and now your kid. Understands Spanish and English but won't talk at all. It looks like traumatic shock of some kind to me. I see a lot of it. It's a shame too, a pretty kid like that."

"What does her mother say about it?"

"Oh, her mother isn't here. Somebody dumped her on our front steps last spring."

"Literally?"

"Oh, yeah. There was a knock, and the night duty woman heard a car burning rubber down the street and there she was, soaking wet, curled into a ball. Somebody'd raped her, naturally. So we took her in and she's been here ever since."

"You didn't call the cops?" asked Marlene.

Duran gave her a pitying look. "Please! The cops leave us alone, and we return the favor. Same with the state social workers. Child Welfare's got enough problems of their own. They know I'm up to code, and that's all they care about. I don't take any government money and I don't want any. Because of that, I get women who won't come to any other shelter."

"You mean illegals."

"Them," Duran agreed, "and others." She did not elaborate and her tone did not welcome additional prying.

"What about Hector?" Marlene asked, looking over at the children's table. Lucy was talking a blue streak and making faces. Hector was giggling; Isabella had a peculiar strained expression on her face, as if she were trying to remember how to smile. Duran followed Marlene's look and said, "Damn, I ought to rent that kid from you. I actually think Isabella's about to crack a grin. Oh, Hector—he's another drifter. Doesn't live here. Shows up a couple times a week for lunch and a talk with Isabella. He says she's his sister."

"Is she?"

"Search me, Jack. She could be. On the other hand, Hector's a bit of a slippery character himself."

"But can't you find out where he's from, his family . . . ?"

"See, you're still thinking like a social worker. Look, you want to hear my take on them? Illegals, pretty sure, but from someplace bad. Salvador or

Nicaragua. See that little shawl she's got? That's from somewhere down there, the embroidery. The white dress too. It's the only thing she'll wear and it's falling apart. The boy's accent is Central American or south Mexico, Chiapas or around there. Anyway, say they came to the big city with Mom and Dad, illegal as hell, live in a shithole, take some kind of sweatshop work. One day Mom and Dad are gone, who knows where. The *migra* got 'em. Or it could be worse, they were mules and they tried to skim some of the product, or maybe somebody just thought they tried to, or the drug people did it themselves and laid it on the dumb *campechanos*. So the kids come home one day and there's cops all around and they run. They know not to talk to cops. Or they were there when it went down, the dealer sent a couple of *choteros* around, and either they did them right there or took them away someplace, cut them up a little to see what happened to the powder. The kids're hiding under the bed. Either way, the kids are on the street, don't know nobody, don't trust nobody. God knows what happened to the girl—I don't want to think about it."

"And there's no clue about where they came from?"

A tired wave of the hand. "No, and I asked around the neighborhood. Nobody knows them or who their parents could've been. Either people don't know or someone's got them really scared."

"So who dropped her off?"

"Who knows? I figure he grabbed her off the

street, raped her a couple of times and got scared, and he was too chicken to kill her and drop her in a dumpster like they usually do. A Good Samaritan. You're shocked? Honey, we get them dropped off here like that all the time."

· "I'm not shocked, Mattie, just reliving. I used to run the Rape Bureau at the New York D.A.'s."

Duran nodded. "Yeah, I remember from the article. You got out and now you're back in it. With a kid too."

"And another on the way."

"Hunh!" Duran's eyes widened and then she smiled. "It can't be displaced maternal instincts, like me. So why? You got money, you're a lawyer . . ."

"I'll introduce you to my husband, the pair of you can bat it around," said Marlene impatiently. "Why don't we leave it that it's just something I need to do just now?"

Duran stared at her for a long moment, a flat, penetrating Indian look, while an amused smile flickered on her lips. Then she muttered, *"A lo dado no se le busca lado."*

"Excuse me?"

"Just an expression," said Duran. "Gift horses. The thing of it is, I could use your help. Let's get the meal cleared away, and we'll take some coffee into my office and have a talk."

Lucy had to be dragged away from the shelter, with many a promise that she could visit Isabella and Hector again very soon. Marlene reflected as they walked to the car how remarkable it was for a seven-year-old to have formed so close and so dominant a relationship with two much older children. It was as if Lucy knew instinctively that both of them were not what they physically appeared to be, that Isabella was deep in some traumatic regression, and that Hector had been severed from his childhood by overwhelming events. In treating them as she would her contemporaries, she was apparently giving them just what they required.

Back at the loft, they found Karp sprawled amid strewn newspaper, watching a football game on television. He was wearing a black sweatshirt with the arms torn off and ragged chinos; moreover, he was unshaven and was actually drinking a beer, probably his third or fourth for the calendar year. It was a rare thuggish look, and Marlene found it erotic. She came over to the sofa and gave him a friendly nuzzle.

"I was getting worried," he said.

"Well, we're safe," said Marlene. "Your family has survived another day on the killing streets."

"A long church? Lots of sins to confess?"

Lucy came dashing over, after dutifully hanging her church-going camel hair on its special peg, and jumped on her father's lap.

"We went to the shelter," she cried, "and I played with Isabella and Hector. They're my new best friends and they're really old too and they have a playhouse and we had lunch, and you know what?"

"What?"

"Ladies could stay there when bad men want to hurt them, and we could stay there too!"

Karp glanced meaningfully at his wife. To his daughter he said, "What if bad men want to tickle them?" and suited action to word, until she shrieked, after which they had some boxing practice until Marlene ordered an instant change out of good clothes.

"What was that about?" Karp asked after Lucy had run off to her room.

"Oh, just curiosity. I stopped off at the East Village Women's Shelter and met Mattie Duran. She runs quite an operation, actually. I think we can work with them: referrals, temporary shelter for our clients, like that. And there's stuff I can do for them too."

"Like?"

"Oh, summonses, tracking down deadbeats," offered Marlene casually. Mattie Duran had suggested a set of other activities, under the general heading of "taking the bastards out," but Marlene did not care to broach these with her husband just now. If ever.

Nor did Karp seem eager to pry. "You had a load of calls," he said.

"On Sunday?"

"Vigilantes never have a day off," he replied and went back to watching the game.

Marlene changed into comfortable clothes and went into her office. The machine tape had a dozen or so blank messages, probably from women who had called and been directed by the outgoing message tape to her new answering service. The others were from Ariadne Stupenagel (six) and from Harry Bello (one).

She called Harry first.

"Where were you?" he asked without preamble when she identified herself.

"In church, Harry. It's Sunday."

Grunt. "We got court tomorrow on Pruitt. I'll pick you up."

"I have it down, Harry. By the way, I made an interesting contact today." She gave him a summary of her visit to the women's shelter, and of the cases Mattie Duran wanted her to work.

"This is what? Like the Pruitt and the other guy?"

"Only if necessary. We'll try reasoning with them, explain the situation. Make sure they understand that we're watching, that if they violate an order or try a break-in or an assault, they're looking at consequences. One or two, Mattie thinks they're beyond that already, in which case—"

A pause on the line. "You need a gun."

Marlene laughed. "Oh, yeah, that and a divorce. *You're* the gunslinger, Harry."

"We'll talk tomorrow," said Harry, and hung up.

Ariadne was at home and clearly waiting for a call. She picked up on the first ring.

"Where have you been?" Stupenagel demanded.

"I've been having my nipples gilded."

"On Sunday?"

"What can I do for you, Stupe?"

"I need a favor. Do you know anybody, like a friend, in the medical examiner's office?"

"Yeah, I know some people. Why?"

"Because this thing with the Latinos who died in jail is heating up. Paul Jackson and another cop are definitely shaking down gypsy cabbies, and they're not gentle about it either."

"How do you know?"

"Because I gypsy-cabbed in drag a couple of nights and I got shaken down and slapped around."

"Jesus, Stupe!"

"Then I hung around the Two-Five and ID'd Jackson. He's hard to miss—the guy's a moose. The funny thing is, I had a feeling I'd seen him someplace before, but I can't recall where."

"Didn't Roland take you around to the Two-Five?"

"Yeah, it must have been then, but there was something else about it too. I'll think of it. Anyway, I went to see Tommy Devlin at Internal Affairs, and he sort of hems and haws and says he can't do anything directly because the shakedowns are part of a separate investigation, being run out of the D.A.'s squad. That's possible, isn't it?"

"Sure. The D.A. squad does a lot of official corruption stuff, but that's usually politicians and bureaucrats. It gets dicey when it's just cops, like God forbid anybody should suggest that the P.D. isn't competent to police itself."

"Yeah, that's what he said. The hack bureau's involved and the licensing division and the medical examiner."

"The M.E. too? How?"

"Well, they suspect somebody covered up on the autopsies. The boys didn't really hang themselves, maybe somebody helped them out. But I can't get a hold of the reports, because they've been impounded pending investigation. So I thought—"

"Stupe, forget it! I'm not going to be party to screwing up an investigation."

"Just ask, Marlene, for chrissake! You can do that, can't you? Somebody must know if something fishy went down."

There was an unfamiliar strain audible in Stupenagel's voice, one at odds with the cool and wheedling tone she used when she wanted to extract information. Marlene asked, "Is there something wrong, Stupe? Are you in trouble?"

A nervous laugh, and, lightly, "Me? Oh, no more than usual." Marlene waited. "Well, actually, yes," said the reporter. "I think somebody's following me."

"Are you sure?"

"Hell, girl, I've been followed by experts. There's two kinds of following: when they want you to know, so you'll get scared off doing whatever it is they don't want you to do, and two, when they don't want you to know so they can see where you go and who you talk to. This is the first kind. I've seen the same dark Plymouth Fury in my rearview or outside my place about ten times in the past couple, three days."

"So complain, Stupe! This isn't some police state hellhole. You want me to help you file a harassment complaint, I'll be happy to do *that* for you."

"Yeah, well, you're probably right. Maybe I still have Guatemala on my mind. I mean, what're they going to do, shoot me?"

ELEVEN

Karp stared at the interview sheet and tried to decide whether Jerome E. Delaney, 66, of East 34th Street in Manhattan, a retired highway engineer, would or would not be constitutionally disposed to find for the plaintiff. He glanced up from the sheet at the man himself and, smiling pleasantly, inquired of him whether he had ever been a party to a lawsuit. He had not. The answer, like the man, was neutral; that is, flames did not issue from Delaney's nostrils when he said it, implying that mere fate, and not an inveterate hatred of lawsuits and those who brought them, had so deprived him. Karp said thank you and made a note. Delaney would do. Karp seated himself and watched his rival, corporation counsel Josh Gottkind, rise for his crack at the venireman.

Karp allowed himself a moment to soak in the atmosphere of the federal courtroom, so different from the rotting premises of the county courthouse, where he had spent nearly all of his professional career. Here all the woodwork was beautifully tended oak, unimproved by etched graffiti; the murals told their allegories of justice triumphant unmarred by peeling paint and mildew stains. Even the judge, the Honorable Joseph C. Craig, seemed to draw from the august surroundings a dignity greater than that of his confreres of the lower bench, reflecting the acknowledged fact that decisions about serious money were inherently grander than deciding whether Joe had stabbed Phil forty times over a ten-dollar bet.

Of course, Craig would've been dignified anywhere, Karp thought as he studied the judge, a thin, small man in his middle sixties. He had a large head carried on a slender neck, and a long, thin nose that looked red and damp at the tip. With his sharp, bright blue eyes peering out of their nest of wrinkles, he seemed like nothing so much as a heron, a heron staring down at a pool full of frogs before deciding which one to have for lunch.

This was the first day of jury selection and would probably be the last. Federal jury selection was an expeditious process compared to that in the state courts, and Karp was happy that it was. The judge asked the basic questions that might disqualify jurors for cause, and the lawyers' questions had to be submitted in advance. Karp was not himself a voir dire maven, although he knew that many lawyers believed it to be among the most critical aspects of a trial. Many lawyers said they could pick a plaintiff's jury or a defendant's jury; some lawyers didn't try cases at all but merely advised others on how to select. In contrast, Karp's belief was that once you had disposed of frank prejudice or special interest, all juries were more or less the same. His only selection rule, which he had learned at the feet of the old bulls of the long-lost Homicide Bureau, was "no singletons on a felony jury." You shouldn't, if you wanted a conviction, have one black, or one woman, or one of any identifiable caste, because the odd man out was more than likely to feel isolated and threatened and therefore to vote against a convicting jury, hanging it. This rule did not, of course, apply in a civil case.

And you could outsmart yourself with a too-clever selection strategy. Gottkind, for example, was now asking Mr. Delaney whether he felt that physicians were more credible than other people. A stupid question. What sort of answer did he expect, "Yeah, sure"? Delaney, if selected, would perhaps start the trial in the belief that the defense counsel thought him a jerk. Karp left one ear open and studied the next information sheet. They needed two more jurors to make up the six-person panel, plus two alternates, and Karp expected that this group of twelve venire-men or the next would suffice.

Gottkind finished with Delaney, and Karp rose again, to smile at, and briefly question, the next prospective juror. Her name was Sonia Delgado, a restaurant manager, who had also never gone to the bar of justice for any reason, but was clearly a person of Hispanic ancestry. It was obvious by now that Gottkind thought that a largely Hispanic panel would be favorable to at least one of his clients, Angelo Fuerza, at that time the highest-ranking Hispanic on the City's payroll. Karp briefly wondered whether he should use one of his peremptories on Mrs. Delgado, and decided not to. For all he knew, Fuerza might be the spitting image of her despised first husband.

When the questioning of the current lot was complete, both Delaney and Delgado made it on to the panel, and that was it for the panel itself. It was now the second day of May. The suit had been filed the previous August. Judge Craig had studied all the motions submitted, the opposing interpretations of state statute and the precedents of constitutional law, and judged that the case had merit under law. He declined to dismiss; he had ordered the facts to be tried; and here they all were, only two hundred and seventy days later. Blinding speed.

As Judge Craig prepared to address the lucky winners, Karp turned to his client and said, "Murray, I heard something pretty disturbing the other night. Are you aware that there's a corruption investigation going on out of the D.A.'s squad that involves the medical examiner's office?"

Karp watched the other man's face carefully as his words registered. He thought he saw puzzlement and dismay only; there was no telltale flush of uncovered guilt.

Selig said, "What investigation? What're they investigating?"

"Some Latino kids, early part of last year, up at the Two-Five, died in custody. You guys did the autopsies and passed them as suicides, two of them, and the third as natural causes."

Selig's brows remained corrugated. "Yeah, I recall

the incidents. I didn't do them myself, but they were done under my supervision by competent people. The hangings were genuine. The marks made by a suicide hanging are completely different from those made by strangulation or garotting with a cord. It's Autopsy 101—a no-brainer. Who told you we were being investigated?"

"Marlene, actually. She got it from a reporter friend of hers who's looking into the deaths."

Selig shook his head vigorously. "I've never heard anything about it," he said, and then, seeing the doubtful look on Karp's face, added with more heat, "I swear it, Butch! I never heard anything about any investigation—in general or in regard to those autopsies."

Karp nodded and swallowed hard. He did not think Selig was lying, although that did not, unfortunately, mean there was no investigation. Selig, he had discovered in the past nine months, was a thoroughly decent man, but one whose reserves of observation and focus were entirely consumed by the narrow demands of his profession. At his work, literally nothing escaped his attention. Away from the steel tables, nearly everything did. It was actually possible for Selig to have missed being investigated.

Karp patted Selig on the shoulder and said, "It's okay, Murray. I believe you. But something may be up and I need to check it out. I'll let you know what I find."

The new prospectives were seated. Karp turned his attention to the information sheets once again.

A short walk and a world of class away from the Federal Courthouse, Marlene sat in the chair provided for witnesses in Grand Jury Room B, in the New York County Courthouse, and told an assistant D.A. and the twenty-three members of the grand jury what Rob Pruitt had done to her. Pictures were exhibited of her damaged face. After she was done, Harry Bello got up and told his fable. There was no cross-examination, since grand juries have neither defense lawyers nor judges. They belong to the district attorney and represent the limpest possible trip wire against arbitrary prosecutions. Almost always, when the D.A. so requests, they bring in a true bill of indictment, and they did in this case, in less than five minutes.

Marlene lingered to share some thoughts with Ira Raskoff, the kid A.D.A. in charge of the case. Although most of the people who man the trenches in the D.A. last as long in the memory of the office as faces seen from a departing subway train, there were exceptions, and Marlene was one of them. As was Butch Karp. Marlene traded shamelessly on her notoriety and her husband's still bright and fearsome rep to fix in young Raskoff's mind that this particular case was not your ordinary bullshit barroom assault charge, of which he cranked through dozens each week, but special, and that its outcome would be observed. This particular defendant was going to do hard time, at least three years, which result would redound to Raskoff's favor with the grandees of the

Felony Trial Bureau, while failure to obtain it would have dire consequences. Raskoff got the point and promised to keep Marlene informed.

When Marlene and Harry left the courthouse, Foley Square was cold in the bone-withering way that March can be cold in New York and swept with sheets of chilling rain. Marlene had intended to walk home, but now she allowed Harry Bello to lead her to his old Plymouth, illegally parked in a judge's slot at the side of the building.

They got in and Bello raced the engine to pump some warmth into the car. Marlene relaxed, fumbled out a cigarette, longed for it, and replaced it in her bag. She was over six months pregnant and slowing down a hair. Instead, she fiddled with the radio dial, searching for music to soothe her savage breast. She found someone singing a Puccini aria and left it on. The song ended. It was then that she realized that they had been traveling far too long. She looked out the window. They were on the West Side Highway heading north.

"Harry, where are we going?" she asked.

"Weehawken," said Bello.

If Harry Bello had been a regular person, Marlene would have asked him why they were going to Weehawken and he would have said why, and they would have taken it from there. But Marlene knew that Harry expected her to know already why they were going, as if the trisyllabic name of the unlovely Jersey burg already contained, in the fashion of the ultra-fast code bursts sent down from spy satellites, the complete story. And she knew that if she just demanded an explanation in the conventional way, Harry would look at her funny and think she was slipping, and so the trust between them, which besides the person of Lucy Karp was the only thing that held Harry to the normal world, would fray a little and Harry would withdraw another notch into the chaotic depths of Harryland.

She was used to this, however, and it took her less than a minute to figure it out and respond, "I said, I don't need one."

Because she had gone back to the last substantive conversation she had had with Bello, over the phone, during which she had told Harry about Mattie Duran and what Mattie wanted her to do, and Harry had said, "You need a gun," and she had declined and this was Harry not taking no for an answer.

"She's got a sheet," said Harry, dismissing her last statement and making another jump. This was an easy one. Of course, Harry would have used his cop sources to check out Mattie Duran. Marlene was not surprised at what he had learned. She waited.

"Forty-six months in Texas for bank robbery," Harry added, switching to Real Mode. "Guy I talked to down in El Paso said she popped her old man too, but they didn't prosecute."

"Why not?"

"It's Texas. They thought the guy needed killing. Had a couple of partners in the bank thing. Both killed in a shoot-out with the Rangers. They never recovered the loot. Something like eight hundred K."

Harry looked at her significantly and she moved her head slightly, indicating that she hadn't known all of that. He seemed about to say something, but at that point he had to maneuver the tricky exit from the West Side Highway and onto the ramp leading to the Lincoln Tunnel.

Marlene ruminated as they sped through the filthy tiled pipe. Harry's information explained a lot about Duran: how she was able to run the shelter without public money, why she was wary of the authorities. The parricide thing was a bit of a shock, though. Marlene did not recall ever meeting anyone— socially—who had killed one of their parents. She wondered whether she should, and by what means she might, bring it up in conversation with Duran. Meanwhile, it was clear that Harry thought that her relationship with Mattie required an increased level of protection, and she wondered why.

Harry read her mind, of course, and said, as they emerged into gray daylight and rain, "People disappear."

"That's her job, Harry. It's for the women's protection."

"Men too," said Harry.

"Wait a minute, Harry. You think she does hits on people?"

Harry did not deem this worthy of an answer, and left Marlene to her unpleasant thoughts as they emerged into freezing rain in Weehawken. After a drive of about ten minutes through broken and deserted industrial streets, Harry pulled the car through a sagging gate in a chain-link fence topped by rusty barbed wire. There was a low concrete-block building on the site, which bore a small, faded sign announcing that it was the home of the Palisades Rod and Gun Club. Harry parked and led Marlene through a door marked OFFICE.

A chubby man in his late fifties rose from behind a cluttered desk and shook Bello's hand. Bello introduced him to Marlene as Frank Arnolfini. Marlene looked around the small, veneer-paneled room. For a rod and gun club, it was remarkably light in the rod department. Shelves held shooting trophies and the little banners they give out at conventions. A glass showcase counter was full of handguns, and a rack held rifles and shotguns. The walls were decorated with posters supplied by arms and shooting accessory manufacturers, and the sort of plaques and photographs that people accumulate during a long career with the New York Police Department. Arnolfini was an ex-cop and a part-time gun dealer.

After some chat about how bad the weather was and how they were both doing in retirement, Arnolfini turned to Marlene and said, "Harry tells me you're interested in a weapon."

"Actually, Harry's interested in me getting a weapon. I can't stand the idea myself."

Arnolfini chuckled understandingly. "Yeah, well, a lot of ladies are that way. But there's really nothing to be scared of if you have the proper training. We run a pretty good handgun course here for women."

"Uh-huh, but as it happens, I'm not scared of guns,

and I'm a natural shot." Arnolfini and Bello exchanged looks. Arnolfini shrugged and said, "You want a carry gun, you're probably in the market for a semiauto, a nine, right?"

"How big is it?" asked Marlene shortly.

Arnolfini smiled in a way that confirmed Marlene's impression that she was about to be patronized.

"Well, that would depend," he said. "There's all different kinds."

She felt a wave of bitchiness rise within her. She didn't want to be here, she didn't like guns. That she was here, and that she probably was going to buy a gun, and carry it, stemmed from her decision to go into an enterprise that might require her to shoot somebody. Having to lie in a bed she had made was not something Marlene was fond of doing.

Arnolfini went to the handgun cabinet, took out a selection of semiautomatic pistols, and arranged them on a felt pad on top of the glass.

"These are all good nines," he said. "Your Browning Hi-power, a little old but still a classic, your Beretta 92F, pricey but a great gun, your Heckler P9S, *very* pricey but the best; I can give you a deal on this one. And here's your Smith 669 in stainless. A good piece, and under six hundred bucks."

When Marlene made no move to handle any of the weapons, Arnolfini picked up the Smith and held it out to her.

"Try it. It's real light."

Marlene took it and let it dangle from her hand like a wet dish towel. "It's a brick," she said.

"It's only twenty-six ounces empty," replied Arnolfini. "Look, here's something maybe you don't get. The heavier the pistol, the easier the recoil. For a woman that's something to think about."

Marlene put the Smith down on the pad. "Smaller. I'm not going to carry anything that big all the time, and if I don't have it on me all the time, I might as well not have one at all."

"You ain't going to get much smaller than that in a decent nine."

"What about an Astra Constable. A .380?"

Arnolfini shook his head. "Nah, you don't want anything smaller than a nine, Marlene. Believe me. You need the stopping power."

"I shot a man through the lip once with a Constable. It stopped him pretty good."

The gun dealer gave Bello a look and Bello nodded gravely. The gun dealer shrugged and bent down behind the counter again.

"I don't carry any Astras, but you want light, this is light." He put a small, angular pistol on the pad. "It's a Colt Mustang Pocket Lite in aluminum alloy. Twelve and a half ounces."

Marlene picked up the gun, worked the action, and squeezed off a dry-fire shot. "Fine. I'll take it."

"You don't want to fire it?" said Arnolfini.

"I'll trust you it works," she said.

"Shoot it, Marlene," said Harry.

She met his eyes and looked away. He was serious about this, and it came from his concern about her safety, which it was not in her heart to despise. She nodded and said, "Okay, let's shoot."

Arnolfini led them through a hallway to a firing range, a four-stand affair that took up most of his building. He turned on the lights, a rack of space heaters, and a blower. An icy breeze wafted over them, its chill hardly deflected by the gusts from the heaters. Arnolfini broke open a box of .380 semi-wadcutters, and they all worked silently for a few minutes loading three clips. The gun dealer snapped a silhouette target to a traveler and sent it twenty-five yards downrange.

Marlene bellied up to the barrier, slipped muffs over her ears, and without preamble, in her usual casual way, began firing. She shot two clips of five into the target's chest and, for a lark, shot the last clip into the head. Arnolfini flipped the traveler switch and brought the target back.

"Very nice," he said with new respect in his voice. The chest shots fell into two neat patterns, neither larger than a playing card. The five head shots were somewhat more dispersed, but still impressive shooting.

"Of course, it's a lot different on the street," he added. "The guy's moving, it's dark, maybe he's shooting back. That's why you want a weapon that'll put him down with one hit, which this little thing probably won't do. It's really a backup gun."

"Yeah, well, I'm a sort of a backup person, Frank," said Marlene lightly. "Harry's going to do the heavy killing, aren't you, Harry?"

She saw the shock on his face, and immediately wished she were a thousand miles away with her tongue cut out. How *could* she have! Bello turned away and walked out of the range.

Back in the office, Marlene took out her checkbook and examined her bill for the Mustang, two extra clips, a nylon belt holster, and a box of Federal 90-grain jacketed hollow points. Arnolfini explained that she was getting the cop discount since she was with Harry. It made her feel worse.

"You want one of these?" the dealer asked. He was holding a shiny .22 revolver. "For the price of a box of rounds? I bought out a guy last month. Made in Brazil. Not a bad little gun for plinking, but I can't sell 'em."

Marlene was too tired to refuse. "Yeah, sure," she said, "throw it in." But the shiny gun had reminded her of Lucy's cap pistol—and the reality of keeping weapons in the loft. "Have you got a gun box, a safe, with a lock?"

He had several, and Marlene bought a green one about the size of a file drawer, with a push-button combination lock. Harry helped carry it out to the car.

"I'm sorry, Harry," she said when they were sitting in the car. "There's absolutely no excuse for me saying that kind of shit to you."

"Forget it," mumbled Harry as he started the car.

"No, listen, you need to hear this! Look at me, Harry!"

Bello stopped the car and looked at her, his face

its usual mask. Marlene spoke quickly and in a low tone, as in a confessional. "I have problems with this, Harry. And they're coming out in sneaky little digs like that in there. It's driving me up the wall, and I don't like the way I'm acting and feeling behind it. This gun thing. First, it's going to drive Butch crazy all over again, having a gun in the house, and I'm going to have to deal with that, and then, for me personally, I don't *like* being armed, or maybe it's I like it too much. Maybe it's the same thing, if you know what I mean. It was one thing, sort of exciting work, getting Pruitt and stopping the other guys we've been handling this past couple of months, but it's something else completely, dealing with guys who want to kill their girlfriends and we might be in the way, and we might have to shoot them first. I killed one guy, and it almost wrecked me and I had dreams about it for weeks—did I have to do it, did it have to go down that way . . . ?"

"The way I heard it," said Harry, "was you didn't have a choice. The guy was shooting at a cop."

"Right, right, of course, but you always think, maybe you set up the situation. Anyway, that's the point, what you just said, this business might put you in a situation where you're getting shot at, and I have no right to be in a position where I can't help you out. So I'm packing, but . . ." She shook her head, as if trying to jar sense into it, and then made a gesture of futility with her hands, saying, "It's a fog, Harry. I mean, what the fuck . . . what'm I doing? What're *we* doing?"

"One day at a time," said Bello.

"That's a platitude, Harry," she snapped.

He stepped on the accelerator and moved the car down the street. They drove back to the tunnel in silence. In the roar of their passage through the tube, he said, and his words were low-pitched so that she had to strain to hear them, "You'll get used to it. You'll probably never have to use it. Frank, there, the gun expert? Thirty-five years in Bed-Stuy, never shot one. You have to, you'll do the right thing."

"You say that, but how do you *know* that, Harry?"

"I'm here, right?" he said.

The rain did not let up all that afternoon, and when the sun went down it changed to sleet, driven by a nasty east wind. It was, however, positively halcyon compared to the weather within the loft when Karp discovered how Marlene had spent her Jersey morning.

"You brought *guns* into our home? *Guns?*" was his anguished cry. This was at the dinner table. Marlene had made a favorite dish of Karp's, veal parmigiana, which that barbarian considered the epitome of Italian cuisine and which she rarely degraded herself to prepare, but did this time, feeling queasily like Lucy Ricardo.

"Don't raise your voice!" she said.

"Why not? You'll shoot me?" he shouted.

"Lucy, dear," Marlene said, "if you're finished, you can go to your room now."

"Can I see your gun, Mommy?" Lucy asked, her eyes widening.

"*May* I see your gun, Mommy?" said Marlene automatically.

"*May* I see—"

"No, you can't," said Marlene. "What you *can* do is get ready for your bath, and then you can watch *Gilligan's Island*."

"Oh, why don't you show it to her, Marlene?" said Karp nastily. "Let her play with it, even. She will anyway, sooner or later."

At this Marlene turned upon her husband a look of such bone-chilling malevolence that he shut up. After Lucy had run off, she said, "How *dare* you suggest that I'm endangering my child! How dare you!"

They locked gazes and ground teeth for an interminable-seeming moment. Then Karp sprang to his feet, knocking over his chair with a clatter. He had his big fists clenched and appeared to be looking for something to break.

"Shit, Marlene!" he shouted. "Why are you *doing* this? Why are you fucking up our life with this shit?"

"I am not doing any such thing," responded Marlene in a voice unnaturally calm. While Karp gaped and glared and shot flames from his nostrils, she continued, "You object to what I'm doing. It upsets you. A couple of years ago, you dragged this family off to that hellhole in D.C., taking Lucy away from her friends and her relatives without a moment's thought . . ."

"Wait a min—"

". . . without, as I say, a moment's thought, and as I recall I did not scream or yell or insult your integrity or your love for your daughter, or me . . ."

"I didn't—"

" .. whereas I have given this a great deal of thought. Are you going to sit down and listen?"

Karp picked up his chair and sat down in it, after the manner of men who are tied into similar chairs with paper targets on their breasts.

"As I say," Marlene resumed, "a great deal of thought. I didn't want to get a gun at all. Harry thought I needed one—let me finish this, please!— because he was concerned for my safety. I decided to get one because I was concerned for *his* safety. We're going to get in the way of domestic violence from time to time, and I intend to back him up just like he backs me up, and I need a gun for that. As far as safety goes around here, I have a gun safe, in which the guns will sit, locked and unloaded when they're not attached to my body. I also intend to show them to Lucy and let her handle them so she knows what they are and what they can do." She leaned back in her chair and crossed her arms.

"Is that it? You're finished?"

"For the nonce," she replied.

He sighed and rubbed his face. It had taken Karp a long time to learn that in domestic disagreements, the point was not, as it was in the courtroom, to win, but rather the restoration of felicity. This apparently required a different set of skills from those he had honed to a diamond edge, and it was clear to him that he had still not got it right. "I said," he said, "I was sorry a million times about Washington, and you keep bringing it up whenever I give you shit about something you want to do. It's not fair."

Marlene thought about that for a little. "You're right," she said, "it's not. I'll try to lay off of that."

"Okay, and I'm sorry I said that about Lucy and the gun. It was a cheap shot." He sighed again. "But."

"Yes?" she said, a long, drawn-out yes.

"I don't know what 'but.' Sometimes I think I'm inside this, ah, plastic bubble, and if I can just push through, everything will be clear and I'll just accept everything. I mean, I'll stop worrying about you and the kid the way I do. I mean, if you're here, I'll love you, and if you're gone, you're gone and I'll be sad. But no churning stomach all the time. And sometimes I think, I've done it, and I'm through, but then something like this goes down and I realize there's *another* bubble outside the one I just went through. And I think things like, she's acting crazy because she *wants* me to stop her. That's not true, is it?"

"No. Of course, if I was really crazy, I wouldn't tell you the truth, would I? Or would I? Tell me, do you trust me?"

"Oh, yeah," he said immediately. "With my life. I trust your integrity. I trust your decency. However, it's my learned opinion as a professional criminal justice guy of long standing, and some reputation, that you're into something that's way over your fucking head. That's not a trust thing, that's a judgment thing. I could be wrong."

"Thank you for that opinion. I will consider it in my chambers."

"You do that," said Karp.

Both of them had on their faces the kind of shy smiles they wore when they realized that they had yet again escaped the shoals and riptides and were back on the fair, broad seaways of marriage.

"So," said Karp brightly, "what kind of gun did you get?"

"A Colt Mustang .380. The guy threw in a cheap revolver too."

"Well, *mazeltov*," said Karp with a bland smile. "Use them in good health." He stood up. "I think I'll help Lucy with her bath."

In all, a good day, was Marlene's thought when, toward midnight, she floated into the antechamber of sleep. Karp had given her one of those violent fucks she dearly loved, and which she thought one of the ways in which a good marriage discharges otherwise unappeasable aggression and discontent. She was sore and lightly bruised, and Karp, now breathing huskily beside her, had numerous flaming bite marks on him, at least one of which, she hoped, would show above his collar the next morning.

At this point the phone, her closely guarded private number, rang next to her ear. She snatched it up on the first ring. There was a woman on the line.

"Is this Marlene Ciampi?"

"Yes?"

"This is Harlem Hospital Center Admitting. Do you know a person named"—she pronounced it wrong, carefully—"Ariade Stupenagel?"

"Yes, Ariadne. Has something happened to her?"

"Yes, she's in the E.R. now. She doesn't have health insurance, and when we asked her for a responsible party, she gave us a card with your name on it."

"What happened to her?"

"Um, ma'am, are you the responsible party? Otherwise, you know, I can't, um, discuss—"

"Yes, yes, I'll be responsible," Marlene snapped. "What was it—an accident?"

"Uh, no, ma'am," said the woman. Marlene could hear paper rustling. "We have police involvement in this case. This is an assault case."

TWELVE

"They picked her up by the Mount," said the detective. "That's up at the north end of the park near 104th Street, east. It's used as a composting area. Real deserted."

"How did you find her?" asked Marlene. They were sitting on plastic chairs in a crowded hallway in Harlem Hospital's E.R., surrounded by sick or bleeding people, some on gurneys, some slouching exhausted in the same sort of chairs. Marlene was in the sweats, sneakers, and leather jacket she had thrown on after getting the call. The detective was dressed in a rumpled blue suit and a damp tan raincoat, a chunky, sad-eyed black man. He seemed intelligent and concerned. Marlene had identified herself as the victim's closest friend, a former D.A., and a current private investigator. The detective was therefore somewhat more forthcoming than detectives usually are when interviewing people connected to victims.

"We got a call at the precinct," he said. "Anonymous, of course."

"Of course. What precinct? The Two-Five?"

"No, the Two-Three," said the detective. "Anyway, a night like this, she would have died for sure, exposed like she was. We're treating it as attempted murder."

"She was naked?"

"Underpants, socks, and sneakers."

"Raped?"

"We're checking that. It looks like a gang thing to me. Some of these kids are pretty nasty little suckers."

"I doubt that," said Marlene. "That it was a kid gang."

The detective looked at her sharply. "Oh, yeah? Why is that?"

"Ariadne is six-one and strong. She isn't your typical New York housewife or secretary. She carried a nine-inch Arab dagger almost all the time and she knows how to use it too. For the last ten years or so she's been playing risky games with guerilals, bandits, and secret police all over the world. She could eat the average gang of kid muggers for breakfast."

"You think she was a target? It wasn't random?"

"I'd bet on it."

The detective wrote something on his notepad. He asked, "So she had enemies."

Marlene snorted a laugh. "You could say that. Ariadne enjoys pissing people off. She thinks it's her professional responsibility as a journalist."

"Like who, in particular?"

"I don't know," said Marlene after a brief pause.

"Take your pick. Last year she exposed some nasty connections between American officials and the generals who're murdering Indians in Guatemala. She did a piece recently on stalkers that might've gotten some people annoyed."

"Uh-huh," said the detective, writing. Then, casually, he asked, "By the way, how come you thought the call came in to the Two-Five?"

Smart guy, thought Marlene, and was about to tell him Stupenagel's interest in the cabbie suicides, and the involvement of Paul Jackson, but thought better of it. It had been some time since she had spoken to Stupenagel about it; maybe the whole thing hadn't panned out. And the woman had not mentioned being followed after that one time. And, more to the point, she didn't know this guy, or his connection, if any, with the cops out of the Twenty-fifth Precinct who were supposedly doing the shakedowns.

"I don't know—Two-Three, Two-Five—I guessed it was one of the East Harlem precincts, considering where you found her."

The detective grunted, wrote, asked a few more questions and then flipped his notebook shut. He handed Marlene a business card. Lester Moon, Detective Third Grade. She gave him one of hers.

"Call me if you think of anything else," said Moon with a meaningful look, and strode off through the deep misery.

Marlene managed to track down the harried Panamanian intern in charge of Stupenagel's case, from whom she learned that her friend had survived surgery; that her internal bleeding was under control; that her broken bones had been set; that she was out of immediate danger; and that he had another patient he had to see right away.

Marlene then marched into the administration office and obnoxiously flashed her checkbook and her gold Visa card to attract the attention of various civil servants, through whom she arranged for Stupenagel to be transferred from Harlem Hospital Center to Columbia-Presbyterian. The Columbia College of Physicians and Surgeons supplies interns to both hospitals. They send the ones with good American M.D.'s to Columbia-Presby and the ones from third world countries holding degrees from places like Guadalajara U. to Harlem. Marlene knew this, and she had no compunction about buying her friend's way out of a public hospital, and thus supporting a dual health-care standard she would have abstractly opposed at any cocktail party. Then she went home and cried and awakened Karp, who comforted her and wisely refrained from expressing his constant fear that the next midnight phone call would be about Marlene.

It took three days for Stupenagel to recover her senses enough to converse for any length of time. On each of those days, after taking care of Lucy and dropping her at school, Marlene had come, and sat through the visiting hour, and chatted inanely to the unanswering, white-swathed figure on the hospital bed.

When she arrived on the third day, Stupenagel's

bed was propped up and her eyes were open. They were ringed with yellow-violet bruises. Much of the rest of her face was concealed by plaster, except for a rough hole at the side of her mouth, through which she could suck nourishment and carry on a slurred conversation.

"How are you, Stupe?" asked Marlene, sitting in a chair by the bedside.

"Oh, I'm having a ball. Dope's pretty good. Nurse said you're paying the freight for this. Thanks, but you don't have to. Call my dad." She gave Marlene a telephone number with a 216 area code, and Marlene wrote it down.

"You want to know what happened, huh?"

"Sure," said Marlene.

"So would I," said Stupenagel. "The last thing I remember I was in my apartment. I had just come back from uptown, I'd taken my coat and my boots off, and I was drinking a Bloody Mary I'd just fixed. I remember thinking I wanted to call you. Drinking the drink, and then I woke up here. First thought after waking up, it was some kind of explosion. Gas. Seems like not. I got pounded, they tell me."

"Yeah. You don't remember anything?"

"Nope. Traumatic retrograde amnesia, they call it. A cute kid doctor came in this morning when I came to and explained it all to me. Some of it may come back over the weeks. He said."

"What's your guess, then?"

"Hmm. Where to begin? Well, I'm working on an exposé of the Guatemala thing, a long piece for *Har-*

per's. Somebody down there might have heard about it and sent somebody up here to do some Central American public relations on me. Unlikely, but possible. There's the stalking piece—one of the guys I mentioned might have been brooding . . . an old boyfriend . . . shit, I don't know, Champ—"

"What about the Two-Five shakedown business?" asked Marlene.

"What business was that?" responded the injured woman vaguely.

"You know, Stupe, the gypsy cabs, the suicides in jail, that guy who roughed you up—"

"Oh, God, of course! Jackson! Something just broke on that, but I can't remember . . ."

Marlene waited some time, but Stupenagel did not finish the thought. Finally she said, "Meanwhile, can I do anything?"

A rattling sound came from behind the bandages, a sad attempt at laughter. "*Now* she asks!"

"Right," said Marlene, refusing the proffered guilt trip. "Every time you get your face smashed in, you have a free crack at my professional services. What do you want me to do?"

"Check out the D.A.'s investigation of the shakedowns."

"There isn't any investigation, not according to the former chief medical examiner."

"You talked to him?" There was a surprised squeak in the muffled voice.

"No. He happens to be a client of my husband's. Butch asked him."

"Hnnh. He might be in on the scam, then."

"I doubt that. I mean, Butch doubts that."

"Oh, well then, it's the gospel. Okay, maybe you can get your hands on the original ausotsy—whoops, goddamn, I'm so fucked up—*autopsy* reports. We can show them to somebody, see if these kids really killed themselves."

"Okay," said Marlene, "I'll try. Is that it?"

No answer. Marlene leaned closer. "Stupe?"

"Mmmm? What?"

"You drifted off."

"Yeah. I do that. Call my dad, okay?"

"Sure. Get better now, okay?"

Stupenagel closed her eyes and her hand twitched, but whether it was in farewell or a random spasm Marlene could not tell.

From a phone booth in the hospital, Marlene called Mr. Stupenagel at his office in Cleveland. The man was calm and low-key about the disaster, asking for information, getting what Marlene had, thanking her politely, and signing off. It was clear that he had been waiting for such a call for a long while. Then Marlene called the morgue at Bellevue and asked to speak to Dr. Dennis Maher.

"Peg o' my heart!" said a light Irish voice in her ear.

"Hello, Denny. How's it going?"

"Ah, flourishing, flourishing, my dear. They're dyin' to get in here!"

Marlene laughed dutifully at the ancient joke. "Why I called, Denny, is I need some help."

"Unto the half of my kingdom. As you're aware, my practice is largely with the silent majority, but I could brush up a bit for you, Marlene. Would it be a wee gynecological problem, he said hopefully?"

Marlene ignored this. "Would you be free for lunch today? My treat?"

"Oh, let's see now—shall I gnaw upon a stale tuna sandwich from a machine in an office reeking of formalin, or shall I dine in splendor with a beautiful woman, her paying the tab? Oh, God, these decisions!"

"I'll take that as a yes. How about Malachy's on Twenty-third?"

"Would that be the saloon with the largest selection of unblended Irish whiskey in the whole of this great city? Why, I don't believe I've ever entered the door."

"Twelve-thirty," said Marlene, laughing, and hung up.

Denny Maher was part of the great Irish Medical Migration of the 1960s, in which the Irish Republic's decision to combine brilliant training with rotten salaries redounded to the benefit of New York's best hospitals. Maher was one of the few forensic specialists in this wave, and the M.E.'s office had snapped him up. At thirty-six, he was single and a drinking man, characteristics not unrelated to each other. Marlene liked him. He had been something of a pet of the D.A.'s office for years, a big reason being his status as the purveyor of Olde Medical Examiner, a fruit punch made with absolute alcohol purloined from the morgue, which had long been the centerpiece of bureau parties at the old D.A.'s.

He arrived ten minutes late at the saloon, looking the same to Marlene, who hadn't seen him in a couple of years. A slight man, he had a boyish, freckled face and crinkly red hair. His eyes were watery blue, trimmed with the decorative red stigmata of the serious lush.

Maher kissed Marlene on the cheek loudly, said a variety of flattering, and false, things in his consciously adopted stage Irishman's brogue, ordered a whiskey, drank it, ordered another, a different malt, for purposes of comparison, drank that, compared the two, declared the second superior, ordered another of the second to reward the firm, ordered a steak, ate it washed down with a pint of Guinness, all the while talking delightful nonsense, and then, pushing away his plate, his face flushed red, his eyes rolling, asked, "And now, my benefactress, what is the little favor that Dr. Maher, late of Trinity College, Dublin, can do to repay all this magnificence?"

Marlene said, "I want you to find and steal three autopsy reports." She explained the situation and why she needed them, adding, "The word is, there's something fishy about them, and the D.A.'s office has taken them in as part of an investigation."

Maher gave her an inquiring look. "Wherever did you hear that?"

"It's around," answered Marlene. "Why, aren't you aware of it?"

"I am not, which is the same as saying the creature does not exist. As you know, m'dear, I have no life. I am totally dedicated to my profession. Many and many's the night I've labored until dawn in those grim precincts . . ."

"You mean, sleeping it off?"

". . . labored, as I say, and never a whisper of it have I heard. However, this canard on our glorious abbatoir shall not go unchallenged while Maher draws breath. I shall . . . exactly what was it that you wanted, my girl?"

"Steal these three files." She inscribed a business card with the names Stupenagel had given her and the dates of death, and slid it across the table.

Maher glanced at it and put it away, saying, " 'Steal,' madam, is not a word that sits comfortably on a gentleman's tongue. However, since it's your own dear self and a matter of honor, Maher's your man. And another drink to the success of the enterprise?"

Marlene paid the tab and left Malachy's with Maher's promise to call that evening with the results of his search. She took a cab and arrived home to the usual hysterical greeting by the big black dog, whom she fed, and then checked her service. Among the messages was one from Mattie Duran. Marlene returned it immediately.

"You remember Vickie Sills?" said Duran without

preamble. "You met her when you were here. She's got a problem you could help her with."

"Vickie . . . ?"

"The knee. The pit bull?"

Marlene recalled the knee. "What's up?"

"I got her into a two-family house in Bensonhurst. The husband apparently found out where it was and paid them a visit last night."

"What went down?"

"The usual. He tried to break in. Had that damn dog with him. She called the cops, but by the time they got there he was gone. Now she's terrified and doesn't want to go back. She's here now with the kids."

"What do you want me to do?"

"Take her out there again, calm her down, sit with her. He'll be back."

"And then what?"

"Use your imagination," said Duran. "Show him his errors."

"Good plan," said Marlene. "I'll be by in a little while."

Marlene called the service and left a message for Harry, telling him what she had planned. She changed into her pirate clothes—the jeans no longer buttoning but coverable with the sweater—applied her patch, walked the dog, shopped for supper, dropped off some shirts at the Chinese laundry on Mott, and then it was time to pick up Lucy, who was delighted to learn that they were going to visit Isabella at the shelter.

At the shelter, Marlene played for a while with her daughter and the silent girl in Isabella's cardboard hut in the playroom, which Lucy thought hilarious. Marlene and Isabella were the babies and Lucy was the Mommy, provoking breathless fits of giggles from Lucy and vague Mona Lisa smiles from the older girl. Lucy also imposed on her mother for some sleight-of-hand demonstrations, and this developed into a full-scale magic show involving all the other kids as well. Coins jumped out of ears to the satiety of all. Time flew. It was past five before Marlene thought of her meeting with Mattie Duran.

Entering the little office, she got a long, humorous, appraising look. "I like your outfit," said Duran.

"It's designed to strike fear into the hearts of my enemies," said Marlene. "Those that don't laugh. It's going to be a real sketch in my eighth month."

"Yeah, well, Ernie Sills is no laughing matter."

"This is the husband?"

"Yeah," said Duran, wrinkling her nose. "He's a baker. Skinny little nasty guy with a nasty dog. He used to set the animal to watch her when he was at work. She couldn't go out, and her folks couldn't visit. When he got his load on, he used to make it chase her and the kids around the house. A real joker, Ernie. She finally called me and I went over there with the Animal Control people and got her and the two kids out of there. He got his dog back from the pound, by the way, before he thought of looking for his family. First things first."

"You ever talk to him?"

"Hell, no!" Duran snapped, and seemed surprised at the question. "Why should I, the bastard?"

"I don't know—he could have a story. It would be something to find out what type he is. He can't be very happy if he behaves like that."

Duran gave her a withering look. "Oh, save it for church!"

"I thought the point was that we weren't supposed to," said Marlene calmly.

Duran lowered her heavy brows and gave Marlene thirty seconds of the Indian stare. Then she said, "Honey, you want to be a social worker, get those unhappy families back together, you have definitely come to the wrong rancho. Why do you think I got quarter-inch steel plates and heavy window grating on this place? You think it's a fashion statement? What we got here is the people nobody else will take because their old men threaten to shoot up and burn down any place that takes them in. Send them to jail? Yeah, sure, they send them to jail, three months, a year; then they're right back out doing the same number. Of course, if they're solid citizens, like your friend Ernie Sills, they get probation and R.O.R.: don't do it again, boy, you hear? Yes, Judge, I sure won't."

"I only meant—"

"No social work, Marlene. Protection and deterrence, that's the business."

It was irritating to be lectured like this, especially in terms that Marlene had once herself used at the D.A. Without much thought she put in, "You sound like a cop, Mattie. Which is surprising, considering you did all that time . . ."

Duran's face darkened to the color of damp rawhide. "You've been snooping," she said in a tight voice.

"My partner, actually. Harry is very particular about who we do business with, and, you know, we're *detectives*. I figure you kept the loot, which is how come you can run this place. Where did you stash it, anyway?"

"No comment. I guess you heard about the other thing."

"Killing your father? Yeah, that too."

Duran relieved herself of a great sigh. "He wasn't my father. My father died when I was four. He was my stepfather. Not that it matters, but he started fucking me when I was eleven. When I was sixteen, he started chasing Carmen, my half sister. She was ten at the time. So I stuck a gun under his chin while he was sleeping one off on the couch and blew his brains out. I never lost a minute of sleep over it either. Carmen's a nurse in El Paso, married, two kids. Very respectable. We don't talk. You want to do some social work at *that*, now?"

"No. But here's the thing: I set up a guy and had him beaten half to death and put in jail. Maybe it was necessary, maybe not. And I took some lumps too. But I didn't like it at the time, the setup part, and my husband didn't like it, and I sort of half think he was right. So I've decided that I'm going to try as hard as I can to resolve these cases peacefully. No, let me finish! I know other people might have tried, but the point is, *I* have to try, personally. That doesn't work, I guess I can get as heavy as necessary. Which is heavy enough. The other thing is, my partner thinks you had guys whacked, which—I said, let me finish!—is your business, but I don't want to hear about it, and if it gets stuck in my face so I can't avoid it, I'll rat you out."

Duran was glaring at her, her face getting steadily darker; Marlene glared back, feeling, having said her say, more at ease with herself than she had in a long while. It had taken a good deal of the sting out of owning a gun.

As if reading her mind, as well as making up her own, Duran relaxed and, with a curt nod of the head, said, "Okay, it's your play. Meanwhile, assuming nice don't work for you, do you have protection?"

Marlene smiled. "As the nun said to Father Feeny. Yeah, I have a gun. How about yourself? I bet you have a big one."

At this Duran laughed out loud, a hearty noise that blew the sour tension out of the room. She reached into a drawer and put a pistol on the center of her desk.

"Wow! That's very impressive. May I?"

Duran nodded. "It's loaded."

"I guess," said Marlene, who stood and picked it up. It was the most famous pistol in history, a Colt .44 Peacemaker, the one nearly everyone in the world has seen hundreds of times from early childhood in the hands of film cowboys and gunfighters. And like

nearly everyone else who has ever picked up a Peacemaker for the first time, Marlene tried to twirl it on
her finger. She found it was a lot harder than Hoot
Gibson made it look.

"Here, give it to me—you'll drop it and break your
toe," said Duran. She took it from Marlene butt first
and did a snappy finger twirl, forward, back, and
forward again, and mimed sticking it into a low-
slung holster. "My grandfather's," she said. "He was
a rodeo cowboy. And yeah, this is the one I used. I
buried it before I called the sheriff so they wouldn't
take it."

"Incredible!" said Marlene. "And here you are in
the big city, the world's only feminist chicana desperado. This is why they call you the Durango Kid,
right?"

Duran snorted and slipped the thing back into its
drawer. "Not such a kid anymore," she said.

"Me neither, now that I think of it," said Marlene.
"Don't you dare laugh, but I have to go home and
feed my husband."

Duran laughed anyway, long and loud.

Marlene went home, opened her gun safe, and
took out her gun. She read the little manual supplied
by Colt, field-stripped the weapon according to its
directions, and cleaned it with the little kit the gun
dealer had tossed in. As she was reassembling it, she
suddenly noticed that the sounds that Lucy had been
making while playing had ceased. By design, the
playroom shared a wall with Marlene's office so that

she could keep tabs on what her daughter was up to while working at home.

"Lucy? What're you doing?" she called out. No answer. She stopped what she was doing and listened carefully. At the same time she became aware of eyes on her back. She spun around in the swivel chair. No one. The door was closed. Then she raised her eyes up the rear wall of the office. At the top of this wall, where it joined the ceiling, was a long window, designed so that light from the street could pass from Marlene's office into the playroom, which had no other natural light. There was a face in the window, grinning down at her from twelve feet up.

Marlene put the gun down and walked out her door and into the playroom. Lucy had placed her miniature desk on a toy chest and two chairs on top of that to reach the high inset window, on whose sill she now crouched.

"What were you looking at?" asked Marlene when she had helped the girl down and given her a stern lecture about neck breaking and the sorrows of the quadriplegic life.

"Nothing." Embarrassed down-gazing.

"You wanted to see my gun, didn't you?"

Nod.

"Okay, come on in. But next time ask me. Don't be a sneak."

Marlene gave Lucy the standard gun-safety lecture and, after explaining how they worked, allowed her to handle both pistols, unloaded.

Lucy pointed at the shiny revolver. "That's my favorite kind. My one is like that."

"Yes, but you understand the difference," said Marlene sternly. "This is not a toy. And you are never, never, never—"

"I know, don't touch it without you," said Lucy, idly swinging the little revolver by its trigger guard. Then, of course, she had to try twirling it like a cowperson, and then Marlene had to show her how to do it, and fail, provoking laughter, and then the two of them traded the pistol back and forth, laughing like lunatics and seeing who could be the stupidest and clumsiest gunfighter.

"Oh, Jesus," said Marlene, wiping her eyes, "if your father ever saw that, God, playing with guns, he'd go nuts. Let's keep this under our hats, okay?"

Lucy gave her a sidelong look. "Isn't that being sneaky?"

"Hey! *I* give the moral instruction around here, *capisc'*?"

Lucy giggled and said, *"Shen gao huang di yuan,"* in a singsong trill.

"Right on, whatever it means!" said Marlene. "Let's go cook dinner."

"This was an excellent dinner," said Karp, smiling at his family. And it was: tomato soup made with actual tomatoes and basil, broccoli salad, a London broil sliced paper-fine and wrapped around fresh *porcini*, with madeira sauce, and a strawberry shortcake with real whipped cream.

"I whipped the cream," said Lucy, not for the first time.

"Yes," said Karp, "and I thought that was the best part of the dinner. I wish we could have your whipped cream on everything."

Much proposing of horrible things to have with whipped cream, giggling until our milk gushes from our nose. Sent from the table, still giggling.

"She's been a maniac all day," said Marlene. "I don't know where she gets her sense of humor. Both of us are as dry as toast."

"Meanwhile," said Karp, "I hate to say this, but being fed like this arouses my suspicions. Am I going to get hit with something?"

"Yes, I figured you would feel like that—because of the infamous Gun Meal—but really, it's not the same, because then I was being smarmy and embarrassed, and making up to you by cooking something that you like but that I think is garbage, whereas in the present instance, I was really enjoying doing this one. For the man I love."

Karp cocked a disbelieving eye at this, which Marlene pretended to ignore. She asked, "And how was *your* day, dear? Trying?"

Their old joke. Karp grinned and said, "Since you ask, I had a pretty good one. The evildoers took some lumps."

"Did you do Bloom?" asked Marlene, who had not been following the case closely at all.

"Oh, God, no—it'll be weeks and weeks before we get to him. Right now we're just preparing the ground, digging the pits, sharpening the bamboo stakes. For instance, today I had Mrs. Ortiz up there, Fuerza's administrative aide. Been at Health since before penicillin, in her early sixties, plain as a post, she's going to retire soon, so they can't offer her anything or shaft her too much."

"She helped you out?"

"Oh, yeah. She knows where all the bodies are buried. Anyway, the basis of this charge was that Murray hired a bunch of associate medical examiners without Fuerza's knowledge or approval. Broke the law, in other words. What actually happened was that Murray needed the examiners to keep up with his caseload, he went to Fuerza for approval, Fuerza told Mrs. Ortiz to find the money in the general Health Department budget, which she did, and Murray began recruiting. Fuerza actually wrote a note to him recommending a pal of his for one of the jobs. We also have a letter to the Mayor's Office, signed by Fuerza, backing the recruitment of four pathologists."

Marlene looked puzzled. "That's silly. Why would they make a charge like that if they left that kind of paper trail?"

"Why indeed," said Karp. "That's the wacky thing about this whole case. Anyway, what they'll argue here is that Fuerza stepped in to protect the City from liability after the recruits were promised jobs illegally by Murray. But the dates are wrong, and the Ortiz testimony nails it down that Fuerza was in on the deal from the beginning. All the charges are like that. They say he disclosed confidential records; he didn't and we can prove it. He failed to produce a report on office organization; he did, and Fuerza's on record at the time as saying it was a good report. He left the City without proper notice—"

"What!"

"Yeah, they had to scrape the barrel for that one. It's all picky shit like that, but the important thing is that Fuerza confirmed all of it in deposition, and now I'm going to have witness after witness, document after document, impeaching his sworn statement. When I get him on the stand, I'll totally destroy him."

"And the Mayor too?"

"Nah, I'm going to go light on the Mayor. The Mayor will be very cooperative. Basically, his line will be: 'I just did what these guys told me to do,' not particularly inspiring leadership, but not culpable. Fuerza will take all the shit."

"And Bloom," said Marlene.

"And Bloom," said Karp. "Oh, my, yes."

Marlene rose and began clearing, and Karp helped her. In companionable silence they scraped dishes and loaded the dishwasher.

"By the way, I have to go out tonight," said Marlene in the midst of this.

Karp bit back a needling remark, something he was getting a good deal of practice at, and said coolly, "Oh, no problem. Where are you off to?"

Marlene answered blandly, "In all honesty, I have to see a man about a dog."

THIRTEEN

Vickie Sills was a small woman in her late twenties, with short auburn curls and skin the color of Redi-Whip. She would have been unobtrusively pretty if not for the dark smudges under her eyes and her generally dilapidated air. Her children, a boy (Jamie), five, and a girl (Tiffany), three, were whiny and clinging. They were terrified, naturally, of the dog, Sweety, whose friendly efforts to smear them with drool had been rebuffed with hysterics. The children had been calmed and fed on Beef-a-Roni. Sweety now lay sulkily in a far corner.

The apartment in which Marlene now sat with Vickie, on a worn red plaid sofa, was the sparely furnished downstairs of a two-family brick house on a quiet street off Avenue S. It smelled of old paint, steam heat, and Vickie's incessant smoking. Marlene, who was dying for a cigarette, reckoned that she had already inhaled the equivalent of half a pack, as had the Sills children. Her fetus was shriveling without deriving a particle of pleasure, and she was starting to resent it.

Nor was Vickie a fascinating companion, her conversation consisting mainly of anecdotes illustrating the cruelty of life, with herself the chief target of fortune's fell arrow. Marlene got the uncomfortable feeling that Vickie would probably have put up with Ernie's little ways had they not included her own mutilation in the jaws of his pet. She drew the line there—not a poster girl for women's lib, Vickie. She was relating the story of how her ex had chortled as his pit bull tore apart Tiffany's little kitten, when a car door slammed on the street outside. Vickie stopped in mid-sentence, and her face turned, amazingly, even whiter.

"That's him!" she squeaked.

"Let me check," said Marlene, rising and going to the front windows. In the light of the street lamps she could see a fairly new red Mercury sedan double-parked and, coming around the front of it, a small, wiry, tan man with short, curly hair and a lowering brow. He wore a black Jets duffel coat over baker's whites. His walk was oddly stiff, as if he were trying to keep from falling over forward, and at first Marlene imagined that he was staggering drunk, but as he emerged from between the parked cars, she saw that he was being pulled along by a big, white pit bull terrier on a steel choke collar.

"Vickie, take the kids and go into the big bedroom," Marlene said. They vanished. Marlene heard heavy steps and the scrabbling of claws on the concrete stoop. Pounding on the door: the knob rattled and the door shook in its frame.

266

"Vickie! Goddammit! Open the goddamn door!"

Sweety rose slowly to his feet and stretched. His nose twitched, and a ripple zipped down the muscles of his back.

"*Prego*, Sweety!" said Marlene, and the dog came alert and took up a position on Marlene's left side. Marlene opened the front door halfway and confronted Ernie Sills and his slavering companion.

When Sills saw who it was, his eyes narrowed and he snarled, "Who the fuck're you? Where's Vickie?"

Marlene said, "Mr. Sills, you know you're under a court order. Please go away and leave your wife alone."

"I *said*, who the fuck're you?" Marlene could smell the fumes of beer as he shouted this into her face.

"My name is Marlene Ciampi. I'm helping Vickie and the kids get settled."

"She don't need no help," said Sills, putting his hand against the door. He let his dog's chain out a little, and the pit bull leaped at Marlene through the doorway, its teeth snapping a few inches from her leg.

"Mr. Sills, if you try to push in here, you're going to be in a lot of trouble."

"Ah, go fuck yourself, y'one-eyed bitch," he snapped and threw his shoulder against the door. Marlene had to give way, and the man and dog rushed past her into the L-shaped hallway that led to the living room.

The pit bull saw Sweety before his master did, and its lunge threw Sills off balance. He went down on one knee and lost the dog chain. Marlene closed the front door.

A snarling white blur, the pit bull flung itself at Sweety's throat and buried its teeth in the loose folds of skin that defended the mastiff from just such an attack. Of course, it was a hopeless gesture: sixty-pound terriers, however tough, do not go up against one-hundred-ninety-pound Neapolitan mastiffs. Sweety opened his huge jaws, engulfed the back of the pit bull's neck, and jerked upward, ripping away a chunk of skin and muscle. The pit bull's jaws remained locked on his throat. Sweety took another bite. Blood and bits of flesh sprayed around the hallway, patterning the floor and the walls.

"Hey . . ." said Sills.

The pit bull's spine was exposed; the mastiff clamped his teeth around it and crunched. The pit bull's body twitched in spasms and it lost control of its bowels and bladder, but its teeth remained locked tight, even when Sweety shook himself violently. The white body hung from his neck like an obscene lavaliere. The whole thing had taken thirty seconds.

Ernie Sills, frozen in place from the first instant of the dog fight, now rose and started to back away in the direction of the door.

"Sweety, *assalite!*" shouted Marlene.

In an instant, despite the dead dog hanging from its neck, the mastiff was on the man, smashing him to the ground. Sills landed on his back, with his head jammed up against the door frame.

"Sweety, *afferate!*" ordered Marlene. The mastiff

clamped his jaws around the man's throat. Marlene walked slowly over and knelt down by the man's head. She was shaking with adrenaline and took a moment to calm her breathing.

"How do you feel, Mr. Sills?" Marlene asked mildly.

Only gasps came from Sills's throat.

"Sweety, *non tanto!*" said Marlene. The dog's jaws relaxed, but not very much.

"I asked you how you felt," said Marlene.

"Ahh, not . . . not good," said Sills, his eyes rolling in his head. The bloody dead muzzle of his dog was pressed up against his cheek.

"No, I bet you're not," said Marlene. "It's no fun to be attacked by a big dog. Do you understand how Vickie felt when you got your dog to chase her? She felt just like you do now. Look, you pissed on yourself. You must be very frightened. Aren't you frightened, Mr. Sills?"

"Wha—whadyou want?"

"I'm giving you an experience, Mr. Sills, the same experience you've been giving your family. You're being attacked by a big animal, and your pet has been torn apart in front of your eyes, just like you did to your daughter's little kitten. How do you like it so far?"

There was no answer. Marlene said, "Sweety, *più strettamente!*" The dog's jaws clamped tighter, and Sills jerked and made noises.

"You have to answer me, Mr. Sills. How do you like it?"

"Don't. Don't like it. Jesus, make it let go."

"Sweety, *non tanto*! That's good, Mr. Sills. You don't like it, and your family didn't like it when you did it to them. Now, I don't know what you're thinking right now, Mr. Sills, because I don't know you. Maybe you're thinking that you're going to get back at me, or your family, and that somehow you're going to be able to continue doing like you've been doing. Maybe you're the kind of person who's completely out of control. I sure hope not, for your sake, Mr. Sills. Because things have changed. And I hope that this experience—I mean, lying here in your own piss with your dead dog squashed against your face—will have a good effect. You remember when you barged in here, I said that if you did, you would be in trouble, and here you are, in trouble. Is this enough trouble for you? Answer me!"

The tone of Marlene's voice was enough to make Sweety utter a diesel-ish growl. "Yeah, yeah, enough . . ." yelped Sills.

"Fine. Now, look: I'm not forcing you to do anything bad; I'm just trying to get you to do the right thing. You've got a problem dealing with anger, you have a little drinking problem, you can find programs to help you out. I hope you do. But meanwhile, you have to be nice to your kids; support them; be polite to your ex-wife. You know, be a man! I think you can do that, don't you?"

"Yeah . . . sure," said Sills.

"I'm delighted to hear it," said Marlene cheerfully. "And I'm going to let you up in a second, and I'm not even going to call the cops and report that you violated your protective order, because I don't want you to go to jail, maybe lose your job. Here's the thing, though, Mr. Sills: if I hear you're giving Vickie a hard time, I will find you. I know where you live and where you work. And we'll share another experience, only this time the dog will eat your face right off your skull—nose, eyes, ears, the works. Look into my eye, Mr. Sills, and tell me that you believe me. And make me believe you!"

"And then?" asked Maggie Duran over the phone.

"Nothing much," answered Marlene. "I gave Sweety '*Lasciane*' and he backed off and Sills got up and ran out of there without a word. Burned rubber too."

"Hot damn, girl! You've made my month!"

"Glad to hear it," said Marlene a little sharply. "It was extremely unpleasant. I had to use a kitchen knife to cut the fucking dead dog's jaws off of Sweety, and then Vickie went hysterical when she saw the mess. The place'll need to be repainted, and then I had to stop by the animal emergency room on First Avenue to get my dog stitched up."

"Send me the bill."

"I intend to," said Marlene, and shortly thereafter she closed the conversation.

It was nearly one in the morning, and Marlene had stripped and showered and taken a hot soak in her converted electroplating tank and thrown her clothes into the machine before calling Mattie Duran with her report. Now she was lounging in her office, in her kimono, feeling faintly nauseated from the after-effects of violence and wondering whether the stress was hurting the baby, and cursing yet again the scientists who had condemned cigarettes and alcohol for the pregnant.

She saw that the message light on her machine was on, and so she punched the button and listened to messages from her mother, Ariadne Stupenagel, and Denny Maher. The last was the only one who was likely, nay, certain, to be up and talkative at one a.m. and so, consulting her Rolodex, she dialed the morgue and asked for the extension of the lab room that Maher used as a home away from home.

"Peg o' my heart!" said Maher when he heard her voice.

"Did you get it?"

"It?"

"Oh, Denny, don't tell me you forgot!"

"Oh, now, wait a minute, it's coming, it's coming . . . ah, sure, and how could I forget a promise to the likes of yourself? You'll be interested to know that something is definitely amiss in regards to the three young Ibero-Americans, late of this city. Someone has snatched the autopsy reports, and the lads're being cremated—"

"Oh, crap! We're screwed, then, right?"

"Would have been, absent the wiles of the cunning Maher. Little did the villain know that the photo lab keeps the negatives of all the autopsy shots and the reports are microfilmed. I looked them up and had some glossies made for you. I could have them framed. Something for the den . . . ?"

"What do they show?"

"A pair of poor hanged boys and one without a mark on him."

"The two were definitely hanged?"

"Oh, yes, if the marks on their necks aren't just painted on. The position of the ligature marks, you see, the classic invert V, up and past their ears. Very different from garotting, where they run right around like a slice in a sausage, or manual strangulation, where you see the thumb marks. And they're deep as well: these boys hung by their own weight, for certain, my sweet."

"Crap!"

"Oh? And did you want them not to be hanged?"

"Yes. I mean, no. I mean . . . Christ, I don't know what I mean anymore. It's one-thirty in the morning, and I'm totally wiped, and my dog just ate another dog—no, don't say it, I know, it's a dog-eat-dog world—and I'm too frazzled to think straight right now. Look, Denny, can you courier those pictures and copies of the actual reports over to me tomorrow—I mean, later today? Maybe I can make something of them. And Denny? Try to find out who might have lifted those original shots, or if the morgue people recall anybody asking questions about those three autopsies."

Angelo Fuerza made a good appearance on the witness stand. He wore a gray pinstripe and a benign expression, looking like a decent professional man, a family doctor. His thick, heavy-framed black horn-rims and his neat, dark rectangular mustache gave his face a defining horizontality, like an equals sign escaped from a math text. His movements were small and precise; you would take your kid to him for the flu and do what he told you to do.

Dr. Fuerza was, in fact, a family doctor. Some fifteen years previously, he had settled in the Morrisania section of the Bronx, in the first wave of Puerto Rican migration, and started a pediatric clinic catering to Hispanic families, and had stuck it out through the growing blight. Early on he had learned how to corral public money, and his organization, El Centro de la Salud de los Niños, had become a key principality in the City's multibillion-dollar health empire. Money and politics being inextricably linked in the City, as elsewhere, Dr. Fuerza had become a politician too, a man who might be depended upon to deliver votes in return for largesse at budget time. He had survived several investigations, and it was inevitable that, when the time came to appoint the first Hispanic health commissioner, Dr. Fuerza would get the prize.

Looking up at him now, Karp felt the stirrings of sympathy. Here, he understood, was a man who had done a lot of good, who, through thoughtless political loyalty, was about to fall into a blender in full public view. Karp did not much enjoy acting the whirling blades, but on the other hand the doctor had committed numerous perjuries and was doubtless about to commit others. Karp glanced over at the Health Department counsel, Ira Nachman, a thin, elderly man, also a perjurer. Nachman knew he was in trouble, if Fuerza didn't. He kept licking his lips and shuffling documents.

Karp consulted his master sheet one last time as Fuerza was sworn in. In a case as complex as this one, it was essential to tell the jury a coherent story, with well-marked chapters and conclusions. Fortunately, the defendants had done most of the job for him, for the two memos, one each from Fuerza and Bloom, with their neatly bulleted points, comprised the totality of the charges for which Selig had been fired. The Mayor had already testified that he had relied exclusively on these charges in forming his decision, and that otherwise he thought that Murray Selig was a prince. Each charge thus had to be isolated, examined, and proven false, and not only that, Karp had to show that, in devising and maintaining these charges, the defendants had acted with reckless disregard for what they knew to be the truth. Thus, as each charge fell amid a tangle of prevarication, Karp would be hammering ever deeper into the collective mind of the jury one critical fact: that the dismissal was an arrant frame-up.

The first charge on the Fuerza memo was that Selig had demanded patient records from a Mt. Zion hospital drug clinic, violating federal confidentiality laws, and that he had made persistent demands for same in the face of the hospital's refusal.

Karp approached, had the witness identify himself,

had the witness agree he had made the charges, read the first charge, had the witness confirm he had made it, asked the witness whether he knew that the patient whose records Dr. Selig had requested was deceased and the subject of a forensic examination (he did), and whether he was aware that such requests for patient records were routine (he did).

Karp handed Fuerza a letter and asked him to read it and describe what it was about. Fuerza shifted in his seat and looked at his counsel.

He read it and said, "It's from me to Mt. Zion, asking for the medical records in this case."

"And in it you declare that such requests are not violative of federal confidentiality statutes, isn't that so?"

"Yes."

"In fact, by this letter, you yourself obtained the records?"

"Correct."

"So you believe that there was actually no violation of confidentiality law?"

A slight hesitation. "It was my counsel, Mr. Nachman's belief. I signed the letter on his advice."

"And did you believe at that time, when you signed the letter, that Dr. Selig's request was violative?"

"No, not at that time."

"Thank you. Now let's move to July, when you wrote the memo to the Mayor. Did you believe then that Dr. Selig had violated federal confidentiality rules?"

"I was following advice of my counsel, Mr. Nachman."

"Please answer the question, Doctor. Did you believe then that Dr. Selig broke the law in reference to this deceased patient?"

"Yes."

"Your counsel changed his advice, then?"

"No," said Fuerza. His eyes, magnified behind the thick lens, were starting to shift at Nixonian velocities.

"No?" asked Karp in the tone usually reserved for a schoolboy's whopper.

"I mean, yes. His advice was that it was a violation."

"Which one was a violation? Dr. Selig's original request or the request that you yourself signed and sent to Mt. Zion?"

"His," answered Fuerza desperately.

"I see. Let me understand this. His request was illegal. Your request supporting his request for the identical records was not. Is that what you're telling us?"

"No."

"Sorry. Then exactly what are you saying, sir? It's right when you do it and wrong when Dr. Selig does it? Or that it's right for both of you in January, but wrong for Dr. Selig in July?"

"I relied on advice of counsel," said Fuerza weakly.

"So I gather," said Karp. He paused to let the jury

get a full whiff of the horseshit. "Turning now to the next charge . . ."

Things went in similar fashion throughout that day and the morning of the next, Karp working the witness like a big tuna on a hook, using the past testimony of the minor witnesses and Fuerza's own deposition to sink the barbs deeper, throwing up the astounding paper trail that Fuerza had left, a trail that up until early July of that year demonstrated that Angelo Fuerza was as happy with Murray Selig as a boss could be with a subordinate. As the hours dragged, the tuna weakened, it lolled by the boat awaiting the gaff. Fuerza's voice became duller. He misspoke, contradicting himself. He hardly seemed to care what he said, if only the torment would end. Gulfs opened between what he had said at deposition, and what the witnesses had said, and what he was saying now. He became sulky; he took refuge in advice of counsel, blaming the lawyers, making himself look like a puppet, and a stupid puppet at that. The tuna knew it would never see blue water again; it was thinking Star-Kist, Bumble Bee, Chicken-of-the-Sea.

The final charge was the "leaving town without notification charges," an anticlimax that left several of the jurors rolling their eyes and shaking their heads. Karp trotted out the file of letters that Selig had written documenting his absences from duty, inquiring of Fuerza with respect to each one whether he had seen it (the redoubtable Mrs. Ortiz having confirmed this in detail) and, getting an affirmative answer to each, asked on what specific occasion Dr. Selig *had* been absent without leave. To which Fuerza replied that he could not name any. No further questions. Karp turned his back and walked stiffly back to his seat.

Naomi Selig was in court that day, and after Fuerza was dispatched, she and her husband and Karp went to nearby Chinatown for lunch. Naomi chose Lee's, a big, touristy Cantonese joint on Mott that Karp, who practically lived in Chinatown, had never been to, and also took charge of the ordering, informing Murray what he liked and what didn't agree with him, and promising Karp that he'd love whatever arrived. She also gave a stream of advice to the waiter about how she wanted the food prepared. Karp thought that he would have strangled the woman after a week of marriage, but it was clear that Selig doted on her, and didn't mind, in fact positively enjoyed, being managed.

"I think we're doing very well," said Naomi after the food had arrived, looking at Karp. "You wiped Fuerza off the map, the rat."

"Well, he was an easy target," Karp allowed. "There was documentary evidence contradicting all the charges except one . . ."

Naomi uttered the name of the vice-president who had died under odd circumstances.

". . . right, that one," Karp continued. "But even there we had two docs who'd been at the meeting and contradicted the charge. But we can expect them, when it's their turn, to drag in some guy who'll swear Murray carried on for an hour about how the great man spent his last moments popping his rocks."

"This duck is too soggy," said Naomi. "It should be crispy on the outside. Even if they do, it's their witness against ours."

"True, but . . ."

Naomi caught his tone and returned a sharp look. "But what?"

"Scuttling Fuerza was the easy part. The Bloom charges didn't leave a paper trail. Bloom's a better bureaucrat than that. Also, we have the where-there's-smoke-there's-fire problem with the jury. Even if we're able to show that the charges per se are all trumped up, the jury's going to be thinking, if this guy's such a sweetheart, why did all these senior public figures go out of their way to screw him? We don't have the answer to that."

"I do," said Naomi. "Sandy Bloom, that *momser*!"

Karp nodded, suppressing irritation. "Yes, I agree. And we've said that to one another over and over again, and we're still not any closer to anything I can tell a jury. I can oppose the individual charges, like I did with Fuerza, but at the end of the day I'd like to be able to stand up there and say, 'Ladies and gentlemen, these *momsers* tried to screw an honest man because . . .' and it can't just be 'because he's a son of a bitch according to the plaintiff's wife.' "

Selig chuckled at this, but Naomi was not amused. She gave Karp the Look, to which he responded with a disarming grin. She decided to return to the original subject. "Assuming we never learn the reason, what happens?"

"Well," said Karp, "in that case, after we destroy the substantive charges, they get a free throw at Murray. I've explained this, right, Murray?"

"Yeah," said Selig around a mouthful of lobster Cantonese, "the chickadees. And the snake."

Naomi's eyes widened. "What? Chick-a-whats?"

"These are legal terms, Naomi," said Selig with a wink at Karp. "Butch thinks they'll bring something in from left field to blacken my name. Like, I beat my wife."

Mrs. Selig's unamusement increased; she was not used to being winked at, nor was she accustomed to remarks of that nature from her husband. She moved to redress the balance. "Well, if that's the case, we're home free; Murray's only vice is leaving his dirty underwear for the maid to pick up."

Murray blushed and coughed and swallowed some water, and Naomi breezed on to topics of more general interest. "Speaking of beating, you remember, Murray? That woman whose name I can never remember got beaten in the park the other night, the one who wrote that piece in the *Times* about Butch. She had something in the *Voice* late last year. Terrible! This city . . ." She lifted her eyes to heaven and expertly snagged the last sweet-and-sour shrimp.

"Irene somebody," offered Selig.

"No, it wasn't Irene, Murray. Something much weirder."

"Ariadne Stupenagel," said Karp.

"That's it," said Naomi. "As a matter of fact, that article was the reason we thought of you in the first place. You'd think somebody like that would be smarter than to go into that end of the park in the middle of the night."

Naomi and her husband then drifted into a common upper-middle-class New York topic, Nothing Is Safe Anymore, including the usual vignettes about previously "safe" buildings raided by no-goodniks, friends who'd been mugged, and the extreme measures they all had to take to protect themselves. Karp nodded and put in a phrase or two, not really listening. Something nagged at the edges of his mind, some connection waiting to be made. He began to feel slightly dizzy and claustrophobic, but whether from the MSG in the food or Naomi's chatter he could not tell.

They finished eating; the waiter came and cleared. Selig wanted to order pineapple ice cream; Naomi mentioned his arteries; Selig asked who was the doctor. Naomi said it was his funeral, but not to expect her to attend. Selig asked Karp whether it would hurt his chances if he beat his wife just this once. In this way the conversation came around to the phrase Karp was waiting for, all unknowing.

"Speaking of damaging material," said Selig, "did you ever find out whether there was anything to that story about a D.A.'s investigation of the M.E.?" Karp didn't answer. "Butch?"

"Huh? Oh, right—no, that seems to have been a

rumor . . ." He stopped talking, his face slack, his eyes staring at nothing. The Seligs shared a concerned look.

"Butch, is . . . something wrong? Need a Gelusil?"

Karp snapped to, showing intensity now. "No, I'm fine," he said. "Look, Murray, I want you to come back to my place after court this afternoon. There's something I want you to take a look at."

FOURTEEN

Karp and Marlene sat at their round dining room table and watched Murray Selig look at photographs of corpses. Marlene had turned the track lighting up to its highest setting and brought her halogen desk lamp in from her office, so that the cozy domestic space shone with the unforgiving light of the autopsy room. As Selig studied each picture with the aid of a hand lens, Karp studied Selig. The man was not happy. Oddly enough for someone who had been fired for purported deviations from procedure, Selig was in fact a procedural fanatic. He did not at all like being asked to view unofficially obtained autopsy snaps, and even before he sat down to look at them, he had argued vehemently against the possibility of coming to any valid conclusions from photos alone.

Forty minutes passed. Karp got up once to go to the bathroom, and Marlene went to her office to call her service and answer some calls. Business was brisk, although many of the calls were from women who wanted their exes beaten up on general principles or frightened into coming across with child support. Returning to the dining room after several unpleasant conversations with angry women, Marlene found that Selig had put his magnifier down and removed his glasses.

"Done?" she asked.

Selig rubbed his eyes and looked up at her bleakly. "As done as I'm going to get. Are you two going to tell me what this's about? I'll tell you right now, I don't like it at all." In his mild way, he was quite angry.

Karp said, "Murray, first you have to tell us, is there anything fishy about the finding of suicide in these?"

"Fishy?" Selig looked away. Karp knew from past experience that Selig was extremely loath to contradict the findings of other pathologists, especially any who had worked for him in his former position.

"Yeah, fishy," Karp pressed. "Did the two kids who supposedly hanged themselves really do it?"

Selig put his glasses back on and furrowed his brows. "It's really impossible to state authoritatively without an examination of the bodies," he said sententiously, lifting the stack of photographs and letting them drop.

"Murray, damn it!" Karp said, his voice rising. "You're not in court on this. You were clucking like a mother hen looking through those pictures. Will you please for crying out loud tell us what you saw!"

"I don't see why—" Selig began huffily, but Karp cut him off with a look and a warning snarl.

"Okay. There was no reason for Dr. Rajiv to have noticed it, but seeing the Ortiz and Valenzuela shots together . . . look, here are the posterior photographs. It's the ankles."

Both Karp and Marlene stared at the backs of two pairs of dead men's legs.

"What are we supposed to see?" asked Marlene.

"You can see them better with the lens. Notice the transverse bruising on the posterior surface of the Achilles tendon. The bruising runs around the foot just distal to the medial malleolus."

They looked and agreed that there was a mark there, in the same place on both corpses.

"What does it mean?" asked Karp.

"Well, the funny thing is, the marks on the throats of the two men are just right. They were made by hanging: that is, their bodies, the neck tissues, that is, were pulled with their own weight, at least, against the suspending fabric. There's the characteristic inverted-V bruising. But the marks on the ankles are like mirror images, if you will, of the neck bruises. Which could suggest that, well, a rope was passed around the ankles and force applied in a direction opposite to that exerted at the neck."

"Murray, in plain English," said Karp, "are you suggesting that there might have been foul play here?"

"Let's say it's a plausible hypothesis," said Selig carefully. "If you wanted to fake a suicide hanging, there are two ways you could do it. One is, you tie somebody up and actually hang them from a fixed point, like in an old-style execution. The other way is do the whole thing horizontally. You tie a rope around their neck, tie that to a solid object, tie a rope to their feet, and heave. You'd need considerable strength to do that, though, or some mechanical help. To get the neck bruises to look right you'd need to exert a force equal to the weight of the victim, in these cases in the hundred-and-thirty-pound range."

"I don't understand," said Marlene. "Why would anyone go through the trouble of killing someone that way?"

Selig shrugged. "Hell, I don't know. People do funny things to people. If you just showed me the picture cold, without knowing it was a prisoner, I would've said a sexual ritual gone wrong. Knowing it's a prisoner, I'd guess . . . torture? A little sadism? The killer wanted to be in control. The pulling part, I mean." He cleared his throat and there was a moment of silence while they all thought.

"Gone wrong," said Karp at last, almost to himself.

"Yeah," said Selig. "And now that you've dragged me up here to show me this stuff and bullied me into speculation, would you mind telling me what this is all about?"

"One more question, Murray," said Karp. "You didn't do these autopsies yourself. Why not? A prisoner death? Two prisoner deaths?"

"When did they occur?"

Marlene told him the dates.

Selig wrinkled his brow. "Oh, right. It's because in late April and early May I was laid up. I threw my back out playing tennis. I played two sets with no problems and then I reached down to pick up some balls and that was it. For about a month I couldn't take standing up to do an autopsy."

"Uh-huh, they got lucky," said Karp. "And by the time you got back, the M.E.'s office had declared them genuine suicides, and we know you hate to second-guess your people. But, even with photographs, just now, you spotted this . . . discrepancy. If a full-scale investigation had taken place about these deaths, and you reviewed this material, you *definitely* would have spotted it, right?"

"Of course. Why, what are you driving at?"

"How about your successor, Dr. Kloss?" asked Karp, ignoring the question. "Would he have spotted the phony hangings? From photos?"

"What? How should I know what he would or . . ."

"Come on, Murray! Would he have?"

Selig huffed a great breath and threw up his hands. "Honestly? The guy's a hick county pathologist, he doesn't have serious experience with the variety of situations that I've had. Besides which, between us, the guy's a *patzer*. So, no, he probably wouldn't have. And the point of all this is. . . ?"

"The point of all this, Murray," Karp said with a wolfish smile, "is that he wouldn't and you did, and somebody *knew* you would, that you would have made it a *point* to do a jailhouse suicide autopsy, and that's why you got canned."

Selig's face paled and he opened his mouth to

speak, but nothing emerged. He made a helpless gesture with his hands and shook his head.

"Yeah, I know," said Karp. "It's hard to believe that we're looking at a cover-up of a police murder Murders. But it's the only thing that makes sense."

"You're implying," Selig said in a strained voice, "that Bloom was . . . *involved* in this?"

Karp nodded. "Right. For some reason he couldn't afford a finding of foul play in these cases, which he knew was a possibility as long as there was an independent M.E. on the job—you, in fact." Karp sighed and rubbed his face.

"Meanwhile," he continued, "now that we know this, we're in potentially deep trouble with respect to your civil case. I don't know exactly what violation we've all just committed here, examining illegally obtained forensic records, but until we have the whole story, this session is going to have to be kept dark. I just spent a whole afternoon convincing a jury that Murray Selig follows procedure to the letter, and now I've conspired with you to make an end run around strict legality."

Selig frowned. "Then why—?"

"Obviously because I made the call that finding out about the genesis of this . . . plot was more important than keeping pure on minor procedure. That'll turn out to have been the right call once we get the whole thing pieced together. Then Bloom will have a lot bigger worry than winning a civil case. We can make up a plausible fairy tale for the judge about how you came to cast your eye over these pictures, but your sin will seem so tiny compared to Bloom's that it won't matter."

"The whole thing," said Marlene, quoting him. "You mean, why he'd cover up for a bad cop?"

"Exactly. He's certainly not doing it out of misguided loyalty. These cops must have something big on him, something worse than accessory after the fact to murder."

"I can't believe this," said Selig, stricken. "The D.A.? Look, surely there's somebody we can go to who could deal with this officially?"

"Like who?" Karp challenged. "I can just see it. The discredited medical examiner, fighting for his job? concocts a smear against his accuser with no evidence other than his own opinion that some illegally obtained photographs point to murder rather than suicide, an opinion his own staff rejected. Gorgeous! No, Doc, we're going to have to get a lot deeper into this and find the reason Bloom did something this dumb. And until we find out for sure what it is, none of this"—he picked up the autopsy photographs and dropped them on the table—"ever happened."

"So, what did you find out? Did you get the records?" Stupenagel was sitting up in bed, sipping through a straw from a large pink plastic pitcher that Columbia-Presby Hospital had filled with ice water, and Marlene Ciampi, her visitor, had filled with a quart of daiquiri mix and a half pint of Bacardi. Stupenagel was a good deal perkier than she had been the week before. Much of the bandaging had been removed, revealing a face colored like a relief map of Nepal, with many amusing mauves and ochres, joined as by railroads with lines of black stitchery.

Marlene hesitated before answering. Her friend observed it. They had cut down her meds enough to restore the old gimlet eye. "What's the matter? Did you get it or not?"

"Yeah, well, I did, Stupe, but there's a situation here."

"What kind of situation? Were they phony suicides or not?"

"Yeah, they were, apparently, but I can't really talk about it. It involves one of Butch's cases."

Stupenagel put down her drink and fixed Marlene with her ghastly raccoon eyes. "Excuse me, there must be something wrong with my hearing. Did you just say that you're intending to cover up a couple of murders so that hubby can win a case?"

"Oh, for chrissake, Stupe, don't be dumb!"

"Okay, I'll be smart. Let's see how much brain damage I've suffered. A case, she says. What case could that be? Well, old Butch is suing the City because they fired what's-his-face, the medical examiner—no, don't tell me . . . Martin? no, Murray . . . Selig! So, we have a medical examiner and phonied autopsies. Let's say, Marlene gets these records from . . . somewhere—an old friend of hers, or Selig's maybe—and Marlene gets Selig to look at them, tell her what he thinks. But no, why should Selig do something faintly crooked just to help Marlene, who's just doing a favor for a poor, decrepit friend? And besides, hubby would never allow it, the last thing he wants is his client doing something naughty, and so . . ." She paused for effect. "That must mean that the murders of these kids have a *connection* with the case, that helps make the case that Selig was framed. Oooh, I'm getting goose bumps. This is even a better story than I thought. So what's the connection? The M.E. gets fired because . . . because somebody is afraid that an independent medical examiner will spill the beans on the gypsy cab murders, and they want a malleable schmuck in there. So who's the somebody? Two candidates: the Mayor and the D.A. How am I doing? Getting warm?"

"No comment," said Marlene stiffly. Then, in a feeble attempt to change the subject, she asked brightly, "So, when're you getting out of here?"

"Marlene, don't be a jerk."

"I bet you'll want to take a nice vacation back home in Ohio," Marlene continued. "Say, a couple of months, spend the holidays with the folks, get some skiing in . . ."

"In Ohio? What is this message I'm receiving here, Champ? You don't want me to write this story? Mayor or D.A. covers for killer cops?"

"Not 'don't write it,' but wait. The story isn't complete, and if it leaks halfway it's going to warn the bad guys, one, and two, not that you would care, but it'll screw up Butch's case, fuck a really decent guy, and put a big crimp in our extravagant income. Butch

is hanging out on this case—his boss didn't want him
to take it in the first place—"

"Why not?"

"Because he's tight with the Mayor. It was embarrassing to have one of his people sue the City and
His Honor personally."

"So the Mayor is running this cover-up?"

"No, Bloom," said Marlene quickly.

Stupenagel raised an eyebrow, a disturbing sight
with her face in the condition it was in. "Why
Bloom?"

"Because," Marlene began, and then stopped when
she realized that it had never occurred to either her
or Karp that it was anyone other than Bloom. "Because, ah, the Mayor has no real contact with the
M.E.'s office. The D.A.'s office is involved with it
every day."

The reporter's face twisted into a disbelieving grimace. "Marlene, that makes no sense at all. If Selig
is actually being fired to help cover up a crime, then
either the Mayor or the D.A. could be the source of
the cover-up. Or both of them together."

"It's not the Mayor," said Marlene, sounding more
confident than she now felt.

"Why not? I can think of a lot of things that the
Mayor might like to cover up. A fifty-four-year-old
confirmed bachelor? Maybe Vice caught him in an
alleyway with an underage leatherboy. No, you're
just fixated on Bloom, you and Butch, because he
tried to fuck you. This is the last act of this vendetta

that those two have been running for the last—what is it now?—eight or so years."

"Bullshit, Stupe! The Mayor's guy said he barely knew who Selig was until Bloom began needling about how he had to be canned."

"The Mayor's guy? Oh, *there's* an unimpeachable source! So, meanwhile, tell me what Bloom's supposed to be covering up that's important enough for him to help a bad cop shitcan a pair of custody murders!"

"We don't know yet," said Marlene weakly.

"You don't know yet," the reporter mocked. "But you don't mind asking me to sit on my story indefinitely until something turns up."

"You wouldn't have a damn story," snapped Marlene, "if I hadn't got those pictures, and if Butch hadn't got Murray to look at them."

"Yes, but what have you done for me lately? Sorry, Marlene, but for the next three to six weeks I'm going to be huddled in my room like the Phantom of the Opera with nothing to do but work the phone and pound keys, and this just became my only priority. I mean, I don't expect to be dating much until they fix *this*"—here she indicated her damaged face— "speaking of which, somebody's going to pay for *this* big-time, not so much because of me personally, but because—and I know you think I'm totally cynical and don't believe in anything, but I do and this is it—because you're not supposed to beat up on the press, at least not with your fists, not in this country anyway, and I say this as someone who's spent most of her adult life in countries where it's practically the national sport. And so, while I feel bad about Selig and Butch and anybody else who might get singed in the back blast . . ." She left the sentence hanging.

Marlene said, "All right, let me appeal to your journalistic instincts, since you've all of a sudden turned into Ida Tarbell, girl muckraker: grant me it'd be a better story if it was complete, if we knew who had set up the firing, and what the cops had on him to make him do it."

Stupenagel paused for barely a second. "Granted. And. . . ?"

"I'll find out for you," said Marlene. "I'll find out and wrap the whole package up for you like a fish, and you can relax and get better."

"Your concern is touching," said Stupenagel. "How long do you think this miracle will take?"

Marlene pulled a figure out of the air. "Five, six weeks."

"Mmm, would that be just enough to get a judgment in re: Selig?"

"I have no idea," said Marlene stiffly.

"I bet." Stupenagel took up her drink again and sipped it until the straw sucked dry. "I don't know, Marlene, it's an interesting offer, but . . ."

"You haven't heard the downside," said Marlene. "You don't have the photographs, and all you have to indicate that the jail deaths weren't suicides is my word about what Selig said. Shaft me on this, and not only will you not get the autopsy shots, but I'll deny this conversation ever took place, nobody will admit anything about any murders, and when I do figure it all out, I will deliver the *whole* story, with evidence, to whomever I figure will piss you off the most. Jimmy Dalton, for example."

Jimmy Dalton was a police reporter for the *Post* and a male chauvinist of citywide reputation. Stupenagel slammed her drink down on the bedside table, making the ice in it rattle like maracas. She glared at Marlene for what seemed like a long time, and then abruptly burst into laughter. "Goddamn, Champ—playing hardball with your old buddy! Jimmy Dalton, my ass! Okay, deal. Go get 'em! Don't get killed, though."

"I have a gun."

"No kidding? Can I see it."

"Oh, shit, Stupenagel! You're worse than my daughter."

From the hospital Marlene journeyed downtown by cab to the courthouse on Centre Street. She passed through the guarded entranceway to the part of the building that housed the D.A.'s office, using for the purpose an expired pass from the days when she'd had a right to be there. There was a search point in the main entrance for regular people, and she did not want to have to explain her pistol. Once in the courthouse, she filed some protective orders for clients, attended a hearing for a man who had violated one, and generally behaved like a lawyer for the rest of the morning. When the courthouse emptied out for lunch, she bought yogurt and coffee at the ground-floor snack bar, returned to the D.A.'s offices, and took the elevator to the sixth floor, where she entered a cubicle and made herself at home.

She was on the phone when the office's official occupant, Raymond Guma, walked in, sucking on a toothpick. Guma was a short, tubby man in his late forties, with an amusingly ugly monkey face and a mop of thinning black curls. He frowned when he saw Marlene sitting in his chair, speaking over his phone.

"Hey, didn't we finally get rid of you?"

Marlene continued with her phone conversation, but reached into her shoulder bag and pulled out a long white box: a fifth of Teacher's scotch. She placed it on the desk and gave Guma her brightest insincere smile.

Guma seated himself in a visitor's chair and ostentatiously twiddled his thumbs while humming loudly without tune. Marlene finished her conversation quickly.

"Anybody I know?" asked Guma, indicating the phone.

"Could be. A gentleman who won't take no for an answer. I was arguing the prudence of doing so."

"Or you'll get your goon to dance on his face? I been hearing stuff about you, Champ. You keep it up with the heavy shit, you gonna give the Italians a bad name."

"Sorry you don't approve, Raymond."

"You know me, a woman's place is in the home." He removed his toothpick, examined it, and flicked it into a large brown glass ashtray in which two White Owl butts already nestled. "How's Butch, by the way? I hear he's making out like a bandit."

"We're doing okay. Look, Goom, I need a favor . . ."

Guma tapped the white package. "Ah, see, here I was thinking, you're sorry for all the mean things you said to me, you decided to retire from being a witch, come by with a little present for an old pal . . ."

Guma's tone was sarcastic, but Marlene sensed a genuine sadness underneath it, the sadness of someone who had worked in an office for a long time—it was nearly twenty years for Ray Guma—and had worked with a group of people, had shared struggles with them, triumph and defeat, and had seen them pass on, with many a promise to keep in touch, which promises had trickled out into a few uneasy evenings after work. In fact, neither she nor Karp had much in common with Guma outside the work of the D.A. Guma, divorced, estranged from his kids, was into after-hours clubs and cocktail waitresses. Impulsively, Marlene got up from behind the desk and planted a wet kiss on Guma's mouth.

"Hey, Goom, you know we love you. Butch has been real busy, but as soon as we get a break, you'll come over, you'll eat, drink some wine. I'll make pasta fagiol'."

Guma's face broke into a smile, and he made a friendly grab at her ass. She allowed the familiarity. Guma was harmless.

"This must be some favor. Who do I have to whack out?"

She sat on the edge of the desk and said, "It's nothing, really. I just need you to call Fred Spicer and find out whether the D.A. squad is running an investigation on the medical examiner."

"That's it? Whyn't you ask him yourself?"

Marlene laughed. "Because Fred wouldn't tell me there was a fire if the building was burning down. You know Fred."

"Yeah, I do. Okay, I'll make the call." He rose and picked up his phone, then hesitated. "Just a second— how come you want to know?"

"It's a long story, Goom."

He replaced the phone and sat down again. "That's okay. I got time." He grinned, showing crooked, gap-spaced teeth.

Marlene sighed and spun out the tale, omitting any reference to Ariadne Stupenagel, which was something like painting the Last Supper without Jesus, but necessary, since some years back Ms. Stupenagel had taken up Ray Guma during a period when he had information about a story she was writing and, after it was published, had dropped him on his head. Thus, in this version it was Marlene, working for Karp, who had discovered the phony suicides, and she made it sound as if the sole point of the inquiry was helping Butch with the Selig case.

When she was finished, Guma asked, "You really think some cop at the Two-Five killed a couple of beaner cabbies?"

"Hey, how should I know, Goom? I'm out of the business. My only concern right now is seeing if someone is trying to pin fucked-up autopsies on Murray Selig."

Guma gave her a hooded look and dialed his phone. Spicer, the longtime chief of the D.A. squad, was in, and Guma spent the obligatory time talking Knicks and Rangers, after which he put the question. Marlene was able to follow the answer via Guma's end of the conversation. When he hung up, she said, "No investigation?"

"None that Fred knows about. Of course, it might be somebody else doing the investigating."

"No, Guma, the people at the morgue told her—I mean, told me—that the guy said he was from the D.A. Besides, who else could it be?"

"Well, if a cop's involved, it could be I.A.D."

She shook her head. "No, Devlin at I.A.D. swears they got nothing going on. And plus, they bought the suicide story, so why would they be poking around to see if it was legit?"

"I don't know, kid. The snakes are a devious bunch. I tell you who you could talk to, though— Johnny Seaver."

"Seaver? That name rings a bell. A cop, right?"

"Yeah. He's on the D.A. squad."

"He is? I don't remember him at all."

"He came on after your time," Guma explained, "earlier this year, maybe April, May."

"And why is he important?"

"Well, for one thing, he transferred in from the

Two-Five, so if anything is going on funny up there, he might have a clue. Another thing, he made detective second real early for no reason anybody could see. That means he's either got a rabbi way up at the tip of Police Plaza—"

"Or he's a snake?" Marlene was confused. She knew that the NYPD recruited cadets right out of the academy to work in its Internal Affairs Division, policing the police, and that these men tended to be promoted early to make up for the hardships of spying on brother officers, but she couldn't understand why the bosses would waste a snake in the small D.A. unit charged with investigating public corruption and doing humble chores for the A.D.A.'s.

"Not exactly," said Guma. "He could be a snake on ice. He got blown in some cop sting, and they wanted him parked out of the way until they figured out what to do with him. Why I say that is that Fred told me he just showed with a name-requested letter from Bloom, which means it came from pretty high up in the cops: superchief or above."

Marlene glanced at her watch. If she didn't leave right now, she was going to be late picking up Lucy. She gathered her bag. "Okay, I'll give him a ring," she said, and then leaned over and patted Guma on the cheek. "*Paisan*, thanks a million for this. I'll call you, okay?"

"Yeah, whenever. By the way, you ever see that friend of yours, you know, Queen Kong?"

"Ariadne? Yeah, from time to time."

"Yeah, well, next time you see her, tell her *fuck you* from me."

At the school Marlene extracted Lucy from a knot of Asian girls, refused Lucy's whispered request to show them the gun, and walked to the car. She noticed Miranda Lanin playing with another group in the schoolyard and then spotted her mother coming down the street. Marlene waved and smiled, to which Carrie returned a stiff nod of recognition and walked on by. She had not seen Carrie Lanin since her tormentor had been convicted, and clearly the woman was not interested in renewing their relationship.

"Are you still friends with Miranda?" Marlene asked her daughter as they entered the yellow VW.

"She's too babyish," Lucy pronounced dismissively. "I have another tooth loose."

"We'll alert the tooth fairy. So, who do you hang with now? Janice Chen?"

"Sometimes. But my special best friend is Isabella. Are we going there now?"

"Yeah, I thought we'd drop by," said Marlene. She started the car and pulled carefully around the waiting schoolbuses. "Isn't Isabella a little old for you, dear? She's—what?—fifteen?"

"She's fourteen. Her birthday's in January."

"Really? She told you this?" Nod. "What else did she tell you about herself?"

"Um, stuff. Could we have a birthday party for

her? When she gets fifteen, you're supposed to have a big party," she said.

"Well, we'll see, but honey, you know Isabella—well, if she's talking to you, then you're the only one she talks to. Besides her brother, Hector. We don't know where she comes from or who her parents are or what happened to her, so if you know any of that stuff, it's really important for you to tell me."

"She got raped," said Lucy.

Marlene gasped and stared at her seven-year-old child.

"Um, dear, what do you know about rape?"

"Everything," said Lucy blithely. "I read it in a little book in the shelter. It had pictures. It's when bad men hurt ladies with their penis."

Marlene gulped and it was a moment before she found her voice. "And did Isabella tell you how this happened?"

"Bad soldiers shot her daddy with guns and cut him up, and then they ran away, Isabella and Hector and Isabella's mommy. On a boat. They had to sit under the fish, and she was real scared."

"This was in Guatemala?"

"No, in San Fanisco. That's where she lived."

"San Francisco?"

"Uh-huh. Then they came here and the bad soldiers chased them and Isabella got raped. And they raped her mommy too, and all the ladies got raped and they burned down their houses. That's how come she doesn't have any clothes or toys. We could buy her some clothes for her birthday, couldn't we, Mommy?"

"Yes, of course—but, Lucy, did Isabella tell you her last name? Or where her mommy lives?"

Lucy shrugged and turned her face toward the side window. After a minute or so, she said, "She's not supposed to tell 'cause of the bad soldiers. Hector says she has to stay at Mattie's shelter until Hector is big and has a gun and kills all the bad soldiers. Then they could go to school."

At the shelter Marlene sent Lucy to the playroom and went to see Mattie Duran.

"They killed my cat," Mattie announced when Marlene entered.

"Oh, shit! Megaton? When?"

"Last night. He got out through a window and went down the escape. We found him all cut up on the sidewalk in front this morning. The bastards!"

"You know who did it?"

"Oh, it has to be one of our gentleman callers. We get cruised pretty regularly by guys chasing our residents. One of them must have seen the cat come out." She moved a pile of papers off a rickety side chair and gestured for Marlene to sit. "So, I hope you've got a cheery story for me, like, you ripped some shithead's lungs out."

"I don't know about cheery, but interesting. It's about the mystery girl." Marlene recounted the garbled story she had heard from Lucy.

"It's amazing," said Mattie when she was through,

"nine months with her lip buttoned, and then she spills it all to your kid." She seemed almost affronted.

"But what do you make of it? It seems like a . . . a fantasy, or a bad dream."

"Lots of those down south," said Duran. "Nightmares, with real blood. No, I think it sounds like what Isabella remembers, or as much as an American seven-year-old could take in and tell you. Isabella got caught in a raid in Guatemala or El Salvador, her father was killed, and she escaped with her mother and brother. Then something else happened, here in the City, and the family split up."

"What, you think some Central American regime actually sent agents up here to chase refugees?" asked Marlene, her tone incredulous.

"It's been known, girl. The Chilean junta killed a dissident in the middle of Washington, D.C., a couple years back. If the family all saw something they shouldn't have . . ."

Marlene was at that moment thinking about Ariadne Stupenagel and the possibility that she was barking up the wrong tree looking for her attackers in a New York police station.

"But what about the San Francisco part? You think they chased them across the whole country?"

"That's where you're being gringocentric," said Duran with a tight smile. "I doubt very much that she meant the city in California. There must be a couple hundred places in Latin America called San

Francisco something-of-another. I think she was talking about her hometown. I could check."

"Yeah, and look: if Isabella's talking to Lucy, maybe we should arrange to give them some more time together. Why don't I invite Isabella home with me tonight? Hector too."

After a brief pause Duran shrugged and said, "It's okay by me. If she'll go."

FIFTEEN

Isabella would come, it turned out, nervously and with many a hesitant step, out of the shelter, into the yellow car, and up to the loft. Hector, her perhaps brother, invited himself along. They sat together silently in the backseat while Lucy chattered like a tour guide, pointing out the neighborhood attractions. Hector held the girl's hand, stroking it gently and whispering in some hissing language that Marlene could not make out from the driver's seat. It was not Spanish.

Somewhat to Marlene's surprise, neither of the shelter children were the least bit frightened of the dog, Sweety. Hector pulled its loose skin, and when it licked Isabella's face, it elicited a ghostly smile and a near giggle, after which banana bread with butter and Ovaltine were served in the kitchen.

"We have big dog. Had," said Hector, patting Sweety and surreptitiously slipping crumbs into the slobbering maw. "He was nice."

"Oh? Where was this?" asked Marlene, feigning mere politeness. "Where you used to live?"

"Uh-huh. Our house."

"Really? Where was your house, Hector?"

Hector turned his face away from her and looked around the loft with interest. "You got color TV?"

"Yes, we do," said Marlene. "So, Hector—you had a big dog. Do you have a dog where you live now?"

"No, the soldiers shooted it." The boy leaped from his chair and mimed shooting, with appropriate sound effects. "Is dead. Could we watch your TV now? A-team! A-team!" He leaped about the kitchen, spinning and kicking, playing all the parts in an action drama and humming suitable stirring background music. Before Marlene could stop him, he had snapped a clumsy karate kick at the table, which shook, bringing a glass half full of tan milk crashing to the floor. The dog jumped to its feet, snarled, and flashed teeth, never an amusing sight. Hector froze in a crouch. Isabella ducked under the table, her eyes shut, her hands covering her head. The first one to break the tableau was Lucy, who rose calmly from her chair and, tugging Marlene's shirt to get her attention, whispered in her ear, "He doesn't like grownups to ask him questions. It makes him sort of crazy."

Then Lucy scooted under the table and started to coax Isabella out. After that, and after cleaning the spill, they went to the room designated "gym" and played with Karp's rowing machine and Marlene's boxing stuff. Marlene changed into sweats and put on speed gloves and did a punching-bag demo, which impressed Hector no end, and then he tried to bat the bag around, not doing too well. Then Marlene lowered the bag on its well slide to give Lucy a crack at it. Lucy's expertise did not sit well with the boy, and he began slamming the body bag around, grunting and cursing under his breath. Marlene let him punch until he was sweaty and exhausted. It seemed to do him some good. He smiled and said, jerking his chin at Lucy, "I'm stronger than her."

Throughout, Isabella watched from a corner, wide-eyed and silent as a carved saint.

Marlene left the children in Lucy's room and went into her office to pay some bills and check her messages. After some time, she heard laughter, Lucy's high-pitched giggle, Hector's semi-manly chortle, and another, lighter laugh, one she hadn't heard before. She rose from her chair quietly, went next door, and peeked in. They were all on Lucy's bed, having a tickle and pillow fight with the stuffed animal menagerie. Lucy was making the animals talk, her usual nonsense, but clearly the height of wit to the other two. Isabella was laughing, and was utterly transformed by it, converted by an interlude of safety and nonsense from an icon depicting early death into what she really was—a child robbed of childhood.

Marlene gently closed the door. She was not as a rule sentimental about childhood, rather medieval about it in fact, un-American, which is what tends to happen to you when you run a sex-crimes unit for a while, and which accounted for much of her daughter's social precosity. Nevertheless, for an instant the horror beat in past the shield of ordinary life, the sure knowledge of what millions of people were doing to millions of children all over the world, not just in benighted nations like the miserable homeland of her two foundlings, but doubtless within a long throw to home plate of where she now stood, millions shrieking in pain, little spirits crushed under brutal heels, the ravaging of innocence, the great unfinished project of the twentieth century. Her eye watered and she had to struggle to suppress a painful sob.

Karp walked in, whistling. She went to greet him at the door, and hung on his neck and kissed him with intensity.

"What? I did something right for a change?" he asked when they came up for air.

"No . . . just . . ."

"What? Tell me."

"Nothing. Just . . . *life*."

An unusually loud gale of laughter floated through the loft.

"Lucy has guests," Marlene explained. "I think I'll allow an overnight."

"On a school night? Who is it? Janice?"

"No. A couple of kids from the shelter. They're sort of refugees."

They walked arm in arm back to the bedroom, where Karp began to change out of his court clothes.

"So, nice kids? What're they, Lucy's age?"

"No. They're older. She's about fourteen, he's about twelve. As to nice—that's probably not a good word. She's practically a zombie most of the time from some kind of traumatic damage. He's got a lot of anger, probably for a damn good reason. But playing with Lucy seems to help them, and Lucy, needless to say, is in paradise—big kid friends. Janice Chen is not in it."

A louder gale of laughter. "Lucy is making the animals talk," said Marlene.

"Always a crowd pleaser," said Karp, now dressed in jeans and a sweatshirt. "Let's check it out."

They walked down to Lucy's room. Karp beat a tattoo with his knuckles on the door and flung it open, crying, "What's all this laughing? No laughing allowed!"

Lucy giggled and said, "Hi, Daddy!"

Isabella froze and crouched in the corner of the bed, her face blanching and stiff with fright.

Hector sprang from the bed and stood between Karp and Isabella, his eyes darting, looking for escape routes, or weapons.

Lucy was the first to catch on. She put a comforting arm around the boy's waist and with her other hand stroked his arm, and told him in a soothing voice that it was only her daddy and that he wouldn't hurt them. Then she suggested that they all help Mommy make dinner. As she walked by the stunned Karp, she held out her arms and he picked her up and kissed her. She whispered in his ear, "They hate men."

"What the hell was that all about? When I came in to Lucy's room?" Karp and Marlene were sitting in their living room watching *Key Largo* in black-and-white when he asked this question, which he had carefully avoided during dinner and the lengthy process of bedding down the three children.

"Yeah, good thing he didn't have a knife," said Marlene. "They probably have bad experiences around strange guys bursting into rooms. Lucy tells a garbled story they apparently told her about being attacked by soldiers and her getting raped. He's a little confused about where all this happened, though, here or down there."

"They're orphans?"

"No one seems to know. Hector apparently lives on the streets and runs by the shelter every once in a while for hots and a cot." She sighed. "A heart-breaker—number eighty-nine thousand and four. Why are you looking at me that way?"

"I'm thinking about how you got Sweety. Picking up strays."

The mastiff, hearing his name, lifted his head and sniffed loudly, and then dropped it heavily to the oriental rug at their feet, where he was constructing a sizable lagoon of spittle.

Karp threw his arm over Marlene's shoulder and kissed her hair. "Are you thinking of adding an orphanage to your empire of good works?"

"Empire is right," she said. "Harry's got six cops working moonlight for him. He's a changed man."

"Really? I thought the cops couldn't stand him."

"As a cop, no. Harry doesn't fit the mold of the Job. They don't mind taking his money, though."

"You're making money?" said Karp incredulously.

"Yeah, smarty pants, we are. Mattie has money for the shelter people, some of her own, and some from foundations. And we have some celebrities—well, semi-celebrities. It turns out stalking's a problem for them big-time. I got that model, she pays us a retainer. A rock singer. A woman on the pro-tennis tour. And Karen Wohl. I just saw her the other day."

"This is a name I should recognize?"

"If you watch *Lust for Life* with us housewives. She plays Mary-Beth, the one with amnesia who's going out with her brother, unbeknownst. Nice kid. Some scumbag's sending her mash notes, I'll kill you if I can't have you, the usual. Anyway, Harry'll be opening a little office next week, in a loft on Walker. Speaking of money, how was your day?"

"We did good," said Karp after a moment's reflection. "I had James Warneke on the stand in the morning. He's the A.D.A. who supplied Bloom with the information about Murray and *People* v. *Lotz*."

"That's the snails in the snatch one?"

"Uh-huh. Mr. Warneke's memory proved to be foggy under examination. It turns out that Dr. Selig never actually hinted, implied, suggested, or in any way spoke in such a way as to lead a reasonable man to believe that he thought that the deceased had inserted snails in her vagina and thus that no possible disrespect for said deceased had ever been uttered. Then there was all the bullshit about lost evidence and the incompetence of the tour doctor, the hired physician on the case. I believe I was able to show that Mr. Warneke's training was deficient in that he did not appear to know what standard procedure for handling evidence was at a crime scene. We established beforehand that the cops are responsible for securing evidence at the crime scene, not the M.E., and further that the relevant evidence was not lost, although the poor schmuck didn't know where it was for a time. As far as the competence issue goes, we established that Warneke had used the damn tour doctor as an expert witness in Lotz's trial, praising his expertise to the skies."

"Seriously?"

"Yeah. Not a prepared witness. The whole thing's a zoo. The guy reflected the excellent training he got from his boss."

"Whose knowledge of criminal procedure is proverbial," said Marlene. "What happens next?"

"Same as with Fuerza's charges. Bloom made four: the Lotz things, one in *People* v. *Mann*, where Selig was also supposed to have lost evidence, *People* v. *Ralston*, where we have a young lady A.D.A. who says that Selig publicly humiliated her and refused to make himself available for testimony, and a couple, three charges in *People* v. *Girton*, which—"

"Girton? Isn't that the one where the gay guy killed his lover and confessed? Last year, right?"

"That's the one."

Marlene looked puzzled. "Correct me if I'm wrong, but didn't Murray *solve* that case? He was the one who redid the autopsy and showed that the guy who confessed really did it."

"Uh-huh. Girton walked into a precinct in tears

and confessed that he murdered his lover. The cops looked it up and found that the M.E.'s office had declared it a suicide and kicked the guy out. He kept coming back, and they kept giving him the boot, until the one detective they had there who wasn't brain-damaged figured there might be something in it and called Selig. Selig had the vic dug up and re-autopsied him and sure enough, the guy'd been strangled manually. Girton went with a plea of temporary insanity. I have his lawyer scheduled to testify that if not for Dr. Selig's skills, the case never would have been made."

Marlene laughed. "And they're dragging this out to demonstrate Selig's *incompetence*?"

"Yeah, I know," said Karp. "It's like the rest of it—makes no sense. The thrashing of wounded beasts. Anyway, a week, ten days from now, I'll have Bloom up on the stand. Then we'll see." He paused for a moment, then added, "Speaking of faked suicides, I need to get going on those kids who died in jail, but I'm not sure how to start. For sure I can't involve Stupenagel."

"Why not?" asked Marlene, although she well knew.

"Because if somebody went up and told her that the suicides were faked, she'd want to know how they knew, and that would lead to knowing that my plaintiff conducted an unofficial and probably not strictly lawful study in this very joint where we're sitting, which would be splashed all over the press in the middle of the trial in which we're painting him as the picture of probity, and that—" He stopped and looked at his wife's face. "Oh, shit, Marlene! Tell me you didn't tell her!"

"I didn't! She asked me about the autopsy records she asked me to get, and I had to tell her something or she would've tried to get them some other way and found out that we already had them. She guessed the rest. Don't look at me that way! It's her job and she's good at it."

Karp groaned and threw his head back against the sofa. "She's going to print this, right? When?"

"She's *not* going to print it. She said she'd hold off if I got the whole story and gave her the exclusive." She summarized the heated discussion she had had with Stupenagel at the hospital. Karp listened patiently until Marlene got to the reporter's suggestion that the Mayor might be involved in the cover-up.

"Oh, horseshit! It's Bloom."

"I'm just saying what she said."

"Don't tell me you agree with her?"

"I didn't say that. I just said it was a possibility. There was once a pretty good A.D.A. who used to say, 'Don't fall in love with your theory of the case.' "

It was, in fact, one of Karp's sacred maxims. He thought for a while and then announced, "Okay, fair's fair. I'll check it out. So, are you going to pursue this for us?"

"Us?"

"Yeah. You're a P.I., remember? I'll put you on the payroll. That way, anything you find out will be protected by confidentiality of counsel." He saw her hesitation and added vehemently, "Come on, Marlene! Otherwise it'll be a pain in the ass—we're working on the same case and keeping secrets from each other? It's not like we're in an office and I'm your boss. Besides, if you don't do it, I'll have to bring in somebody fresh who doesn't know the players and has half your brains and Stupenagel will get impatient and blow us out of the water."

After a brief but uncomfortable silence, Marlene nodded and said, "Okay, but no kibitzing! I run the investigation my way, me and Harry, and we tell you what we find."

"No problem," replied Karp sincerely.

"Okay. Let's start with where we are now. Paul Jackson is the obvious suspect. I.A.D. isn't investigating him actively because there's supposedly a hold on Jackson coming down from the D.A.'s, because of some big joint corruption investigation, but I talked to Guma and he says Fred Spicer says there's no investigation, which means . . ." She paused and stared at Karp. "What the hell does it mean?"

"It means that Bloom is generating the heaviest possible cover for Detective Jackson, and he's doing it directly, without involving his official people. God! What in hell could the little fucker have done?"

"Him or the Mayor; Bloom could be covering something the Mayor did."

"Yeah, yeah," agreed Karp for form's sake, "the Mayor too. By the way, Bloom didn't even tell Wharton. I saw that during deposition. When I asked him what happened in May to make him want to fire

Murray, he went white, and Wharton was obviously totally unprepared for the question. This is a very private party."

Karp rose and began pacing, his face blank with thought. He mumbled to himself in time with his steps, "What did he do, what did he do?" He stopped and spun, facing Marlene. "It was May. What happened last May? About the middle of the month. That's when it all started."

"The gypsies died before that," said Marlene.

"Exactly. They killed the two kids, hanged them somehow. They must have been scared shitless of a serious investigation. Everybody knew they were shaking down cabbies; the whole thing was set to blow up, and then they lucked out. They caught the D.A.—sorry, the D.A. or the Mayor—doing something that gave them a lock on any conceivable investigation—except an investigation cranked up by the one person they couldn't control. . . ."

Marlene slapped her thigh, a whipcrack sound that stopped Karp's musings.

"Seaver!" she cried. To Karp's puzzled stare she added, "They. You keep saying 'they.' I just realized who the other guy besides Jackson had to be, because Stupe got ripped off by two cops. A private party, you said: yeah, but not just Jackson and Bloom. Guma told me Bloom name-requested a cop from the Two-Five, a cop who got promoted mysteriously fast to detective second, a cop who's working in the D.A. squad, the same D.A. squad pulling this phony investigation routine. It's John Seaver. I'll bet he pulled those autopsy files from the M.E. And . . . I'll bet when we check, we'll find that Seaver's partner up at the old Two-Five was . . ."

"Paul Jackson," they both said in unison, and laughed.

Karp sobered quickly. "Fine, say Seaver and Jackson are it; what does that buy us? We have no evidence, no witnesses . . ."

"Stupe can ID them ripping her off as a cabbie."

"Uh-huh, a reporter's word against two cops. No, that's the problem, Marlene. We can't proceed in bits and pieces like in a normal criminal case. We need the whole enchilada, with proof, or we have nothing."

"I'll talk to Seaver," said Marlene. "Maybe he's bursting with remorse."

"Do that. I'll call Phil DeLino in the morning and lay this out for him, maybe it'll rattle some cages. If the Mayor's involved in any way, Phil'll start sniffing for a deal. If not, maybe we can get His Honor to start distancing himself from Bloom."

After that, they talked details: who would do what and when, and who would mind the kid, the companionable bargaining of married life, in which Karp found himself remarkably able to forget that his wife's career involved dealing with extremely nasty armed persons. Marlene made a pot of tea and they settled in to drink it, and munch on biscotti, and watch Bogart get the girl and send the bad guys to perdition.

"Do you think our life is becoming too much like

a movie?" said Marlene as the final credits rolled. "Excessively romantic?"

"Having second thoughts?"

"Oh, yeah," admitted Marlene, "and third and fourth ones. Don't think it doesn't cross my mind in the middle of some of the things I've been doing lately that I could be drafting contracts in some cozy office. Still, *somebody* must be living lives like they do movies about. I mean, Don Quixote was crazy, but there *were* actually knights, weren't there?"

Karp gave her a look that mingled love and apprehension and then adopted a more cheerful expression, replying Bogartly, "Whatever you say, shweetheart."

The next day Marlene dressed in civilian clothes, a plum-colored wool suit, with Ferragamo pumps and her glass eye, and went uptown to Dr. Memelstein's office for her six-month maternity checkup, where she received something of a shock, such that on leaving she repaired to a nearby cocktail lounge, where she ordered a Jameson's up, soda on the side, which, when it came, she decided not to drink, but sat there for a half hour, sipping the chaser.

She then called Harry Bello from a phone in the place.

"Harry, it's me. John Seaver, D.A. squad. Did you know him when you worked there? He started in the spring of last year sometime."

"To talk to. Why?"

"What's he look like?" asked Marlene, ignoring the question.

"Five eight, one sixty, brown hair, brown eyes, mustache, dark complexion. A dresser. Could be some P.R. in there. Why?" More insistently.

"Harry, I'll tell you the story later. Let's meet for lunch at the office. Bye."

After this, she took a cab down to the courthouse on Centre Street, where, using her old ID, she inveigled herself into the D.A. squad offices and lay in wait for John Seaver.

This is a guy in trouble, was her first thought when he walked in. He was a dresser, though. He wore a blue-gray Italian suit, with what was probably a Sulka, and the little tasseled loafers with the gold trimming that all the boys in narco like to wear. The face didn't fit the jaunty outfit: it had gone yellowish and soft-looking, like something was rotting it from inside, and the eyes were deeply shadowed. John wasn't getting his eight hours, Marlene concluded.

"Detective Seaver? I'm Marlene Ciampi," she said, standing in his path before his cubicle door and holding her hand out for him to shake. Which he did, limply. "I wonder if you could spare me a minute."

When they were seated in his space, she said, handing him a card, "I used to work here, but now I'm in private practice with Harry Bello, who used to work a couple of doors down. We've been retained by Bohm Landsdorff on the Selig case. You're familiar with it?"

"Uh, not really."

Marlene smiled charmingly. "Oh, well, neither am I, to tell the truth, but they asked me to clean up one little item, which is this investigation that the D.A. squad is apparently, supposedly, running on the medical examiner's office. Now, I've already checked through official channels, Lieutenant Spicer and all, and he doesn't know anything about it, and the defendants in this case, um, the Mayor, and the D.A., Mr. Bloom, they sure haven't shared any information about any investigation, like they're supposed to." She paused.

"Excuse me," said Seaver, "I don't understand why you're talking to me. If there's no investigation—"

"Oh, yeah, but see, Detective Seaver, the thing is, even though there's no investigation, *you've* been investigating. That's what sort of threw us."

"I have?" Coolly said, but Marlene saw his throat working.

"Uh-huh. You went down to the M.E.'s files and flashed your D.A. squad ID and pulled three sets of autopsy records and told them that it was part of an investigation." Guessing, but who else could it have been?

Seaver had to clear his throat. "No, I didn't."

Marlene breezed on, as if he hadn't spoken. "Yeah, and we thought it was kind of strange that it was you, considering the nature of the autopsies. The dead people, I mean. We thought, hey, if they thought there was something phony about the suicides, and if they thought that Dr. Selig had somehow screwed up in calling them suicides, why would they involve the very detective who arrested these kids? And probably interrogated them at the precinct. Or maybe it was just a funny coincidence."

Seaver was trying to assemble a shit-eating grin on his sallow face, but the pieces kept getting lost. "I really don't know what you're—" he started, but Marlene continued:

"Yeah, actually, you do. And we also contacted Tom Devlin at Internal Affairs. He's not interested in the suicides, because the M.E. said they were legit, but he was *real* interested in a gypsy cab shakedown racket up by the Two-Five, until he got orders from the D.A. to stop it, because it was part of a bigger investigation, a bigger investigation that does not seem to exist. Very peculiar. You wouldn't have any perceptions you'd care to share with me on any of this, would you, Detective?"

Seaver licked his lips, which looked raw and much chewed. "No, you lost me there. Look, I don't really see where I can help you, and I got things I have to do, so—"

"No problem," said Marlene cheerily, "I appreciate the time, and as a matter of fact, I have stuff to do too. But, you know, I'm sure we'll be running into one another again because, as I'm sure you know, as a professional detective, that when somebody's put together a really fancy scam, they always leave a few threads loose—hey, we're all human, right? You can't think of everything. But when somebody else starts to pull those loose threads, it's really hard to keep the whole thing from coming unraveled. Now, whoever put this together figured that Dr. Murray Selig would be the one pulling the threads because, you know, between you and me, Detective, two of those kids were murdered in custody—the suicide findings don't bear a second look—so, the thinking was, get rid of him and you're home free. And, really, it should have worked out fine. They had no way to figure that Selig would hire just the lawyer who had a wife whose friend was an investigative reporter investigating the mysterious deaths of a couple of gypsy cabbies, and that they would all put their heads together, and the whole thing would come unglued. By the way, pounding on Ariadne Stupenagel was a serious mistake, because it confirmed that the gypsy shakedowns were serious enough to kill somebody for. Another little pull on the tangle. In fact, I would say that in a little while all the principals in this scam are going to be running around like maniacs looking for some kind of a deal, and I would also say, speaking as an attorney now, that the very first person to come clean about the thing would get the best deal going. Wouldn't you agree, Detective?"

"I wouldn't know," said Seaver. His color was bad, and he seemed not to be able to stop swallowing.

Marlene rose. "So long, Detective Seaver. Call me if you think of anything that might be useful." She left him staring at her back.

It was a good while before he was able to begin stabbing a familiar number into his phone with shaking fingers.

* * *

"Twins?" Karp exclaimed.

"Yes, each with a little heartbeat, and didn't I need a drink when I heard it, and wasn't I a good girl not to have one?"

Karp shook his head and stared wonderingly at his wife. "Did you find out? I mean, girls, boys, mixed. . . ?"

"No, Memelstein offered to do a sonogram, but I said that if God wanted us to know that stuff in advance, He would have supplied us with little glass portholes." Marlene sat down in the bed. "My God! We'll have three children!"

"We can afford it," said Karp practically, sitting next to her. "Or will, if we win this case."

"Seaver has three kids," said Marlene musingly. "There was a picture on his desk. Three kids, no wifey. Probably a divorce. Maybe he's got money problems. It's probably why he went into it with Jackson, the shakedowns. The guy doesn't seem the type; I mean, a little easy graft, but nothing heavy—not murder, anyway. He's coming apart behind it."

Marlene filled Karp in about her interview that morning. "Will he crack, you think?" he asked.

"Maybe. When the hounds start getting closer. Which I will endeavor to arrange. Jesus, three kids!"

SIXTEEN

In examining notionally hostile witnesses, Karp had found that a kindly tone and punctilious courtesy answered better than the showy browbeat favored by many in his profession, unless, of course, he thought some jerk was trying to slip a whopper past him, in which case he could adopt a mien that could blowtorch paint. That lacking, he had learned, a civilized manner kept the judges happy and prevented any unwanted sympathy for the witness stirring in the breasts of the jury. Most remarkably, it also made most witnesses less hostile. Considerations of policy are almost never as strong as the natural human desire for respect and kindness.

Beyond this, the present witness, Assistant District Attorney Marsha Davis, inspired actual sympathy in Karp. Davis was a tall woman in her late twenties with a well-cut head of dark hair framing an unfortunate large-nosed face, short on chin and equipped (as if to make up for that deficit) with what seemed like more than the usual number of large, equinoid teeth. Ms. Davis had been the A.D.A. in *People* v. *Ralston*, a homicide case brought to trial in the previous year. According to Bloom's memo, Ms. Davis had complained that Dr. Selig had failed to return numerous telephone calls, that he had been insulting to her at a meeting in his office, at which another doctor had been present, and that he had not appeared in court when he should have, although he had been given four weeks' notice of the appearance, his failure to appear having disrupted the Ralston murder trial.

During the course of her testimony this morning, Karp had charmingly drawn from Ms. Davis that *Ralston* had been her very first homicide case, that she had received no specialized training in prosecuting homicides, and that she was unfamiliar with the practical operations of the medical examiner's office.

"Ms. Davis," said Karp, "how many assistant district attorneys are there working felonies?"

"I don't know. Maybe three hundred, something like that."

"Three hundred. And how many chief medical examiners are there?"

She narrowed her eyes: a trick question. "One."

"Do you think it's reasonable to expect the chief medical examiner to be at the beck and call of every assistant district attorney?"

"No, but . . ."

"For example, was there ever a time in your career where the lack of contact with the medical examiner's office impaired the prosecution of one of your cases?"

"No," said Davis, and seemed mildly surprised at her answer.

"Thank you. Now, you have indicated that three days before the trial in *Ralston* was due to start, you called Dr. Selig's office and told his secretary that you wanted him in court at nine-thirty on Monday, January 13, and that his secretary called you later in the day and said that Dr. Selig had a conflict and could not be there. What was your reaction to that?"

"I was angry."

"Yes, I'm sure you were. Because you had informed his office, I think it was, four whole weeks before the trial that you wanted him there—is that right?"

"Yes."

"Ms. Davis, how long did the trial in the Ralston case last?"

"Thirteen days."

"I see. Ms. Davis, did you imagine that the chief medical examiner of the City of New York was going to hold his calendar completely open for thirteen days waiting for your call for this one trial?"

A long pause. Ms. Davis had clearly not given the issue much thought. At the same time, although somewhat more vaguely, she understood that Karp was giving her the sort of training she had never once received from her own superiors. She said, frankly, "No, I guess I didn't think of that."

"Did you learn why Dr. Selig could not attend your trial at the time and place you desired?"

"He had a conflict, another trial."

"Another trial. I see. Now, did the district attorney's office, to your knowledge, make any attempt at coordinating its homicide cases so as to insure that Dr. Selig's time was efficiently used?"

"No, not to my knowledge."

"Thank you. Now, turning to the meeting you attended in Dr. Selig's office, in the presence of Dr. Prahwah, the forensic specialist from Detroit, whose testimony we heard the other day. Dr. Selig mentioned that fact, the lack of coordination, did he not?"

"Yes, he did."

"And the substance of his remarks was the inefficiency of the current arrangements of the district attorney's office with respect to trying homicides, was it not?"

"Yes."

"Would you say that Dr. Selig used vivid language in regretting the disbandment of the former Homicide Bureau by the present district attorney, Mr. Bloom?"

"Yes, quite vivid," said the witness with a slight smile.

Karp smiled back, all friends now. "And you reported this vivid language, language quite insulting to the competence and acumen of the district attorney, to your superior, Mr. Sullivan, one of the Felony Bureau chiefs?"

"Yes, I did."

"During this conversation in his office, did Dr. Selig at any time insult you personally, or hold you up to contempt before the eyes of his guest, Dr. Prahwah?"

"No, he did not."

"And when you asked him technical questions related to the Ralston case, did he answer them properly and professionally?"

"He was rather short with me. Impatient."

"Impatient. I see. How impatient, Ms. Davis? About as impatient as you would expect one of the most eminent forensic specialists in the United States to be when answering questions from a young and inexperienced prosecutor whose training has been neglected by her superiors?"

"Objection!" said Corporation Counsel Gottkind. "Calls for a conclusion."

"Withdrawn," said Karp. "Impatience, then, but no insult, no unprofessionalism?"

"No."

"In other words, Dr. Selig reserved all his criticism and insulting language for the way Mr. Bloom runs the D.A.'s office, is that true?"

"Yes."

"You won your case in the Ralston matter, did you not?"

"Yes."

"And Dr. Selig did at last testify at that trial?"

"Yes, he did. He came on after the defense had completed their presentation."

"And what was the quality of Dr. Selig's testimony?"

"It was excellent," said Davis in a positive voice. She had accepted the persona that Karp had provided for her: an intelligent woman working way over her head who had been sandbagged by her boss

"It was excellent. So, contrary to the allegations

made in the district attorney's memo, Dr. Selig's failure to attend the trial when you wanted him to in no way, quote, disrupted the conduct of an important murder trial, unquote?"

"No," said Davis. Her eyes shifted to where Conrad Wharton was sitting, glaring arrows at her, and quickly looked away. Then she added, "As a matter of fact, it was probably an advantage to have a prosecution witness at that time, after the defense had already been on."

"Thank you. No further questions," said Karp.

"You might as well shut us down, Marlene," said Harry Bello.

"Why? Because they're cops?"

She was pacing in a fury in front of Harry's desk. The desk was on the second floor of a Walker Street loft building that had just been renovated for commercial use. Harry's desk was under a nice Sam Spade-ish semicircular window that looked out on Walker just off Canal. Marlene intended to have an eye painted in gold leaf in the round center pane of the window. Assuming they stayed in business.

Harry's voice was impatient as he explained; Harry did not like explaining things. "We run on favors, Marlene. From the cops. From other investigators, ninety percent of them ex-cops. Word gets out we're doing a number on these two"—he shrugged—"pack it in."

Marlene was about to object that Seaver was ready to crack, that these particular cops were a disgrace to the Force, but thought better of it. Harry was himself a disgrace to the Force, and the Force had sheltered him, allowing him the opportunity for a few more episodes of brilliant service and an honorable retirement. It was the way things were with the cops; Marlene was a crusader but not an idiot. She moved on to other business.

"Karen Wohl?" she asked.

"Hubert P. Waley. Three-oh-six West Forty-ninth."

"Great! How?"

"Spotted outside the TV studio. My guy followed him. Got a Karen Wohl museum up in his crib. Typewriter that wrote the love letters, drafts. It's him."

"How did he know to follow him?"

Harry got up and went over to a file drawer, where he pulled out a file and handed it to Marlene. One of the two phones on his desk rang, and he picked it up. Marlene looked through the file, and her question was answered. There was a brief surveillance report noting that Waley had been seen standing at the same place across from the entrance to a Sixth Avenue TV studio; there was an eight-by-ten photograph of him along with it, and it was easy to see what had attracted the attention of Harry's moonlighting detective. Waley was a pear-shaped white man in his late twenties, with heavy black-rimmed spectacles, a flat, pasty face, and lank hair cut forties-schoolboy fashion. He was carrying a paper Macy's shopping bag. He might as well have been wearing a T-shirt inscribed "stalker" in red letters.

Harry got off the phone. Marlene tapped the file folder. "Contact?"

Harry held his hand palm down across the desk and waggled it slightly, fingers spread. It meant that in Harry's judgment this person was so flaky that a reasonable approach to him would be unavailing.

"What's the plan?" she asked.

"Report his ass. Get an order."

"Okay, I'll take care of it tomorrow. What else?"

Harry passed her a flat black object the size of a cigarette pack.

"A beeper? Gosh, Harry, this is getting so professional I got goose bumps."

"Use it," said Harry. "And Marlene . . . ?"

"Uh-huh, I know, Harry—stay away from Jackson and Seaver."

Marlene walked down to Canal, where she stopped at Dave's for an egg cream and a phone call. The call was to Tom Devlin, Stupenagel's contact at the NYPD Internal Affairs Division. She established herself as an anonymous snitch, providing a checkable fact (the theft of the autopsies from the M.E.'s office) and a tantalizing lead (that, whatever he had heard, there was no ongoing D.A. investigation of the gypsy cab shakedowns). She hung up, leaving him panting for more. It was stirring the pot, building the pressure on John Seaver and, perhaps, Paul Jackson, although Marlene thought that the big detective might be an entirely tougher customer than his former partner. Enough pressure and they might do something dumb. In any case she was, in a technical sense, staying away from directly investigating the two cops. In this way Marlene thought she was satisfying both her husband and her partner. She did not want ever to be in a position where she had to choose unambiguously between them. She was not at all sure how she would choose.

"We need to talk, Phil," said Karp. He was on the phone with Phil DeLino, speaking into one of a bank of phones on the ground floor of the courthouse, squeezed between a cigar-fuming bail bondsman and a whining drug merchant. "Let's have lunch. Today."

"Gosh, Butch, today's rough," said DeLino. "Can't it wait?"

"No, unless you want to read it in the papers. I'll meet you in Wing Fat's in twenty minutes."

The Wing Fat Noodle Company is a steamy, small room about the size and shape of a boxcar, slotted into an alley off Mott Street in Chinatown. It is permanently open and caters largely to illegal Cantonese manual workers. Its menus are mimeographed in Chinese only, and while it tolerates the white ghosts, it does not welcome them. It is one of the best public places in Manhattan for an indoor private conversation between non-Cantonese.

"Try the pork lo mein," said Karp, who was one of Wing Fat's rare Caucasian regulars. DeLino, who had never been to the place, looked around nervously and said, "Yeah, sure, whatever." Karp pointed at an item on the menu and held up two fingers. The scowling waiter nodded curtly, slammed a steel quart-sized pitcher of scalding tea down on the table, and left.

"I notice you didn't ask them to hold the MSG," said DeLino.

"Hold the dog meat is what you say here," said Karp. DeLino smiled tightly; Karp continued. "Phil, we got a bad situation, and I wanted to talk to you before anything happens, because even though we're on opposite sides of this lawsuit, I think you're basically a straight shooter and you wouldn't be mixed up in something like this."

"I'm flattered," said DeLino with a genuine smile.

"You should be," said Karp, straight-faced. "Okay, we have determined, to my satisfaction, that in March and April of last year two Hispanic prisoners, gypsy cab drivers, in custody of the Twenty-fifth Precinct, were murdered by police officers and their deaths disguised as suicides. They were passed as suicides by the medical examiner's office at that time, but we were able to make the autopsy reports available to Dr. Selig, and he has indicated that, in fact, this finding was in error. The prisoners were killed. They were killed by two detectives who've been running a shakedown of gypsy cabbies for months. We have independent confirmation of that, of the shakedowns." Karp paused to let that sink in. The waiter brought a pair of steaming bowls and slapped them roughly on the table.

"You'll recall," Karp continued, "that the first time we talked about this case, I asked you why Murray got canned. The only conclusion I can come to is that this is the reason. Somebody couldn't afford to have a first-class independent forensic expert in that slot, accent on independent. Somebody blocked any investigation by I.A.D. by claiming that the shakedowns came under a broader investigation run directly out of the D.A.'s office, but there's no such investigation. I presume you see the implications of all this. I also presume that you know me well enough to know that there's no way I'd be party to concocting a plot like this to gain an advantage in a civil case, especially one in which I seem to be beating the pants off you guys." Karp filled in a number of confirming details and started to slurp his noodles. DeLino didn't touch his.

After a minute, DeLino said, "It's not the Mayor. You're implying a massive criminal cover-up to protect two bent cops. The Mayor spends half his time on the mat with the Patrolmen's Benevolent Association and that Irish mafia up at Police Plaza. There's no way in hell they could offer him anything politically that would justify this."

"What about non-politically? He was felony naughty and these two shitheels caught him."

"It's barely possible," DeLino admitted, "but extremely, extremely unlikely. What could they have caught him doing? The guy has no life. He lives on his salary and spends ninety percent of his time on public business. His sex life is . . . let's just say his sex life does not involve felonious behavior. Is there graft? Yeah, as long as we're letting our hair down, there's the usual schmeering of bagels, but absolutely nothing, even if every tricky contract the City ran in this whole administration was blasted across the *Times*, nothing that would justify protection of murder. Plus, I'm telling you, and this is the key point, to my own certain knowledge, this firing idea did not originate in His Honor's bald little head."

Karp was glad to see that DeLino did not try to score lawyer's points with respect to Karp's statement of the facts. He said, "Well. I tend to believe you, which leaves—"

"Fucking Bloom! Oh, shit! What a mess! God, I'm sick!"

"Yeah, but you know, I've known Bloom long enough not to be that surprised. The guy has no moral center."

DeLino was still shaking his head. "But, Jesus! The D.A.!" He took a deep breath. "Okay—first, I owe you a big one. I will . . . take steps to minimize the damage to the Mayor's office from this shit. You think it'll come out—the whole mess?"

"Without a doubt, once we get the complete story. We're doing that now."

DeLino stood up abruptly and put some currency on the table. His lo mein was untouched and cooling in its bowl. "I need to get back right now. Thanks, and Butch? Remember Jack Keegan?"

"Of course." Jack Keegan had been the chief of the Homicide Bureau in the glory days before Bloom, and one of the men who had taught Karp how to prosecute homicides. He was a man with a monumental reputation for skill and probity.

"He's casting for a judgeship," said DeLino. "He needs Bloom's recommendation, and the word I have is that he's planning to appear as a defense witness. He's going to blast Selig."

"My God!" Karp exclaimed in disbelief. "Jack Keegan shilling for Sandy Bloom?"

"Yep," said DeLino with a tight grin. "Now you know how *I* feel."

"I have here," said Karp, "a copy of a letter from you to Dr. Murray Selig, dated January twentieth of last year. Are you familiar with this letter?"

The district attorney took it from Karp's hand as if it were a used Kleenex. It was the third day of his testimony. The courtroom was packed with spectators, including a larger than usual contingent from the press. In some mysterious sharklike fashion, the press smelled blood, and the reporters were more than usually avid for it, Bloom having spent a significant amount of time cultivating them. Nothing delights reporters as much as nailing people who have gone out of their way to be nice to them.

Bloom was holding up fairly well, considering the battering he had received. Karp had used his time with Bloom on the stand to go through the four cases that figured in the charges in Bloom's memo, not so much to demonstrate their hollowness, which he had already done with other witnesses, but to show that the district attorney had no real idea of how his office operated in homicide cases, and thus was not qualified to judge how Dr. Selig did his job.

Bloom glanced at the letter and shrugged. "I sign a lot of letters"—meaning, how can I expect to remember this trivial crap? He smiled at the courtroom, but turned off the teeth when Judge Craig snapped from the bench, "Just answer the question!"

"Yes, this is my letter," said Bloom.

"Thank you," said Karp. "Would you read the indicated passage to the court?"

Bloom read, in a bored monotone, "Dear Dr. Selig, I would like to thank you very much for your superb participation in *People* versus *Ralston*, which has just concluded with convictions on all counts. Marsha Davis, the assistant district attorney in charge, tells me that you enabled her to understand the significance of the medical testimony in the case, and the forensic issues that arose during cross-examination, enabling her to respond most effectively in a way that would not otherwise have been possible."

"Thank you. So Dr. Selig was competent, highly competent, in January, and fit to be dismissed, a disaster, in July—in your considered opinion?"

"Yes," said Bloom confidently, ignoring the inherent absurdity of that answer. He had learned something from Dr. Fuerza's miseries and was prepared to brazen out the conflict between the golden opinions of winter and the poisoned barbs of summer.

"So Dr. Selig's performance must have deteriorated in those six or so months?"

"Not necessarily. I was apprised of facts that I did not know when I wrote that letter."

"The facts do not exist, as we have seen here in testimony after testimony."

Bloom smiled. "The facts are for the jury to decide."

Karp smiled back and turned to the jury to show them he was happy. "Thank you, sir. I stand instructed. But the facts aside, isn't it your judgment that we are dealing with here, based on your understanding of how the criminal justice system ought to work, in comparison to which Dr. Selig's performance—pardon me, his spring and summertime performance—falls seriously short?"

"Yes, in my judgment."

"Mm-hmm, now returning to the Ralston case, you cited Dr. Selig for disrupting the trial by not appearing at the appointed time. Would you care to tell us how this disruption occurred?"

"Objection, Your Honor," said Wharton. "Repetitious. We've had all this before."

"Your Honor," said Karp, "the purpose of this line of questioning is to determine the qualification of the witness to make a judgment on the performance of Dr. Selig during trial."

A moment of stunned silence. Then Wharton burst out, "This is preposterous, Your Honor. The witness is the *district attorney.*"

"Plaintiff has made no stipulation as to the expertise of the witness in trial procedure," said Karp equably. "His official position is no guarantee thereof."

The ghost of a smile flickered over the judge's chalk-line mouth. "Overruled. Proceed, Mr. Karp."

"Thank you, Your Honor. Mr. Bloom, would you give the jury some sense of how exactly this disruption was accomplished?"

"Well, basically, you arrange your witnesses, when you're trying a case, in a certain way. You want to get all the medical witnesses onto the record before you call the defendant, for example."

Karp struggled to keep his face neutral. He moved slightly so that he obscured the line of sight from Bloom to the defendant's table. "I see, so the prosecution wants to get all its ducks in a row before they call the defendant up there to testify, is that what you're telling us?"

"Yes."

"Tell me, Mr. Bloom, is it normal for the prosecution to call the defendant to testify?"

Wharton objected and the judge quashed him instantly. He seemed fascinated with what was happening.

Bloom's noble forehead creased slightly. It sounded like a trick question. But it couldn't be; on TV the defendant was always yapping up there on the stand, while Perry Mason was finding the real killer. "Only when necessary," he said. A good compromise answer.

"Mr. Bloom," said Karp, his voice rising, "are you not aware that the Fifth Amendment to the United

States Constitution absolutely forbids the prosecution to call the defendant to testify?"

"I . . . what I . . ."

"And are you aware that this prohibition is central to our whole process of justice, the trial system that you as district attorney have the responsibility to manage?"

"Yes, what I meant was . . ." Bloom's mind went blank. He didn't know what he meant. His eyes met Karp's. Karp might have been looking at a patch of vomit.

"You've never tried a homicide case, have you, Mr. Bloom?"

"No, but I've—"

"And so you are utterly incompetent to pass judgment on any aspect of how homicide cases are run, including the role of the medical examiner, isn't that so?"

"No, my subordinates—my subordinates informed me—"

"Your subordinates. But your subordinates didn't fire Dr. Selig, did they?"

"No, the Mayor did."

"And the Mayor relied primarily on your advice, didn't he?"

"He took it into account, but—"

"Because you're the expert, the expert on the criminal justice system, right?"

"I felt it was necessary," said Bloom lamely.

"Why? Why, Mr. Bloom, was it necessary to fire Dr. Selig? What occurred between winter, when he was brilliant enough to prompt letters of commendation from the D.A., and July, when he had to be fired?"

"I don't know what you mean."

"No? What happened at the end of May that made it absolutely necessary for you to get rid of Dr. Murray Selig, a great and *independent* medical examiner and put your own creature in his place?" Karp had slowed his delivery, lowered the timbre and raised the volume of his voice, making it as much like that of Jehovah in the desert as he could manage, all the while staring at Bloom and delivering the unspoken message: "I know!" The D.A.'s paint was crisping nicely.

"What was it, Mr. Bloom? *What was it you did not want Dr. Selig to discover?*"

"Nothing! *Nothing!*" Bloom's voice had cracked on the repetition on this word. Wharton rose to object. Murmurs began among the spectators; the jury was transfixed, frozen, each juror frantic to know what the *nothing* was that was clearly *something*. The murmurs grew. Craig frowned and struck his gavel.

Karp said, in his most carrying voice, "Your Honor, the plaintiff's case is concluded." He turned on his heel and walked back across the bloodied sands. Spanish maidens threw roses.

SEVENTEEN

Marlene had just picked up Lucy and was looking for a parking place near D'Agostino's on Sheridan Square when her beeper went off. Marlene cursed under her breath and turned to her daughter, sitting in the seat beside her.

"I've got to call Uncle Harry, Luce. You stay in the car and watch Sweety. And don't leave it for any reason, understand?"

"Did that lady get found?"

"I don't know, baby, I sure hope so." Marlene double-parked and ran into a cigar store to make her call. It was inevitable that sooner or later one of Marlene's clients would be attacked by a gentleman acquaintance. She knew that, but it did not diminish her wrath or her pain. The previous evening the actress Karen Wohl had left her East Fifty-second Street apartment, telling her roommate that she was going to meet some people at a restaurant. Her doorman got her a cab, and that was the last time anyone had seen her. There was an all-city search in progress, for the woman and for her admirer,

Hubert Waley, whom Marlene had instantly fingered for the cops.

"They found her," said Harry. His tone made her belly lurch.

"How bad?"

"Bad. He wrapped her and dumped her by the river in East Harlem. He's in custody at the Two-Five."

"I'll go," she said. Tears were flowing down her cheeks and she made no effort to hold them back.

"You're sure?"

"Yeah, my client, my fuck-up—I need to be there."

"It happens, Marlene," said Bello.

Marlene said an abrupt good-bye and hung up the phone. She did not wish for comfort.

"Where are we going, Mommy?" asked Lucy when the yellow car was speeding up the East River Drive and it was therefore clear that they were neither going shopping nor returning home. Marlene snapped a glance at her daughter. The child's eyes were shaded under a grubby tan Stetson that she had taken over and which she was wearing with the only skirt she would willingly put on for school, a white leatherette garment with a fringe. A pink western shirt with pearl buttons and the flower-embroidered shawl she had borrowed from Isabella completed the bizarre outfit.

"I have to go by the police station."

"That lady got killed, right?"

"Right."

"Are you going to look at her dead body?"

"No. But they caught the man who killed her, they think, and they want me to look at him and say if it's the right man."

"Then they have to kill him too, right?"

Marlene sighed and wiped her eyes with a tissue. "No, honey, it's too late for that. They'll just put him in jail for his whole life. Maybe."

There were several TV vans and a crowd of reporters on the street outside the Two-Five. Marlene parked in one of the spaces reserved for unmarked cop cars and placed on the dashboard an "NYPD Official Business" sign that Harry had saved from his former life. Holding Lucy tightly by the hand, she pushed through the crowd, identified herself to the uniforms at the door, and entered the building.

In the lobby, an officer with sergeant's stripes on his arms and a rack of decorations over his breast pocket approached her and asked politely if he could help. Marlene introduced herself and said, "I'm here on the Wohl murder. They want me to ID the suspect as the man who's been stalking the victim."

"Okay, that's Detective Mancuso, the second floor. Just go up . . ." He stopped, aware that the woman was staring at him strangely. "Is something wrong?" he asked.

"Ah, no," said Marlene. "I just noticed your name tag. You're Joseph Clancy, aren't you?"

"Guilty," said Clancy, smiling. He looked down at Lucy, who was staring at him wide-eyed, and wiggled his fingers. He said, "Hiya, cutie! That's a neat outfit. You gonna be a cowgirl?"

"A cowgirl detective," offered Lucy. "My mommy is a detective too."

Clancy looked back at Marlene, wrinkling his brow. "I'm sorry, do I know you?"

"Not really. But you know a friend of mine, Ariadne Stupenagel. The reporter? You've been a subject of conversation at our house." Marlene thought Clancy was less than pleased to hear this.

"Oh, yeah. I heard she got hurt. How's she doing?"

"Much better. She's writing away."

"Anything ever come of that story she was doing?"

On impulse, and in service of some more pot stirring, Marlene replied, "God, yes! She thinks it's going to be the biggest exposé since Knapp."

But Clancy responded to this information with a noncommittal nod and a grave look. The massive Knapp Commission study of corruption in the early seventies was a familiar and painful memory to the cops. He turned his attention back to Lucy. "Hey, cowgirl—how about you and me go for some ice cream while your mom does her business?"

"Oh, that's very kind of you," said Marlene, "but . . ."

"No, really, it's no trouble," said Clancy, offering his hand to Lucy, who grasped it. "I got four of my own, and it might take some time to organize the lineup for this scumb—this suspect."

Marlene went upstairs and met Detective Mancuso, a quiet, burly man who reminded her a little of Harry

Bello. He was brushing plaster dust off his desk. He grinned sheepishly and raised his eyes. Marlene followed the gaze and saw that the ceiling was falling down in chunks.

"The place is collapsing," said Mancuso. "It's worse by the cells and the interrogation rooms. It's the beams—dry rot."

Marlene was not interested in ceilings. She asked, "How did he do it?"

"A cab. He got himself hired by a cab company and cruised back and forth with his top light off until he saw her waiting."

"He confess yet?"

"Nah. He loved her and he would never hurt her."

Marlene hung around for three quarters of an hour, observing the detective work of the Two-Five. She looked for Jackson, but saw no one who answered the description given by Ariadne. She did see one person she recognized—the crime reporter Jimmy Dalton, a squat, bald man who gestured broadly with a dead cigar while he talked to one of the detectives. Dalton looked up, saw Marlene, clearly recognized her, and then pretended he hadn't, which was odd.

She was wondering what to make of this when Mancuso came by and said that the lineup was ready. Marlene had no trouble picking the unremarkable little toad, Hubert Waley, out of the group.

When she went by Clancy's desk to collect her daughter, she found Lucy sitting on the sergeant's desk with a cop hat on in place of her Stetson, sucking on a lolly, her face liberally smeared with the remains of an Eskimo Pie.

"You've ruined her appetite for the next month," said Marlene.

"I fingerprinted, Mommy," said Lucy, holding up a smeary official print sheet.

"Not for the last time, the way you're going," said Marlene sourly. Turning to Clancy, she was about to offer conventional thanks, but, somewhat to her own surprise, she found herself lowering her voice and saying, "Look, Sergeant, I may be out of line here, but we need to talk."

"About what?" said Clancy, frowning.

"You know about what. John Seaver. Paul Jackson. The D.A. covering for them. They looked at the autopsies again. The dead cabbies were murdered, right here, on your watch. The shit is about to hit the fan on this whole thing, and my friend Stupe says you're a nice guy, and while I know about the famous blue wall, this might be a good time to get yourself some cover on the side, just between you and me."

Clancy's face was stiff. Marlene indicated with a movement of her head the large framed picture of a blond woman and four children on Clancy's desk. "You need to think about them, Sergeant, not a pair of bent cops."

An odd look came over Clancy's face, one Marlene could not readily interpret. Resignation? Relief? In any case, he said, "Not here." He scribbled something on a piece of paper and slipped it   her low.

She looked at it: an address in Woodhaven, in Queens.

Karp was home when they arrived. Marlene heated some leftover pizza for Lucy, who begged and was allowed the rare treat of eating in front of the TV, and whipped up a brace of Spanish omelettes, which they had with big chunks of Tuscan garlic bread. They exchanged the day's news.

"They brought out their old crock doctor today, Feinblatt," said Karp.

"The one who heard Murray say the Great Man died in the saddle with his boots on?"

"That's the one. I killed him on cross. It turns out that what he remembered was not what Murray actually said at the conference, but the newspaper speculation surrounding the death—the Veep was found alone in his town house with an attractive woman, he had his shirt off, stuff like that. We had three witnesses who were there testify that Murray never said anything like that. Besides, if the chief medical examiner had said publicly that the vice-president had died during sex, it would have made headlines around the world, and it didn't."

"How's Murray holding up?"

"I think he's recovered. It's hard to shake up somebody who likes to dissect rotten corpses. He screwed up by not telling me all the jobs he's taken since he got canned, but on the other hand, I had those big-time lawyers up there saying they wouldn't touch him as an expert witness because of the firing. Plus, he didn't get the Suffolk County job, which we brought out on cross. It may hurt us on damages, but not much. He's still got badge of infamy with respect to getting any major C.M.E. appointment. Face it, they have no case on the facts, they have no case on the law; the only thing they can do at this point is smear."

"That's why Keegan," she said.

"Yeah, Keegan," said Karp glumly. He fell silent and pushed the food around on his plate.

"You're going to have to tear him up?"

"Oh, hell, no! Keegan? What'm I going to do, impeach him? On what grounds? No, besides . . ."

"What?"

"I feel terrible for the guy. A man like that, sucking after Bloom." He paused, thinking both of Keegan and of himself. "Ambition." The word came out like a blasphemous oath.

"So what will you do?"

"I don't know," said Karp, suddenly blithe. "Appeal to his better nature, I guess." He looked at his wife benignly, and seemed to absorb for the first time that she had not changed out of her downtown outfit, that and the hurried meal.

"You're going out?"

"Yeah," she said, "I'm going to Queens to talk to Joe Clancy."

"Uh-oh. That sounds serious."

"We'll see how serious. I think mainly he's thinking about jumping ship and he wants to know how long is my rope."

* * *

Sergeant Clancy lived in a post-war brick bungalow in Woodhaven that was barely distinguishable
from the post-war brick bungalow in Ozone Park, a
mile or so to the southeast, that was still home to
Marlene's parents. And although Clancy was about
her own age, or a little older, she found his home
more like that of her parents than her own. There
was a living room, in which she was now seated,
with the good set of furniture, the blocky sofa, the
two graceless armchairs, all covered in a chicken-
blood satin, the mahogany coffee table, the china cabinet, and side tables. The Clancys had gone for the
fake Duncan Phyffe instead of the fake French Pro-
vincial her folks had. Marlene had a glass of Pepsi
in her hand, with a cocktail napkin around the base
and a coaster for the coffee table. Mrs. Clancy, a
worn, pale, blond lady, with a tendency to speed,
had supplied this, together with five minutes of small
talk. Kids, schools, and churches. The Clancys were
Holy Family people; the Ciampis were St. Joseph's.
Oh, you must know . . .

The two girls and the older boy were trotted past
for admiration; the retarded child was not, nor was
he mentioned, although there he was in the large
color photo portrait of the whole family (the sergeant
in uniform, with decorations, the rest of the family
dressed for Easter at church) that hung over where
the mantel would be if the house had been grand
enough to have a fireplace.

"I'll go get Joe," said Nora Clancy when the conversation flagged. Marlene was studying the portrait when Clancy walked in.

"That was a couple of years ago," he said from behind her. "James, that's the baby, is in the Southampton Institute, out on the island."

"For Down's syndrome?"

"He had hydrocoele too," said Clancy too quickly. "Water on the brain. He needs a lot of care. Everyone else is just fine, though, like you saw. Can I get you another drink? Or something stronger?"

"I'd love one, Sergeant . . ."

"Hey, I'm home—call me Joe."

"Okay, I'm Marlene. I'd love one, *Joe*, but I can't drink right now—I'm six months gone."

A peculiar look came over Clancy's face when she said this, and Marlene briefly wondered whether he found something accusatory in her remark, as if the Clancys' prenatal regime had been short of perfection and there was the result, the gnomelike creature up on the wall. But the look faded in an instant, and Clancy plopped himself down in an armchair, waving Marlene at the sofa.

"So, why are we here?" he asked.

"Because the shit is about to hit the fan, Joe. D.A. or no D.A., those guys are going down. And we got two dead kids in jail. On your watch."

Clancy rubbed his face and looked at her bleakly. "Jesus God, what a mess! Okay, how much do you know already?"

Marlene told him about the autopsy photos and what they revealed, about Stupenagel being shaken down by Jackson and Seaver, about her interview with Seaver, about the reasons for believing in the complicity of Bloom in protecting the two men, about Bloom having had Selig fired to ensure that the medical examiner would be incapable of uncovering the true fate of the cabbies. All she left out was that it was Selig himself who had examined the autopsy photographs. Clancy listened in silence, nodding, his face grave and pale.

When she was done, he said, "Okay, let's say I'm disgusted but not surprised. Jackson I know pretty well; we were in uniform together at the Two-Seven before I made sergeant and he got his gold potsy, but I just know Seaver by rep. Paul's got a little problem with his hands. He likes to tune up the skells; you know, perps and the lowlifes."

"And others as well?"

"Yeah, that too. Generally not an equal-opportunity kind of cop. He got some reprimands, but it never went further than that. The guy had something like seventy-five good felony collars. So they balanced it off."

"You never wanted to be a detective yourself?"

Clancy rolled his eyes. "Get real! I like regular hours. I have a *life*. You got any idea what the divorce rate is in plainclothes? Besides, the promotion's faster in uniform, and there's more slots open for you at the top. I'd like to be chief of patrol."

He said this calmly and without arrogance. And why not? thought Marlene. A hero, a good Irish family man; it was entirely possible, provided he had an effective rabbi up at Police Plaza. Somehow, Marlene figured Clancy had taken care of that too.

She said, "Okay, Jackson was rough. Was he always bent?"

"Yeah, Paulie took. Not like guys in narco, not big-time, but he took. The problem with Paulie, though, is in the brain department. He's not too swift there, you know?"

"So Seaver came up with the plan, you think?"

"No question. Paulie just liked to pound meat, but Seaver needed money bad." Marlene looked a question and he added, "He likes sports action. Compulsive. The guy bets on soccer games, for cryin' out loud! His wife ditched him, so he's got child support to pay. By the way, this is all hearsay. Neither of them exactly unburdened themselves. But it's known around the house. I even heard they got themselves a string of girls on the stroll over by 'Tenth, near the park."

"Okay, they were bent," said Marlene. "They shook down gypsy cabbies and some of the poor bastards started to make waves. So they yanked some of these guys off the street to put a little fear into them, and ended up killing Ortiz and Valenzuela. So, the question is, how did they get the D.A. to cover them? What did they have on the D.A.?"

Clancy made a helpless gesture. "Hey, I'm not in on the whole story, Marlene. This I don't know, but you got to figure, everybody needs money, right?"

"Oh, come on Joe! Sanford Bloom rolling over for a couple of hundred a week? The total of what they ripped off in a year wouldn't pay the maintenance fees on his duplex. No, they caught him doing something real bad. In the spring of last year, around April, May. Anything ring a bell?"

Clancy shook his head. "Not a blessed thing, Marlene."

"What about Stupenagel getting beat up?"

"The same—not a whisper. Of course, the kind of job I have, I wouldn't hear much from the detectives. As far as seeing something? You got to understand, a patrol sergeant's practically a railroad train. It's a clockwork job—roll call, paperwork, make your beat tour, coffee from the same joint every night. It's not hard to keep something from a patrol sergeant. In fact, you could say it's a well-developed art." He paused, smiling slightly at his joke. Then he said, "I wouldn't put it past Jackson, though. Seaver, I don't see him involved, in that or in any murders."

"Why not?"

"Because the guy had a name as a candy ass. A bleeding heart. I mean, he might let Paulie do whatever, but he wouldn't touch any rough stuff himself."

Marlene nodded. This only confirmed her impression of John Seaver as a man without the cold-bloodedness necessary for violence. Ariadne's story of Jackson shaking her down also supported that view; Jackson had used his hands, Seaver had stood by.

"So you think Jackson hanged those two kids by himself?"

"If they got hanged, Jackson could have done it. The guy's strong as an ox. He could have cuffed the kids flat on the ground and then tied a shirt or a sheet around their necks and stood on a table or something, and then just hauled up. Was that how it was done?"

"Something like that." Marlene felt no need to tell Clancy about the ankle abrasions Selig had found on both victims.

"What do you think will happen now?" asked Clancy, worry in his voice.

"What I guess is that once I.A.D. gets another look at those two autopsy reports and puts it together with the other information—and that story about the D.A. squad running a big investigation won't hold up—then they'll move to suspend Seaver and Jackson. Seaver will crack. He almost cracked with me, and I'm nobody. The state A.G. will suspend Bloom, or maybe he'll be forced to resign, and then the merry show will begin."

"You went to I.A.D. with this?" asked Clancy, his face growing tight.

"No, of course not," said Marlene, growing somewhat stingy with the truth. "My sole concern is with Dr. Selig's civil case. But clearly the cover-up led to the firing that's the basis of the case. Once that comes into the open, the defendant's case collapses totally."

"And Selig wins big bucks." Clancy uttered a rueful snort. "This is all about money, isn't it? Just money."

"Of course," said Marlene, as innocently as she could contrive.

*   *   *

Jack Keegan looked smaller up on the stand than Karp remembered him being in his office. He still had the blocky, Irish good looks, the iron jaw, the big nose, and the bright silver wavy hair. Maybe everyone looked smaller on the stand. Or maybe it was what Keegan was doing up there that shrank him, at least in the eyes of his one-time disciple.

It was now what Karp estimated to be the last week of the trial. Spring had returned, signaled in the windowless courtroom by the flowering of light print dresses on the three female jurors and on the spectators, and by the absence of that close odor, compiled of steam heat and disinfectant, that permeates New York's public buildings in the winter, and also by a certain quickening in the pace of the trial. After Selig's long agony on the stand, in which, as Karp had predicted, the defense had asked him to account for every penny he had earned since his dismissal, to the end of demonstrating that being fired was the best thing that ever happened to the Selig bank account, the others called by the defense had been quickies: the crock doctor and a set of anti-character witnesses, of whom Jack Keegan was the best and last.

Gottkind put him through his paces through the late morning hours. Yes, Dr. Selig had been abrupt; he had been arrogant; he had often not returned phone calls. Your witness.

Karp rose. "Your Honor, it is five past twelve. I wonder if it would be convenient to break for lunch at this time, so as not to interrupt my cross-examination of this witness?''

It was fine with Craig. The defense did not object. The judge gaveled the adjournment and turned to converse with a clerk. The jury filed out and the courtroom filled with the familiar rattle of chatter. Karp walked over to Keegan, who stuck out his hand. Karp took it and looked into the older man's eyes. They were almost of a height, Keegan somewhat shorter but bulkier, a football rather than a basketball guard.

''Come and talk to me for a minute, Jack,'' said Karp.

Keegan nodded gravely and started to follow Karp out of the courtroom.

''Your Honor!'' Gottkind was dancing in front of the presidium and waving his hand, like a third-grader asking leave to go pee. ''Your Honor, I must protest. Plaintiff's counsel is interfering with my witness.''

Craig looked up from his conversation, annoyance on his face. He focused his heron's stare at Karp. ''Mr. Karp?''

''Judge, Mr. Keegan is an old friend and colleague. I only wanted to have a few words with him, of a personal nature.''

''It's irregular, Your Honor, and I will register a protest on the record.''

''That is your right, Mr. Gottkind,'' said the judge dismissively. Amusement crept into the sharp blue eyes. ''Mr. Karp, may we trust you not to suborn, bribe, or intimidate the witness during this colloquy?"

"I will not, Your Honor."

The judge nodded and went back to his conversation. Karp led Keegan to a quiet corner. They traded compliments on how well each other looked, and chatted briefly about old friends. Keegan asked about Marlene, Karp asked about Mary Keegan. A nervous silence; then Karp said, "Damn it, Jack, what the hell are you doing up there?"

"They asked me," said Keegan lightly. "Would I say that Murray Selig is an arrogant son of a bitch? Yeah, he *is* an arrogant son of a bitch."

"So am I, Jack. So are you. So was Phil Garrahy, for that matter. It's a character flaw of people who know what the hell they're doing. But Selig wasn't canned for being arrogant. He was canned because he ran afoul of one of Sandy Bloom's dirty little schemes. And you're up there giving credence to it. Why?"

Keegan's face started to flush dangerously. "You said it right, Butch. You *are* an arrogant son of a bitch, and self-righteous with it. Sometimes you need to go along to get along—you still haven't learned that, son. You're growing a little long in the tooth to be an *enfant terrible*."

"It's the judgeship, isn't it?"

There was a long stare after this. Keegan dropped his eyes first and assumed an amused look. He held out his hand. "Good to see you again, Butch," he said. Butch shook the proffered hand, convinced he had seen for an instant a flash of shame in Keegan's eyes.

After the lunch break, Keegan took the stand.

"Mr. Keegan," Karp began, "when you served as head of the Homicide Bureau, I was one of your assistant district attorneys, was I not?"

"Yes."

"And you had the responsibility of training me to prosecute homicides—I was your student, in a sense, and you were my teacher, weren't you?"

"Yes." He paused, smiled. "You were my best student."

"Thank you." Karp turned slightly so that his remarkable peripheral vision could take in the jury. They were lapping it up. "And part of that training was in how to work well with the medical examiner's office, wasn't it?"

"Yes, indeed."

"And as part of our work we had much to do with Dr. Selig when he was a senior assistant medical examiner there? Hundreds of cases?"

"Yes, certainly."

"Now, as part of your teaching, did you ever warn me that Dr. Selig was hard to work with, incompetent, and lacking in any respect whatsoever?"

A longer pause. Keegan seemed to square his shoulders. He answered, "No, never."

"And was there ever, to your knowledge, a homicide case involving Dr. Selig in which he did not carry out his duties with the very highest professional standards?"

"No, none."

"And did any of the problems you adverted to this morning in your testimony, the missed phone calls, the so-called 'arrogance,' ever, to your knowledge, hinder in the slightest degree the successful prosecution of a single homicide case?"

"No. None that I can recall."

Karp waited three beats and said, "Mr. Keegan, would it surprise you to learn that many of the young lawyers who sat at your feet during those years, being trained to be the best homicide prosecutors in the world, may have considered you yourself somewhat abrupt and arrogant?"

Keegan smiled broadly. "No, it would not surprise me in the least."

Karp grinned back. "Thank you. No further questions."

Keegan left the stand. Karp didn't know whether the expression on Conrad Wharton's face was worth a judgeship, but it was one of life's sweet moments nonetheless.

"The defense calls Dr. James T. England," said Gottkind.

Karp felt a sinking sensation. He grabbed his tattered yellow note sheets, looked in vain, tossed them aside, shuffled up the list of defense witnesses he had been supplied. No England. He stood. "Your Honor, this witness is not on the witness list, nor on the list of deponents."

Craig beckoned him forward with a thin finger. He

advanced, followed by Josh Gottkind. At the bench Gottkind said, "Your Honor, Dr. England came forward voluntarily. He called me yesterday and said he had important evidence relevant to the plaintiff's character."

"This is outrageous, Your Honor," said Karp hotly. "Are defendants to be permitted to drag smearing witnesses out at the very last moments of the trial?"

"They did not 'drag,' Mr. Karp, nor pursue, it seems, if what Mr. Gottkind says is true. Is it true, Mr. Gottkind? This is a spontaneous appearance by a concerned citizen?"

"Yes, Judge," Gottkind answered quickly. "He's been following the case in the papers. He felt obliged to come forward."

"I take exception, Your Honor," said Karp formally.

"Exception noted," said Craig. "Bring on your witness."

"Who the fuck is this guy, Murray?" asked Karp in a whisper between clenched teeth as the witness took the stand.

"He's a big shot on the state medical board," Selig whispered back.

"What did you do wrong that he knows about?"

"Nothing! No, really, Butch, I got no idea why the guy is up there."

They soon found out. Dr. England was a man in his late sixties, dressed in an old-fashioned and unseasonable brown three-piece suit and extremely shiny brown wing tips. His face was white and long, the thin silver hair combed tightly over the skull. With his wire-rimmed glasses he looked just like the antique doctor in the ads drug companies ran in glossy medical journals, the one sitting at the child's bedside.

Dr. England testified that he had chaired the Committee on Professional Conduct of the State Board of Medicine in the revocation hearing of a Dr. Stephen Bailey. Bailey was one of the many Dr. Feelgoods who had sprung up in the seventies, dispensing various reality-altering pharmaceuticals essentially on demand to a well-heeled clientele. It was alleged that Bailey had taken to attending house parties in upstate Sullivan County bearing little bags of such meds, distributing them freely to all who asked. Dr. Selig had been called before the board as an expert on toxicology; the board had to determine whether some of the doses of diet pills and such that Bailey had administered were, in fact, dangerous.

"And did Dr. Selig think that Dr. Bailey had prescribed dangerous doses?" Gottkind asked.

"He did not," said England with a tone and a look that showed what he thought of the opinion. "Dr. Bailey retained his license, largely as a result of Dr. Selig's testimony."

"And during that testimony, what, if anything, did he say regarding dosage of the drug amphetamine?"

"He said that he did not know what all the fuss was about, because he had taken massive doses of amphetamine in medical school to help with studying and it hadn't harmed him any." Murmurs spread briefly through the court.

"What did you think of that?"

"I thought it was gratuitous, frivolous, and unprofessional," said England, his face glowing with righteous satisfaction.

Karp whispered to Selig, "Did you say that?"

"Oh, God, of course I didn't say that."

"What did you say, then?"

"Hell, Butch, how can I remember my exact words? It was nearly five years ago."

England's testimony ground to a halt. The defense rested. Karp checked the wall clock. He rose. "Your Honor, I have no questions at this time, but I would like to call Dr. England back first thing on Monday when court reconvenes."

The judge's eyes flicked at the clock too. He knew the pickle Karp was in. He also knew that it was a gorgeous spring day and that if he left now he could roll up a mess of paperwork and get in a full set of tennis before dark. And it was Friday. And the jury could use a little break; he had driven the case hard for eight weeks.

"Well, I don't see why we can't break now, as Mr. Karp suggests. You can do your cross Monday, Mr. Karp, and then we can begin summations. I trust that neither of you will be so long-winded as to make me regret this indulgence." The court tittered politely. The gavel fell.

"How bad is this, Butch?" asked Selig nervously.

"How bad? It's a disaster, Murray. It's the end of

the trial and I got no way to impeach the fucker, because the transcripts of license revocation hearings are sealed, and there's no time to get an order to unseal them, and it's the weekend anyway, and what's in their minds now is you're a junkie who let a dope pusher keep his license.''

EIGHTEEN

"Cheer up, Butch, it can't be that bad," said Marlene soothingly. He was acting like a baby, and it was starting to get on her nerves. They were in their living room, waiting while a casserole warmed.

He groaned and began to tell her again how bad it was, but she interrupted him. "Look! Stop kvetching already! The main thing is, is Murray telling the truth?"

"Oh, crap, Marlene, how do I know? He says he didn't say that flip stuff about speed, but you know Murray. He likes to shake up the civilians from time to time with tales from the crypt. It's something he *could* have said. But that doesn't matter. We need the transcript of that hearing to impeach England, and we don't have it."

Marlene thought for a minute or so. "You say the transcripts are in Monticello, in the county courthouse?"

"Yeah, why?"

"It's only about three hours away. I could run up and get them."

"No, Marlene," Karp explained, "you're not lis tening. They're sealed records. It would take a court order to unseal them. It's the weekend. I already called the courthouse; the guy there told me Monday's the earliest they could start to look for them, and Monday's too late."

"Would Craig write you an order?"

"I guess so, but what good would it do? The place is closed."

"Closed places can be opened," said Marlene archly.

He looked at her, at the all-too-familiar expression on her face, and then slowly raised his hands to cover his ears. "I don't want to hear this, Marlene."

"No, you don't, but you want the transcripts by Monday, and this is the only way to get them. Get the order to cover your ass with the judge and . . . I don't know, I feel the need for some country air. Maybe I'll take a drive upstate this weekend with Harry."

"La-la-la-la-la-dum-di-dum," sang Karp. He kept his hands over his ears, his body hunched as if to avoid blows, as he walked sideways out of the room.

He passed Lucy on the way out and got a startled look.

"Why is Daddy acting goony, Mommy?"

"Because he's a goon. Come here, I want to talk to you." Lucy sat by her side on the sofa.

"Look, Daddy's having some bad problems with his big case, and I have to help him this weekend. I have to go out of town, so—"

Lucy's face crumpled. "Nooooo!" she moaned. "You promised you would take Isabella and me and Hector to the zoo and to Rumplemeyer's for sundaes. And go shopping. You promised!"

"I know I promised, but this is an emergency. *I* know! I bet Daddy will take you."

"Nooo! It's not the same. Isabella *hates* him."

"Dear, there's no reason for Isabella to hate him because he's never done anything bad to her. Maybe it would be a good thing for her to start getting over her fear of men, hmm?"

"You *promised*!" wailed Lucy. Tears covered her tender cheeks.

"I'm not going to discuss it anymore," said Marlene firmly. "You can call Isabella at the shelter and tell her your father will take you, or you can wait for next week."

Lucy uttered a shriek of frustration and flounced out.

"What was that all about?" Karp inquired, wandering back in.

"Oh, nothing. Lucy's being unreasonable again. I told her I couldn't take her to the zoo because I had to go . . . someplace."

"Oh. You know, I wrote down the information on the Dr. Bailey revocation hearing, the dates and all, on a piece of paper and I can't remember where I left it. It might be on your desk."

"Yes, it might," said Marlene. "It's probably filed under 'Arrant Hypocrisy.' "

"Yes," agreed Karp. "That, or 'Keeping Daddy Out of Jail.'"

She was parked with Harry Bello in front of the Sullivan County Courthouse in Monticello, New York, a small two-story brick building. They sipped coffee and made plans. Marlene slipped a vitamin pill from her jacket pocket into her mouth and washed it down. It was early Saturday morning; they had left the City just past dawn, and her stomach was starting to grumble for real food.

"This does not look like Fort Knox," said Marlene.

Harry grunted in acknowledgment and got out of the car, carrying a cheap plastic briefcase. He went up to the glass door of the building and knocked, long and hard. A middle-aged, hefty man in a gray uniform came to the door, shook his head, and tapped the sign that listed the courthouse hours. Harry reached into his pocket and pulled out an ID wallet. He flashed a shield at the man.

Police departments throughout the nation produce miniatures of their shields, and cops exchange these at conventions. Harry was flashing an NYPD detective's shield, which, if you weren't all that familiar with the full-size model, looked authoritative. It wasn't *precisely* impersonating an officer. The guard opened the door; Marlene saw Harry speak to him for a moment, and then they both went in.

She went around the back of the building. There was an alarm, but she had to assume it was off. She was dressed neatly in slacks, a tweed jacket, low boots, and a white turtleneck with a Liberty print scarf, an outfit that tried for the appearance of old, weary money—at the opposite end of the social spectrum from lady burglars. She picked the lock to the back door and went in.

It took her a half hour to find the right room, and another to find the right filing cabinet. It took two minutes to pick the lock thereof, ten minutes to find the appropriate file, and fifteen minutes of flipping pages until she found the pages containing Selig's testimony. She cranked up a copy machine and started making copies.

"What are you doing here?"

Marlene jumped and nearly dropped the file, but she completed the copy of the last page she needed and slipped the copies, folded, into her breast pocket.

"I said, what are you doing here? Who are you?" The guard moved closer. Marlene replaced the file, closed the drawer, and turned to face him.

"Sorry, national security," she mumbled and started to move past him. He held up an arm.

"What?"

She pulled a red capsule from her pocket, held it in front of his face, and then tossed it into her mouth. "Cyanide," she said. "I have to kill myself if captured. You've seen the lights in the sky? No? Other people have. This is big, Officer, we're talking extraterrestrials, the Soviets. The Kennedy assassination? Just the beginning. Look at this!" She popped out her glass eye and waved it in front of his face. He blanched and backed off a step.

"High-technology device. Where does it come from? We don't know. I got to go now, Officer, that or you got a corpse on your hands and a world of trouble from the Agency. I haven't taken anything, I haven't harmed anything. Just let me disappear and forget you ever saw me."

He gaped. She pushed past him and in a minute was out of the building and into the car.

"Take off, Harry! I flim-flammed him, but I don't know how long it'll hold."

Harry drove away. "Sorry. He went through the whole mug book."

"He bought the story you were chasing a fugitive who used to live here?"

"Yeah. You get it?"

Marlene adjusted the rearview and replaced her. eye.

"Got it."

"You get it?" asked Karp.

"Got it. Murray was right, he's clean."

"I don't know what you're talking about. How surprised I'll be when I find just the material I need on the floor of my office on Monday morning. Meanwhile, will you marry me and have my babies?"

A long clinch. When normal breathing resumed, Karp said, "Speaking of babies, Lucy's in a bad mood. She tried to call that friend of hers at your shelter, and they told her she wasn't there. Is that standard? Maybe she has to be on a call list, like jail."

"I don't know. Let me call them. I'll talk to Mattie."

But what Mattie Duran said, when Marlene got her on the line, was, "No, Lucy's right. She's not here. She disappeared sometime last night or early this morning. It took us awhile to catch on, because we figured she was in her box, but when we looked, she wasn't there. I thought she might be with you until Lucy called."

"She just walked out? How could that happen!"

"Hey, this is a shelter, not a jail. We're set up to keep people out, not in."

"And you have no idea where she went?"

Marlene could almost hear the shrug over the phone. "Not a clue. She came, we took care of her, to the extent that she let us, and she went. It's not the first time it's happened to us either, with street kids."

"Yeah, but Isabella is not your regular street kid. Is Hector around?"

"Not lately. Look, it's possible that they found a parent or relative—"

"Do you believe that, with what you know?" snapped Marlene.

"Not really, but Jesus, Marlene! What can you do? It's the big city."

"I'll think of something," said Marlene. "Keep in touch and call me if you hear anything, okay?"

Lucy was still stiff with her the next morning as they got ready for church. The child clearly blamed Marlene for her friend's disappearance: if she had not broken her promise, they would have gone to the zoo and for sundaes, and the world would not have been turned upside down. And Marlene, of course, felt the same at some level, despite the illogic of it. She had given up trying to explain it all to Lucy. Time would doubtless heal her when Isabella returned, something Marlene intended to insure. In the meantime, Marlene was going to church with more than her usual burden of guilt, so much so that she chose to go early to Old St. Pat's and stop by the confessional to have her tank drained. The nave was purple-draped for Lent, which suited her mood.

She parked Lucy with the good sisters in the church basement and waited at the confessional, while a heavy, dark woman in a lace head scarf and black dress and a skinny old man in a shiny suit used the booth, and then she went inside.

The slide snapped open, she said the ritual words and then began. Of the Seven Deadlies, Marlene specialized in wrath and pride. She was not envious of anyone; sloth had never been a concern—the opposite, in fact; she felt she had way more than enough worldly goods, avarice not a problem; she longed for booze and tobacco occasionally, but did not obsess about them, or food, which left gluttony out. Lust? Well, yes, on the impure-thought level, but she always worked her fantasies out in the sanctity of the marriage bed, in regard to which she considered that neither Father Raymond nor the Holy and Apostolic Church needed to know the squishy details. She was at present, of course, blameless in the use of contraception.

"I've had anger," she continued. "I want to kill men, to keep them from hurting their families, from killing women. On four occasions I have committed acts of violence or caused them to be committed. I have stolen, three occasions. I have lied, under oath on two occasions, and on many other occasions. I have—" Here she stopped. What was the sin in respect to letting down Isabella and going to Monticello instead?

"I broke my word to a child in order to perform an illegal entry in order to help win a case for my husband, and now that child has run away and she may be in grave danger."

This must have startled the usually phlegmatic priest, for he cleared his throat and asked, "Do you mean that your own child has been lost?"

"Oh, no, Father," answered Marlene. "It's a young girl, a refugee. Isabella . . . I don't know her last name. She was staying at a shelter I've been working with, and my daughter grew attached to her. She vanished the other day, along with her brother, we think, and I'm worried sick about her."

"I see. Continue, please."

Marlene's confession petered out into venialities. She received a hefty penance and left. Later, at the rail, she felt the pressure of a stare, and looked up to find that it was the priest looking at her with a strange intensity. This was more than odd. Marlene had never shown any interest in Father Raymond as a person, nor he in her. She did not participate at all in parish life. In this she was content, for although any number of heresies tempted her from the true path, donatism was not one of them. Unlike many of her contemporary coreligionists, Marlene was indifferent to the character of her priest, treating him purely as a spiritual utility. As far as she was aware, he returned the favor.

She was even more surprised when, after the service, he approached her outside the sacristy as she was about to pick up Lucy, and beckoned to her. He seemed nervous and distraught; curiously, these emotions seemed to give life to what Marlene had always considered an utterly unmemorable, middle-aged face.

"I wanted . . . my, this is difficult! I wanted to let you know that Isabella is safe and well. As is Hector."

Astounded, Marlene blurted out, "Whaaat! How the f—I mean, Father, how do you know? Do you know the kids?"

"Yes. Hector I know quite well. In fact, he often stays here at the church. A very sad child. Much abused and, you know, not quite right in his mind. I've only seen his sister once. A beautiful child, and devout. The one time she was here—"

Marlene interrupted, "Please, Father, where are they now?"

The priest hesitated, clearing his throat several times, an irritating sound. "Well, I saw Hector just last evening. Isabella is . . . in good hands. She's away from the City, in fact, which I think is a good thing."

"She's in danger, isn't she?"

"Hector certainly thinks so. He calls them soldiers, but we believe they are agents from . . . the regime, in her original country."

"Guatemala," said Marlene.

The priest looked surprised. "She spoke to you?"

"No, but we figured it out. As far as I know, she only spoke at any length to one person, my daughter, Lucy. And her brother, of course." She gave him a close look. "Is he here now?"

A significant pause. "I really couldn't say," answered the priest uncomfortably. "He often comes into the rectory in the evenings."

Marlene changed the subject. "Do you know anything about their parents?"

"Not a thing. Hector is remarkably tight-lipped about it. Fear of authority, and no wonder! I haven't notified the juvenile people about him for that reason. I think if I did he'd run completely, and live a . . . depraved life, on the streets. You know, the Church used to care for strays like him all the time, informally. Maybe there's something to be said for it, the personal or spiritual approach, rather than everything being bureaucratic."

Marlene gave him a smile so bright that he blinked. She couldn't have agreed more.

In the car, Marlene asked Lucy, "What did you learn about today?"

"The forgiveness of God," said the child shortly.

"And do you forgive me?"

"I guess," said Lucy without enthusiasm. "I miss Isabella."

"So do I. Father Raymond says he knows where she is and that she's safe."

Lucy's face lit with interest. "Where is she?"

"He wouldn't say. I think he promised that he wouldn't."

"Are you going to find her? Please, Mommy!"

"You know, I think I will. I think that if she's being chased by the kind of people I think she's being chased by, they're not going to be slowed down much by a bunch of nuns. And I'd like to see if she has any relations in town. It would help a lot if I knew her last name. You don't happen to know, do you, Luce?"

"No," said Lucy. Aha! thought her mom.

Later, having served a mighty breakfast of French toast, and his lordship having gone out to shoot hoops in the Village, Marlene was washing up and handing the dishes to her daughter for drying when she remarked, "You know, I was thinking: it's pretty easy to decide between doing bad and doing good, but it's a lot harder to decide between two kinds of good. Like, I broke my promise to you, but I really helped Daddy, and like, it's wrong to tell a lie, but sometimes we tell lies to avoid hurting people's feelings."

"White lies," said Lucy.

"Yes. Look, put down that plate and look at me. You're seven, which is supposed to be the age you become capable of making moral choices. Let me ask you to make a moral choice. I think Isabella told you her full name, and you promised not to tell anyone else. I think that some very bad men from her old country are chasing her, and that's why she ran away. Now, *I* think that if I had her full name, I could find some relative who might know what the danger was, or where Isabella was, so I could help protect her. Now, maybe nothing will happen. But maybe you keeping your promise prevents me from finding her before the bad guys do. You have to choose, and you have to bear the moral responsibility for whatever happens."

"But she'll *hate* me if I tell."

"Yes, she might. In which case you have to decide whether you want Isabella safe and hating you, or loving you and hurt or dead."

Marlene's heart broke as she watched her daughter's eyes fill with tears, but she held her tongue and resisted the urge to sweep the child into her arms and roll back the implacable years. Suddenly, Lucy sniffed loudly and turned away and ran clattering out of the kitchen. She was back in a moment holding out at full arm's length a piece of folded notebook paper. Marlene took it and spread it out.

Around the outside of the page was a garland of lush flowers, heavily outlined, executed in colored pencil. Birds in yellow and green, beautifully rendered in the same bold style, were set among the blossoms. In the center was written, in a smooth, antique, schoolroom hand: *Lucy, Yo Te Amo, Su Amiga, Isabella Concepción Chajul y Machado.*

Marlene swallowed a lump and said, "Good call, Luce. Now, do you happen to know her mommy's first name?"

"Corazon," said the child, and then collapsed, wailing, in her mother's arms.

"That sounds like a Maya name, that Chajul," said Ariadne Stupenagel over the phone. "You say they're Guatemalans?"

"We think so," said Marlene. She had called Stupenagel for help with finding out where a Church-connected underground would stash a kid from Guatemala. Stupenagel was one of two people she could think of to call, and the other one, Mattie Duran, was unlikely to have any Church contacts.

"Where from in Guatemala?"

"We don't know that either. Lucy was babbling something about San Francisco, but apparently there are dozens of—"

"Could it have been San Francisco *Nenton*?" Stupenagel asked carefully.

"Possibly. Why?"

"*Jesus!*" A shriek.

Marlene had to take the phone from her ear. "What?"

"Marlene, in November of the year before last, a special unit of the Guatemalan Army, trained by the U.S. government, entered the village of San Francisco

Nenton and massacred the entire population, 434 men, women, and children. Or so we thought. God, I've got the trembles, Champ! If this fucking kid is an eyewitness to the Nenton massacre . . . my God, the junta would go crazy if they knew she was wandering around in the States. And you say she's got a brother to confirm it? Christ, Marlene, you got to find her. And let me have first crack at her, of course."

"Of course," lied Marlene. "But look, what about my original question?"

"Oh, who they'd shunt her to for cover? God, I couldn't begin to figure . . ."

"What about those nuns you mentioned that time—the Sisters of Perpetual Dysentery? Are they in the States?"

"Damn! You're right, I must be getting senile. I've been so focused on this cab driver thing. They're the Sisters of Perpetual Help."

"I never heard of them," said Marlene.

"No, they're small, and they only turn up where nobody else'll go. A daughter house of the Poor Clares, I think. They're all R.N.'s or nurse practitioners, plus they're all cross-trained in mucky stuff—agronomy, sanitation. They jump out of airplanes too. A far cry from the penguins. They have a rest house someplace in Jersey. Just a sec, I'll get it for you." Clunk and rustlings. "Yo. It's in Chester, Pee Ay." She read off the address. "By the way, speaking of the cabbies . . ."

Marlene brought her up to date, closing with her

visit to the Twenty-fifth Precinct and her conversation with Clancy. Marlene heard the scratch of note taking. "Oh, also," she added, "you'll be interested to know I saw Jimmy Dalton up there schmoozing with a couple of dicks, waving his stinky—"

"What?"

"Jimmy Dalton at the Two-Five. I thought—"

"Thanks, Champ—look, keep in touch, this is great, gotta go." She left Marlene staring puzzled at the dead phone. She pushed down the button and called Harry Bello.

Hector Roberto Chajul y Machado, aged twelve, slipped from the basement room in the rectory of Old St. Patrick's, where he had passed the night, and walked north on Mulberry Street until he came to Houston, where he turned east. He paused at the corner and, as he did habitually, turned to see if someone was following him. He saw no one and went on his way. He saw no one because the man who was following was very good.

The boy entered the Lexington Avenue IRT subway station on Houston. In the dank underground, he checked to see that he was unobserved and then darted under the turnstile. He took the Lex up to 116th Street, left the subway, and walked to a tenement at 117th Street. At the third-floor front apartment, he listened carefully at the door, as he had been taught. There were no sounds. He drew out a key that hung around his neck by a long, dirty string, opened the lock, and went in.

From his perch on the stairwell, one floor above, Harry Bello heard the boy cry out. In an instant he was down the stairs and through the door. Like most tenement apartments, it had a railroad layout, living room, kitchen, and a narrow hall leading to two bedrooms and a bath. The place had been tossed, and crudely too. The couch in the living room had been overturned and slashed, the small television knocked off its table and tossed into a corner. Harry moved into the kitchen.

Hector was in the center of the room, surrounded by ruin. The refrigerator and the pantry had been emptied, the food containers broken and spilled onto the floor, which was covered with a swill of liquids, rice, corn flakes, dried beans, and broken crockery. The counter drawers hung open, their contents scooped out and strewn in piles beneath them.

The boy cried out when he saw Harry and grabbed a long knife from a pile. He charged but slipped on the mess and fell to his knees. Harry stepped on the knife, knelt, and hugged the boy to him.

"Listen! I'm not here to hurt you. I didn't do this. I'm Lucy's godfather. *Soy el padrino de Lucy. Comprende?* Lucy!"

Hector stopped struggling. They both stood up. Harry asked, "Do you know where your mother is?"

He nodded. "She's working."

"You got a number?" Nod.

"Okay, let's call her."

"The lady say not to call."

"Yeah, well, this is an emergency. Give me the number."

Harry called and got an irate woman who told him that Corazon had not shown up for work that morning, and that she was highly inconvenienced, and that as far as she was concerned—

Harry hung up. "Hector," he said, "I'm going to look around here for a minute, and then you and me are going to go up to Lucy's house and you're going to stay there for a while. And then we need to go get your sister and bring her back to the City. I think you all need to stay at Lucy's until we figure out who did this and who's after you."

"The soldiers," said Hector.

"Yeah, them." Harry started to go through the trash from the kitchen drawers. People whose equipage does not run to desks and filing cabinets use kitchen drawers as a depository of sorts. Harry found a bank book, electric and phone bills, but no pay stubs and no personal papers. He also found two keys on a ring, which caught his eye, because they had red embossed-tape labels on them. The labels read "800 18 Fr" and "800 18 B." He thought for a while and then made a phone call, and asked a cop he knew to use the reverse-number directory on the phone number he had just called. The cop gave him an answer. He grunted thanks, and when he left the apartment with Hector the keys were in his pocket.

Shortly after passing the Joyce Kilmer service plaza on the New Jersey Turnpike, Harry thought of the keys. He reached them out of his pocket and tossed them to Marlene, who was in the passenger seat of the tan Plymouth.

"Funny."

Marlene looked at them, as always trying to stay in step with Harry's jumps. "Work keys," she reasoned out loud. "Somebody's apartment; she's a maid. But not her current employer?" Harry nodded. "So: another employer, or a former employer, to whom she didn't give back the keys, because . . . she ran? She was canned under unpleasant circumstances?"

Harry shrugged. "Front and back. And no letter."

Marlene inspected the key labels. She had a peculiar feeling, almost a déjà vu, something tugging at her mind. "Front and back doors means either a private residence, something in the burbs, or an apartment in an old-fashioned, high-tone building. The 800/18? Eight hundred Eighteenth Street? No such place in Manhattan. Or the eighteenth floor of 800 some avenue? Oh, I see, you think the floor having no letters after it means there's only one apartment on the floor, so, somebody with money." She laughed and handed the keys back. "Or maybe she just picked them up on the street." But she didn't believe that.

The Sisters of Perpetual Help were housed in what used to be a cheap motel, one of several along a strip of mixed zoning cut off from the rest of Chester, Pennsylvania, by the roaring mass of the I-95 freeway. The motel signs had been removed, and a black and white sign with the name of the order had been placed in the window of the former motel office. Here Marlene and Harry entered.

A rugged-faced young woman with short brown hair, wearing a modest blouse and jumper combination, looked up and smiled and asked if she could be of help. Marlene explained who they were and asked if they could see Isabella Machado. The young woman looked blank, and said that she had no information about a guest with that name, but if they cared to wait, she would refer them to Sister Gregory, who was out at the moment. If they wanted to get something to eat while they waited, the restaurant in the motel across the road was open. You understand, things are always a little slow on Sundays. They understood, but short of rousting the place with drawn guns, they could do nothing, and so they said they'd be back and traipsed across the street to the Keystone Motel, 24-Hour Service, Truckers Welcome, an arc of aqua-colored huts terminating in a diner-like office and restaurant.

Several truckers had, in fact, been welcomed at the Keystone, as witnessed by their rigs parked in a row on the motel's large gravel lot. There were also private cars in slots in front of three of the huts.

They went in and sat at the counter. Marlene was not hungry; she ordered a bran muffin and coffee. Harry ordered a cheese steak, the specialty of the house.

"What are you staring at, Harry?"

"The Fury with the New York plates in the lot there."

"What's wrong with it?"

Harry bit into his sandwich and chewed for a while. Then he said, "It looks like an unmarked."

Marlene frowned. "Harry, that doesn't make any sense. Why would an NYPD car be parked in a motel lot in Chester?"

Harry shrugged. He didn't seem interested in his sandwich anymore. He stared at the black Fury some more and then abruptly rose, slapped some bills on the table, and walked out. Marlene ran after him.

"It *is* an unmarked," said Harry, shading his eyes with his face pushed up against the glass of the Fury's window. He stared at the door of the cabin number twelve, the one closest to the car, as if trying to see through it.

"Come on, Harry," said Marlene. "It could be a fugitive bust, a police convention, anything . . . come on, I want to see Isabella."

He gave her a scornful look and stalked away. Marlene looked at the car and then at Harry's retreating back. She tried, and failed, to see what an NYPD car had to do with Guatemalan hit squads while she trotted to catch up with Harry. He had an idea, and since he was Harry Bello, it was probably a good one, but she had no clue as to what it was.

Sister Gregory was a wiry little woman with close-cropped steel-colored hair. She appeared in the ex-motel office in a greasy mechanic's coverall, of a blue slightly paler than her eyes, which regarded them with a curious mixture of sweetness and suspicion from behind smudged, round spectacles. She explained that she had been fixing the boiler. Isabella who? She shook her head, as did the nun behind the reception desk.

They showed her their P.I. cards and explained who they were and what they wanted. The sister looked at these closely and returned them with a look that was kind but unsympathetic. Marlene remembered that look well from parochial school in relation to sloppily done French exercises.

"I'm sorry," said the nun. "You know, anyone can get these made up."

"Sister, do we look like Guatemalan assassins? Isabella is a friend of my daughter." Faint smiles, regrets. A memory blossomed in Marlene's mind. She rummaged in her bag and extracted the drawing Isabella had done for Lucy. The nuns studied it, conversed briefly in undertones, and returned it.

"Wait here," said Sister Gregory.

They waited. They heard running steps. Sister Gregory burst into the office, flushed and angry.

"She's gone!"

"What! When?" cried Marlene.

"She was at lunch," said Sister Gregory. "It must have been sometime after that. Somebody broke in the bathroom window."

Harry's eyes met Marlene's for an instant, and then he was gone, running out of the office and across the road. A passing semi blocked Marlene from following him, and by the time she got to cabin twelve at the Keystone, Harry was pounding on the door with the butt of his .38 revolver.

He used the pistol to smash the window, reached in, and released the lock and door chain. He turned his head and shouted to Marlene, "Get out of here! Call the cops!" Then he went in.

Marlene drew her .380 automatic and followed behind him. The bathroom door opened and Marlene had the impression of a huge shape filling the doorway, a big man, swarthy, with stiff black hair, wearing a white T-shirt and blue slacks. The blood was pounding in her ears. Something was shouted, but she couldn't make it out. She shifted to her left to get a clear line on the big man.

Who moved, a great leap, like a forward going for the paint. Harry's gun went off, twice. Marlene stopped, stunned by the sound.

The big man had Harry down on the floor. They were grappling for the gun. The back of the man's white T-shirt had a large, round red circle in its middle, like a Japanese flag. Harry fired again. A window shattered. Again. A chunk flew out of the ceiling tile. In a corner of her frozen mind, Marlene knew that Harry was trying to expend all his bullets, because the man on top of him was stronger than he was and in a few more seconds would wrench the pistol away. Another shot.

"He's got the gun, Marlene! Run!"

The big man struggled to one knee, and Marlene saw that indeed he had the pistol in his hand, holding it by its short barrel and cylinder. He turned to look at Marlene. His eyes were bulging; his face was pale and covered with sweat, and she could see a larger red stain on his chest, spreading around two dark holes in the cloth.

Marlene shot him in the face. His head jerked, but he didn't fall. There was a hole in his cheek, below the left eye. Incredibly, he rose slowly to his feet. He swayed slightly and looked at the pistol in his hand, as if he barely understood what it was for. Marlene shot her remaining four bullets into his chest. The big man took a step backward; again he looked stupidly at the pistol in his hand, turned it around, and pointed it slowly in Marlene's direction.

Then, like a man returning after a hard day's labor, he took a step backward and sat down on the edge of the bed. He opened his mouth, loosing a gush of bright blood. He toppled sideways and slid off onto the floor.

"Are you okay?" asked Harry, getting up.

Marlene was on her hands and knees, retching into the tin wastebasket. She brought the spasms under control, got to her feet.

"Yeah, just great," she said. "You?"

"My arm's fucked up, but I'm okay. Jesus, the thing that wouldn't die." Marlene went into the bathroom. She rinsed out her mouth at the sink. Fortunately, the mirror had been shattered by a bullet, so that she didn't have to look at herself. When she came out she made herself look at the corpse.

"Christ, Harry, who the hell *is* he?"

"Was he," said Harry. He was going through the

items on the bedside table: a .38 Chief's Special in a woven belt holster, a wallet, a pair of sunglasses, a set of keys, and a black leather badge folder. Harry flipped open the badge folder, revealing an NYPD detective's gold shield and ID.

"Paul Jackson," he said. Half consciously, he slipped the shield into his pocket.

The name barely registered with Marlene. "My God! Where's Isabella?"

They quickly searched the motel room. Nothing. Harry grabbed the keys from the nightstand and ran out to the car. He opened the trunk.

Harry tried to wave Marlene off, but she pushed forward and looked into the trunk. The marks around the girl's throat were the same as those on the young men in the autopsy photographs.

Marlene screamed. She shouted curses, not the sexual and scatalogical obscenities of the Anglo-Saxons, but the dreadful blasphemies of Sicily, in Sicilian. God was a dog. God was a pig. The Madonna was a whore. Jesus was the son of a diseased whore. She pissed in Christ's wounds. She cried, great heaving sobs, and smashed her hands again and again against the roof of the car. She tore at her hair. Harry grabbed her and held her still, while the sirens grew in volume.

Harry dealt with the local cops. Marlene sat in Harry's car and shivered. Harry had given her his suit jacket to wear because she had started shivering. It was stained down the front with Jackson's blood. She had her hands thrust deep into its side pockets.

Her hands closed around something hard and angular, and she drew out the two keys with the red labels and looked at them dumbly.

Then her mind started to function again. A building at 800 some avenue and an apartment on the eighteenth floor. Yes. She had, in fact, been in that very apartment. In less than a minute she had figured the whole thing out.

NINETEEN

"Why am I not surprised?" said Karp. It was two in the morning, Monday morning. Marlene had returned from Pennsylvania an hour earlier, had stripped and plunged into a perfumed bath, ignoring Karp's questions, and then had emerged and related the terrible events of the day, and what she and Harry Bello had made of it all.

"No, 'surprised' is not the word," said Marlene. "Maybe 'stupefied.' Here's a guy who has all the money in the world, he has a powerful position, he's good-looking, personable. He could get all the sex, of any variety, that any man could possibly want. Why does he decide to rape the fourteen-year-old daughter of his maid?"

"Why not? He tried to rape the head of the Rape Bureau, didn't he? And got away with it? And he probably would've gotten away with this one too if Jackson hadn't been such a dumbass and Bloom had remembered to get his keys back."

Marlene sighed and lay back on the pillows. At a certain level, she thought, evil becomes incomprehensible to the rational mind and exists only as agony, a bone cancer to the spirit. Tears were still leaking from her eyes at intervals, as much as she tried to push from her mind the thought of that thin white body curled into the filthy trunk of Jackson's car. There had been no telltale marks on Isabella's ankles. Jackson had hung her from the shower head; her own small weight had sufficed. Murdering the cabbies at the precinct, he had been forced into a horizontal technique, because the fixtures in the rotten ceilings (oh, yes, she remembered now, but she hadn't made the connection at the time) wouldn't have held the weight of even a skinny Central American. Jackson had probably intended to leave her dangling somewhere on the nuns' property, another sad Latina suicide. Clearly not one to let a good idea go, Jackson, not that any of it mattered now. She would have to tell Lucy in the morning. And Hector.

"The only things that're missing," Karp said, "is, one, how Jackson and Seaver were brought into it in the first place, and two, how Isabella got to the shelter."

Marlene brought her thoughts back to the present. "How do you mean?"

"Okay, the girl gets raped. The mother, the maid, finds out. She takes off, quits, gets a new place to live. Does she go to the cops? No, she's an illegal, she wouldn't dare. But somehow Jackson and Seaver find her, and they figure out that Bloom is the rapist. This would be last May. Jackson had murdered Ortiz in March and Valenzuela in April. Fuentes had just died too, and there was an investigation heating up. So they go to Bloom and they say, we got the girl you raped, make sure there's no serious investigation of the guys we killed. It was manna from heaven, finding that girl. Anyway, Bloom says something like, hey, I can't control the determination of murder, that's the M.E.'s job and he's an independent bastard. So they, Seaver probably, says, get rid of him, put your own guy in there. And he does. All the dates check like clockwork. Still, there's something missing on how the two of them got on to the rape in the first place."

"Yeah, but how she got to the shelter is easy," said Marlene. "Bloom obviously says to them, okay, deal, but you have to get rid of the girl. She has to disappear. So Seaver takes her to the shelter and leaves her on the doorstep. That date checks too."

"Why Seaver?"

"Because if it was Jackson, he would've killed her," said Marlene. "He did kill her, may he burn in Hell forever. No, Jackson says, we got to whack the girl. Seaver says, hey, I'll do it, you did the two spic cabbies, it's only fair. But Seaver's a softy; he doesn't like rough stuff, and also he's being a clever boy, because it gives him an edge, Bloom ever starts saying, 'What rape was that, Detective?' So he drops her at the shelter instead and tells Jackson and Bloom she's buried out in the Meadowlands someplace."

"So how did Jackson find her after all this time?" Karp asked.

"Ah, fuck if I know," said Marlene groggily. "We

haven't quite penetrated to the bottom of this yet. We'll find out the whole thing when they grab Seaver, though. He'll talk." She clicked off the bedside light, and they lay awhile in the semidarkness, in the pale moonlike glow of the street lights filtering through the blinds on the wide bedroom windows. "What'll this do to your case?" she asked, suddenly remembering the ostensible cause of the entire cascade of revelations.

"I don't know," said Karp. "When the press gets hold of what happened down there, it's going to really hit the fan. I'll have to think about it in the morning."

In the morning, as Karp had expected, the shooting death of an NYPD detective in a Chester motel room, the murdered illegal-immigrant child, and the involvement of a faintly notorious one-eyed feminist private detective made an irresistible story. Even the staid *Times* gave it page one, although below the fold. What Karp had not expected was what the *Times* ran above the fold, in a two-column piece on the left side: Murder Alleged in Custody Deaths of Gypsy Cabbies, read the headline, and the byline read A. A. Stupenagel. Karp devoured the piece on the subway going downtown to his office, muttering curses and imprecations in so energetic a tone that, although the car was crowded, a cautious circle opened up around him.

The core of the story was, of course, the reconsideration of the autopsy evidence; Murray Selig was identified by a 'reliable source close to the plaintiff' as the pathologist who had discovered foul play. (There was a brief review of the Selig civil case in a sidebar.) The article was enriched by the tale of the kickbacks from the cabbies, Seaver and Jackson being named, together with the other corruptions they had battened on. Stupenagel had made much of her personal adventures in disguise as a gypsy and of being roughed up personally by the late Jackson. Other "sources" were quoted suggesting very strongly that the two rogue cops were being protected for some reason by the D.A. himself. The D.A. himself had refused comment. The Police Department was quoted as saying that the investigation of the deaths and of the extortion racket would be reopened.

If Karp was less than pleased by the story, Judge Craig was furious. He called both counsel into his chambers before court opened that morning.

"This *farrago*, Mr. Karp, this *mess* of charges, did you have anything to do with planting them in the mind of this reporter?" asked Craig, tapping the unfolded copy of the *Times* on his desk with a clawed digit.

"No, sir," said Karp honestly. "The reporter is a friend of my wife's, who's a private detective who's been helping us with our case. We had Ms. Stupenagel's assurance that this story would not be published until after the trial, or until we had the full story of why District Attorney Bloom was so anxious that my client be dismissed. I'm very distressed to see it out prematurely."

"And do you now have what you call the full story?"

"Substantively, yes, sir. I believe I do."

"And would you care to vouchsafe it to the court?"

Karp glanced over at Josh Gottkind, expecting some sort of objection, or even a motion for a mistrial, but Gottkind's face was as bland as Buddha's. Karp felt a wash of relief. Phil DeLino had done his work. The Mayor was pulling away from Bloom, as from a fouled anchor. Karp said, "Obviously, we would expect this material to form the basis of a formal criminal investigation, but in broad terms this is what we know."

He told the story into a stony silence. When he was done, all Craig said was, "Do you intend to bring any of this material forth in my courtroom?"

"No, sir," answered Karp. "We've rested our case. We think it's sufficient."

"Mr. Gottkind? You have a comment?" asked Craig.

"Yes, Judge. We would ask that the jury be instructed to ignore the press allegations as they bear on the dismissal."

"Thank you," said the judge. "If that's all, let us repair to the courtroom and finish this wretched thing."

It took Karp twenty minutes to demolish Dr. England with the transcripts Marlene had brought back from upstate. Karp had England read Selig's statements verbatim, by which it was clear to all that Selig had not flippantly derided the large doses of amphetamine dispensed by Dr. Bailey, but had positively denied that he had any clinical expertise at all as to what constituted a normal dose, and mentioned, merely as an aside, that he had occasionally taken 15 mg. orally as a med student.

That concluded the case for the defense. After a brief recess, Karp rose and began his summation, which took almost four hours to deliver; the transcript ran to 256 double-spaced pages. He read over each charge in the original language of the memos, and then construed the stigma on Dr. Selig's professional abilities that the reader was supposed to gather from that language. Reminding the jury of the charges was essential, because the stigma arising from the charges was the basis of the claim for damages. Then he demolished each charge, summoning up the testimony he had elicited and adding choice phrases from the transcripts. He omitted any mention of the growing scandal in the Twenty-fifth Precinct, or the possibility of a connection between the firing and someone wanting to cover up two murders in custody, but the networks and the papers were full of the story; the stink of it hung in the courtroom, too heavy by far for Judge Craig's admonitions to disperse it. Closing, Karp asked for reinstatement, back pay, and damages totaling two million dollars if Selig were reinstated, and up to thirty million, depending on what lesser jobs, if any, Selig was able to get.

Gottkind asked for an adjournment so that his own

summation would not be interrupted, which request Craig granted. It would take the morning and part of the afternoon of the next day, after which Karp would have a chance to rebut. That meant that Craig would charge the jury on Wednesday, which meant that the trial would probably conclude this week. Karp looked up from his note taking and regarded his client. Murray was pale, drawn, diminished, and Karp sincerely hoped that the money would make up for this, to some degree. A wretched thing, indeed.

"Stupe, goddammit, how *could* you!" yelled Marlene over the phone as soon as she knew who was on the line.

"Sorry, kid—like the Mob says, it's nothing personal. No way I was going to be scooped on this one, not taking the kind of lumps I took. As soon as I knew Dalton was nosing around the Two-Five—"

"You're still a total shit."

"Thank you. How's the trial going?"

"Fine, despite your best efforts," Marlene snarled. "They're doing summations. Butch expects a verdict Thursday or Friday."

"Oh, so they didn't throw it out because of my story, huh? What a bunch of fraidy-cats you all turned out to be!"

"It was only because we found out what was really going on. The Mayor wants to get the thing behind him as soon as possible, and cut any connection he has with Bloom."

"Oh, so it *was* Bloom!" exclaimed Stupenagel.

"What was he doing? It couldn't have been something to do with that Guatemalan kid who got killed? By the way, what happened down there in Chester? What was it like killing Jackson?"

"Actually, Stupe, I was just about to call Jimmy Dalton and give him the whole story," replied Marlene with the nastiest tone she could manage, and hung up.

The phone rang again immediately. Marlene let it ring ten times before she picked up.

"You weren't serious about calling Jimmy, were you?" asked the reporter.

"I don't know, Stupe. As long as we're being bitches, why don't you give me a good reason why I shouldn't?"

Marlene was only playing with the reporter, so it was with considerable surprise that she heard Stupenagel say, "I know where Corazon Machado is."

"How? How do you even know her name?"

"You forget my contacts in the Guat community, dearie. As soon as your girl's surnames were on the wire, I started pumping. It was hard, because the Machados all really are witnesses to the San Francisco Nenton massacre. But I convinced the community to help because it's obvious they need protection."

"So where is she?"

"In Miami. At the Krome Avenue Detention Center, en route for Guatemala and certain death. I'm flying down there tomorrow to talk to her. The story

I get is that someone ratted her out to *la migra*. Any idea who that could be?"

"Bloom, obviously. He called in some favors and got her processed on a fast track. Quasi-legally, of course, but who gives a shit about another greaser shipped off? Look, Stupe, I got to get off and call Butch. He might be able to do something."

"Wait a minute! You were going to tell me—"

Marlene hung up and redialed the federal courthouse.

In the break after Karp finished his summation, a clerk handed him a sheaf of phone messages. Most of these were from the press, which he tore up and trashed. One was from Marlene, marked urgent. One was from Bloom.

He went to a public phone and called Marlene first. He spoke with her for five minutes, and then hung up and called a number in Washington, D.C. He spoke briefly, then terminated the call, and called a number in Miami, where he did the same. Then he returned Bloom's call. As he dialed, he noted that the number was not that of the D.A.'s centrex board, but Bloom's private number, the one his friends called, the one that rang on the special phone on his desk.

"Let's talk," said Bloom when he picked up and Karp announced himself.

"We're talking."

"Not on the phone. Come by this evening. Say six? We'll have some privacy."

Karp was about to say something violent and obscene, but stopped himself. The sentiment would be better expressed face to face. Besides, he was truly impressed with Bloom's apparently inviolable chutzpah. He said, "Okay. Six," and hung up.

Karp walked into the D.A.'s private office at a quarter past six. The outer office was deserted; Bloom had left word with the guard below to let him up. The D.A. was sitting behind his desk, with only the desk light on. The blinds were drawn. The scene was almost parodically *noir*; Karp idly wondered why Bloom had arranged it that way, and decided that he could not understand it, which was also true of nearly everything else the man did. Bloom's face was in shadows, but did not appear to be dripping sweat, nor were the eyes wild and bulging with terror. Bloom looked as he always did, prosperous and comfortable. He was in shirtsleeves, with yellow suspenders. He had a long cigar in his hand.

"Sit down," said Bloom, gesturing to one of his leather and steel sling chairs.

"What do you want?" said Karp, not sitting.

"I want to put this all behind me," answered Bloom.

"What is this 'all'? That you raped a child? That to conceal *that* you covered up two murders by the police? That you connived to have a decent man fired to cover *that* up?"

Bloom waved his cigar dismissively. "First of all, I didn't rape anyone. And besides, the kid is dead and so is the man who killed her For all we know, Jackson was the rapist. So we can cancel all that out. The Selig thing—I want to tell you I regret that. I was misinformed by my staff."

"You didn't do it to cover up Jackson's murders, you're saying."

"Of course not!"

Karp was interested to note that Bloom's famous imitation of moral outrage remained intact. "So why are we here?" Karp inquired.

Bloom essayed a smile, not a pleasant expression to see. "Why not? After the battle's over, we're all colleagues, right? Members of the bar? I won't pretend that I like you personally, and I know you as sure as hell don't like me, but we've always been able to work together. I'm thinking chief assistant district attorney. I'll handle the politics, you run the office."

"You're going to jail," said Karp.

A short barking laugh from Bloom. "Don't be stupid! There's not a shred of—"

Karp kept talking, to himself it seemed, but out loud. "You're trying to distract me with this moronic offer. From what? There are only two people who can put you away. One is John Seaver, but I sense that you've already gotten to him. He's a flexible man, Seaver. Why should he piss off the D.A., especially when there's no confirmation of any accessory to murder charges and he can lay it all off on his dead partner? The other is Corazon Machado. Who knows what kind of physical evidence she kept?

That's probably part of what Jackson was looking for when he tossed her place, that and information about where the girl was. Well, he found that, all right, but he missed your apartment keys. Maybe he missed something else. So you got some of your friends in immigration to frog-march her out of the country. Even then it'll take some time to process her, and you don't want either me or Marlene to spend time looking for her, so you come up with this . . . scheme, offering me this job."

Here he paused and rubbed his chin and gave Bloom a look of the type we bestow on the two-headed calf or the baby with scales and fins floating in murky fluids at the carnival side show. "I can't figure you out," Karp said, genuine puzzlement in his voice. "You really think this is just another peccadillo you can wiggle away from, and that I'll sort of be party to it. Even though you tried to rape my wife."

"I didn't—"

"*Shut the fuck up*! And in a way, I don't blame you. I've been covering your ass for years. Your corruption. Your incompetence. Your actual crimes. I guess I thought I was doing it for the office. I'm really a sort of good German, in a way, and you saw that, and used it. But now, now you're going down. See, what I did, a couple of hours ago, is that I called another corrupt fuck I know, who happens to be a U.S. congressman who owes me a big one, and I got him to spring Corazon Machado, pending a full investigation of her case, and I called a P.I. I know down there to pick her up and take care of her. She's

flying back here in the company of a newspaper reporter who speaks fluent Spanish. I bet they'll have a
lot to talk about on the way up. The papers'll be a real
interesting read tomorrow morning. I can't wait."

Bloom said nothing. His face had started to twitch
around the eyes.

Karp took a deep breath and looked around the
office. He said, "They'll have to fumigate this place
with a flame thrower before they let the next guy in
here," and then he turned and walked out.

"What did he say then?" asked Marlene.

"He didn't say anything," said Karp. He shifted in
bed, trying to ease the pain in his knee, the result of
a day spent mostly on his feet. "I just walked out.
To tell you the truth, I was getting nauseated just
being in the same room with the bastard. I mean
really, physically. My stomach was heaving, I wanted
to hit him so bad. The worst thing was thinking it
was partly my fault that he's still in there. I should
have knocked him out that first time, years ago."

"Oh, wah! You're not a plaster saint. I want a
divorce."

"Oh, yeah? You think you can do better?"

"Of course. They're lining up out there for one-
eyed, eight-fingered babes with three kids. They'll
have to use velvet ropes to control the crowds."

Karp laughed, swooped his head under the covers,
and lifted her nightgown. He nuzzled her swelling
belly. "How're Heckle and Jeckle doing in there?"
he asked, and things might have developed in an

interesting manner had not the sound of knocking, light and tentative, sounded on their bedroom door. Karp groaned. "Oh, Christ, not again!"

"What is it, honey?" Marlene called. Karp reluctantly emerged from the steamy cavern. Lucy entered, looking forlorn. "I'm too sad to sleep," she said in a weak voice.

Marlene patted the bed and Lucy climbed up next to her. Nothing had been kept from Lucy about the events in Chester. It was Marlene's firm belief that there was no enormity that would scar a child's mind worse than a secret that could not be discussed in the family. Snuggling in next to her mother, Lucy asked, "Is Isabella in Heaven yet?"

"Yes," said Marlene confidently. "She probably has one of the good seats too."

"Is she an angel too?"

"Arguably," said Marlene. Lucy sniffled and began to weep silent tears. Marlene hugged her closer and said, "Look, I know you miss her, Luce, and I miss her too, but she's gone. You have to cry and remember her, which you did, and then it's time to stop crying and just remember."

"Hector isn't crying. He just stares at the ceiling. He says he's going to kill the soldiers."

"It wasn't soldiers who killed Isabella, Lucy. It was a policeman."

"And you and Uncle Harry killed him. I'm *glad* he's dead and he has to go to Hell."

"Well, you may be glad, but I'm not. It was horrible. I threw up."

"You did? Because of the blood and goosh?"

"Partly that, but it's a horrible, horrible thing to kill a human being. It's *not* like on TV. You only do it when it's necessary to stop something worse from happening. The bad policeman would have killed Uncle Harry and me, so . . ."

"It wouldn't have bothered me," said Lucy boldly, and then started to weep again. "*Why* did he have to kill her?" she wailed. "I thought police were *good* guys."

"Most of them are, baby."

"Like that one who got me ice cream when you were seeing the scumbag?"

"Yes, Clancy."

"Uh-huh. I was wearing my scarf from Isabella with the flowers, and he said it was pretty, and he asked me all about Isabella, how old she was and where she lived. I told him she lived in the shelter but she slept over my house a lot. He was nice."

"Yes, he was." Marlene bent over and kissed her daughter once on each eye, a magic kiss to stop the tears, and then got out of bed and lifted her up. She carried the child down to her own bedroom and tucked her in, and then checked next door, where Hector was sleeping on a cot in the playroom. He lay still, but Marlene was sure he was not asleep.

She was halfway back to bed when it hit her, so hard a thought that her stomach churned and she grew light-headed. Walking unsteadily, she went to her office and called information. She dialed the number she got and managed to pry from a sleepy night nurse the information she wanted. Then she rummaged through the slips of paper on her desk until she found the right one, and dialed again. Her fingers were trembling.

After ten rings a man's voice answered, rough with sleep.

"Yeah?"

"Oh, Clancy," Marlene said. "Oh, Clancy, you piece of work, it was you, all the time, you, and all of us just dancing around the helpful Sergeant Clancy."

"Who the hell is this?"

"It's me, Marlene Ciampi, Sergeant. Joe. You remember, the one with the charming daughter, with the scarf. You recognized the scarf, because you'd seen it before. It was you who fed Isabella to those two monsters, wasn't it? One of your guys must have picked her up on the street after Bloom raped her and brought her to you, clutching that scarf, the only thing she had from her miserable country, and you must have thought that she came from heaven because your lummox Jackson had just killed another little spic and you knew that one you could explain away, but two was a bit too much, even for a fine Irish hero like yourself. And it was your racket all along, wasn't it? God, how could I have been so *stupid!* When was there ever a racket in a precinct where the night-shift patrol sergeant wasn't up to his neck? It must have been a shock to know she was still in circulation, and not only in circulation, but real close to someone who was investigating the scam you set up to cover the murders your boy pulled off. Oh, you shouldn't have worried, Clancy! I *never* would've thought of you. And what threw me off, you know, was that you weren't a gambler like Seaver or a sadist like Jackson. You were a fine family man with a great misfortune, and you stuck your great misfortune in the Southampton Institute, which I just found out charges every year a little over nine-tenths of your total annual salary. Good thing you didn't have to live on your salary, Clancy, you bastard! Does your nice wife know, Clancy? That you bought her relief from her little idiot with blood money? Because you murdered her, Clancy. You murdered Isabella Machado, just as sure as if you used your own hands. And you're going down for it, Clancy. I.A.D.'s on Seaver already, and he'll spill his guts. Oh, yeah, you're going down, you scumbag!"

Clancy had been utterly silent during this. Now he spoke. "Seaver's dead. He ate his gun at eleven-fourteen this evening." The voice was calm and unruffled, the voice of a man who had done what was necessary to protect his family. Marlene could think of nothing to say. There *was* nothing to say. He was going to get away with it. "Don't call here again," he continued. "If you call here again, I'll have you charged with harassment." The line went dead.

Marlene stood up. Her chest was tight and a sheen of sweat covered her face and body. She turned around. Lucy was standing there, staring at her, her face unreadable. After a few moments the child let loose a great sigh, turned, and walked off to bed.

TWENTY

In the morning Hector was gone. Marlene called the church and then the shelter, but neither Father Raymond nor Mattie Duran had seen him. Oddly, Lucy seemed altogether less morose this morning and did not ask any questions about Hector. The day passed without event, and without word of the boy.

The next morning, the Thursday, Karp was preternaturally cheerful at breakfast, a sign of nervousness on a day when a verdict was in the offing. He expressed confidence. Craig had given a good charge the day before, most of the law had gone Karp's way, but, of course, with juries . . . Karp refused to think about what would happen to him if they lost.

An especially warm kiss sent him on his way. Marlene dressed and went to the gun safe for her Colt. She was going to move a woman for Mattie that morning. Harry was busy with some celebrity in midtown. As she removed her pistol, she checked, as always, to see that the boxes of ammunition and the little nickel .22 were in their places, and then carefully shut and locked the safe's door.

It was pouring outside, a heavy spring rain. She took Lucy to school and then bought a paper at a stand, holding it over her head as she dashed to her car to read it. Ariadne's story was on the front page, in the center above the fold, with a picture of Bloom and one of a thin and tired-looking Latina woman identified as Corazon Machado.

BLOOM DENIES RAPE CHARGES IN GROWING SCANDAL

On the jump page was a supporting piece: the state attorney general, Milton Veers, had appointed a special prosecutor to look into the charges that the district attorney had been involved in a conspiracy associated with the Twenty-fifth Precinct extortion rackets. The lead editorial demanded that Bloom step down as D.A. until these allegations, and those from Mrs. Machado, were put to rest. Below the fold was the story of Seaver's suicide. It was decorated with leaks from the brass at Police Plaza regarding the investigation of corruption in the Twenty-fifth. Marlene noted that, apparently, the corruption was widespread and involved drugs and burglaries as well as prostitution and extortion. She offered a prayer that some of it would stick to Joseph Clancy.

Marlene shifted her fugitive woman without incident, and then drove back to the Walker Street office to do some paperwork and return calls. She was just considering whether to place an ad in *Cosmopolitan* when the private line rang.

"It's me," said Karp. "Reinstatement, back pay, and two point one million. They were out for six and a half hours. I'm jelly."

"Congratulations, baby!" said Marlene with real feeling. "Oh, good for you! Murray must be ecstatic."

"Yeah, he's fairly jolly. We're in my office, drinking champagne. I have Naomi's lipstick all over me."

"Not on your fly, one hopes."

Karp laughed. "Yes, a smudge or two, but let's not get petty, Marlene. Oh, speaking of sloppy blowjobs, I seem to be back in Jack Weller's good graces. He was effusive. The Mayor is now playing himself as a wronged victim of the evil manipulator, Sandy Bloom, and Weller is joining the chorus. Now it's good for the firm to have made a principled stand defending a fine public servant. Can you believe this?"

"Easily. So, no more talk about leaving, huh? We're filthy rich forever. On to Goldsboro?"

"Ah, shit, I don't know, Marlene," said Karp, sobering. "Since this case I have less enthusiasm for cleaning up the piles of poop left by major corporations. And between you and me, dear, Goldsboro's hands are not entirely clean."

"What? And B.L. is going to defend them? I'm shocked. *Shocked!*"

"Yeah, right. Oh, also, did you hear? Jack Keegan didn't get his robe. They gave it to Jerome Oster."

"Who he?"

"Nobody special—some law school professor. This will kill you, though: he's married to Milt Veers's sister."

"The A.G.," said Marlene, recalling the article in the paper. "Sandy's covering his ass, you think?"

"Bet on it! But it's not going to work this time. Look, fuck Bloom anyway. We want to celebrate tonight. Can you set up a sitter and we'll pick you up in Murray's car around seven?"

It was more than agreeable to Marlene, who could not recall when last she had spent an evening on the town that did not involve packing heavy-caliber firearms. She collected Lucy at school, noting with pleasure that she was again playing with her old friends, Janice Chen and Miranda Lanin.

Lucy was fed and sent downstairs to stay with neighbors. The only problem was what to wear; she was now swollen enough so that none of her good skirts would close. She chose a blue beaded suit with a long jacket and faked it with safety pins at the waist. At least she had a bag and shoes to match this outfit, and if anybody bitched she could shoot them with her gun.

The evening was a success. The Seligs were roaring, Karp was more relaxed and happier than Marlene had seen him in some time, thanks in part to a whole glass and a half of Dom Perignon. They went to Le Cirque. *Le tout* New York seemed to pass by their table, showering congratulations on Murray, on Naomi, and Karp, the man of the hour. Nor was Marlene excluded from the general approbation: an extremely famous actress approached her hesitantly in the ladies' and gushed about how much she admired her and what a wonderful job she was doing with those poor women; it hardly diminished Marlene's sense of well-being when she followed this with a detailed description of what her ex, the bastard, had done to her. They exchanged numbers.

In the morning Marlene was up early, having passed the evening happily enough on soda water, while Karp, the wretched sot, was still snoring. He was to be allowed to sleep in.

She roused Lucy, started the coffee, and switched on the little kitchen television set to the *Today Show*. The weather; an author pitching a book; a review of the breaking news. Marlene was cracking eggs into a bowl when the mention of a familiar name brought her out of the pleasant trance of domesticity. She looked up at the screen: a color photograph of Joseph Clancy in his blue uniform, with medals. They cut to tape from the night before. A police radio patrol car sat at the curb on a street in Spanish Harlem, the yellow tape holding back a crowd. The passenger door of the car was open. The camera dwelt lovingly on the thick, dark stains spreading over the back of the seat.

The on-scene reporter, a studious black man, reappeared, saying, "Although there were numerous witnesses to the crime, the street was crowded because of an auto accident on the next corner, and, according to police, the stories conflict. Some witnesses said it was a tall teenager in a gang jacket. Others said it was a middle-aged man. Some said it was a thin child not more than twelve. All we know for sure is that an hour ago, *someone* stepped from the crowd, fired four bullets into the head of Sergeant Joe Clancy as he waited for his driver to fetch their usual coffee and donuts from the convenience store behind me. A police hero is dead, four children are without a ather, and no one knows why."

Marlene left the eggs in their bowl and walked down to her office. She consulted the Rolodex where she kept business cards, and made a call, and left a message. Then she finished scrambling eggs and making toast. She called her family to the table. Her heart was gelling in her chest. The phone rang. She dashed down to her office to pick it up.

"This is Detective Moon. You called me?"

"Yeah. This is about the mugging, the attempted ᴄnurder? My friend Stupenagel?"

A pause. "Yes, well, Ms. Ciampi, see, that case's ᴅeen cleared. We believe that Paul Jackson did that. I've already spoken with your friend and she agrees."

"Oh, good! That's what I was going to say. I didn't want to leave any loose ends. Oh, gosh, here I am bothering you with a case you already solved, and you're probably busy with this terrible murder. Sergeant Clancy. God, I was just talking to him the other day."

"You knew Joe Clancy?"

Marlene explained why she had been at the Two-Five, omitting, of course, the rest, and then said, "My God, three thirty-eights in the head! At least he didn't suffer."

Another pause. "Um, where did you hear they were thirty-eights?"

"Gosh, I don't know. Didn't they mention it on TV?"

"They were wrong if they did. Twenty-two's. They thought it was a Mob hit at first. Then everybody's talking about this little kid. Look, I got to run, Ms. Ciampi. Thanks for your help."

Marlene mumbled a good-bye. As soon as the phone was down she went to her gun safe. It took her two tries to work the combination. Her vision blurred; her face felt like a bag of blood.

She reached in and pulled out her chromed .22. Oh, you clever child, she thought, stifling the mounting horror. You heard me yelling at Clancy on the phone, you and Hector both, and you put your little heads together, didn't you? You spied from your window up there and got the combination and then swiped the pistol and gave it to Hector, and then you put your little silver cap pistol in there so it wouldn't be missed until Hector had a chance to use it. And you remembered what Clancy had said about running on a schedule. He knew just where to find him.

Marlene replaced the cap pistol where she had found it and closed the safe. She took several deep breaths and pinched her cheeks to get the color back into them. Karp and Lucy were at breakfast already, Karp in his ratty plaid bathrobe, unshaven and happy, Lucy neatly got up in her white leather skirt and a shirt with tiny red checks, chatting to her father about something silly. Marlene forced a smile and sat down, poured some coffee.

"I think I'll take the whole day off," said Karp. "I think I should get a day off every time I make three quarters of a million dollars."

Lucy was impressed by the figure. "I could get a pony!"

"Of course, m'dear," said Karp expansively. "We'll train it to go down the fire escape, and it can sleep in your bed."

And more nonsense of the same sort, Marlene dying inside, laughing away.

They stopped at the school. Lucy opened the door to get out, but Marlene stopped her. "Luce, could I ask you something? You tell me the truth, don't you? I mean, if you did something really bad, you'd tell me, wouldn't you?"

Lucy did not squirm or avoid Marlene's gaze, but looked her boldly in the face and replied, "If it was something about you and me, I would. Like if I promised to do something and you asked me did I do it and I didn't I would tell you."

"But what if it was, like, a crime? Would you tell me?"

Lucy thought about this for some time. "I would if you asked me and I thought it, well, it wouldn't hurt anybody." She hesitated. "But God is the judge of everything, isn't He? Sister Theresa says, God judges the truth in our hearts."

Marlene felt a stone rise in her throat; she had

made this and would have to live with it. What a rocky path, she thought, and then she said, "Listen! A great man, a priest, said this a long time ago: *La falsità non dico mai mai, ma la verità non a ogniuno.* It means, I never, never tell a lie, but the truth is not for everyone. Do you understand that?"

Lucy smiled a small Sicilian-Jewish smile. "Of course, Mommy," she said, and she sang the short Chinese phrase she had used months ago when they had played with the guns. Then Marlene watched her darling little accessory to murder in the first degree run across the pavement into first grade.

And Marlene thought that, yeah, God would judge, judge her and judge Lucy, and she imagined herself arguing at the Throne, probably against a Jesuit, that yeah, it was murder, but here was Clancy, still a hero, instead of a disgraced slimeball, out of a job or in jail, and there'd be an inspector's funeral and the Emerald Society would play "Flowers of the Forest" on the pipes, and they'd fire a salute and the pale woman would get the flag folded into a blue, starry triangle, plus the pension, plus the insurance, and without a doubt the Department would pass the hat so that little what's-his-name could stay in the fancy institution, and besides, the son-of-a-bitch deserved it, and let God sort it out, because she, Marlene Ciampi Karp, could not.

"Hector's back," said Karp when Marlene returned with Lucy that afternoon.

"Really? When?"

"A little past noon. He just walked up the stairs and knocked on the door. I fed him some tuna and he went and sacked out. The poor kid looked beat."

"Did he say anything about where he was?"

"Oh, yeah! Hector? Hector likes to keep it close. Oh, also, his mom called. We had a nice talk in broken English. I don't think we should have any trouble getting her settled here. Stupenagel has taken her up."

Marlene forced a conventional smile. "Oh, that's nice," she said. Superconducting magnets were pulling her toward the gun safe.

He had replaced the real pistol, the good boy. She took it out and sniffed the muzzle, which stank of burnt powder. She slipped the thing into her bag and headed for the door.

"Hey, where're you going?" called Karp.

"Oh, stupid me, I left something I need at the office. I'll be back in twenty minutes. No, you stay here, Sweety!"

She drove to West Street, to the abandoned pier where gays held parties on summer nights. She walked to the end of the wooden structure, sat down on the edge, and disassembled the pistol. Then she compounded a felony by throwing each piece as far as she could in different directions, there to join generations of other murder weapons on the bed of the slow and stately Hudson.

The next day, Saturday, was the first real hot New York day of the year. Marlene Ciampi was wearing a T-shirt that said Ray's Pizza, in white on blue. Her daughter was wearing one with the line about a woman needing a man like a fish needs a bicycle, in black on yellow. Behind the daughter trailed a wire cart loaded with soiled laundry, and behind that trailed the huge black dog.

They were walking down Mott Street in China-town. The rain of the past week and today's heat had summoned forth the traditional rich scents of the district—anise, hot oil, rancid meat, rice water, and steam, all on top of that ineffable odor, clean New York. There was a potsy court drawn on the pave-ment in pink chalk, and Lucy left her cart and picked up a filthy bottle cap from the gutter. She tossed it for a turn of ones-ies.

Marlene watched Lucy bounce fairy-light through the squares. She looks like a regular kid, she thought, clinging to the hope that this was indeed largely the case, that her offspring was not, in fact, an embryo Duchess of Malfi.

They went into Wing's Hand Laundry and passed the dirty stuff over the scarred counter, receiving a blue ticket in return and a brown paper package of clean stuff. Marlene paid, and they were about to leave when she had a sudden thought.

"Lucy," she said, "say your Chinese saying to Mr. Wing."

"*Shen gao huang di yuan,*" said Lucy. Middle high high high low.

"Do you know what that means, Mr. Wing?" asked Marlene.

Mr. Wing had to think for a moment, because the saying was in Mandarin and not Cantonese, but it was a familiar saying nonetheless, one he had lived by all his life.

"It means: The mountains are high, and the Emperor is far away," said Mr. Wing, and then wondered why the white ghost woman with the little girl and the demon dog was laughing until tears sprang from her eyes.

Don't miss

Robert K. Tanenbaum's

latest thriller featuring

Butch Karp and Marlene Ciampi

IRRESISTIBLE IMPULSE

Available October 1997

from Dutton

ONE

In the early hours of the 5,742nd year since the creation of the universe, Dr. Mark Davidoff, M.D., stood in the crowded, marvelous, immense nave of Temple Emmanu-El on Fifth Avenue, and belted out *"Ain Kelohanu"* in a lusty voice, and thought that so far the universe was working out fairly well. He was young (young-ish), healthy, and rich, an internist like his father and grandfather before him, possessing all his hair, a Jaguar Van den Plas, a ten-room condo on Central Park West, a wife and two blossoming Davidoff-ettes. Around him standing and singing were his people, in whom he was well pleased, the upper crust of Jewish New York, a group as prosperous and secure as any Jews had been since collapse of the caliphate of Cordova.

The song and the service ended. Davidoff crowded out with the rest, for the temple was packed for Rosh Hashonah, the beginning of the High Holy Days, when it was appropriate for Jews of Davidoff's degree of religiosity to seek solidarity and, it might also have been, exculpation for countless Sundays of Chinese food, countless Sabbaths at the office or on the links.

He knew many of the people milling around the cloakroom, and there was considerable hand shaking, and "good-Yonteff"-ing, before Davidoff, enclosed in camel-hair coat and cashmere muffler, was able to leave the synagogue and emerge out into the bright, crisp day. He was about to walk down the avenue, to where he would stand a better chance of finding a cab home, when he heard his name called and saw the very last person of his acquaintance he would have expected to see standing in front of Temple Emmanu-El on Rosh Hashonah.

Vincent Fiske Robinson stood out in that particular throng like a Hasid in Killarney. He was tall and slim with a face both sculptured and sensual, set with sky blue eyes and decked with fine blond hair worn swept back from a widow's peak. Mark Davidoff had blue eyes and blond hair too, but not, of course, *that* kind of blue eyes and blond hair. Davidoff moved through the crowd and held out his hand. Robinson's hand in his felt hot and damp.

"Vince. Long time no see," said Davidoff with an uncertain smile. "What are you doing here?"

"I came to see you, man. I called your apartment, and your wife told me I'd find you here."

"Yeah, I didn't figure you were thinking about conversion . . ." Davidoff began in a bantering tone, and then stopped, automatically checking out the other man with a diagnostician's eye. Robinson seemed flushed and overheated despite the chilly

air. He looked as if he had dressed in the dark—
he was wearing grubby jeans, a worn blue button-
down shirt, and sneakers, over which he had
thrown a lined Burberry. "You okay, Vince?" Davidoff asked.

"Yeah. No, actually, I'm in a bit of a mess. Actually, a gigantic mess. The thing is, could you do a
consult for me? It would really help me out."

"A consult? Vince, it's Rosh Hashonah. Can't it
wait?"

"Actually, no, it can't," said Robinson. "It's personal. My nurse, one of my nurses, actually, she's
my girlfriend . . . she's in my apartment, very sick,
very, very, sick . . . I was . . . could you, you know,
take a look at her?"

"Vince, what is this? You have an emergency, call
911, get her into a hospital . . ."

"No, actually, I don't think that would be appropriate in this case. That's why I came here."

Davidoff was about to refuse when he registered
the desperation in Robinson's eyes.

"Please, Mark. I really need your help."

This was new and, Davidoff could not help feeling
with a little thrill of self-satisfaction, not a mien that
Vincent Fiske Robinson had ever adopted with Mark
Davidoff when the two of them had been at Harvard
Medical School together. For a brief period the two
students had shared a group house in Cambridge,
during which Robinson had given Davidoff numerous unspoken lessons about the difference between
New York Jewish aristocracy and *Aristocracy*. There

was no actual anti-Semitism, of course, not that you could put your finger on, only a humorous, casual condescension. That Davidoff studied hard and got top grades, while Robinson did not seem to study at all, but eventually received the same degree, and got a good internship, too, was also the subject of considerable comment on Robinson's part, charming comment, for Robinson was certainly the most charming man in Davidoff's experience. Even when he had pissed you off, and made you feel like, for example, a grubby Jewish grind, it was hard to remain angry with him. Unaccountably, on this cold New York Street corner, an image from a dozen years past flashed across Dr. Davidoff's mind: spring in Cambridge, a Friday, the Friday before the dreaded human physio exam, himself surrounded by books and notes, glancing up from his desk as Robinson pranced by, swinging a lacrosse racket, a white sweater draped around his neck, and a pale laughing girl with a blond pageboy haircut draped on his arm. Somehow, the current situation, Robinson begging Davidoff to help him out of a mess, balanced out that long-ago scene on some cosmic and inarticulable scorecard.

So Davidoff smiled and said, "Sure, Vince, I'll have a look at her. Let's go."

Robinson lived on the East Side, of course, a duplex in an old brownstone in the Sixties off Madison. They walked there in silence.

"Shit, Vince!" he cried when he saw the woman in Robinson's bed, and felt sick himself. She was a lovely woman, or had been. Pale hair framed a fine-boned face, with a wide, inviting mouth. Davidoff found himself thinking once again, just for an instant, of the laughing girl in the Cambridge hallway. He cleared his throat to gain control of his voice, and said, "When?"

"This morning. She was, um, like that, nine, nine-thirty."

" 'Like that'? You mean *dead*, Vince. That's the term we docs use for a person in this condition. How long was she sick?"

"A day, a day and a half. She was fine Friday. We went out for dinner, came back here, went to bed, and mooched around Saturday morning. We were going to go out biking in the afternoon, and she said she wasn't up for it; she said she felt feverish, head-achey. I thought, flu. Saturday night she started spik-ing a fever. One-oh-three, one-oh-four. I couldn't bring it down. I gave her a shot of penicillin Sunday morning. Sunday afternoon she was sick but coher-ent. We joked, you know, we're playing doctor. Jesus, Mark, she's twenty-eight! Never been sick a day. I figured, viral pneumonia, liquids, bed rest, antibiotics to keep the secondaries down. Sunday night I went to bed in the guest room, and I came in to see how she was, seven, eight this morning, and she was in coma. I panicked, and . . ." He made a helpless gesture.

"Okay, so let me understand this: you wake up, find your girlfriend dead, and your first thought was to come get *me* for a *consultation*, I think you said?

Right. We've consulted. She's dead. I agree. So, what's going on here, Vince?"

"It's . . . I need a certificate, Mark," said Robinson. He was looking off into the distance, his eyes shying from both the dead woman and the other man. "I want you to declare her."

"You want me to *declare* . . . ?" Davidoff felt the first stirrings of anger. "Ah, Vince, correct me if I'm wrong, but didn't Harvard give you one of those nice posters with the Latin? I got mine framed. Why the hell don't *you* write out the god-damn certificate?"

Robinson gave him a brief look, in which Davidoff read both despair and shame, and then turned his face away again. "I'm involved with her, Mark, you know? And, well, I've been giving her things."

"Things? What kind of things?"

"Oh, megavitamin shots, diet stuff, stuff to help her sleep. She was a troubled person."

Davidoff took a deep breath and bit off what he was about to say. He went over to the bed and examined the dead woman's arms and thighs.

"This is a junkie, Mark," said Davidoff, his voice now quaking with rage. "What the fuck are you try-ing to get me into?"

"She's *not*, she *wasn't* a junkie! I told you, she was a troubled girl. I was trying to help." He turned to face Davidoff, and he seemed a different person from the elegant figure Davidoff had envied for a dozen or more years. He was literally wringing his hands, and his eyes were wet and red-rimmed. "She has a

family, Mark, you know? A mom and dad? I just . . .
I want her to go out decently. I loved her. Mark, I'm
begging you . . . do you want me to go down on
my knees?"

Davidoff believed that he would have. He felt a
wave of loathing, and an intense desire to get out of
this apartment, away from this man, and, what was
worse, he felt a tincture of self-loathing too, because
some part of him was enjoying the sight of Vincent
Fiske Robinson brought low.

They stood that way in silence for what seemed a
long time. At last Davidoff let out his breath in a
huff and said, "Okay, shit, give me the thing and I'll
sign it. I presume you have one."

"Yeah. God, Mark, I can't tell you how much I
appreciate this."

"Viral pneumonia, huh?" said Davidoff as he cast
his eye down the single-sheet form that Robinson
handed him. "Why not?" He signed his name and
dated the death certificate in the spaces provided.

"Well, Vince," he said, handing over the paper. "I
wish I could say it was nice seeing you, but . . ."

"Thanks a million, buddy," said Vince, the famous
perfect smile appearing for the first time that afternoon. "Look, I'll call you, we'll have lunch."

Davidoff said nothing, nor did he offer to shake
hands. Outside the apartment, in the fresh, cold air
again, he took several deep breaths. Vince Robinson
had never called him for lunch before, although they
had been working in the same city for at least a dec-
ade. He doubted Robinson would call him now, and

found that he was glad of it. He would have been even gladder had he observed the expression on Robinson's face as he walked out.

There were only four people who were allowed to interrupt, by a phone call, a bureau meeting of the Homicide Bureau of the New York District Attorney's office: the district attorney himself, John X. Keegan; the bureau chief's wife; a detective lieutenant named Clay Fulton; and the chief medical examiner of the City of New York.

"Excuse me, guys, I got to take this," said Karp, the bureau chief, to the twenty or so people assembled in his office as he lifted the phone and punched the flasher.

"Butch? Murray Selig," said the voice.

"What's up, Murray? I'm in a meeting," said Karp.

"Yeah, sorry, but I thought you should hear about this one personally."

Karp turned to a fresh page on his yellow pad and poised his pen over it. "Okay, shoot."

"The dead woman is a nurse, Evelyn Longren, twenty-eight, cause of death, viral pneumonia. All right, that's the first thing. Pneumonia, they call it the old man's friend; it takes the debilitated, the elderly, and babies. We don't expect to see a twenty-eight-year-old woman die from it. Next, the attending physician was Mark Davidoff, who, let me tell you, has a rep as one hell of an internist. His dad is Abe Davidoff, head of internal medicine at Columbia P. and S., for years. Next, we have the death took place in a private residence, not a hospital. And finally, the date of death was this past September 21. Davidoff signed the death certificate on September 21. Interesting, no?"

"No. Murray, I'm not following you. What's so special about the day?"

"What's so . . . ? *Oy vey*, what a Jew! Schlemiel! It was Rosh Hashonah. So I'm asking myself, Why is a Jew, one of the biggest internists in the city, attending a woman with viral pneumonia in a private house on Rosh Hashonah? Believe me, Mark Davidoff don't make house calls."

"She was a friend. He was doing a favor."

"Uh-uh, Butch. If it was a friend, and she was developing complications, he would've had her in a hospital before you could turn around. And he would have seen the complications in time. This is a young, healthy woman. There are no contributing factors on the certificate either—no fibrosis, no asthma, no staph."

"So he made a mistake. I know you think doctors are perfect, Murray—"

"Mistake? Butch, listen, if you saw Larry Bird pass to the other team six times in one game, what would you say? He made a mistake? No, you'd say something was fishy. The Mark Davidoffs of this world do not lose young, healthy viral pneumonia patients in private houses."

"So what happened, Murray?"

"Hey, you're the investigator. I'm just passing it on. But I'd like to cut that lady up."

"I bet. Okay, Murray, thanks for the tip. I'll look into it and let you know."

Karp hung up and turned back to his meeting, focusing his gaze on a nervous young man standing at the foot of the long table whose head was occupied by Karp himself.

"Okay, Gerry," said Karp, "take it from the witnesses again."

Gerald Nolan, the young man, resumed his explanation of the evidence in a homicide case called *People* v. *Morella*, one of the thousand or so ordinary killings that ran through the New York County D.A.'s homicide bureau in the course of an ordinary year. This particular one was: felon gets out of prison, finds his wife shacked up with another man, kills both. That was the People's story. The defendant Morella's was different, hence the forthcoming trial. The purpose of the exercise, and of the withering criticism that Karp and his senior assistant D.A.'s would shortly apply to the young man's case, was to bring home to the people in the room, and the criminal justice system, and to the city at large, that murder was never ordinary, that it retained its unique status among crimes.

Watching the young man do his spiel, Karp reflected, not for the first time, on the peculiar historicism of the scene. Fourteen years ago, more or less, the infant Karp had been standing down at the end of this very table, presenting his first homicide case to a group of men (men only then, of course) who were accounted the best criminal prosecutors in the nation, and the current D.A., Jack Keegan, had been sitting in the chair, the actual chair, that Karp now occupied as head of the Homicide Bureau. One of Keegan's first acts on assuming the position on a gubernatorial appointment had been to track down the chair and the table. The office was the same old bureau office too, a much better office than Karp had occupied the last time he had run the Homicide Bureau. Keegan wanted to send a message too about the unique status of homicide and that a new day had dawned at the D.A.'s, or rather a reprise of the old days, when the legendary Francis P. Garrahy had reigned as district attorney.

This public presentation of homicide cases had been part of the tradition then, and Karp was trying to reestablish it in all its brutal splendor. He looked down the row of faces to see how they were reacting to the young man's presentation. Doubtful but still polite expressions adorned most of the faces. A rather more various bunch of faces nowadays, of course. When Karp had started in the late sixties, the bureau had been staffed with the gentlemen who had started in the Depression, when a steady job at the D.A. had been among the best places a young Jewish or Irish lawyer out of Fordham or N.Y.U. could find. Under Tom Dewey and Garrahy they had faced down and broken Murder Incorporated, and challenged the Mob, when the Mob ran New York. These old bulls had all left when Garrahy died, left or been driven off by his successor, the exiguous and unlamented Sanford Bloom. Karp thought that this Nolan kid was lucky not to have been up there back then; by this time the old bulls would have been hooting and throwing balled-up papers at him.

Karp still had a couple of people on his staff who remembered the golden age. Ray Guma, sitting just to his left, was one of them; Roland Hrcany, Karp's deputy bureau chief, sitting halfway down the table, was another. Most of the other A.D.A.'s were young, eager, bright, and, in Karp's opinion, almost completely unprepared to try homicide cases. Training had not been a big priority of the previous management; for that matter, neither had homicide trials. This was changing, but slowly, painfully, and in the nature of things, it was these people who were going to bear most of the pain. Fortunately, Karp had a willing sadist in Roland, whose current twitchings, subvocalized profanities, and nostril flarings informed Karp that the bomb was about to go off.

Roland Hrcany brought his massive knuckles down on the table twice, like the crack of doom. Hrcany had the physique and mien of a television wrestler, with white-blond hair worn long to the collar and a face like a slab of raw steak. Nolan froze in mid-sentence.

"Ah, Gerry," said Roland, "this Mrs. Rodriguez, the neighbor, seems to be your chief witness. In fact, she's your only decent witness, am I right?"

"There's Fuentes," offered Nolan.

"Oh, *fuck* Fuentes!" snarled Roland. "Fuentes is the vic's sister. Morella used to beat the shit out of the wife before he went upstate. Fuentes'd say he was

Hitler. No witness. So, you going to trial with Rodri-guez, Gerry? Is that what you're telling us? With no gun? Where's the fucking gun, Gerry?"

"He had a gun," said Nolan. "We had a witness who saw him with it . . ." He started leafing franti-cally through his papers, seeking the name of the witness who had seen the D. with a gun.

"Hey, he had a gun? Nolan, *I* had a gun once too. Maybe *I* killed Carmen Morella and what's-his-face, the boyfriend, Claudio Bona," said Roland. "Anyway, what's Ms. Rodriguez's story? Did she get along with Carmen okay? Did she ever fuck Claudio? Did she ever fuck Morella? What about her kids? They selling any dope up there on East 119th Street?"

Guma said, "Yo, and I hear old Claudio was pretty tight with the Columbians." Everyone looked at him. Guma had a reputation as a man from whom orga-nized crime in the City held no secrets. Nolan's face was blotched red where it was not cheese-like.

"I . . . um, there was no evidence of drug, um, involvement," he stammered.

"No evidence?" said Roland. "Did you check? Did you check with Narco? With Organized Crime? No, you didn't. You don't know shit about Mrs. Rodriguez either, just her statement. You know what you got? You're on your knees saying, 'Be-lieve the Rodriguez woman and not the D.'s wit-ness, the cousin, Morella's cousin, who says he wasn't anywhere near the place when the shooting went down.' "

"There's the forensics. He was there."

Roland hooted. "The forensics! My sweet white ass, the forensics! Schmuck! It was his *apartment* before he went upstate. The vic was his *wife*! *Of course* there're fucking prints and fibers. There's going to be his prints and fiber on her *snatch*! No, look: let me tell you what you did, sonny. You didn't build a case with your own hands. You just bought what the cops dragged in, and what the cops did was they caught this case, a couple uptown spics get whacked, no biggie, they check out the husband did time, got a violent sheet on him, and case closed. Well, fuck them, that's their *job*. *Your* job, which you didn't do, was to construct a case that would stand the test of no reasonable doubt. What we got instead is something any little pisher in Legal Aid with two weeks' experience could drive a tank through."

And more of the same, with Guma joining in, and a couple of the more confident of the group picking like vultures on the bones of the case. Nolan grew paler and quieter; he stopped making objections, and scribbled notes, nodding like a mechanical toy. Karp ended his misery by suggesting that he needed some more time to prepare, and after that the meeting dissolved. Everyone filed out with unusual rapidity, as if fleeing one afflicted with a purulent disease. Nolan was silently gathering up his papers when Karp said, "Gerry, the reason why we do this is that we figure it's better you get it here than in court, in front of a judge."

Nolan looked up, his lips tight, his chest heaving

with suppressed rage. "I got twenty-eight convictions," he said. "I don't like being treated like a kid out of law school."

Karp had heard this before. "It doesn't matter what you did in Felony, Gerry. This is the Show, the majors. It doesn't matter you could hit the Triple-A fastballs. Homicide is different, which is the point of all this."

"Morella did it."

"I'm sure," said Karp. "But like I've said, more than once, it's irrelevant that he did it. The only question is, Do you have a case of the quality necessary to convict? And you don't. So get one and come back with it."

Nolan gave him a bleak look, stuck his file folders under his arm, and walked out.

Karp was sure that Nolan would be back, and with a better case too, because Karp had picked him as being the kind of skinny Irishman who never gives up. Nolan was an athlete. He had been a J.V. quarterback at Fordham, although someone as small as Nolan should never have gone anywhere near a football field. In fact, all the people Karp hired were athletes of one kind or another. It was a tradition. Roland was a wrestler and running back. Guma was a shortstop who, before he got fat, had been offered a try-out with the Yankees. Karp himself was a high-school All-American and a PAC-10 star before an injury to his knee ended his career. The other twenty-two attorneys on Karp's staff included enough football and basketball and baseball players to field complete teams, and good teams, in each of those sports. The three women on the staff included a UConn power forward, a sprinter, and an AAU champion diver. The one wheelchair guy played basketball. A jock sort of place, the Homicide Bureau; Karp believed, on some evidence, that no one who did not have the murderously competitive instincts of a serious athlete could handle the rigors of homicide prosecution, or the sort of coaching delivered by people like Roland Hrcany. The sports credential impressed the cops too, which didn't hurt.

The phone rang. Karp picked up, listened for a moment, said, "I'll be by in a minute," and hung up. He stood, and from long habit tested his left knee before he allowed it to take weight. It would undoubtedly hold, being made of stainless steel and other stuff he did not particularly want to think about. Karp was six feet five, with long legs and very long arms, at the ends of which were wide, spider-fingered hands. His face was wide too, and bony, with high cheekbones and a nose lumpy from more than one break. He still had his hair at thirty-seven, and he kept it shorter than was fashionable then, at the start of the eighties. The two surprising features were the mouth, which was mobile and sensual, and the eyes, which had a nearly oriental cast and which were gray with gold flecks: hard eyes to meet in a stare, hard eyes to lie into. Karp walked out of his office, told his secretary where he was going, and (a daily masochism) took the stairs two flights up to the eighth floor, where the D.A. had his office.

The man behind the D.A.'s desk was an older version of the sort of man Karp was, although of the Irish rather than the Jewish model. Jack Keegan's skin was bright pink rather than sallow like Karp's, and his hair was thinner and silver. The eyes were blue, but they had the same expression: bullshit me, laddie, at your extreme peril.

Without preamble, when Karp walked into his office, Jack Keegan roared, "Rohbling, Rohbling, Rohbling, bless his tiny evil heart!"

Karp came in and sat in a leather chair across from his boss's desk. The furniture was as close a match as possible to the decrepit City-issued suites favored by the late Garrahy, and as far as possible in style from the slick modern stuff with which the awful Bloom had surrounded himself. "What now?" Karp asked.

"Ah, nothing, I just wanted to blow steam at someone," said Keegan. "Political crap. I just received a call from our esteemed Manhattan borough president, a credit to his race, as we used to say, who informed me that he would take it very much amiss if we agreed to a change of venue."

"And you informed him . . ."

"I informed him, politely, that we had just nailed the little shit and his lawyer had not yet asked for one, but if he did there was no way we would go for it; nor was there a conceivable reason for any judge to grant it, this being New fucking York, and if you couldn't pick a fair jury from that pool, good night, Irene."

"This is the race thing."

"This is. The black community is concerned. They see this nice rich white boy from the North Shore with a funny hobby that involves killing elderly black ladies. It makes them irate. They're worried about what the esteemed gentleman called 'legal tomfoolery.' They want this guy dangling from a lamp post, and failing that, they want his white butt upstate forever." Keegan took a Bering cigar from his desk drawer, pulled it from its silver tube, and stuck it in his mouth, unlit. "So. Anything new?"

"Not much," said Karp. "We ordered a psychiatric evaluation and Bellevue says he's competent. Grand jury should start next week sometime. I think we want to expedite this—"

"No joke. Red ball on this one."

"Okay, it's the beginning of November. Five counts of murder are going to take some time to present, so let's say we arraign on the indictment before the end of the month, and then motions—say forty-five days?"

"Say ninety days, if you're lucky. This is Lionel Waley you got here on defense, the Duke of Delay."

"Okay, that rolls us well into next year. So we'll figure jury selection to start up in March."

"Yeah, that'll be a delightful experience, too. It took a full month to select a jury for Bobby Seale.

Count on at least that. Roland is going to do it, I presume. The actual trial."

Karp had been waiting for this. He met Keegan's gaze and answered, "No. I'm going to take it."

Keegan's eyes narrowed, and they stared at each other for an unlikely length of time. Then Keegan pursed his lips and examined the pale green wrapper of his cigar. He said, "You know, Butch, when I got to be D.A., I fondly imagined that my subordinates would do what I told them to do. I was mistaken, although I recall that when Phil Garrahy was in this chair, we all tried to do pretty much what he told us. Now, I think I've mentioned a time or two that as a bureau chief you can't take trials—"

"You used to take trials."

"May I finish? Thank you. And especially you can't take a horrendous long trial like Rohbling is going to be, not and rebuild the Homicide Bureau, and run it, and keep on top of everything else you have to do. And have a life. You've got three kids."

"You had four kids and you did it."

Keegan's face dropped a shade into the red zone. "Yes, damn it, back in the sixties, when we had half as many homicides, and a dozen men in the bureau with twenty, twenty-five years' experience, who didn't need their noses wiped like your people do, and, frankly, before Warren and the Supremes got into the act, when we could do things to move cases through that we can't do now. There's no comparison." He held up a meaty hand to check the expostulation he could see forming on Karp's face. "Look, there's no point in discussing it. I think I've made myself clear on this. On the other hand, you're the bureau chief; I don't intend to second-guess you. But here's something to think about: if this case goes sour, there will be a shit storm of uncontrollable fury directed at both you and me. I have to face an election in a year's time in a city where nearly half the electorate is non-white. So all the things we're trying to do to bring this office back from perdition will be at risk. You need to understand that aspect."

"I do," said Karp. "I can handle it."

Keegan replaced the cigar in his mouth and stared at Karp down its length, as along a gun barrel. "You ever go up against Lionel T. Waley?" he asked.

"No. You?"

"I did. In 1963. This is before he became the nation's greatest criminal lawyer, as I believe he actually calls himself."

"Is he?"

Keegan grinned. "Well, he wins a lot of cases. He's up there with Lee Bailey and Nizer. You know what they say: if you can't get Bailey, get Waley. Of course, Lionel says it's the other way around."

"Did you win?"

"I did not. He whipped my young ass. This was the Sutton case, a classic society killing. Is that a blank look? Babs Sutton, department store heiress? No? How soon they forget. Jesus, that whole world is gone. Café society, so called. In any case, Babs, or as the society columns used to say, the Princess

Radetsky, was married to this playboy, Prince Ladislas Radetsky, and of course the prince continued to play, and Babs found him in their suite at the Waldorf, on top of a sixteen-year-old whore. She took out, if you can believe it, her pearl-handled .32 and gave him five through the chest."

"She *walked* on this?"

"Oh, yeah. Waley gave them the defending the sanctity of the home horseshit. Driven to madness by the violation of the nuptial bed was how he put it. Had a jury full of decent Catholic women too, and he dressed the defendant like an understudy for the Little Flower. Oh, it was rare! My mistake was thinking that the facts spoke for themselves. Wrong, at least with Waley. You're sure you don't want to think it over?" He shot Karp another gun-sight look over the cigar.

"No, and this is going to be a team thing too. I don't intend to do it all myself."

"Oh, well, *that's* a relief," said Keegan and laughed. "Jesus! Well, I knew you were a stubborn Jew son of a bitch when I hired you. I have only myself to blame. What I should do is call Marlene and get her to bang on your head. How is she, by the way?"

"Fine, I guess. We tend to pass in the night."

"I presume she's still . . . you know." He made a shooting gesture with his hand.

"Uh-huh. Apparently the business is flourishing."

Keegan shook his head. "What a world! And her a mother with three children!"

Excerpt from IRRESISTIBLE IMPULSE

"What can I say, Jack? It's important to her. I'm married to her. I love her. Case closed."

"Well, yes," said Keegan. "I didn't mean to pry. Except, if there's any mercy left in the world, the next time she shoots someone, it'll be in Brooklyn. Outside the fucking County of New York."

"It's my daily prayer," said Karp.

FREE BOOK OFFER

Now that you've read FALSELY ACCUSED,
get a free Robert K. Tanenbaum paperback
when you purchase his new Dutton hardcover,
IRRESISTIBLE IMPULSE!

(available November 1997)

To receive your free book, mail:

- Proof-of-purchase from the front flap of IRRESISTIBLE IMPULSE and the UPC number from FALSELY ACCUSED
- Dated receipt(s) for the purchase of FALSELY ACCUSED and IRRESISTIBLE IMPULSE
- Your name and mailing address
- $2.00 for postage and handling (check or money order payable to Penguin Putnam Inc.)

Mail to:
PENGUIN PUTNAM INC., Dept. AG PRS
375 Hudson Street, New York, NY 10014

Name _____

Address _____

City_____ State_____ Zip _____

Choose one of the following Robert K. Tanenbaum novels as your free book:

___ **JUSTICE DENIED**
___ **MATERIAL WITNESS**
___ **REVERSIBLE ERROR**
___ **IMMORAL CERTAINTY**
___ **DEPRAVED INDIFFERENCE**